Amber & Dusk

LYRA SELENE

Scholastic Press · New York

Library of Congress Cataloging-in-Publication Data

Names: Selene, Lyra, author.
Title: Amber & dusk / Lyra Selene.
Other titles: Amber and dusk
Description: First edition. | New York : Scholastic Press, 2018. | Summary: Raised in the Dusklands where her power to create illusions was regarded as a curse, Sylvie has traveled to Coeur d'Or, where the Amber Empress, the cruel Severine, rules in hopes of finding her legacy—but the court is full of dark secrets and deadly intrigues, and Sylvie, now renamed Mirage, must learn to hone her magic, and find her way past the enmity of the empress to claim the place that is hers by right of birth.
Identifiers: LCCN 2017051321 | ISBN 9781338210033
Subjects: LCSH: Magic—Juvenile fiction. | Secrecy—Juvenile fiction. | Identity (Psychology)—Juvenile fiction. | Empresses—Juvenile fiction. | Sisters—Juvenile fiction. | Adventure stories. | CYAC: Magic—Fiction. | Secrets—Fiction. | Identity—Fiction. | Kings, queens, rulers, etc. —Fiction. | Sisters—Fiction. | Adventure and adventurers—Fiction. | Love—Fiction. | Fantasy. | GSAFD: Adventure fiction. | LCGFT: Action and adventure fiction.
Classification: LCC PZ7.1.S37 Am 2018 | DDC [Fic]—dc23 LC record available at https://lccn.loc.gov/2017051321

10 9 8 7 6 5 4 3 2 1   18 19 20 21 22

Printed in the U.S.A.   23
First edition, December 2018

Book design by Elizabeth B. Parisi and Mary Claire Cruz

To Mom and Dad,
for encouraging me to dream
of impossible worlds

ONE

The sun had not set on the Amber Empire for a thousand tides. But that didn't mean my world knew nothing of darkness.

Or violence.

The Skyclad platoon bore down on the convoy beneath a sky spackled with blood and charcoal. Bright metal armor glinted red in the twilight. Hoofbeats on packed earth echoed the drum of my heart against my ribs. I reached for the amulet at my neck, letting the familiarity of its skin-warmed planes calm my twisting nerves.

I wasn't the only one who was afraid. Voices of laborers and free travelers rose in panic as the soldats approached. Women drew tight the curtains of their wagons. Men shouted for children scurrying among the mess of tents and cook fires and freight drays. Livestock brayed and squawked.

Only Madame Rina was still. She stood in front of the biggest transport with feet planted wide and dark braids dancing in the hot breeze. She didn't flinch as the platoon drew close enough to see the wild eyes of the mounts and the silvery dristic armor protecting the bodies of the soldats.

"Luca!" I called, although I couldn't drag my eyes away from the approaching platoon. "Luca, where are you?"

"Here, Sylvie." The gentle touch on my shoulder reassured me, but when I turned toward my friend, his normally laughing face was tense and serious. His hazel eyes darted, barely registering his mother's stalwart figure at the front of the camp. "Where's Vesh? Have you seen my brother?"

"He was playing with the other children, last time I saw," I murmured. Vesh was younger than Luca by nearly twelve tides, and rarely strayed far from his older brother's protective eye. "Luca, I'm sure he's fine."

"Fine," Luca agreed. The certainty of the word didn't reach his eyes. "Listen, you stay here. Don't move. Let Maman do the talking. I'm going to find my brother."

"Luca, wait—"

But he was already gone, swallowed up by the permanent twilight. I breathed deeply through my nose and tried to calm the thrumming of my heart. The Sisters of the Scion—the religious sect who raised me—swore my unsanctioned journey to the Amber City would be cursed with misfortune. But I never imagined that menace might come from the Amber Empire's own troops. The Skyclad—the Amber Empress's elite force— were said to be born with a weapon in each hand. Unflinchingly trained. Merciless. Their famed armor was bright and pale as the azure heavens above the distant Meridian Desert.

The platoon thundered to a halt at the front of the camp. The captain dismounted in a flurry of dristic and blue, tossing her reins to a lieutenant and dragging off her helmet. She was a tall woman near Madame Rina's age; grey threads sparked in the brown hair knotted at the nape of her neck. Laugh lines etched her face, but her eyes were forged of hard metal.

"You." The captain glared down her nose at Rina. "This is your convoy?"

"Aye." Rina's voice rang with authority. "Chartered and bonded, these last seven tides."

"Your papers."

Madame Rina thrust a sheaf of parchment into the captain's gloved hand. I hadn't seen the documents since I'd first joined the convoy, but I remembered what they looked like, inked and beribboned.

Madame Rina's bond permits and Charter Writ.

"Everything is in order, I assure you," said Rina. "What quarrel could you possibly have with me or this convoy?"

"No quarrel," the captain grunted, not looking up from her rough perusal of the documents. "We search every convoy with free travelers in this quadrant."

"Since when? My charter grants both bonded laborers and free travelers right of passage along this route."

The captain fixed Madame Rina with a stare. She raised a slow hand toward one of her soldats, and bent a finger.

The soldat broke formation. Shifting patterns of light and shadow danced across the pale metal of his armor. One swift kick sent an iron cook pot lurching off its stand. Boiling water poured across livid embers. Steam billowed to the sky, wafting the stench of seared meat and wet wood across the camp. Somewhere, a child wailed.

I clutched harder at my pendant, biting down my fury. Anything I said would only make this worse. Until I got to the Amber City, my words meant nothing.

Worse than nothing, since I was technically a refugee. The Midnight Dominion—the darkness beyond the reach of our static sun—had been creeping into the Dusklands for tides, sending shadows to swallow light and drive frightened Dusklanders from their homes into the Amber Empire.

But I wasn't running from the darkness at the edge of

nowhere—I was running toward the light at the heart of the empire. I was going to Coeur d'Or, the imperial palais in the Amber City.

But that wouldn't matter to these Skyclad soldats.

"My orders are not your concern, Dusker," the captain said. "But by all means, continue to question them."

Rina's eyes narrowed to slits, but her expression relented.

"Better. Now, tell me—where did this convoy originate?"

"Piana. A village near the edge of the Dusklands."

"Its destination?"

"The Amber City."

"Purpose?"

"It's an ore convoy. Our freight is ambric—a little dristic and kembric too, for trading."

"And who are these folk?"

"My bonded labor, mostly. The rest are free travelers—merchants and herdsman who have paid for our security and company along their passage west."

"Any Dominion refugees?"

Rina hesitated for barely a second before shaking her head no. But the captain saw her hesitation. Everyone did.

The captain swept back her pale cloak and planted her palm on the hilt of her sword.

"Who?"

For one awful moment, I didn't know what Rina would say. The metal clasp of my amulet dug into my palm, but I didn't take my hand away.

Finally, Rina clenched her jaw and shook her head again. "No refugees here, Captain."

A cold smile crept across the captain's face. "We can do it that way too."

The captain raised a gloved fist. Her soldats snapped to attention.

"There are refugees here," she barked. "Find them. Anyone who stands in your way is in defiance of Imperial Law."

Swords rang from scabbards. Helmets snapped down. Booted feet stamped hard-packed earth. The platoon of armored soldats bore down upon the camp.

Panic sprinted ahead of the Skyclad onslaught. Parents rushed for their children. Free travelers reached for meat knives and shovels: anything that could be used to defend themselves. But the soldats were more interested in terror than violence. Laborers were shoved aside to sprawl in the dust. The canvas sides of ore transports tore beneath steel, scattering glowing nuggets. A keening scream splintered the air, then ceased abruptly.

I dived for Rina, who was standing frozen amid the chaos. I grasped her shoulders and yanked her gaze away from the scenes of cruelty and destruction.

"Madame Rina!" I hissed at her. "You have to do something!"

But her gaze was blank and terrible.

"Vesh?" she asked. "And Luca? Are my boys safe?"

"I don't know!" I fought the urge to slap the older woman. "But they're not the only ones who could get hurt if we don't stop this!"

"How?" she asked, and turned away, as though she knew her question had no answer.

I gritted my teeth so hard I thought my jaw might crack. I pushed away from Rina, casting my gaze toward the Skyclad captain. She stood a few strides away with her back to me, arms loosely clasped behind her cloak. Calm. Contained.

I couldn't contain the rage boiling up inside me.

"You!" I shoved all my anger into the word and threw it at the captain, closing the distance between us. "Stop this! Stop it now!"

"I will stop," said the captain. "When someone tells me which of these groveling mongrels was puked up by the Midnight Dominion."

"You're sick." My words rang harsh. "There are no refugees here! Why would you do this to innocent people?"

"I'm doing my duty," she said, turning at last to look at me. "No one is truly innocent. And innocence certainly doesn't pay a soldat's commission."

Fury painted fire along my bones.

The Sisters always swore the Scion would punish me for my sins: my anger, my ambition, my tenacious dreams. But I always thought those features made me stronger.

My secret unfurled gauzy wings inside me.

I caught my lip between my teeth and chewed. Standing up to a Skyclad captain was dangerous. But so was running away from the Sisters, choosing uncertainty over mediocrity and power over poverty. So was traveling halfway across an empire with barely more to live on than crusts of bread and Luca's kind smiles.

There were many kinds of danger. And there were worse things than facing it.

I knew what I had to do.

I squeezed my eyes shut and reached for a single glowing memory: the moment that changed my life.

A dingy, frigid room. Dull, livid light illuminating a sheaf of parchment lined in handwriting so elegant I barely recognized the language. And the Imperial Insignia, ornate and unmistakable—a sunburst bigger than my hand, stamped in amber wax and gilded with kembric. I concentrated on the memory until I could see nothing but the seal, glowering in the bruised dusk.

I forced my eyes open and swallowed down the scorching tang of fear. I stepped toward the Skyclad officer.

"Stay your men, Captain," I snapped, threading my voice with as much command as I could muster. "Your business here is done."

The woman's brows slashed together. Dread kicked my ribs with dristic-toed boots.

"Do you wish to die, girl?" A smile wove the lines of her face into a savage tapestry. "They say it is a great honor to die on a Skyclad's sword."

"And yet, an honor that is beneath me," I snarled, drawing myself up to my full height. I held out an imperious hand, and made the captain see something that wasn't there.

A sheaf of parchment appeared in my hand. An illusion, fashioned from memory and forged in the kaleidoscope crush of my heart. The ink glimmered blood-red and the paper rustled in the breeze, densely woven and fine. And the Imperial Insignia of the Amber Empire glared from the top page, heavy and solid and glittering like a tiny sun.

I held my breath, ignoring the low humming in my ears and the strength sapping from my limbs.

The Skyclad captain took one look at the seal. Her face drained of color. She swept into a bow so low the hem of her silvery cloak stirred up puffs of dust.

"My deepest apologies," she gasped. "I had no idea someone of your station was traveling with this ore convoy. Forgive me!"

She saluted briskly, spun on her heel, and strode forward into the melee.

"Stand down!" she shouted. "Our authority here has been revoked! Return to your mounts at once!"

The order rippled outward through the camp. One by one, soldats lowered their weapons. Free travelers fell back with gasps and cries as the armored men and women turned away to their horses with blank, impassive faces.

I sucked in a deep breath of smoke-smudged air and glanced down at the document in my hand. The edges of my vision curled like flame-eaten parchment as the illusion evaporated, bleeding into wisps of color and form. Within seconds, nothing remained of the Imperial Insignia. Panic burst hot in my veins, but the Skyclad officer kept her gaze diffident and her back angled toward me. She hadn't seen the official seal of the empire melt away into nothing.

I shoved my hands into my pockets, praying to the Scion I'd done enough.

The captain swept me a final salute before mounting her horse. Within moments, the Skyclad platoon was gone, shards of bright metal choked beneath a billow of yellow dust.

Dizziness clutched at me. I forced myself to turn and face the camp.

The damage was bad. Broken glass glittered along the edges of gaping transport windows, mixing with shattered chunks of ambric ore. Tents were nothing more than shredded wisps of canvas. Livestock lay slaughtered and broken, dank blood dampening parched earth. The guttering tongues of scattered cook fires licked at the debris of wagons torn to pieces.

I was so transfixed by the wreckage that it took me a moment to register the heavy press of a hundred eyes. I lifted my gaze, dreading what I knew I would see.

Laborers and free travelers were scattered across the camp-site, crouched between overturned transports and cowering in the comfort of one another's arms. And everyone—man, woman, and child—was staring at me. Suspicion gave their eyes sharp edges.

What had they glimpsed, amid the chaos, to make them look at me like that? Had they seen a nameless Dusklander conjure an Imperial Insignia from thin air? Or was it enough that they had watched a penniless orphan singlehandedly banish a platoon of armed Skyclad soldats into the dusk, and walk away unscathed?

Humiliation tinged with old resentment caught in my throat and choked me. Whatever its cause, their palpable suspicion felt all too familiar—I'd spent my life glimpsing it in the grimaces of superstitious Sisters and the sidelong glances of dirt-smudged villagers. Hearing it in the voices of cruel children who couldn't understand where I fit into their narrow worlds.

Freak. Witch. Monster.

A hand fell on my shoulder. I spun, my heart vaulting.

Madame Rina.

"Come, child," she murmured. Her face was unreadable in the dusk. "You've done nothing wrong. We'll find a way to fix this."

I gave a slow nod. But as Rina turned to pick her way through the ruins of her precious convoy, I didn't have the heart to tell her that what the captain had said was true: No one was truly an innocent.

Especially me.

And nobody could fix that.

TWO

The bell for second Nocturne pealed. Though the exhausted camp had mostly cleared away the evidence of the Skyclad attack, the soldats' presence lingered in the air like a bad smell.

I perched on the roof of the biggest ore transport, staring across the plains and trying not to think about what had happened. The sun glared from its spot above the horizon, livid and unmoving. A handful of raindrops splatted into the dusty earth as thunder rumbled behind me, clouds darkening the sky above the Midnight Dominion to a frantic violet.

Dominion. The vast, unexplored land beyond the reaches of our eternal day. A land wreathed in impenetrable shadow and fathomless myth. A land where the darkness had a will of its own, reaching fingers toward the light to snatch away the living.

I grew up in the Dusklands, mere miles from the seething border of Dominion. Abandoned on the steps of their cloister as an infant, I was raised by the Sisters of the Scion, who sheltered me from the shadows of Dominion prowling closer and closer to civilization. A begrudged home, with a hundred averted eyes and a thousand superstitious platitudes about sin and expiation, but a home nevertheless.

The Sisters never predicted me discovering a secret meant to stay hidden. The secret lurking in my bloodline. The secret that drove me far from the only home I ever knew toward a world bursting with possibility.

"Oi!"

A deft figure clambered up the side of the transport. I caught a glimpse of black curls and golden-brown skin.

Luca.

Just spans older than me, Madame Rina's son was the only friend I'd made on this cursed journey. Heir to his mother's chartered ore convoy, Luca had spent half his life traversing these brittle, sun-reddened plains. He'd been the one to catch me when I attempted to stow away in the convoy at Piana, the mining town near the edge of the Dusklands.

It had already been nearly a span since I'd run away from the Temple of the Scion, and although I'd tried to secure passage to the Amber City with half a dozen convoys and caravans, everybody took one look at my hungry eyes and torn dress and turned me away without a second thought.

"Not enough coin," the kinder guides said, pity slicking the lie and making it easier for them to swallow.

"No Duskers," the blunter ones said, pointing to the crude signs etched into the prows of their transports. "Imperial Law. Refugees might be carrying Dominion taint."

I gritted my teeth and tried to explain there was no such thing. Dominion shadows might hunt and kill, but they were just shadows. And the people fleeing toward the light were just people. But my words did nothing to lessen the fear slithering behind their eyes as they glanced toward the horizon.

I watched Madame Rina's convoy for three days as it stock-piled ambric and other provisions. Her transports numbered nearly twice the other convoys, and the smaller wagons carrying kembric and dristic were rarely touched—there was no demand for those precious metals out here on the edge of nowhere. I didn't relish hiding between crates and stealing food from hardworking laborers for six spans, but I was running out of other options.

I waited until third Nocturne before dashing across the shadowed stockyard and hurling myself beneath the canvas siding. I froze, squinting into the dense shadows. I almost didn't hear the whisper of leather ties against canvas as the door behind me fell open, splashing violet light across the floor of the wagon.

"Can I help you?" said a voice, crisp with laughter.

I spun. Silhouetted against a sweep of fire-scorched clouds, he was easily the best-looking boy I'd ever seen. He had none of the waxen, dull-eyed pallor of the Dusklanders I'd grown up with; energy seemed to pulse out of him, brash and buoyant in the seething dim.

"I was just—" My tongue was suddenly too fat in my mouth. I didn't have a good reason to be here, and we both knew it. "Looking for something I lost?"

"That so?" His eyes gleamed with amusement. "And how did a fine lady such as yourself happen to misplace sixteen quintals of raw kembric ore?"

I licked my dry, cracked lips as I rolled lies and truths and excuses around the ragged furrows of my exhausted mind. For all my bravado during that past span, I had very little left to lose. Desperation made me brave, or maybe a little mad.

"I'll tell you," I promised, giving my chin a vain twist, "in exchange for free passage to Posette and the return of half my riches."

Luca had laughed until his face turned purple, then dragged me into his mother's tent and insisted she accept my contract as a free traveler, despite my lack of coin or supplies. And to my surprise, Madame Rina had rolled her eyes in resignation and drawn up the paperwork.

Now Luca plopped down beside me. Below, in the center of camp, someone had lit a bonfire, and the crimson glow sent ruby sparks glinting from the tri-metal bar bisecting Luca's ear—his signat, the mark of his profession. He dug his elbow into my ribs. "Where've you been? Avoiding cleanup duty?"

His tone was light, but I remembered the hunted look in his eyes when he couldn't find his brother, Vesh. Both boys survived the attack unharmed, but something twisted in my stomach and kept me from returning the jibe.

"I tried to help," I muttered. "But I figured I'd be better off staying out of everyone's way."

Luca chuckled. "Why?"

"Because I saw the way everyone was staring at me."

Luca's shoulders stiffened. I instantly regretted my petulant words.

"Sylvie." Luca's hands were gentle, unknotting my fingers and unclenching my fists. "Look at me."

I hesitated, then obeyed. Sometimes I thought Luca was born to laugh, with his broad white smile and eyes that crinkled with humor even when he was trying to be serious.

He wasn't laughing now.

"You saved us, Sylvie." Luca's voice was soft but clear. "I saw the way you stared down that Skyclad captain. Without you, we might be dead. We all know it—Vesh, Maman, me. *They* know it too. But they don't know *how* you saved them. What you did or said to drive the platoon away. They don't know who you are. And that frightens them."

"I didn't—"

"Listen. Out here—where the dust twists itself into monsters, and mirages dance on the horizon, and the shuttered eye of the Scion stares down on us from Matin to Nocturne—we fear the things we cannot fathom. We use that fear as a shield against the dusk and hope we can survive long enough to understand. It's not about you."

I swallowed a bitter retort. I knew he was right. I knew it when I was a strange, lonely child in a shoddy Duskland village full of roughnecks and bullies. I knew it at the Temple, where the Sisters shunned me in favor of the cold, silent comfort of prayers and penance. And I knew it when I held out my hand and made the Skyclad captain see something that wasn't there.

"I know, Luca." I forced a smile and buried the old resentment. "I'm just tired of being a castoff. My parents abandoned me. The women who raised me despised me. The villagers feared me."

"Is that why you're going to the Amber City? To start over without hate or fear?"

I tore my eyes away from Luca's inquisitive gaze and glanced back toward the western horizon. Toward the sun, frowning from its rusty throne. Toward the Amber City, where I'd find either a world where I truly belonged . . . or more disappointment.

"You ask me that every Nocturne, Luca," I reminded him.

"And every Nocturne I hope you'll finally tell me," he retorted. "Now come down off here—it's getting late."

"I'm not ready for bed."

"Who said anything about bed?" A warm breeze kicked up the edge of Luca's tunic and ruffled his hair. "Noémie's telling the Meridian tale. By the bonfire."

"Again?" I wrinkled my nose. "I don't want to listen to that same old story."

"Yes, you do." Luca jumped into a crouch and wrapped his arms around my waist, sweeping me off my feet. I let out a surprised whoop when the world tilted upside down, spinning the sun in a blurry circle.

"Luca!" I was breathless with laughter. "Put me down!"

Finally, he set me gently on my feet, then vaulted off the top of the transport in a spinning leap. I gasped, but he landed neatly and took off at a run.

"Coming?" he called.

I dragged my dark tangle of dusty, sun-faded hair into a knot on the top of my head, then clambered off the transport.

The camp hummed with tension. Free travelers and workers clustered in knots, sipping from the precious stores of tize, honeyed wine imported from the Sousine Coast. The bonfire burned low, choking down offerings of battered wooden wheels and shattered furniture. One of the slaughtered animals roasted on a spit above the embers, a grudging boon from a cursed day.

A cluster of children scattered around my legs like wind around a tree trunk. One bouncing mane of coal-black curls caught my eye.

"Vesh!"

The boy skidded to a stop, his eyes brightening before he threw his arms around my waist and knocked me off-balance. At least this boy wasn't strong enough to lift me off my feet and spin me around.

Yet.

"Sylvie!" Vesh took a bite out of whatever he was holding in his hand, then talked around a mouthful of food. "Did you see the Sky-horse people?"

"I did." I crouched. "Did you?"

"No," Vesh said, a frown creasing his liquid eyes. "Luca made me hide beneath one of Maman's transports. So I didn't see nothin'."

"Luca was only trying to keep you safe," I explained. "He's a good brother, you know."

"Say that to my face!" Luca danced out from behind me and swept his little brother onto his shoulders. The younger boy shrieked with laughter, clinging to Luca's neck as he frolicked toward the edge of the fire.

A smile crept onto my face. I never had a sibling, but even if I did, I couldn't imagine being as close to anyone as Luca was to Vesh. Not only did they resemble each other physically—with their coloring and easy laughs—but even when they were apart they seemed to move in the same manner, and with the same intent. Two marionettes, fashioned from the same material and moved by the same hand, dancing always to the same silent rhythms.

Melancholy tugged at my heart. I reached for the amulet around my neck—the only thing I truly owned, the last relic of the anonymous parents who discarded me like trash at the edge of the daylight world. The pure ambric glowed dully between my fingers, and I wondered what it would feel like to belong. To be part of a family, whether by blood or by choice.

Part of me wanted to ask Luca, but with his warm eyes and quick smile, I couldn't imagine him ever knowing what it felt like to be unloved.

THREE

The sound of strings being plucked pulled me out of my bitter reverie. Noémie—a storyteller who'd joined the convoy at Posette—knelt by the bonfire, her fingers deftly tuning the wizened knobs of her ancient luth. Behind her, her dancer daughter Audé had begun to stretch, lifting a lean leg above her head as her husband, Henrique, grasped her waist for balance.

Finally, Noémie swept a hand toward the crowd, fingers splayed.

"Listen!" she cried, voice sonorous.

We listened. The only sound was the crackle and purr of the fire.

"Listen!" Audé and Henrique paced slowly forward, the outlines of their long limbs sinuous in the flickering firelight. "Listen, and hear the beginning of the longest day. Listen, with your ears. Listen, with your eyes. And listen, with your heart."

A warm hand brushed mine. My pulse jumped, and I sliced my eyes to the side. Firelight heated Luca's gaze as he leaned in, his lips nearly grazing my ear.

"Thought you didn't want to hear this story again."

"Who says I'm here for the story?" I teased.

I turned back toward Noémie, pretending not to see Luca's cheeks flush dull red.

"Long before the Amber Empire," she began, "or the Midnight Dominion, or any of the lands today, the world was ruled by two gods. The Sun, and the Moon. The Sun was a beautiful god, and where his holy fire fell, the earth was fruitful with joy and plenty. His heart was generous, so every day he spun around to all faces of the world, drenching new lands in light."

Henrique performed a dizzying series of graceful pirouettes. The bonfire scattered sparks.

"The Moon was a beauty like no other, a bright creature shining like polished dristic embedded with diamonds. When the Sun left behind darkness in his wake, she lit the sky with her calm, pale light."

Audé's arm arched above her head, and in her open hand nestled an opal, sparking with a cold, muted glow. The children cooed with delight and leaned closer, but Audé twisted the stone away into the folds of her silken dress.

"The Sun loved the Moon with a passion. But the Moon was indifferent to his gaudy light. Still, the Sun chased the Moon around the world, and whenever he caught her he touched her hand or stole a kiss, hoping to win her heart." Henrique and Audé orbited each other in the dusk, their steps so light they almost seemed to be floating. "But the Moon always ran away again, and the Sun became bitter and jealous.

"The Sun decided if he could not be with the Moon, he would kill her. But he could not bear for the Moon's pain to be on his own conscience. So he searched as he spun, until he found a man strong and ruthless enough to do the terrible deed in his stead."

We all leaned forward, caught in the haze of legend and fire sparking between Noémie's words and the dancers' choreography.

"The man's name was Meridian, although you may know him by other names. Scion. Evening Star. Skybender. Some say he was a god himself. Or even a demon." The fire popped, and someone gasped. "His legacy was strong, stronger than any who have walked the world since. He could summon the rain from the skies, or command a wind to cease. The dirt trembled when he walked, and the waters shivered away from his touch.

"The Sun saw all this and knew Meridian would do as he asked. He summoned Meridian to his skyborne palais, and gave him three objects. First: a net woven from fine golden filaments, to capture the Moon. Second: a spear made of metal forged so hot it would never break, to pierce the Moon's chest. And third: a vial made of glass, to catch the blood from the Moon's heart.

"Meridian rode his flaming chariot across the sky in pursuit of the Moon. For a tide and a day he chased her. Finally, she could evade him no longer. And in the velvet night, surrounded by a thousand weeping stars, she turned to face Meridian. But even as he lifted his spear to strike the fatal blow, Meridian saw the Moon's exquisite form, bathed in pale light and near enough to touch. Overcome by adoration and unable to murder something so beautiful, Meridian turned the spear on himself, piercing his heart with the deadly metal.

"Meridian's flaming chariot plummeted, and with him fell his terrible tools. The net, delicate and golden, spread across the lands of men. *Kembric*." Audé sent a glittering chain of burnished kembric spiraling into the dust. "The spear drove veins deep into the Meteor Mountains. *Dristic*." A polished bracelet of the strong, silvery metal slipped off Henrique's wrist and landed with a puff. "And the shattered glass vial, stained with Meridian's own blood and infused with his great power, pierced shards deep into the heart of the world. *Ambric*." Audé blew across her palm, and a billow of shimmering amber dust swirled up to fly above the empire that was its namesake.

"Meridian hurtled to the earth. The Moon fled deep into the comforting darkness of night. And the shameful Sun, wracked with terrible guilt for his evil deed, turned his face from the world, hiding within the flaming towers of his palais. And from that day forth, the daylight world became as you know it. The Sun does not traverse the skies. The Moon remains hidden in the shadowy gloom of the Midnight Dominion. And Meridian—Meridian is lost."

I leaned forward, gripping my knees as a shiver teased my spine. This was my favorite part of the legend. The familiar words never failed to raise the flesh on my arms and tickle the hairs at the nape of my neck.

"Some claim Meridian is not dead, but merely sleeping. Deep within the bosom of Midnight he sleeps, waiting for a time when mankind needs him most. Only then will he awake from slumber and use his legacy to force the Sun to rise and set once more.

"But some say Meridian is neither dead nor sleeping. Meridian, impassioned by the beautiful Moon, trekked deep into the shadows of Dominion to seek forgiveness from his love. There he shines still, a bright star at the Moon's side. And one day, when darkness spreads across the land and Midnight rules the earth, he will watch as the vengeful Moon finally snuffs out the light of her greatest enemy. And the Sun will shine no more."

A sudden hush sifted secret fingers through the dusk. The only thing I heard was a low, distant humming in my ears. A humming like—

Unease grasped my throat. I glanced down at my lap, and sucked in a sharp breath.

A pennant of shadow yawned between my hands, velvety and fathomless. A million brilliant flecks of light danced within the darkness, still and cold and impossibly remote.

The third bell of Nocturne chimed across the camp, breaking the spell. Children giggled, and Noémie accepted a sprinkling of applause as Audé and Henrique bowed. The free travelers dissipated to their tents and wagons, eager for sleep.

Panic stitched cold threads down my back. I clamped my hands in the folds of my skirts and squeezed my eyes shut. A swarm of invisible insects hummed in my ears. I reached for something to distract me from the vision of an ink-black night studded with diamonds of light. Words and images flickered across my mind's eye.

A bloodstained sun, peering between flags of livid clouds.

Dristic streaks in the hair of a frowning Skyclad captain.

A tumble of black curls above kembric-flecked eyes.

A shining city, and the promise of a new world.

"Sylvie?"

I lifted dizzy eyes to meet a familiar gaze. Warmth stained my cheeks, and I turned to stare into the fire, forcing my breathing to slow.

"Is everything all right?" Luca asked. "You're pale."

"I'm fine," I lied, scrambling to my feet. "I thought I . . . saw something."

"What did you see?" A mischievous smile pushed Luca's frown away. "Was it a *mulo*? A dust devil? They haunt these lands, and if they catch you, they'll use your hair for a necklace and your blood for wine."

"Luca, don't." I hated the peevish tone of my voice, but my ears still hummed, and my fingers itched, and my heart thrummed uneven in my chest. "There's no such thing as a *mulo*, in these lands or any other."

"It was a joke, Sylvie." Luca's smile faded. "Are you sure you're all right?"

"It's been a long day." I scrubbed a hand over my brow. "It's past third Nocturne. I should sleep."

"Of course." Luca stuffed his hands into the pockets of his tunic. "Will you ride with me and Vesh tomorrow? You know how he loves your stories."

"I will." I forced a thin copy of a smile, guilty for being so unkind to my friend. My *only* friend. "I'll even promise to tell a new story."

"A promise I'll hold you to."

I was almost to my patched tent when Luca's voice reached out and stopped me.

"Sylvie?"

I turned.

"Every day I ask why you're traveling to the Amber City. Every day you brush me off with jokes or half-truths. Why won't you answer me?"

In the harsh glow of the silent sun, Luca could almost be a *mulo* himself, a spirit crafted from dust and wind, restless and wild as the parched earth that spawned him.

"Maybe you're not asking the right questions, Luca."

"I've asked every question I can think of." Luca gave his curls a rough shake. "Everything I know about you I had to coax out of you. Even your name I had to guess. You tell me nothing. I just want to know you. Why can't you give me something real, Sylvie?"

"I'm not sure there's anything real to give, Luca," I whispered into the dusk. "Blink, and I might return to the shadows I came from."

I ducked into my tent, tugging the flap closed before I could see the hurt on my friend's face.

I flung myself onto my meager pile of blankets and examined my hands in the gloom of the narrow tent. My slender fingers tingled, and I curled my hand into a fist, watching the tapestry of blue veins beneath my skin pump blood I shouldn't have. Blood I *couldn't* have.

Mother Celeste and the other Sisters swore I was an aberration, a judgment from the Scion himself meant to test their piety. They begged me to stop, praying over my deviant hands as radiance poured forth, impossible as sunshine in that dim-cold dusk at the edge of Dominion.

It's for your own good, they hissed, desperation crowding out the terror in their eyes. *Do not tempt the wrath of the Scion, child!*

And when I couldn't—or wouldn't—stop, they kept me locked in my room for days at a time, conversing in hushed whispers outside my door.

That was the first time I heard the word: *legacy.*

Legacy. A word I barely recognized until a tide ago. A word I'd never uttered aloud. A word that shuddered through my bones with a familiarity I couldn't name.

Legacy meant magic. Legacy meant power. Legacy meant birthright.

Only the aristocracy of the Amber Empire claimed the gift of legacy. It was an inheritance bestowed upon the descendants of Meridian, bloodline of the Scion—the great families who held court upon the Amber Empress herself, in Coeur d'Or, the palais at the heart of the Amber City.

I wasn't highborn. Or if I was, whoever sired me disowned me, dumping me in the shadows at the edge of the world like I was worthless. The thought stoked the ember of rage burning always within me, a bright kernel hard and polished as a ruby.

When I opened my hands illusions spilled out, beautiful and terrible and impossible to control.

Trees of kembric, draped in garlands of jewels.

Bouquets of skyflowers.

Bracelets of stars.

I wasn't worthless. I wasn't an aberration, a freak, a *monster*. I was a *legacy*.

I ran away from the Temple of the Scion because I knew I deserved better than merely being tolerated. Much as I'd tried to follow in their footsteps when I was young, I had never belonged with the Sisters, and they had certainly never loved me. They had taught me many things: that to laugh too loudly in the presence of the Scion was a sin, and that the bruises and scrapes inflicted by the ignorant village kids were my own fault, and that dreaming of anything outside the dank walls of the Temple was too dangerous to be allowed.

They had taught me that being alive was not the same thing as living.

They had tried to stop me from leaving, when I finally fled. They had burned the Imperial Insignia and tried to lock me in my room, panic churning their studied tranquility into chaos. But I'd escaped. Jagged satisfaction tinged with guilt burned through me when I remembered how I'd repaid a lifetime of their indifference.

But I deserved the chance to find where I belonged. To find a world where my gift—my *legacy*—did not frighten superstitious Sisters or enrage cruel children. To find a world forged in sunlight and honed on dreams, as perilous and intoxicating as the colors spilling jewel-bright from my fingertips. To find a world where I wasn't a freak or a monster.

That's why I was traveling to the Amber City: to join the court of the empress in Coeur d'Or. As a legacy of the Amber Empire, I would be embraced and celebrated. I would finally be around others like me, who understood what it was like to *burn*—with magic and wonder and the heady thrill of impossible visions.

I twisted my hands again, and a shower of ghostly petals drifted down to brush against my lips, soft as a kiss.

A kiss that tasted like a promise.

FOUR

A breeze scudded clouds across the somber sun, and the convoy slept.

I huddled at the edge of a guttering cook fire, warming the gristly scraps of dried meat I'd wheedled out of Löic, the kindly drover of one of Rina's transports. I'd tried to be tough, gnawing on bitter ginga root to keep my hunger at bay, but it was getting harder to ignore the jut of my ribs and hipbones. I was running out of food, but so was the rest of the camp. Barrels of tize diminished as stores of lavas and meat thinned.

The convoy had trudged westward for another span, churning our spirits in its wake until they were as dusty as the earth. The hours of Matin bled into Prime, then drifted into Compline and Nocturne until the bells rang out for Matin once more. The sun appeared to creep higher above the horizon, lightening the sky to tangerine. The dusty prairie had finally given way to endless meadows of green maize swaying beneath pristine flocks of cygni soaring overhead. We passed men trudging through stunted villages. Their hair and clothes were black with smears of the soot produced in the smelting of kembric.

But we were still nearly a span's ride from the Amber City.

"Sylvie?" A voice sliced through my tangle of anxiety. "What are you doing out here?"

I whirled. Luca stood in the silhouette of the biggest transport, hair mussed. I clenched my fist around the handle of the borrowed skillet and almost tried to hide it, before realizing it was too late. Luca's sleep-heavy gaze had already narrowed on the meager scraps of meat.

"I told you to tell me if you ran out of food," he growled. He crossed the space between us in a few long strides, his drowsiness dissolving into exasperation. "If this is all you're eating, you're going to starve before we reach the Amber City."

"A romantic way to die," I said, and laughed.

Luca didn't.

"I don't want to bother your family," I explained, sobering. "You and your mother have already done too much for me."

"You aren't a bother. You need to eat."

"I'll never be able to repay you."

"You don't have to repay anything. We want you here. *I* want you here."

I cut my gaze to Luca's. The scudding clouds threw pennants of light and shadow across his face, and I could almost pretend I didn't see the ruddy flush rising in his cheeks. I looked away, and silence stretched out between us, brittle as metal hammered too thin.

"You once spoke of a *mulo*, a dust devil," I muttered, reaching for something—anything—to ease the tension. "Will you tell me the story?"

Luca gusted a sigh, crouching to flip my scraps of meat before they burned. "There isn't much of a story. It's just something Tavendel mothers tell their children to frighten them into behaving."

"I want to hear it anyway."

"They say a *mulo* is born from dust, christened in fire, and cursed with an eternal thirst. Back home, we left saucers of wine in front of our tents, to stop the *mulo* from sneaking inside and drinking our blood."

"Wine?" A shiver curled cold fingers around my spine. "But why would the *mulo* drink the wine when it could sneak inside and drink your blood instead?"

Luca's fire-bright eyes met mine, and he shrugged. "Maybe by paying a demon what he needs, you keep him from stealing what he desires."

A fierce breeze kissed my neck. My palms thrummed, and I felt the dire image heaving through my consciousness. *Dust. Fire. Blood.* I saw its terrible eyes, ringed in fire; heard its silent, billowing footsteps; felt the metallic gnaw of its bloodlust hollowing out my stomach.

"Home," I gasped out, seizing that word and using it as a shield against the dream pummeling strange fists against the prison of my ribs. "You mentioned home. Where is that?"

Luca's brows came together, and he glared into the fire. "It's less of a where than a *who*. My people—we are Tavendel. Time was, we traversed the length of the Tavend flatlands, following the rains to the best grazing. These days, few among us follow the old paths, choosing instead to seek out more lucrative trade in the cities."

I nibbled on a bit of jerky as cautious curiosity surged within me. I'd heard Luca mention Tavendel, but this was the first time he'd spoken of what that meant to him.

"So you were herders?" I asked.

"We bred and grazed horses, yes." A sudden radiance gripped him, and he grinned. "But we were also cartographers, and astronomers, and poets. Vesh ôn Khorin, my grandfather many times over, wrote a thousand poems—quite a few are still famous, sung often among the Tavendel."

I tried on a smile. "Sing me one?"

Luca uncrossed his arms and gazed at the sky. His voice spilled out, timid at first, then more confident. I didn't understand the language, but the fire-fretted melody curled desolate against my skin. Finally, the song trailed away on a soft, low note. I shook myself, and swiped at my suddenly damp cheeks.

"Beautiful," I murmured. "What does it mean?"

Luca shrugged, suddenly shy. "My Tavendel is rusty, and the translation is complex. But it's about something precious being stolen away, and the hollow wind at the edge of heartbreak."

I nodded like I understood. "Why did you and your family leave? Your Tavendel homeland, I mean."

Luca tensed, the muscles in his forearms going rigid as bars of dristic. I immediately regretted my thoughtless question.

"Luca, I'm sorry." I choked on a tough scrap of meat. "I shouldn't have—"

"No." Luca's voice was puckered as an old scar. "It's a story that deserves telling, just so it's never forgotten." He paused, and smoothed his fists open onto his thighs. "I was eleven. Vesh hadn't been born yet. My father had chosen me to follow in his footsteps as a Guardian—I would learn the ways of weaponry so that I might one day be able to protect my tribe from any dangers it might face. But first, I had to be tested. So I was blindfolded and taken into the Chabrol, a maze of rock formations sacred to the Tavendel. They left me there, bound, with no food, water, or map. I had to use my wits, my endurance, and my bravery to find my way home, or die trying."

You were only a child! I wanted to shout. But I bit my lip and listened.

"It took me four days, and by the time I returned I was sun-burned and bleeding and half-dead with thirst. But I didn't get the victor's welcome I had expected." He paused, and the sooty dregs of some ancient shame passed over his face like ashes. "While I was gone, a Skyclad platoon had raided the camp and stolen all our horses. They slaughtered my father, as well as my aunt, uncle, and older cousins. They only spared my mother because she was heavy with child."

Shock and pity struck me mute.

"Maman wept for a week, then went cold and hard as forged dristic. We walked to the nearest sand port in Dura'a, where she sold every last piece of her bridal jewelry in order to purchase a Charter Writ. Vesh was born on that first expedition to the Duskland mines, and we've worked to grow the convoy every tide since." He spread his arms to encompass the tents, travelers, transports, and crates of ore. "And so I will spend my life travers-ing this harsh land, instead of becoming an honored Tavendel warrior like my father wished. All because the Amber Empress's hired thugs didn't feel like paying for fresh mounts."

"Luca—" I dug deep for words to express the roil of disgust and sympathy and fury souring my stomach, but only unearthed platitudes. "I'm so sorry. I can't imagine how terrible that must have been for you and Madame Rina."

For the space of a breath, a pall of bitterness seemed to tower over Luca, twisting his features and hunching his spine. But in another moment it was gone, banished by the sudden carefree blaze of his smile.

"Past is past." He surged to his feet. "Convoy's moving on in two hours—best get some rest."

I groaned out loud, pushing away the uneasy weight of shared sorrow. Luca was right—there was no point in dwelling too long on past tragedy. But as I trailed him back into the heart of camp, I wondered for the first time whether his near-permanent grin masked a different face—a face scarred by misfortune and pocked with spite.

A face I'd glimpsed in the space between heartbeats, and hoped never to see again.

FIVE

I rode in the back of Madame Rina's transport, teaching Vesh a silly guessing game I invented. Brightly dyed curtains swayed in the breeze, casting a patchwork of colored light and shadow. Vesh laughed as I dragged a nub of charcoal across a scrap of parchment, sketching a rough design.

"Horsey!" he shouted, breathless. "Flutterwing! No, wait—giant!"

I shook my head, giggling over the sound of my rumbling stomach.

The transport swayed to a halt. The curtains trembled, and a stack of copper pots fell to the floor with a thud. Voices raised outside, then silence.

Vesh and I stared toward the front of the transport.

"Vesh!" Luca's head popped between two green curtains. Excitement lit his face. "Sylvie! Come out and see."

I clambered to my feet, tamping down a ripple of nerves. Vesh's small hand was hot in mine as I lifted him out to his brother. He was gone before I could blink, sprinting away to find his friends.

"What is it?" I asked, craning my neck.

"You'll see." Luca slid his hands around my waist to help me down from the transport, the touch sending a shiver lancing up my spine. He twined his fingers in mine and tugged. Curiosity and unease warred within me.

Arrayed along a stony arête, the convoy gazed out across a valley. Grass swept away from our feet, dotted with purple heliotrope. The ruddy sun hung a few fingers' breadth above the distant spine of ambric-streaked massifs, and nestled amid gentle foothills sprawled the Amber City, towering and glittering and vast.

We made it.

Sudden panic tore the breath from my throat and chilled my bones. Part of me never believed I'd make it this far. Part of me believed the Amber City was nothing more than a dream, a mythic world conjured up by travelers to soothe the drudgery of an interminable journey. Part of me believed I would wake up one Matin, blanketed in creeping shadows and surrounded by indifferent Sisters.

I blinked to dispel the mirage. The Amber City didn't budge, solid and commanding in its position of majesty across the plain.

So close.

"*Vitza!* Stop gawping!" Madame Rina was a whirlwind of billowing robes and tight braids, rounding up laborers and free travelers like unruly goats. "Do you want to look at it, or do you want to get to it?"

Luca whooped, swinging up onto the roof of the transport as the ambric apparatus belched orange and the convoy trundled toward the distant city. I trotted to catch up, but the air tasted thin in my lungs and I couldn't take my eyes off the distant glitter of domes and spires.

It took us another two days to arrive at the gates of the Amber City, but it might have been an eternity. I did nothing but stare and wonder as the convoy crawled closer. The Amber City was huge. My mind could hardly comprehend the vast metropolis reaching up toward the smoldering sun. The labyrinth of streets and alleyways twisting and converging across the city. The bright smear of the river, its network of canals gleaming red as rivulets of blood.

And surrounding everything, a great wall, with soaring ramparts built from black ironstone and barred in dristic. Sullen ambric lamps pulsed from stern towers, sending shards of red and gold to pierce the sky.

I asked Luca whether an army could ever breach those battlements.

"Any army foolhardy enough to approach the Amber City would have to face ten thousand Skyclad long before even setting eyes on the wall," Luca laughed. "But it makes a statement all the same."

"Is it noisy inside?" I pressed. "Crowded? Where do all the people live?"

"There are different quartiers, see, each with its own character." Luca leaned close enough that his stubble rasped against my cheek. I fought to control my breathing as his hand sketched precise arcs against the outline of the city. "To the south, Unitas: a place of learning where students pore over ancient tomes written in dead languages, staining their fingers with ink and swilling kachua to stay awake."

"Kachua?"

"Like tea, but black and bitter." Luca wrinkled his nose, then pointed to a cluster of glittering spires. "That's Jardinier, where the wealthy clothe their children in the feathers of rare birds and adorn their pets with priceless jewels. That arched boulevard is Concordat, where great fountains spew and the hooves of a thousand Skyclad destriers ring out on kembric-lined streets. North of that is the Mews, where the rich rub shoulders with the poor in vast marchés. You can buy anything: stardust, or the tears of a lovelorn maiden, or a tamed *d'haka* all the way from Dura'a."

"A *what?*"

"A flying desert serpent with wings of flame and eyes so bright they'll make a man go blind."

"Luca, that's not real."

"How do you know?" Luca's smile flashed before he pointed back to the city. "That chaotic mountain of shanties and hovels and ill-made huts, climbing the foothills? That's the Paper City. Slums, where the poor live on top of one another, clambering on roofs and across rickety bridges. Vice goes hand in hand with poverty. You're as likely to get bitten by a starving orphan as a stray dog."

But I was barely listening anymore. My eyes snagged on Coeur d'Or, gleaming at the center of it all. Set atop a rise overlooking the river, the palais of the Amber Empress seemed to shine like a sun. Built from glass and ambric and gilded in kembric, Coeur d'Or dazzled and beguiled. Crystalline towers sent splinters of light dancing across the city. A thousand filigreed arches twisted and spiraled toward the sky.

"And Coeur d'Or? What about the palais?"

Luca's eyes sharpened on mine, and his smile wilted.

"What do you care about coddled aristos dancing attendance on a spoiled empress? My friend Garan is a servant in the palais— you should hear how they prance around in silks and velvets, primping and preening and never venturing beyond the walls of their private paradise." The rusty sun sparked in his eyes and turned his expression harsh. "Those legacied fools don't realize how big the world is. What I wouldn't give to have that blood running through my veins! Maybe I'd find a way to protect the world from evil, instead of holing up in a château in face paint and high heels."

I lowered my eyes, sudden shame battling with the hot thrill singing through my veins. Colors burned the edges of my vision: craggy violet and river red and the intoxicating translucence of seething sunlight through amber. My hands itched, and for the first time since I joined the convoy at the edge of the Dusklands, I actually wanted to show him. Show him the many-hued illusions pulsing at my fingertips, the daydream fancies beguiling my mind.

Coddled aristos. Luca's voice echoed in my mind, dripping with scorn. *Legacied fools.*

I bit down on the colors, shoving them into the cage of my ribs.

"Sylvie?" The brush of Luca's palm against the back of my hand was both a question and a sort of answer. "You're trembling."

I curled my traitor fingers into my palm and stared toward the shining city. I swallowed a wave of sour guilt, ignoring the hurt pooling in Luca's eyes.

I was so close. I couldn't let myself get distracted.

SIX

We felt the gates thunder open in our bones.

The convoy joined the imperial boulevard, steering transports and wagons onto broad flagstones thronged with travelers. Horses stamped as a profusion of livestock squawked and hollered from crates and cages. Women and men of every color and garb jostled for space, and the hum and chatter of a thousand voices crowded my ears and weighed on my chest.

"All right, Sylvie?" Luca's concerned eyes brushed my face. "We're almost there."

"I know," I gasped out. The crush of humanity was nearly too much to bear—I'd never seen this many people in one place.

"Don't be frightened," he said, and grinned. "I've come here so many times I've lost track. You're safe with me."

But when I glanced toward the gleaming domes of Coeur d'Or, I wasn't sure I wanted to be safe.

Through the gates, the city burst with even more sights and sounds. Terraced houses loomed over stately, tree-lined boulevards. A quartet of plumed horses pulled a lavish carriage, gilded shutters pulled tight. Laughing fountains arched beneath looming monuments sculpted from ironstone and gilded in kembric. Tall posts topped with ambric lamps lined the road, hung with banners emblazoned with the image of a face.

Soft, delicate features. Rosy lips curled into a gentle smile beneath eyes violet as the heliotrope blossoms dotting the plains outside the city. Lustrous auburn curls falling beneath a diadem jeweled with a faceted cabochon of purest ambric.

I didn't need Luca to tell me who she was: Severine, the Amber Empress.

I could hardly take my eyes off her. Luca's lips thinned when he noticed me staring, but I gazed at the brightly dyed banner until another reared up to take its place.

We left the dignified boulevard behind, diving into the sprawl of the Mews. Streets and avenues unfurled, reaching in every direction like a many-fingered hand. Vast marchés spilled over sidewalks, colorful tents and stands draped in food and clothing and jewelry and ambric artifices. My nose crinkled at the scent of unfamiliar herbs and spices. Vendors shouted and waved at the convoy, offering up their wares: gemflowers from the Meridian Desert; fur from the mythical white tiger, hunted on the snow-draped peaks of the Meteor Mountains; a lock of the empress's hair, certain to bring good fortune.

Finally, we reached the depot, a dilapidated cluster of store-houses where Madame Rina staged her convoy. Dazed, I gathered my few belongings and threaded through the throng of bonded workers and free travelers hugging and weeping fond goodbyes. Luca and Vesh had disappeared with their mother. I assumed they had business with the comptroller of the warehouse— duties to pay and bribes to dole out.

A trough by the gate held clear water, and I felt suddenly caked in grime after spans on the road. I thrust my hands in the cool liquid, scrubbing at the crusted dirt with my nails. The ruffled surface flung shards of my own image back at me—a blue-grey eye, chapped lips, a length of lank hair. Once, Sister Anouk had admitted I was pretty, with my thick, dark hair and wide eyes. *But sometimes the prettiest people can possess the ugliest souls*, she'd demurred, fading back into the tenets of her faith. *A body is an illusion and a face is a lie.*

What would she think of my soul now, now that my body was dirty and malnourished after spans on the dusty road?

My eyes wandered across the crowded rooftops to the gilded domes of Coeur d'Or, shining above the maze of narrow streets. I imagined pristine jardins and courtyards, ringed in flowers. Glittering hallways, awash in the coral light of a thousand ambric lamps. Elaborate feasts. Gowns. Fêtes.

I clenched my itching palms.

I glanced back at the hunched storehouses. The narrow doors and dark windows. The peeling paint and rusting metal.

I should wait for Luca. I wanted to say goodbye to him, and his strong mother, and his sweet brother. I wanted to tell them how much their kindness meant to me, when I had nothing else.

But then I remembered the look on Luca's face yesterday when he'd spoken of Coeur d'Or. I remembered the brush of his fingers against my hand. His honey-warm eyes, flecked with kembric. The easy brush of curls against his brow. His bright smile.

I bit my lip so hard I thought I might draw blood.

Maybe it would be easier not to say goodbye at all. A poor reward for a good friend, but better than a path to a broken heart.

I turned toward the gate.

"Sylvie!" Luca's shout rang above the clamor of the courtyard.

I spun. Relief battled with regret in the fathomless corners of my heart.

Luca wore only an undershirt—the sweat-damp fabric clung to the muscled planes of his torso. He pushed damp curls out of his eyes and frowned. "Where are you going?"

"I'm leaving." I sucked in a sip of air and forced myself to meet his gaze. "You and Madame Rina have been more than kind to me. I owe you both so much. But I can't impose any longer. I should be on my way."

"Leaving?" The crease between his brows deepened. "Why didn't you tell me?"

"I couldn't find you," I lied, swallowing against the lump swelling in my throat.

"I was just unloading crates with Anaïs."

"Anaïs?"

"The comptroller's daughter," he explained, glancing to the left and raising a hand. I squelched an absurd flare of envy when a voluptuous, golden-haired girl waved cheerfully back. "Many of the bonded laborers and free travelers are staying at the inn next door before moving on. Why don't you do the same?"

"I don't have any money. I can't afford it."

"Then where will you go?"

I opened my mouth to tell him, to explain, but my voice was trapped in my throat.

"Sylvie." Luca grasped my shoulders. The scent of sun-warmed metal and sweat clung to his skin, and my pulse jolted. I wasn't sure whether I wanted to break away, or lean closer. "I don't know where you're going. I don't know why you're here, in the city. But I don't think you know either."

I shook my head, trying to find the words to explain how wrong he was.

"I don't care." He tilted his head. "I know you're proud. But we can take care of you. Me, Maman, Vesh. Stay with the convoy. Stay with me."

My gaze slashed up to meet his. In the faded light, his eyes glinted like coins.

"The ore trade is a hard life," he continued, fervent, "but a good one. Our charter takes the convoy from one end of the Amber Road to the other, traveling through more towns and provinces than you can imagine. You'll see things you've never dreamed of before. Cities made of glass. Oceans with waves of light. Blue men. The infinite sweep of the Tavendel grasslands. I want to show you all of that. I want you to stay."

"Stop," I choked out, finally. "Just stop."

Luca's hands fell from my shoulders. His brow furrowed, and his hands squeezed into fists.

"Please, Luca." I clenched my jaw, still struggling for the right words. "Don't ask me for that. Even if I wanted to, I can't."

"*Why?*" His voice rose in pitch. He shook his mess of dark curls. "I've asked you every Nocturne for six spans, Sylvie. What are you hiding? Why are you here?"

Dimly—distantly—I heard a buzz, like beetles crawling over metal. I rubbed my prickling hands together. And before I could change my mind, I held them out, palms up, like an offering.

"Because of this," I said.

I conjured Coeur d'Or, in perfect miniature. Spires and arches and domes vaulted into the empty space between us, glittering in the light of a faded sun. Spiral stairways. Delicate ogees. Pillars. Fountains. For a moment I could barely believe that I had created this—*this wonder*—from nothing more than imagination and the legacy swirling in my blood.

I sustained the illusion for the length of a held breath. Then the exquisite palais drifted apart like paint washed away by water. A wave of vertigo blurred my vision, and I gasped in a reedy breath.

Only then did I dare look up at Luca.

His head jerked back like I'd slapped him. His nostrils flared with a rough breath. Pain darkened the edges of his eyes before his face shuttered.

"You never told me." It wasn't a question.

"I didn't know how."

"How?" Contempt twisted his face. "It didn't seem so hard a moment ago. What were you afraid of? Did you think I would spit at your feet and call you *witch* or *monster*?"

"No! I just didn't think—"

"I am Tavendel," he interrupted. He trawled a shaking hand through his hair, scraping sweaty locks from his temples. "When we sing, the clouds weep, and our own eyes spill raindrops. When we stamp our feet, *mulos* dance across the plains. When we are cut, we bleed poems full of magic. I would as soon call you a witch as I would disown my own mother."

"That's not it at all," I said, struggling to keep my voice even. "What I just showed you—that's my legacy. I thought you might not understand how much a part of me it is. How it changes the way I see the world. How it changes the way I see *myself*."

"You're going there, aren't you?" He wrenched his gaze toward Coeur d'Or. The palais sparked spears of light into a sky stained with plum and ocher. "You want to join the empress's court. To dance attendance on that horde of sniveling nobles. To find the parents who abandoned you."

"You're not listening to me." I swallowed, dousing a sparking kernel of rage. "I'm already one of them. Coeur d'Or is where I belong. I have noble blood flowing through my veins—the bloodline of the Scion. I deserve this chance to change my world."

"You think your *blood* defines where you belong? You think being highborn means you deserve special treatment?" He sneered. "Our blood is nothing without the will that moves it. You can choose your own life."

"I didn't mean—" I snapped my teeth in frustration, cutting my words to pieces. "I can't control my legacy. It either pushes out of me against my will or makes me tremble with exhaustion. I want to learn how to use this power living within me. Imagine the splendor I could create, the dreams I could make real! The people living in that palais are the only ones who can show me how."

"That's not why you're going." Luca's eyes narrowed to slits of fire. "I just offered you friendship. Security. *Family.* Splendor and dreams are just fancy words for wealth. You want silks, refinement. Fine wines and feasts. Parties that last from Compline to Matin. Kembric dinner plates and high heels. And worst of all, you want *power.*"

"So what?" The words burst from me louder than I expected. "What's wrong with being ambitious? I do want a world full of beauty and grace. I do want power. And what's more, I *deserve* it. It's my birthright, and I'll be damned if I don't claim what's mine!"

Luca rocked back on his heels. I twisted trembling fingers in the fraying hide of my knapsack. Silence stretched between us. Luca finally tore his eyes from mine, staring across the courtyard toward the shadowed warehouse.

"I hope you find the world you're looking for, Sylvie," he said heavily. "I really do. But I've heard the stories about what goes on in Coeur d'Or. Those poisonous courtiers will never accept someone like you. You may claim a legacy, but you weren't born in their world. They will humiliate you with twisted pranks. They'll contaminate your soul with toxic games. You will never truly belong."

Unease gnawed at my ribs.

"So after they leave you broken, think of me. Remember what I offered you—family, security, friendship." His broad shoulders tensed. "More, if you wanted it."

And then he strode away. Disquiet clambered up my throat and choked me with a cold certainty: I hadn't expressed myself well at all.

I didn't want to leave Luca like this. Part of me didn't want to leave him at all. But I'd made myself a promise, back in the grim, pallid dusk—I would find where I belonged. Not just a place to survive, but a place to flourish, surrounded by people who understood the blaze of strange colors staining my soul. A place anchored in beauty and steeped in wonder. A place where magic could bring dreams to life.

Did wanting that world make me vain, or greedy, or ambitious?

Maybe.

But even if it did, was I willing to sacrifice that world for the love of a boy? A boy with heat in his smile and a song on his lips. A boy who'd had his own perfect world stolen away, in exchange for the bitter drudgery of an unwanted life.

I clenched my teeth, sifting my hurt through the shifting sands of my uncertainty.

Luca paused halfway across the courtyard, caught in a narrow swathe of sunlight. Motes of dust glittered like pale stars in the vermilion light. The tri-metal signat in his ear glinted as he turned his head to glance over his shoulder.

"We'll be in the Mews for another half span," he muttered. "Gathering supplies and contracts for the convoy. If you change your mind—"

For a moment I thought he was going to say something else. But then he shook his head and disappeared into the cool, hay-scented dusk of the stables.

Where Anaïs was waiting for him.

I squeezed my eyelids against a prickle of tears. I wouldn't think like that. I was making the right choice.

I cut my gaze toward the center of the city, where Coeur d'Or perched, aloof and ephemeral as an unspoken secret. I still couldn't believe I was here, so far from the dusty, shadowed village where cruel children kicked me for being different. So far from the tomb-quiet Temple where impassive Sisters quelled all my hopes and forbade me from dreaming.

I squared my shoulders and imagined forged dristic pouring into my veins and strengthening my bones. I wasn't that weak, neglected, abused girl anymore. And I'd traveled too far to let regret stop me from finding where I belonged.

So what if I lost a friend? Surely that was a small price to pay for finding a brand-new world.

SEVEN

The gate to Coeur d'Or was a thing of outrageous beauty. Wrought in kembric and shining like a beacon, the portal loomed from the spiked fence abutting it. Gleaming vines of filigree twisted along slender bars. The Imperial Insignia glittered from the ornate finial, the sunburst set with a faceted bijou of ambric that caught the low light and magnified it, splintering radiance across the courtyard. A platoon of Skyclad Gardes flanked the gate, pale armor polished mirror-bright and silvery cloaks stirring.

I tore my eyes from the magnificent gate to look back the way I'd come. The palais occupied a steep hill like a queen atop a throne, and the city spread out below in a vast tapestry, woven with the warp and weft of unfamiliar colors and sounds and smells.

Without knowing the way to the palais—and too embarrassed to ask—I found my way to the gates by sight alone, along alleyways and across parks and up endless flights of stairs. The Amber City was vast and vivid; each new sight and sound shivered through me like the thunderous pulse of a colossal heart.

Satins rippling with sky-lit colors: vermilion and magenta feathering toward a sapphire twilight. A mechanical eagle, twice as big as my head, with articulated wings and ambric eyes as red as the sun. Feral-eyed vendors selling bottled curses and stoppered wealth, mirrored kisses and scented secrets. Clear ponds full of giant lotus flowers, their silky-soft petals pale as the mythic Moon. Jewels and colored glass. Laughing children.

I sucked in a deep breath, letting the sweat dry on the nape of my neck. Up here, the air was clear and fresh—none of the wonderful, shifting scents of the city: perfume and garbage, cooking food and rotting fruit. Up here, everything was expensive and manicured. Controlled.

Perfect.

I curled my fingers into my frayed skirts. My heart beat an uneven pattern against my ribs, and I brushed a strand of greasy hair out of my eyes. A trickle of nerves raised gooseflesh along my arms.

I should have bathed before I came here.

To desire is to sin, Sister Anouk's voice whispered. *Be content with all you have.*

I should have prepared a speech.

Dreaming breeds misfortune. Sister Cathe. *Dominion shadows will seek you out.*

I should have—

No.

I forced the insidious whispers away. I had no reason to feel insecure. I belonged here. The exceptional blood in my veins flowed within the nobles who lived inside the palais. Even the empress herself, whose exquisite face hung in shopwindows and on banners across the city, was of that same bloodline. Meridian's royal, magical line. And if my uncaring parents hadn't dumped their infant in the Dusklands with nothing more than a vague note and an ambric amulet, I would have grown up in this world.

This should have been my home.

I marched forward before I could change my mind.

Beneath their shining helms, the Skyclad Gardes' eyes were flat and distant, registering me as neither threat nor interest. I approached one, taller than me by a head, muscled and power-ful. Another worm of uncertainty wriggled along my spine, and my eyes skittered the length of the tall fence.

There had to be another way. Another gate, or a smaller door, or someone I could talk to—a palais liaison, or—

Stop it, Sylvie, I snarled at the coward sniveling in the back of my mind.

My face swam distorted in the poor mirror of the Garde's breastplate. The soldat finally registered my presence, glancing down her nose at me, a raggedy urchin covered in half the dust and grime of the Dusklands. Her lip curled into a sneer.

"Hello," I stammered, cursing the high squeak that emerged instead of my normal voice. "I'm here to join the court of the Amber Empress as a legacy. The Scion's bloodline flows through my veins."

The soldat cocked her head to one side, a tiny motion that nevertheless nearly sent me running back to the Mews. Smirking, the Garde banged a sword against her shield with an efficient clang, summoning a Skyclad officer from a small hut beside the gate. He strode forward, raising a hand to keep the sun from his eyes. He was young, but he wore his command around him like a cloak, his every movement breathing power and contempt. My skin itched with a chill when I saw his frown.

The Garde clicked her boots and gestured to me.

"A prankster, sir," she muttered.

"A prankster?" The officer's frown deepened. "What manner of prank did the girl play? I see no props or other silliness."

"She claims she is of the bloodline," explained the Garde, dis-dainful. "A legacy, sir. She wants to join the Imperial Court."

The officer's brows shot up toward his hairline before he

schooled his features into passivity. His eyes took in my ragged clothing, my unwashed hair, the grime collected beneath my fingernails. Heat climbed up my neck toward my cheeks.

"And what proof do you have, girl? Writ of birth? Patents of nobility? Anything to prove this absurd claim?"

"N-no," I said, hating the stutter in my voice. Humiliation flared through my veins, and I reached for the soothing planes of my ambric pendant. "All I have is my legacy. I can show you."

"Fine," snapped the officer. His eyes were keen on my face. "Make it good, or you'll be spending this Nocturne in the palais dungeons."

I scrubbed my palms against my skirts. I closed my eyes, listening for that familiar, faint buzzing. My palms tingled. I focused on an image, holding it in my mind's eye until I could see nothing else.

I held out my palms, and showed the officer something that wasn't there.

The same illusion I'd shown Luca: Coeur d'Or in miniature, delicate and gleaming and even more perfect than before. Spires of glass. Arches twisting with porcelain vines. The stunning golden gate, sunlit ambric glinting from the finial. I willed the illusion to hold, but like before, the toy-sized palais melted away in the space of a breath.

I dropped my arms, fighting a wave of dizziness.

The officer stared at the scraps of color evanescing into thin air.

"Worthless trick," he snarled. "Clockwork legerdemain. Ambric and mirrors. I've seen such things before, in the labs at Unitas. A person can even buy such an apparatus in the marchés of the Mews, if one has the money to pay."

Thunder roared in my ears, and I reeled a step back. *No.* I'd imagined a million different ways this day might go. Simply not being believed was never one of them.

"It's not a trick," I said, pouring the last of my strength into the words. "I'm not using a device. It's my legacy. I create illusions."

The officer hesitated, then threw back his head and laughed. The Garde did the same, her straight white teeth gleaming red in the ruddy light. The other Skyclad Gardes within earshot chuckled, shaking helmed heads.

"A worthy attempt," mocked the officer. "Leave now, and I won't punish you for it. Come here again, and I can't promise I'll be so lenient."

He turned on his heel and marched back toward the gate, his cloak swinging in the breeze and his laughter echoing in my ears.

"Wait!" Desperation was a living thing inside me, choking my lungs and squeezing my heart. "I can do better. I'm not lying!"

Something in my voice reached the officer. From across the courtyard, his eyes touched mine, and I thought I saw a glint of uncertainty in his cool gaze.

"Look at me," I ground out.

This time, when I closed my eyes, I let my mind soar through the days and weeks and spans, back to the Temple at the edge of nothing where I was abandoned as a baby. Back to the bullies who kicked me in the ribs when barely formed shapes and colors spilled unbidden from my hands. Back to the sanctimonious Sisters who prayed for hours over my unrighteous fingers.

What if we took them? I once overheard Sister Anouk whisper. She didn't seem to realize the careless cruelty of the suggestion. *The magic would go, and she'd have to stay.*

But I never believed the magic ended with my hands. And I don't think they did either.

I dug my ragged fingernails deep into the skin of my palms. My fingers tingled, but I ignored the feeling, concentrating instead on the space between my ears. Concentrating on the feeling of my skin, covering my muscles and bones. My face.

I hadn't looked into a mirror for a tide. I could almost forget what I looked like—my sable locks; my blue eyes, tinged with grey Duskland shadows. Instead, I imagined another face. A face I'd seen more times than I could count on my journey through the city.

A face with even skin and sharp cheekbones, framed in a luxuriant tumble of dark auburn hair. Lips stained rose red. Luminous eyes the precise color of heliotrope. And a circlet bedizened with a single jewel of flawless ambric.

A swarm of insects droned in my ears. The skin on my face prickled before my cheeks went numb.

I imagined I had that face. I imagined I *was* that face.

I lifted my eyes to the Skyclad officer.

Everything stopped. My breath caught in my throat, and I felt balanced on the edge of something terrible and beautiful and terrifying. I teetered, caught between one world and the next. The past, and the future, intersecting in this single, breathless instant on the cusp of failure and hope.

I toppled.

The courtyard broke out into chaos.

Blood drained from the officer's features. His mouth dropped open, and his palm fell limp by the hilt of his sword. The stocky Garde shouted, then dropped to one knee, her dristic armor clanging loud against the cobblestones. Behind her, other soldats did the same, dropping like a line of Vesh's precious dominos. A muffled whisper sprinted across the courtyard, followed by shouts of *Your Majesty!* and *It's the empress!*

The illusion melted away.

I knew I was me once again.

The officer sprinted toward me, fumbling at the hasp of his cloak. The silvery material bloomed around me, snapping and billowing. He wrapped the silky fabric over my shoulders and face until I couldn't see anything but his shadow, muted on the pale cobbles of the courtyard. I pushed at the cloak, but the officer reached out one gloved hand and captured both my wrists.

"Curse you," he hissed, his words razoring through the shroud of heavy fabric. Then, loudly: "Back to your posts, you ingrates! Have you forgotten your training?"

The Skyclad platoon snapped to attention, shuffling and straightening.

"You," muttered the officer. Polished boots stepped into my limited view. "Nothing happened here, do you understand me? If anyone speaks of this, they will be flogged."

A grunt of agreement. "What will you do with her?"

"Chevalier Devall. He'll know how to proceed."

"Dowser?" A low whistle. "Better hope her mind is stronger than her body looks."

Dread coiled in my belly as the officer tightened his gloved hands around my wrists. I opened my mouth to ask *Who is Dowser?* but the golden gates swung open, silencing me.

I passed between their ornate arms into the glittering heart of the Amber Empire.

EIGHT

Out of sight of the gate, the Skyclad officer ripped the silvery cloak from my shoulders. His eyes weren't kind as he led me swiftly through the evolving labyrinth of the palais compound. Down shallow steps glinting with mica. Through a shimmering copse of jewel-flowered trees. Past a jardin that seemed to breathe in time to the distant chime of crystal bells. Gilded archways. Coiled staircases, golden and white. Stained glass. Mirrors. Chandeliers.

My mind spun at the blur of unfamiliar sights, and though I clung to each new image, I was soon overwhelmed. Struggling to keep up with the strident gait of my captor, I stumbled, my knees cracking against marble. I stared at my grimy hands splayed against the immaculate pattern twisting in the marble. A trickle of dread shivered along my spine, and I scraped my tongue around a mouth suddenly dry and foul-tasting.

"Get up," the officer commanded. I did as he said, swallowing my fear as he dragged me down yet another anonymous hallway. A long line of arms hewn from pale, translucent stone grasped guttering torches wrought in kembric. The officer burst through a hidden door and snapped to attention, raising his arm in a salute.

"Chevalier Devall!" he barked. "Pardon the interruption, but I bring you a matter of some urgency."

I squinted into the room. After all the white marble and gilt and blazing torches, the low-ceilinged chamber was dim and gloomy. A tall figure rose from the corner, face veiled in shadow.

A glowing ember flared, then faded as the person sucked smoke from a curving pipe.

"Is that so?" The man—Chevalier Devall, I assumed—spoke slowly, his deep voice rich and refined. "Please explain."

The Skyclad officer tersely recounted my behavior at the gates, but his words faded as I stared around the new room. A row of curtains shrouded a bank of windows—only a sliver of vermilion bled in from outside, illuminating dust motes suspended in the air. Books thronged jumbled bookcases. Vast spreads of paper swarmed the walls, but in the gloom I couldn't see their contents. Maps, perhaps. The scent of tabak hung like a pall in the room, tinged with a cloying perfume. I smothered a cough.

The officer and the chevalier fell silent, and when I looked up they were staring at me. I pushed a thread of hair behind my ear, and shifted my feet.

"You may go," said Chevalier Devall. The Skyclad officer bowed before stalking from the room. His steps echoed away, leaving me alone with the chevalier.

Anxiety twisted my stomach into a skein of knots. All I could see of Devall was the flare of his pipe. The stench of tabak clambered up my nostrils and sent sickly fingers down the back of my throat. I squeezed my eyes shut, fighting away nausea and a sudden feeling of weightlessness. When I opened them, the chevalier was standing right in front of me.

I muffled a shriek and lurched backward. Devall was tall, and broad in the shoulders. He wore a long, unadorned robe, like a monk or an ascetic. His bald pate was a smooth, deep brown—like polished ironwood—and his features were refined, almost severe. Lines sprayed from the corners of his eyes, and a deep furrow dug between his brows. His black eyes, hidden behind slender spectacles, betrayed no emotion.

"Your name."

"Sylvie, sir," I muttered. "I mean—Chevalier Devall—"

"Call me Dowser," he said. "Everyone else does."

"Dowser," I repeated, bobbing my head like an idiot.

"You traveled far," he said. It wasn't a question.

"Yes, sir," I managed. "From the Dusklands."

"A long journey. From the edge of Dominion to the heart of our empire. Because you believe you are special."

A cold hand stroked my spine, and I shivered.

He's just guessing.

"Maybe you are. But most likely you aren't. Few deserve what they were born with. Even fewer deserve what they weren't born with."

"I'm a legacy, sir," I managed, ignoring the fingers of ice caressing my heart. "I belong here. At Coeur d'Or. At the empress's court."

"Ambition—I like that." A precise smile creased Dowser's face. "But that exhibition you put on at the gates doesn't guarantee you are a legacy. Magic is not the sole domain of the highborn."

My head jerked up, my nostrils flaring.

"Surely you knew that." He studied me, not unkindly. "This world is full of strange things. The bewitching songs of the Gorma can just as easily lure a fish into a trap as they can dash a frigate against the rocks. I've known Aifiri who could bend metal with a touch. Among my people, the Zvar of the Meridian Desert, there are those who can command armies wrought from sand and nightmares. No, the bloodline of the Scion is not the only magic in this world."

"So I've come all this way for nothing?" I clenched my hands to stop them shaking with fury and embarrassment. "But—but I could be a valuable asset to the empress and her court. I create illusions—I can make you see things that aren't there. I could act as a double for the empress at public events, or perform for the people, or—"

"And what of your family?" Dowser interrupted. "Won't they miss you when you abandon them for wealth and prestige? Or perhaps they are in on the plot."

"I have no parents." My tongue was a lick of flame, turning my mouth to ash. "Only a highborn sire or dam who deserted me at the edge of the darkness and never returned."

"Interesting." Swift as a viper, Dowser reached out his hands and placed them on my temples.

"What are you doing?" I tried to jerk my head away, but his grip was like a vise.

"Didn't you wonder why they call me Dowser?" His expression flickered. "Because I dig deep, and what I find is nearly always precious. Now hold still. This won't be pleasant."

My mind imploded.

I might have screamed, but my own voice was distant, like an echo from another time. I fell inward, spiraling. I felt him there—*here*—dredging inside me, digging relentless fingers into the crevices of my being.

Images surged around me, a whirlwind tumble of noises and smells and sights and feelings. I couldn't breathe. I couldn't think. I was drowning beneath the cascade of my own memories.

And at the center of it all was Dowser, watching.

Sifting.

Luca smiling, reaching for my hand. Warmth. The Skyclad platoon. Violence. The shadowed dusk at the edge of nowhere. Home. The bruised clouds above Dominion, bright with slashes of silvery lightning. Frenzy. The slap of a dusty hand on my cheek. Pain. The smack of knees in packed dirt. Misery. Ugly laughter. *Monster.* The pointed toe of a boot in the ribs. Fear. My own urine, warming my trousers and staining the dust. Humiliation. A chilly Prime—
There.

The whirlwind slowed. A dingy, frigid room. Dull, livid light oozed from the window. An ancient desk. Heavy drawers creaking open beneath my hands, empty of anything but dust. One locked. I grabbed a bent letter opener, jamming the tip into the lock. *Snick. Click.*

There.

A sheaf of parchment lined in handwriting so elegant I barely recognized the language. My eyes skittered down the page, but my rudimentary skill in reading could only decipher half the words. *Remit of the empire . . . martial enmity . . . protective custody . . . Order of the Scion.* The sentences didn't make sense. The Imperial Insignia filled my eyes, ornate and unmistakable—a sunburst bigger than my hand, stamped in amber wax and gilded with kembric.

And below that, a signature scrawled in vermilion ink, looping and illegible. A puzzle to my squinting eyes.

The scene whirled away, scattering into dust. I rose, soaring up through the swarm of thoughts and images.

Me. Only me.

I stumbled, and fell to my knees. My breath was a harsh rasp. I swallowed a surge of bile.

Dowser took one shaky step back. His chest rose and fell as quickly as mine. He straightened the immaculate lines of his robe and swept one uneasy hand over his smooth crown.

"Show it to me." His voice was rough with gravel.

"I can't," I whispered, stricken. "They burned it—when I found it, the Sisters burned it. They thought it was the best way to keep me from leaving."

"There's something else. Let me see it."

Recollection poured over me, and I reached with shaking fingers for the only thing I truly owned—the only thing the Sisters never dared take. The only thing that was all mine.

The amulet hanging between my breasts, skin-warmed and timeworn.

I held it out, reluctant. The ambric pendant dangled from its chain, glowing faintly in the gloom of Dowser's study. I'd brushed it with my fingers so often that its sunburst shape was nearly obscured.

Dowser nodded, once. His face hardened with a decision.

"Put it away," he growled. "And get up."

"What does it mean?" I gasped, shoving the amulet beneath my shirt. "Who gave it to me? Whose signature was on that imperial decree?"

"Ambitious, and inquisitive," he said, but this time there was no humor in his tone. "The signature was mine. Now rise."

"*What?*" Surprise wrapped hands around my throat, nearly choking me. "You? How—"

"No more questions. Get up. We're going."

I dragged myself to my feet, cursing my trembling muscles. A waterfall of questions blotted out my thoughts. I came to the city to find the world where I belonged. I swore to myself I didn't give a Scion's eye who my parents were—why should I? They abandoned me, cast me off like nothing. But this—this was new.

Dowser signed the writ passing my guardianship to the Sisters. And even if I didn't care who my parents were . . . I did care *why* they abandoned me.

Dowser swept out of the study, a blot of shadow against the spill of saffron light gilding the marble hallway and stinging my eyes. I hurried to keep up with him.

"I hope you have a better trick than what you showed the Garde tucked up those filthy sleeves," Dowser said without looking at me. "They'll expect something more impressive."

"They?" I felt suddenly dizzy with hope and uncertainty. "Who? Where are we going?"

Dowser twisted to face me. In the ambric glow, his eyes gleamed red as the sun.

"I'm giving you what you said you wanted. I'm presenting you to the Amber Court."

NINE

Entering the Amber Atrium was like waking into a dream of paradise.

The spacious room was airy and full of colors. Potent sunlight streamed in through a curving ceiling paned with colored glass, tossing jewels across the creamy floor. Flowers spilled across walls and along fluted pillars, filling my nostrils with a dense perfume.

Arrayed along a series of shallow tiers rising toward the throne was the Amber Court, strutting and preening like exotic birds. Even the flowers seemed drab and plain beside these courtiers. Everyone was young, and lovely. Silk nestled against velvet, and satin whispered secrets to great sweeping feathers pinned to headdresses or draped along sleeves.

Courtiers lounged along divans and among scattered pillows, lithe and elegant, jeweled fingers waving and fans twisting. Soft chatter rustled the air. A young woman gowned in tangerine strummed at a lyre, while another girl with blue-tinged skin sang. The sound sent a frisson of delight tripping down my spine. A young lord with hair like glass tossed a glittering crystal decanter toward the ceiling, where it exploded in a cloud of glittering fragments. Prisms danced across the floor. When the shards hit the floor, the decanter was whole once more. I stared at a billow of opalescent orbs. A tangle of vines, sprouting roses that bloomed in seconds.

And perched above it all, like an orchid among weeds, sat Severine, the Amber Empress herself.

She was beautiful. Her neck was long and elegant, the imperious tilt of her chin softened by the gentle smile on her ruby lips. Dark auburn hair made complicated coils around her head. She wasn't wearing the famous ambric-set crown, only a simple circlet. The pale fabric of her dress caught a spill of colored light, and for a moment I could almost believe her gown itself was wrought from stained glass.

"Stay here," Dowser grunted. "Don't say or do anything unless I tell you to."

I jumped. I had nearly forgotten why I was here. Nervousness sent threads of fire stitching down my arms to itch against my palms. I squeezed them into fists.

Not yet.

Dowser cut through the jardin of indolent courtiers, severe as a raven among songbirds. He bowed to the empress, then stepped forward to whisper in her ear. She leaned toward him, and for a long moment they were still as a tableau. I thought suddenly of a moldy tapestry in the Temple of the Scion, an illustration of the story of Meridian and the beginning of the longest day.

Dark and light, side by side.

Night, reaching ever for the day, separated only by dusk.

The empress glanced at me.

Even from across the room, those violet eyes fastened on me with all the power and capability of the empire they presided over. I gasped, sucking in a sip of perfumed air. I was pinned to the spot, caught in the space between those eyes.

Finally, she looked away. I took a shuddering step back, my heart racing in my chest. The empress said one last thing to Dowser, then rose to her feet with a sighing sweep of her luxurious gown.

"Come closer, child," she called out, her voice sonorous as the Nocturne bell.

Nobles raised drowsy heads crowned in curls and braids and feathers. Jewels winked from hats and throats and hems and fingers. Red lips twisted into smiles and grimaces. A giggle sprinted around the room like a naughty child.

Embarrassment heated my blood, followed by an icy rage. I took one step, and the sound of my ragged boot on the priceless marble was like thunder in my ears. Another step. I climbed toward the throne. The court scattered before me, flower petals blown before a high wind. Fluttering fans hid smirks and winks.

I gritted my teeth so hard I thought my jaw would crack.

These are your people, I reminded myself. *This is your world.*

But I wasn't as sure as I'd been yesterday.

I paused a few tiers below the empress, and dropped into what I hoped was a passable curtsy. Another delicate laugh scampered to and fro. My fury grew cold and hard and smooth, a river stone polished by tides of wear.

The empress smiled down. This close, I could see she wasn't as young as her banners made her out to be, although she had many tides yet before she turned grey. Thirty, at least. Nearly twice my age, but certainly not yet old.

"So." She waved an iridescent fan in a lazy circle. Her eyes touched mine, but this time there was none of the forbidding power of an empress, only gentle humor. "My Dowser tells me you have an interesting secret to share with my court."

"Yes, Majesty," I forced out, my voice barely above a whisper.

"Why don't you tell us all?" Her fan made a sweeping motion to include the assembled courtiers. "We love a good secret, don't we?"

Someone shouted a mocking "Hear, hear!"

More laughter.

Nausea bloomed in my gut, hot and sour.

"She traveled far, Majesty," supplied Dowser, sensing my discomfort.

They all sense your discomfort, said a nasty voice within me.

"Pray tell us why?" cooed the empress.

"I'm a legacy," I managed. "I've come to join your court."

Stunned silence. Slippered feet shuffled on luxuriant carpets. Whispers coiled behind raised fans. I dared a glance over my shoulder, and saw nothing but eyes staring like livid jewels from a sea of blank porcelain masks.

The empress didn't flinch.

"Delightful!" She dropped me a slow wink. "Perhaps you'll favor us with a demonstration? I've been longing for a distraction from all these dull legacies you see before you."

A feminine titter scraped sharp nails down the back of my neck and struck sparks on my growing anger. They were making fun of me. The courtiers. The empress. Did Dowser bring me here to be humiliated? I sliced my gaze toward the black-robed chevalier, but his expression was shuttered behind the lenses of his spectacles.

Those poisonous courtiers will never accept someone like you. Luca's bitter words echoed in my ears, muffled only by the sick pounding of my own heartbeat.

What if I'd been wrong about where I was meant to belong?

No. I survived tides of indifferent Sisters locking me in my room just so they didn't have to look at me. When the ragtag Dusklander bullies called me *monster* and poked me with sharpened sticks, I snarled back. I escaped the creeping claws of Dominion, traveling spans with no money and little food. All for this—this world of enchantment and beauty and bright-eyed accomplishment. And it was exquisite. Astonishing, not because it existed, but because I hadn't even been able to imagine it without seeing it for myself.

I would just have to prove that I belonged here. That I deserved a place in this sunlit sanctuary filled with jewels and daydreams and perfect faces.

I let my eyes flutter shut. A distant hum drowned out my panicked thoughts. Images crowded against the backs of my eyelids. Colors. Pictures. Emotions. I discarded each in turn. Too small. Too ugly. Too obvious.

Until I was left with only one.

I remembered fire, and lithe limbs sliding through complicated choreography. Charred meat, hard eyes. A plucked luth. A flash of kembric chain and ambric dust.

And a story. A story of a wicked Sun, and an innocent Moon, and the god-king who changed the world forever.

My palms tingled, but I clenched them together, willing the tingle to spread up my arms. To creep toward my shoulders. To tease the nape of my neck.

I spread my arms, and thought of Dominion. That ominous shadow staining the horizon of my childhood home. I imagined it bigger. Purer. Consuming. I poured every ounce of anger and fear and confusion into that darkness. I *became* it.

Night poured out of my hands, thick and velvet. Impenetrable.

I strewed pebbles of silver into the blackness, pricking it with bright points of light.

A high whine filled my ears, drowning out a chorus of gasps. The illusion was barely bigger than the space between my arms, but it was greater than anything I'd ever attempted. Already I could feel it wearing on me.

My arms trembled. My breath gasped.

The ringing in my ears trebled, becoming something like a scream.

Not yet.

I had never seen the moon. No living soul had. So I made it like Noémie had described it, huge and glowing. Silver light streamed through the blackness, pale as marble and sharp as dristic. It sliced through the edges of the darkness and splintered against sunlight, scattering shards of mirrored glass and amber across the Atrium.

I held the illusion for one blistering, aching, tortuous moment.

And then I collapsed.

TEN

I flickered through the dusk. Words and images echoed in my head, distant and incomprehensible. Space seemed to expand and contract, breathing in time to my own exhalations. I tried to move, but I was held fast in the womb-like dark, buoyed by the amniotic embrace of silence and shadow.

Reality came thundering back.

Light and sounds and smells shredded my senses. I lurched onto my elbows.

"She's a fantast!" someone exclaimed.

"Dexter or Sinister?" The clink of coins.

". . . most *certainly* a trick!"

"What does she smell of?"

I tried to follow the flicker of confusing conversation. Smeared faces swam in and out of my sight, blurred and leering.

"Silence!"

The empress.

The conversation died away with a grumble.

"You are a surprise, aren't you?" The empress's smile still oozed benevolence, but there was a tightness around her eyes. "And such a mystery! Dowser claims your bloodline is true, but it seems so unlikely. An outcast, from the edge of the world! Your mother must have been unsuitable indeed for your father to go to such lengths to get rid of you."

The ensuing laughter heated my blood. I struggled to my feet to hide my blush.

"But of course you know a mere legacy isn't guaranteed a place at my court." Her fan flicked, like the tail of an irritable cat. "I've handpicked my court from among the children of my most powerful nobles. Each has something extraordinary to offer. Talent. Wit. *Beauty.*"

She said the last with such languor that it inspired another round of laughter. I rolled a tongue around my dry mouth and bit back scorching fury. Part of my mind screamed at me to run, to escape this excruciating humiliation.

But another part reminded me that if I could only wait—*wait* a few painful moments longer—I might be deemed worthy enough to stay. To walk these halls and call this glory *home*.

"But your legacy is so unusual. A fantast, in the flesh! Perhaps an exception can be made." She tapped her lacquered fingernails. "Perhaps we can even make a game of it. Who fancies a wager?"

A male whoop shattered the silence, and I heard whispers and giggles. To my right, a shower of golden coins arced into a shaft of low light. The courtiers laughed as they shielded their faces from the fall of money. I glared at the kembric écu rolling toward my boots.

Those few coins were more money than I had seen in my entire life.

"This is how it will go," the empress went on. "The girl will join the court, provisionally. She will live among you until Carrousel, in three spans' time. During this period, she will work with Dowser to hone her legacy. Then, at the Fête du Carrousel, she will display what she has learned, and I will personally decide whether she is fit to join my court."

Hope loosened the dristic clamp around my chest.

"Here's the catch." She dropped her voice, and the nobles leaned in. "She has no money. No wardrobe. No breeding. For her to live in Coeur d'Or, one among you must sponsor her. If she earns a permanent place at court, you will be rewarded. If she doesn't, a portion of your personal fortune will be forfeit."

The metal vise tightened, squeezing my heart. I didn't know much about money, but as an untrained legacy I was probably worth little to these courtiers. No sane person would take such a wager.

"Not only that," she continued, a smile coiling in the corner of her mouth, "but whoever chooses to sponsor her also takes her on for their dynasty. Dexter or Sinister. If she succeeds, that dynasty will win my favor for an entire tide. If she doesn't—well, I will let the opposing dynasty choose the forfeit."

Heated conversation sprang up around the chamber, accompanied by a few vicious glances thrown across the hall.

I frowned. Dynasty? Dexter? Sinister? The words spilling from the empress's mouth had devolved into nonsense. I glanced back and forth between the young nobles, a flicker of memory teasing my mind.

Dexter. *Sinister.* Where had I heard those words before?

The image pounced. Another of the Sisters' moldering tapestries, recounting the story of the Scion's prized hounds. The dog that sat at his right hand was loyal but meek. The dog that sat at his left hand was protective but vicious. Their names were Dexter and Sinister.

Right hand. *Left hand.*

And that's when I saw it. Although the divide was not perfect, the courtiers sitting to the empress's right were arrayed in warm, pale colors. Cream. Rose. Apricot. And the courtiers to the left of the throne wore darker, richer hues. Indigo. Steel. Viridian.

A divide, in the empress's court. Two houses in opposition, always pitted against each other.

And me, thrown between them like a bone between two dogs.

"Well?" Severine's voice pealed out above the arguments and insults hissing across the Atrium. "Who will have her? Dexter? Your hearts must bleed for her plight. Or Sinister? Surely you sense the ambition seething within her. Perhaps she will surprise you."

Silence. I forced myself to look around the room, but the courtiers' eyes flicked away from mine like startled flutterwings.

Someone finally stepped forward. A young man, tall and lean and achingly handsome. He wore a doublet of deep violet. Fine brocade glimmered from the sleeves, and silver braid winked across the chest. A black surcoat hung from one louche shoulder, a stark contrast to his slash of white-gold hair.

Hope blossomed in my chest. Someone saw my value. I wasn't going to be cast back out onto the streets after all.

The lord glanced at me. His eyes—pale green edged in dristic—narrowed.

Pain slashed me from head to toe. Sudden. Fierce.

I opened my mouth to scream, but the pain was gone nearly as soon as it came. Nothing remained but a memory of cold, brilliant agony.

The lord's eyes drifted away. His fluid gesture to the empress spoke a subtle language I couldn't understand.

"I will, Majesty." His voice, though soft, rang across the room. "I will sponsor the fantast."

"You, Sunder!" Surprise tinged the empress's voice, and her eyebrows winged up, marring her perfect mask. "I confess you astonish me. You are willing to let her stand for Sinister?"

"You mistake me, Majesty." He bowed. I thought I detected a note of disdain in the line of his back. "I will sponsor her. But I sponsor her for *Dexter*."

"Dexter?" echoed the empress.

The queen's exclamation was underscored by a burst of noise from the Dexter side of the room, accompanied by a hiss of pleasure from Sinister. The young man rose from his bow with a flourish, the sculpted lines of his aristocratic face impassive.

A slab of granite sank into the pit of my stomach. It was one thing to be bandied about like a lame mare at auction. Another thing to be sponsored, but only for the opposing team. This young man—Sunder—was essentially wagering money that I would *fail*. And he was so certain I would fail on behalf of the opposing dynasty that he was willing to forfeit part of his personal fortune in the process.

How rich *was* this young courtier?

"I did not forbid such a thing, so I will let it stand!" The empress raised her voice above the clamor of protestations and congratulations. "Trust our Sunder to always find a way to improve upon a wager!"

She winked at Sunder, who inclined his pale head.

"Nevertheless, if not a sponsor, then the fantast will still need a mentor in Dexter." Her violet eyes scanned the room. "Lullaby. Present yourself!"

A slight girl with gleaming black hair to her waist detached herself from the Dexter side of the room and glided into a curtsy.

"You haven't been at court long yourself. You'll show our new little fantast how she is expected to behave in Coeur d'Or."

"Yes, Majesty." The girl's fluted voice was soothing, loosening the tightness in my chest.

"Keep close to her. I blame you for her mistakes," the empress said, turning back to her throne.

The girl approached on gliding feet, and I saw she was the one I'd noticed singing with the lyre. Against her spill of ink-dark hair, her blue-tinged skin was lovely and otherworldly. Her eyes were also blue, dotted with flecks of green. The expression in them was nothing but mutinous. My ribs clenched as her cool, soft hand circled my wrist.

"One more thing," called the empress. "What is your name, little Dusklander?"

I opened my mouth, but a thread of defiance tangled in my belly. I felt suddenly overexposed and outplayed. The minute I stepped into the Atrium I had ceded all control to these scheming nobles, who didn't seem to care who I was or where I truly belonged. I dared a glance at Dowser, the only person who knew my real name. He wasn't looking at me, but amber reflections danced from his spectacles, and I felt him listening.

I didn't want to tell them. Not the empress, not Sunder, not the girl who radiated anxiety beside me. I wanted to keep something for myself—one thing they couldn't take from me, even as I willingly stepped across the threshold into their world.

My world.

"Rina," I whispered, choosing on impulse the name of Luca's powerful, composed mother.

"A Tavendel name?" Severine's laughter chimed. "How

quaint. Perhaps you meant to present yourself at the stables, instead of the Atrium?"

A wave of amusement rippled in my ears. The empress smiled, pleased by her own joke.

"Well, *Rina*, we don't use our given names in Coeur d'Or. In my world, nothing is more important than your gifts, and how your legacies come together in service of my empire. Each member of the Amber Court has chosen a new name to reflect the spirit of their legacy. Even if you are only with us for a few short spans, I expect you to do the same."

The empress—and the rest of the court—turned waiting eyes on me. I reached for something—*anything*—that would do for a name. A word. A phrase. But only echoes danced in the empty cavern of my mind.

"I—" My voice rasped like gravel in my throat. I ran a tongue across my lips. "I don't know."

"Sunder?" The empress's voice was too sweet. "As her sponsor, perhaps you'll do the honor of choosing in her stead."

The lord stepped forward, and the vise around my ribs tightened. I should have chosen. Something. *Anything*. Because I had no doubt whatever this cold-eyed, pale-haired man chose, it would only be intended to cause me pain.

"She shall be called Mirage," drawled Sunder. "Because, like a mirage, she promises something that is likely not there. And because, with any luck, she will disappear as swiftly as the illusions she creates."

Fire flashed white-hot on my cheeks and roared in my ears, drowning out the accompanying roar of laughter from Sinister. I watched with slitted eyes as Sunder sketched a mocking bow, then turned to clasp gloved hands with a tall girl behind him. Ice-blond hair looped high around her head, and her amethyst gown was edged in black velvet. She favored him with a cool smile, then turned to pin me with eyes like emeralds.

I jerked my gaze away.

"Mirage it is." Severine sank into her chair, her expression suddenly bored. "Now go, the both of you. You have much to attend to. Neither of you will be expected at Salon this Nocturne."

The girl beside me—Lullaby—dropped another deep curtsy. I didn't even make the attempt. Blood stung my palms and rushed hot in my ears.

I allowed myself to be propelled toward the gilded doors at the end of the Atrium. Lullaby's liquid eyes flickered toward mine, silently begging for me to leave quietly. She could probably feel the hot jump of the pulse at my wrist. Or sense the anger and humiliation rolling off me like yet another stench.

As the doors swept open, I skidded to a halt. Lullaby jerked my wrist, but I twisted out of her grasp and turned to face the chamber. Already, the nobles had returned to lounge on cushions and divans, limbs languid and heads swaying.

"And you, Majesty?" I called out. Defiance made me bold, and for once my voice was strong and powerful. "Severine Sabourin, Empress of the Amber Empire, Protectress of the Dusk, Warden of the Shore, and Glory of the Setting Sun? What should I call you, here in Coeur d'Or?"

The empress's smile was sharp: a blade forged from dristic and whetted with secrets.

"If you're very, very clever, little Mirage," she said, "you'll make sure to call me nothing at all."

ELEVEN

The door whispered shut behind us. Lullaby turned on me immediately, her lavender gown billowing.

"What was that?" she hissed in my face. "Are you absolutely mad?"

"Sorry," I muttered. Already that lunatic burst of daring was fading, leaving me hollowed out with unease. "I know I shouldn't have spoken so brazenly in front of the empress, but I—"

"Her *legacy*, you idiot," she spat. "Has your head grown bored of its place atop your neck?"

"What are you talking about?" Confusion chased away the last of my anger. "I don't know anything about her legacy."

"Scion be damned." Lullaby rocked back on her heels to study me with depthless eyes. "You really are a country gamine. Although I suppose you'd have to be ignorant, fighting your way into the palais like you did."

"This is where I belong." I squared my shoulders. "Isn't it?"

Her mouth twisted. She slid her eyes down the empty corridor.

"We have much to do." She turned on her heel, her movements graceful as a dancer's. I trotted to catch up, my ratty boots loud on the tile.

"There are rules here, *Mirage*," she muttered, emphasizing the strange syllables of my new name. "So many rules. I've been here two tides and I still don't know all the rules, much less when I'm allowed to break them. If you have any sense, you'll keep your head down and watch, and listen, and maybe you won't be ostracized or killed."

"Killed?"

"You think this is paradise. That we're all powerful and wealthy and beautiful." Lullaby's voice swelled with caustic humor as she swept through a portico and down a flight of gleaming stairs. "You're wrong. Living here is like living on the edge of a sword. One misstep and your reputation is ruined. And your reputation is the cheapest thing to lose."

Luca's words echoed through my mind. *They'll contaminate your soul with toxic games.* Unease tiptoed into my heart.

"You shouldn't have come." Lullaby's lovely face warped, then smoothed once more. "But you're here now, for the next few spans at least. So. The first rule is never—*ever*—allude to Severine's legacy. And that's exactly what you did when you asked for her court name. You're lucky you're still alive. The last lord who dared ask wasn't so lucky."

A shiver wrenched at my spine. "She had him executed?"

"Worse." Lullaby bared a set of small white teeth. "She set her dog on him."

"Her dog?"

"You're familiar with his name." Her gaze was full of blunt fear. "*Sunder.*"

I stopped in the middle of the room, my head too full of thoughts to walk and think at the same time. Lullaby paused too, the set of her shoulders impatient. Around us, a living chamber of vine-wrapped pillars and leaf-drenched ceilings sighed in time to the trickle of a thousand clear rivulets branching across the floor.

"Sunder. Lullaby. *Mirage.*" I took a deep breath, as though I could absorb all the new information through my lungs. "What do the names mean?"

"The names represent the essence of a legacy. Take me: When

I sing, my song affects the emotions of those who listen. I can just as easily inspire a dance or encourage sleep. So—Lullaby. You are a fantast—your power lies in illusions. While your new name was intended as an insult, *Mirage* is nothing if not accurate."

"And Sunder?"

"Pain." Lullaby walked on, hiking her skirts to avoid the skitter of water across tile. "He can tear flesh from bones, rip limb from limb, tighten your skull until your brain liquefies. *Sunder.*"

I shuddered, remembering the slash of his hard eyes across my face. The shrieking pain in my mind, over nearly before it began.

Sunder. My sponsor. For better or for worse.

I couldn't help but think it was probably for worse.

"And Dexter? Sinister?" I hurried to catch up with Lullaby, who moved much quicker than her high-heeled slippers should allow. "The empress called them dynasties. Are they separated by blood?"

"No. Our dynasty represents our dispositions and motivations. I have seen siblings and cousins split between dynasties. Our dynasty is defined by who we are on the inside, not the manifestations of our legacies."

"So—" I chewed on my lip, remembering the bright garb of Dexter, and the sneering, calculating gazes of Sinister. "Dexter is good, and Sinister is evil?"

"I doubt Sinister would appreciate that judgment." Lullaby's soft bark was barely amused. "It's more complex than that. Take Blaze and Spark, for example. Their legacies manifest in essentially the same way—they both create fire. But while Blaze enjoys setting conflagrations to devour buildings and eat away at forests, Spark prefers sending glimmer-lights to dance spirals against the ceiling. Which of them do you think belongs to Dexter?"

"Spark?" I guessed.

"Exactly."

"But what about me? I didn't get to choose. Sunder sponsored me for Dexter."

"Don't remind me." Lullaby frowned over her shoulder. "Scion knows where someone like you belongs."

I buried a spasm of horror. "And why is everyone so young? No one looks older than twenty-five. Where are your parents?"

"Most of the highborn families keep to their estates, monitoring harvests and trade and taxes," said Lullaby. "Only the most beautiful and talented of the noble children are hand-selected to remain at court. Jewels in a crown."

Lullaby led me down a curving set of steps into a subterranean grotto set behind artfully tumbled boulders and a curtain of ferns. Hidden fountains filled the air with the sweet music of water. The scent of lilies hung heavy.

"Where are you taking me?" I whispered.

"The baths," Lullaby replied, with a faint twitch of her nose. "Now hush, and do as you're told. If you're even able."

Blood heated my face, but something stopped me from releasing the rising flood of angry words. I stared at my new mentor, chosen for me from Dexter at the empress's whim. For all her sharp words and sidelong glances, she spoke to me without scorn, and had answered my barrage of questions with no small degree of forbearance.

She was treating me like a peer. Like an *equal*.

She might find me dirty and rude and uncultured. But she wasn't trying to pretend that I didn't belong in Coeur d'Or.

Rose-scented steam from the baths caressed my skin, promising hot water and perfumed soap and escape from half a tide's sweat and grime. A keen burst of satisfaction warmed my chest, loosening my ribs and conjuring a smile to my face.

I made it. I crossed half an empire to find a world I'd only dreamed of, and it was more spectacular than I could have imagined. Despite Luca's misgivings and Lullaby's daunting words, I knew this was where I was meant to be. My legacy swarmed against my palms, a beguiling promise of a better future yet to come.

I'd made it to Coeur d'Or. I belonged here—I knew that. Now I just had to convince everyone else.

"A bath sounds lovely." I lifted my chin and tossed my head. "Lead the way."

TWELVE

The underground corridor opened into a broad, tiled chamber. Perfumed air caressed my face, hot with steam and lit with a thousand glowing ambric lamps.

Attendants led me behind a screened alcove, where my clothes were stripped away. The way they handled the foul scraps of my ancient dress, I doubted I'd ever see the garment again. I wrapped a panicked hand around my amulet when the attendant reached for it, but the girl pursed her lips and insisted I'd get it back when I finished bathing. She brushed out my hair with deft fingers, then, without warning, drenched me with a spray of lukewarm water. I spluttered and dashed the water out of my eyes, but another cascade drowned out my protestations.

By the time the attendant was finished with me, I was cleaner than I'd ever been. I reached for the robe by the door, but the girl slapped my hands away and gestured for me to return to the main bathing chamber.

I gritted my teeth, fighting a blush as I snatched a hanging towel.

I guess I needed a bath . . . before they would let me take a bath.

Lullaby was already in the steam-swirled pool. I clutched my towel closer when I noticed she was perfectly naked beneath the water. She laughed and sipped from a jeweled goblet.

"Another rural habit?" she asked, quirking a slender eyebrow. "Modesty is a choice, Mirage, but prudishness will get you nowhere in this place."

I sucked in a lungful of humid, fragrant air, then dropped the towel to my feet. I darted down shallow, tiled steps, only releasing my breath when I was safely neck-deep in warm water.

In the shards of light dancing around the chamber, Lullaby's eyes looked paler, and her skin deeper, so that they were both nearly the same color as the water. Her long black hair trailed behind her, twisting like a strange aquatic plant. Her gaze on my face was reflective.

"What?" I demanded. "Is something wrong?"

"Nothing," she murmured, then smiled. It was the first time I'd seen her smile, and it was lovely, like the sun breaking through a dark cloud. "You're passably pretty, you know. Although much too thin. Perhaps things aren't so dire after all."

She ducked her head beneath the water. A stream of tiny bubbles burst upward as she surfaced with a splash and a giggle.

"You seem . . . more relaxed," I ventured.

"I am." The thought seemed to sober her. She pushed sopping hair out of her eyes. "It's the water. I shouldn't let it get to me."

I stared at her, at the tint of her skin, the lively coil of her sleek hair. I'd never seen anyone who looked like her. Not that my life experience was particularly broad.

Lullaby caught my gaze, and blew out a loud sigh.

"By the Scion, you don't know anything, do you?"

"I didn't mean to offend you."

"It's all right." She grimaced. "People talk about it, but usually behind my back. Have you at least *heard* of the Blue Men of the Sousine?"

I had, in Luca's fanciful legends. Men with skin like blue ink; women with the scales of fish, and wings of glass.

"I didn't know they were real," I said. I reached for the twin to Lullaby's glass sitting on the edge of the pool, and breathed the aroma of sweet wine and rare spices. The cool liquid burst on my tongue.

"They are," said Lullaby, "although they call themselves Gorma, and they are neither as fearsome nor as magical as the stories tell. My father was one of them."

"Your *father*? How?"

"My mother is a baronne. She trades extensively in the Sousine Isles, along the empire's southern coast. She met my father on one of those journeys. They loved each other, but he would not leave his home. And she would not give up hers. And so they parted. But not before he gave me these." She touched her hands to her tinted cheeks. "These." She ran slim fingers along the lids of her cool eyes. "And this."

She opened her mouth, and sang. It was a song of overwhelming longing. It rippled through me, and suddenly all I could think of was the water. Of ducking my head beneath the surface. Feeling the warm liquid embrace me. Drifting between the currents. I slid down to the edge of the water. My chin touched the surface. I closed my eyes.

The song broke off. I blinked, my mouth half-open and filled with perfumed water.

"It's beautiful," I whispered, after I'd stopped choking. "I've never heard anything like it."

"Nor had anyone else." Bitterness spoiled the sweet tones of Lullaby's voice. "I only came to Coeur d'Or two tides ago. The empress has known of my legacy since I was a child, but my gift was stained with my father's origins. I wasn't *pure*. She didn't want me. Not until my mother secured trading rights with Lirias."

My brow furrowed at the sudden change in subject. "I don't understand."

"Of course you don't." Lullaby looked away. "Otherwise you never would have come here. We—the children of the empire's wealthiest noble families, gifted with unusual legacies—we are more than her court. We are her crown jewels. Hers to flaunt to the world, and use as she desires. But most importantly, we are her insurance."

"Insurance?" I echoed. I knew the word, but I'd never heard it used to refer to people.

Lullaby hesitated, dropping her voice to a whisper.

"We live here at the empress's pleasure. Our presence guarantees that our noble parents and families behave according to her wishes. Do you understand?"

I struggled to wrap my mind around this new information. "She keeps you all as hostages? But why?"

Lullaby smoothed her mouth into a smile. Her light laugh danced across the rippling surface of the warm water.

"Scion, how should I know?" she asked, loudly. Her gaze moved toward the pale-garbed attendants drifting like phantoms through the haze of steam and perfume. "I never pay attention to politics. Why should I, when there's so much fun to be had here in Coeur d'Or?"

I opened my mouth again, but the sudden flint in Lullaby's eyes silenced me. I subsided into the bath, a whirlpool of questions swirling in my mind. I ducked down, and as the surface of the water closed over my head I felt as though I was drowning in a world I had spent most of my life longing for.

Politics. Lies. Games.

I had yearned to be welcomed with open arms and kind words. No—I had *expected* it. And why wouldn't I? These were my people. This was my world.

But they didn't see it that way. I was an outsider to them—an unwanted complication dirtying the pristine floors of the palais. I could see it in Dowser's calculating eyes, in the empress's gentle, mocking smile. In the sneering gazes of Sinister, and in the pitying glances from Dexter.

I dashed water out of my eyes, and gazed up at marble pillars twisting toward a ceiling of cracked green agate. I breathed deep the scent of cleanliness, edged with the perfume of opulence— pomade and crushed pearls, privilege and entitlement. And I compared it to the taste of my own desire, thick as the sweet wine in my jeweled goblet.

This world still felt right to me. I knew it in the way my blood beat like a drum in my veins, bursting with possibility. In the way my insatiable mind inhaled the incredible magnitude of that first, tantalizing sip of *belonging*. And I knew it in the way my legacy glided soft against my fingertips, sifting shards of color between waves of liquid glass.

I curled my hands into fists, and made myself a promise. If this world liked games, then I'd learn the rules. If intrigue bought friends, then I'd collect secrets. If Dowser could teach me to control the kaleidoscope of colors blooming like jeweled flowers from my fingertips, then I'd endure the tabak stench of his gloomy chambers.

I would not falter.

And whether it was the wine or the wonder, I felt suddenly light-headed; the world pulsed against my eyes, tremulous with promise. I leaned back, letting the warm water buoy me up as the world spun on its axis. I drank in the mosaic of unfamiliar colors, painting their rich pigments upon the cadence of my heart: sun-streaked marble, sapphire water, emerald agate—

Sunder's eyes, green with poison, invaded my mind. I suppressed the shudder running from the tips of my ears down to the base of my spine.

No. Not even a man with pain in his gaze and chaos in his heart could stop me from earning the world I'd always deserved.

THIRTEEN

When the sweet wine was drunk and my limbs were so heavy I thought I might collapse, Lullaby led me to an overgrown courtyard striped in long ruby shadows. Gleaming stone pathways meandered toward terraced villas tucked behind lush foliage and trellised flowers.

"This is Lys Wing," Lullaby said. "All the Dexter girls live here."

"My lady." A severe woman appeared at Lullaby's elbow. The silver tray balanced on her gloved hand bore a slim envelope. "Lord Sunder's steward brought this."

"Madame is the châtelaine of Lys," Lullaby explained. Then, eagerly: "Promissory notes, I hope?"

"Not until the transaction is complete." The woman handed me the envelope without meeting my eyes.

I recognized my new name, inked in a hand so fine it sent a wave of helplessness coursing through my veins. *Transaction.* I turned the envelope over, fitting my thumb beneath the flap.

"In private!" Lullaby hissed at me, eyes narrow. "Are your manners really so vulgar?"

My hands stilled. My cheeks flamed.

"No promissory note?" Lullaby whispered to the châtelaine, a note of desperation straining her voice. "How on earth am I supposed to prepare her without money? Her failure falls on *my* head. I can't possibly afford one new dress for the girl, let alone a wardrobe!"

"Her Majesty has approved a line of credit in the meantime," murmured Madame. "Worry yourself with regard to the girl's wardrobe and comportment. I will handle the financials."

Lullaby inhaled, then stalked away across the shaded courtyard, her silky mane whispering around her shoulders. I hurried to catch up.

Tucked behind a screen of blooming vines, my new chambers were lovely. Coiling pillars braced carved stone archways. Gauzy drapes billowed in a fragrant breeze. Plush carpets caressed my tired feet. But that wasn't what made the chambers so wonderful.

On every surface in the room—from the walls, to the low tables set around the room, to the decorative finials above the door—flowers were painted in a deft, clever hand. Sun-tinged jessamin amid leaves of green. Shy violettes, hiding beneath sills. Gaudy columbine, stained with port. Not even the panes of the windows had escaped the artist's brush; muted sunlight splashed brilliant petals across the polished floor.

"Who did this?" I murmured, spinning in place to soak in the imaginary jardin. "Are all the rooms in Lys like this?"

"No," replied Lullaby. Her voice was choked and quiet, and I spun on my heel to look at her. To my surprise, tears prickled in her stricken eyes.

"Lullaby?" I asked, reaching a tentative hand toward her. "Are you all right?"

"Sorry," she whispered, dabbing moisture from her cheeks. "This was a friend's room. She painted these. The châtelaine must not have had time to remove them before you arrived."

"Why would I want them removed?" Shock made my voice shrill. "Please let Madame know I want them to stay. They're beautiful."

"They are, aren't they?" Lullaby took one more look around the room before setting her jaw. "I'll need to put in a rush order for gowns. Blues, I think, to match your eyes. Be prepared to rise with first Matin. We must transform you into a lady before we can present you at court again."

She half turned. Her gaze narrowed on my chest, where my ambric amulet swayed. She curled her fingers around its time-polished curves. "What is this?"

"Oh." Apprehension coiled a hand around my spine. I remembered the heavy twist of Dowser's expression when I showed him the amulet. What if the pendant meant something to Lullaby as well? "It's just something I wear for luck."

"It looks old." Lullaby released the necklace to thud against my rib cage like an extra heartbeat. Her lip twisted. "And ugly. The empress would hate it. Never wear it again."

Relief tinged with outrage stained my cheeks. Lullaby turned on her heel.

"Lullaby!" I pushed away thoughts of Dowser and the amulet I'd worn since birth. I thought of the vow I'd made myself: my personal pledge to earn my place at Coeur d'Or, at whatever cost. If I wanted this mentorship to work—if I wanted Lullaby to support me, to fight for me to succeed as hard as I intended to fight—then I would need her friendship. I *wanted* her friendship. "Your friend. What's her name?"

Lullaby paused with one hand on the door. Her inky hair floated around her shoulders as she bowed her head.

"Her name was Blossom." Her voice was so quiet I could barely hear her.

"You said these were her rooms. Where is she now?"

Silence hung taut between us, and for a moment I thought

Lullaby wasn't going to answer me. Then her hands tightened on the doorknob, and she fixed me with eyes as forbidding as the shadows cloaking the Midnight Dominion.

"She's gone," Lullaby whispered. "And unless we're both careful, we can expect the great pleasure of following right behind her."

She swept from the room with a whisper of silky skirts and resentment, leaving me alone in a fanciful jardin of made-up flowers, the only memorial to a girl who no longer existed.

A finger of trepidation trailed down my spine. *Gone.*

Whether that meant banishment, death, or worse, I dared not guess. I just knew I would do everything in my power to escape that fate.

My hands shook as I dragged the brittle chain of my amulet over my head. I stared at it, memorizing its soft edges and burnished patina. Then I crossed to my bed and shoved the pendant beneath the soft mattress, ignoring the needle of regret piercing my heart. I already missed the comfort of its warm weight between my breasts.

I would do what needed to be done. If this world required Mirage, then I would forget Sylvie. I would abandon her in the Dusklands with the indifferent Sisters and the cruel, ignorant children. I would say goodbye to her in the bustling courtyard of an ambric warehouse. I would sponge her off and scour her clean, until she was exactly who she needed to be.

I'd gone from *nowhere* to being *here.* The last thing I wanted was to be *gone.*

FOURTEEN

I woke to the disorienting splash of colored light across my face. For a long moment, I thought I was back in Madame Rina's transport, with the livid light of a dying sun peering between colored curtains. But then the bright, clear chime of first Matin pealed through the chamber, and I remembered.

Coeur d'Or. I was in the palais of the Amber Empress.

Excitement tainted with anxiety surged through my veins, and my eyes snapped open. A young woman in a servant's uniform smoothed open another set of drapes, letting a necklace of bright jewels spill across the marble floor.

"Time to rise, my lady," said the girl, bobbing a quick curtsy toward the bed. I glimpsed dark hair pulled away from a soft-featured face. "Apologies, but the châtelaine made it clear you must awaken early this Matin."

"I'm up," I murmured, watching the girl move through the room with practiced efficiency. "Who are you?"

"I'm head of your personal staff, my lady," she replied. "I'll coordinate your wardrobe, activities, and appointments, as well as any other errands you require. Your staff includes two other handmaidens to dress you, plus access to the entire staff of Lys Wing, as necessity demands."

"My—my staff?" The words felt strange in my mouth. Staff meant *servants*. Entitlement waged war with mute horror. *What would Luca think?* I shoved the thought away. "Why do I need so many handmaidens?"

The girl ducked her head to hide the smile stretching the corner of her mouth. "I assure you, my lady, three servants is fewer than customary."

My lady. Those two words wakened a foreign thrill in a chilly corner of my heart. I'd spent more than a few dim, lonely Nocturnes dreaming of servants and soft pillows, hot meals and heeled slippers. I twisted my fingers in the fine sheets and waited to feel guilty.

"Do you have to call me that? It sounds so—so formal."

"And what would my lady prefer instead?"

"My name is—" *Sylvie.* No, it wasn't. I snagged my lip between my teeth. "Mirage. Call me Mirage."

"Of course," she replied, impassive. I studied her face, bleached pale by the faded sunlight streaming through the window. Did she know I was different from the other courtiers? I searched for some sign that she saw me as just another girl—a commoner, like her, from the edge of the daylight world.

But you're not just another girl, whispered the voice deep inside me. The voice that made me run away from the Sisters and stow away on a convoy. The voice that made me leave Luca behind in the Mews. The voice that longed for kembric fancies and dristic smiles; a million ambric dreams honed on sheer impossibility. *You belong here.*

"And what's your name?" I asked, mostly to smother the mess of uncertainty roiling within me.

I saw surprise behind the girl's deferent brown eyes. But then she returned to her task, arranging a bouquet of lilies in a crystal vase.

"My mother calls me Louise, my lady," she said, at last. "But here in the palais they mostly call me 'You, Girl.'"

Horror flickered through me, followed by a flash of amusement. *My servant made a joke.*

"Louise," I said, choking on a laugh. "I think we're going to get on just fine."

"You say that now," said Louise, and a smile transformed her face. "Let's see how you feel after I have a go at your hair."

Two other handmaidens bustled into my chambers, laden with fabric and jewels and enough cosmetics to make my head spin. I jumped out of bed, itching to feel the fabrics beneath my fingers, the sheer breadth of color against my skin. But I was summarily deflected. The girls maneuvered me into layers of garments, pulling and prodding and cinching until I felt like livestock trussed for slaughter. I might be seventeen tides old, but I was apparently not expected to dress myself.

"What do I call you?" I gasped between brutal tightenings of the torture device they'd strapped around my waist. "Louise says I shouldn't ask, but it seems odd. that you've seen me undressed and I don't even know your names."

The girls darted glances at each other. One was tall, with dark circles beneath her pale eyes. The other was plump and pretty, but her fine mouth wore a pout.

"I'm Matilde, m'lady," said the tall girl, her voice timid. "And this is Elodie."

Elodie gave me a tight smile before returning to her task of making my waist as small as possible. Fortunately for her, I'd barely eaten in the past few spans, so I was thinner than I ought to be. The thought conjured up a sudden image of Luca, grinning like a fool as he snuck me tidbits from his and Vesh's dinner. Barely more than crumbs, but more than the nothing I had to eat. A sour hand squeezed at my throat. I clenched my eyes shut and pushed the memory away.

I certainly wouldn't go hungry here.

After I was dressed and cinched to the girls' satisfaction, they began my cosmetics while Louise tore my hair out by the roots.

At least, that's what it felt like.

Louise's touch was even less gentle than she promised. My scalp screamed as she twisted and yanked, grumbling the whole time. My strands were nowhere near her standards, which I imagined were the glossy, thick, impeccable strands of the wealthy and well fed.

"At least it's long," she muttered, and I knew that was as close to a compliment as I was going to get.

Elodie smeared creams across my face, staining my cheeks and lining my lashes until tears prickled at my eyes and threatened to spill down my newly painted face.

"Don't you dare cry," Elodie hissed, her eyes dangerously insolent. And in that moment I realized she must know what I was and where I came from, and that she hated me for striving, hated me for climbing, and most of all, hated me for achieving what she never could.

I pasted a look of cool serenity on my painted face and ignored the roiling sea of pride and shame and ambition carving out my insides.

Finally, the girls moved back, their work finished. Three sets of eyes examined me as I swiveled my head, unused to the heavy weight of my hair. I took a tentative step in my heeled slippers. Dense layers of fabric rustled against the tile. I craned my neck, looking for a mirror.

Instead, I found the face of a stranger in a pane of polished glass. A lady, with blue-grey eyes framed by long black lashes. Lush-dark curls piled high above a flaming splash of vermilion feathers. Lips as red as the rubies strung around her neck. Cream lace frothing above the collar of a carmine gown.

I pressed my palms together, but there was no buzzing in my ears, no restless itch. This was no illusion.

At least, not one made by me. Pleasure swaddled me in warmth.

"You'll do," said Louise, and I thought I heard a note of satisfaction in her dry tone. "Now the lady Lullaby requires you in her chambers for breakfast."

At the mention of breakfast, my stomach growled, hungry as a wild animal. I realized with sudden horror that Elodie had left no room for anything resembling food to pass between the stalwart stays of my corset. She smirked, as though reading my thoughts, then dropped a mocking curtsy before disappearing into an alcove with the other girls.

I sucked in as much air as the corset would allow, and took a tentative step toward the door. Every step was strange in this costume; my body felt as though it had been dissolved and reconstituted in some new configuration. My feet felt small, pointed and delicate. The corset and the tight sleeves of the gown forced my shoulders up and back. The tower of hair balanced on my head required me to hold my neck long and straight. Even my center of balance had changed, tightening my hips and lengthening my spine.

I was newly made.

Sudden melancholy swept over me, prickling my skin with hot little fingers. I spun, searching for something—*anything*—in these chambers to remind me of my old life. Of the old me. But everything I saw was beautiful and spectacularly expensive, crafted with skill and purchased with unimaginable wealth. Even the press of painted flowers was a constant reminder that *this was not mine.*

Why not? I railed against the traitorous thoughts diffusing doubt through my mind. Why should I lament a change I myself had fostered? Why should I apologize for seeking, for striving, for transforming? I was evolving. Every step I took was a step *away* from a life I hadn't chosen, *toward* a life I had. A life bursting with wealth and wonder and a thousand unimaginable possibilities.

The bell chimed for third Matin as I moved out into the shaded jardins of Lys Wing. Half-masked by crimson-streaked clouds, the brassy sun sent spears of muted light to stripe the pebbled pathways. Gentian and cerise slapped against my full skirts, raining petals behind me. The sight of the broken flowers conjured thoughts of Blossom, Lullaby's erstwhile friend.

Gone.

I shoved the thought away as a servant in what I was beginning to recognize as the uniform of Lys Wing bowed me into Lullaby's room.

Lullaby's chambers were laid out like mine, but instead of being decorated in a thousand imaginary flowers, hers were drenched in shades of blue. Cerulean glass paned the windows, striping the walls in aqua. Gossamer drapes undulated in the breeze, casting shadows across the floor. My palms itched with fluid fancies.

"It reminds me of the sea," Lullaby said. "It's soothing."

The rumpled mess of Lullaby's inky hair and her gaping yawn told me she'd just risen. One of her servants draped a dressing gown over her outstretched arms. She meandered toward a low table set with platters of fragrant buns and carafes of steaming liquid, then plopped into a plush chair and shoved a cake into her mouth.

My stomach growled again, louder than before. Lullaby glanced toward me. Her sleepy eyes widened and her mouth popped open, revealing her half-chewed breakfast.

"What?" I snapped, hunger quickly transforming into resentment. When would these people stop staring at me like I was a curiosity?

"Nothing," muttered Lullaby, but her eyes didn't leave my face as she devoured another bun. "Your girls didn't disappoint. You look—well, *beautiful*."

"Oh." Her words cooled the indignation boiling inside me, but only barely. Her loose hair and breezy dressing gown reminded me of the satin prison compressing my ribs. "Why did I have to get primped and prodded at first Matin, when you got to sleep in?"

"Sleep in?" Lullaby snorted. "This is the earliest I've been awake since arriving at Coeur d'Or. Even the early risers don't get up until at least Prime."

"Why not?"

"Because most of us have been feasting and drinking and dancing until the last hours of Nocturne," explained Lullaby drily. "You'll see."

I mulled over this new information as I reached for a bun that smelled as delicious as it looked sticky. But Lullaby slapped my hand away, hard.

"Scion's teeth! What was that for?" I demanded, cradling my stinging wrist.

"You're not here for breakfast," said Lullaby, and I saw a wicked light ignite in her liquid eyes. "And I didn't crawl out of bed at third Matin to watch you stuff your face. You're here to learn court manners, and that's your first lesson."

"I'll be damned—"

"Ladies never curse. Second lesson."

Fire burned my cheeks, and I dug newly buffed nails into my calloused palm. "I haven't eaten since yesterday."

"Then you should have asked your staff to feed you. That's why they're there." Lullaby's eyes softened when she saw the expression on my face. "Oh, fine. I'll tell you what—we'll make a game out of it. Yet another court lesson for you—when there's an opportunity to make a game or wager out of something, take it."

"A game?"

"A game." Lullaby's mouth quirked. "Today we're covering comportment and address. For every question you answer correctly, or task you perform well, I will reward you with an item of food or a sip of tea. Will that do?"

Humiliation battled with hunger. Hunger won.

"I'll play your game," I huffed. Both sides of the wager were in my best interest. I was desperate to master Lullaby's refined graces, and I was starving to boot. Still, pride flared hot in my belly, souring whatever pleasure I'd anticipated in learning how to play courtly games. "But I won't like it."

"Fourth lesson," crooned Lullaby. "Never, *ever* let anyone know you're not enjoying something. That will only make *them* enjoy it more."

And so began the first of many lessons on manners and courtly conduct. Curtsies, *depth* of curtsies, angle of the head, and inflection of the wrist. Unending lists of the types of nobility, and the customary address for said nobles. Duc de Beltoire: *Your Grace.* Comtesse L'Aumont: *Your Ladyship.*

"But *why?*" I asked, around a mouthful of berries Lullaby had grudgingly doled out as the reward for a curtsy she deemed *not the worst.* "If everyone at court uses their dynasty names, why do I need to know how to address them by their official names?"

"It's hard to explain." Lullaby pursed her lips. "Sometimes the most important reason for understanding a courtly convention is knowing when and how the rule may be broken. Does that make sense?"

"Not at all!"

"Comportment matters, but only *really* matters when someone *isn't* doing it. Because when everyone knows the rules of *politesse,* any breach in decorum is always intentional. If I, as the illegitimate daughter of a baronne, know I'm required to curtsy lower to a duchesse, with a deferential twist of my chin, like so"—Lullaby dipped into a graceful, almost obsequious bow—"but I choose instead to curtsy as to a peer, without lowering my gaze"—she adjusted her bow, rising up and adding an insolent inflection to her chin.

"It's an insult," I finished. Realization dawned as I watched the subtle effect of Lullaby's movements. "By going against the protocol of decorum, you're insulting the person you're meant to be paying your respects to."

"Exactly." Lullaby sank back into her chair, sipping on her fragrant kachua. "But most courtiers learn these subtle rules from birth. So trust me when I say you're better off watching and listening until, well, forever. The only thing worse than insulting someone intentionally is insulting them accidentally."

I slid into a clumsy curtsy, trying to mimic Lullaby's gestures.

I felt anything but graceful; with sweat prickling at the base of my neck and unruly tresses slipping out of my careful coiffure, I felt like a dirty swine who'd accidentally stumbled into a stable of fine thoroughbreds.

"Mirage?" Lullaby rolled her eyes at my poor attempt at poise. "I'm going to say that again, in case you weren't listening. Please, *please*, whatever you do—don't insult anyone. Not the empress, not Sinister, not even your servants. Do you understand me?"

I nodded, slowly. But when Lullaby turned away to demonstrate yet another form of social grace, I couldn't help but catch my lip and worry it between my teeth, fighting a rush of resentment and humiliation that was beginning to feel familiar.

I knew this was where I belonged. But would I ever be able to learn the intricacies of a life I wasn't born to? And if I couldn't, how long until the gilded teeth of this opulent court chewed me up and spat me back out into the dusk?

FIFTEEN

W hen the bell chimed second Prime and the sweet buns from breakfast were a fond but distant memory, Lullaby dismissed me back to my chambers. Due to my being a *shockingly rude and graceless rustic*, Lullaby had requested we both be excused from all court gatherings until I was fit to be presented. Which meant we'd be training together, dining together, and—if yesterday was any indication—bathing together.

Lullaby seemed less enthused by the prospect than I was.

"Go explore, or read, or practice your legacy," Lullaby sighed when I asked what I was meant to do until our next lesson. "Sleep, for all I care. Just don't bother me."

So I eased my way along the perfumed paths of Lys toward my chambers. There were signs of life among the residences; delicate laughter wafted from an open window, and more servants flitted between the shadows.

My own rooms were empty save for a breeze sweeping the pale curtains. I let out a disappointed breath; I'd hoped Louise might take mercy on me and unlace the Scion-cursed contraption squeezing my waist into oblivion. I wandered into the parlor area, my heart leaping when I saw the plate of dried fruit and breads laid out on the low table. I sank to my knees, gobbling down delicacies with an aplomb that would disgrace Lullaby.

My chewing slowed when I saw the envelopes laid out beside the decanters of fruit juice. The first was familiar: a small, cream-colored note addressed in a spiky, effortless hand. The delicious bread turned to ash in my mouth when the châtelaine's words echoed in my mind: *Not until the transaction is complete.*

Sunder.

I remembered his sharp, aristocratic profile, his slash of white-gold hair. What exactly did he think he paid for? Outrage soured with shame rolled over me, and I scraped my tongue around my mouth. I pushed the envelope away, ignoring the dread coiling in my belly like a poisoned serpent. I had no desire to learn what my so-called sponsor wanted in exchange for the funds he'd promised.

The second envelope was larger, exuding the faint scent of tabak smoke and leather.

Dowser.

I tore open the letter, letting the envelope flutter to the floor. Heavily inked letters stared back at me, and I squinted with the effort of making out the words.

Mirage—
Welcome to the palais. Your training will begin at once. Make
your way to my chambers at your earliest convenience.
Dowser

A thread of excitement stitched its way down my spine.

Finally. I hadn't forgotten that the terms of my arrangement required me to hone my legacy as well as my courtly skills. How could I? Curtsies and niceties would help me fit in at court, but my true worth—the reason I belonged here at Coeur d'Or—lay in the secret of my blood. My legacy—the gauzy visions spilling from my fingers like half-remembered dreams, jewel-bright but whisper-thin.

Dowser would show me how to improve and control my powers.

A different thought brushed chilly fingers against my heart. Dowser also knew why I'd been abandoned in the dusk. Scion, he might've even been the one who left me there.

That's not why you're here, I hissed at the frigid specter of ancient heartache. Nothing in my past was of any use to me here. I'd come this far using only my wits, my determination, and my legacy. I didn't intend to start looking backward now.

I paused only to shove Sunder's hateful note into the pocket of my skirts before striding out into the jardins of Lys Wing, through the shaded grotto and up a shallow flight of stairs, beneath a veiled entryway and toward—

I stopped, my heeled slippers skittering on the slick floor. This hallway looked unfamiliar. I glanced behind me, but I'd already lost sight of Lys Wing. I tried to conjure up memories from yesterday, when Lullaby led me from the Atrium to Lys, but all I remembered was a jumbled hodgepodge of gleaming floors and burnished ceilings and carved reliefs.

I had no idea where I was going.

And there was no one around to ask.

I took a few tentative steps. A pillared arcade opened out to a vast botanical jardin stretching toward the distant roofs of the Amber City. Grassy boulevards bordered glassy ponds. Pruned hedges twisted into shapes so lifelike I could almost believe they were real: a Skyclad chevalier atop a rearing destrier; a dancing maiden; a strange, hulking beast with a nose so long it twisted like an arm. And beyond that, a pretty wilderness of fruit trees and flowering shrubs whispering secrets into the warm air.

I was so enchanted I almost didn't notice the sound of

footsteps behind me. I whipped my head around, eager to find someone who might be able to show me how to navigate this lavish labyrinth. I spotted a slender, velvet-clad back quickly retreating behind the colonnade of tiered archways.

"Hey! Wait!" I gathered up my cumbersome skirts and dashed forward. The loud staccato of my heels on tile caught the man's attention more than my shouts, and he turned, raising his hands in surprise as I skidded to a halt in front of him.

"Thank the Scion," I gasped between shallow breaths. The corset was cutting off my air supply, and a wicked stitch sliced my side. I bent over, pressing a hand to my rib cage. "I might have wandered forever in this maze if it wasn't for you."

"I beg your pardon?" The gentleman's voice was tinged with concern. "Mademoiselle, are you unwell?"

"No, it's just this damned—" The words died in my throat when I glanced up into the face of the most handsome man I'd ever seen.

He was obviously a courtier, dressed in a stylish dove-grey coat over a shirt of dark blue silk. Ambric and sapphires glittered from the hand he extended toward me, and iridescent feathers in green and blue swept from a rakish hat perched on bronze curls. Hazel eyes blinked from a richly tanned face dusted in freckles. Plush lips parted in surprised amusement.

"This damned *what*?" he prompted, with barely contained laughter. "And is it alone in its damnation, my lady, or can I expect a similar fate?"

"Sorry, I shouldn't have said that," I managed, straightening to my full height. I pushed back an unruly strand of hair and forced myself to stop staring at his perfect features. "I've been admonished that ladies shouldn't curse. I've also been told that ladies oughtn't talk about their underthings."

The man stared at me for a moment longer before throwing his head back and letting loose a whoop of laughter.

"Well, aren't you a fresh breeze in a stuffy room," he smiled. His eyes skimmed my face before examining my new gown, the cobweb-thin bangles whispering around my wrists, the blunt nails on my tanned hands. "You can only be the new legacy everyone is talking about."

"Is it that obvious?" I fought the urge to pull an unladylike face, and hid my rough hands in my skirts instead. "Do I still have dirt stuck under my fingernails?"

"Not at all." His eyes softened on mine. "Rather, I cannot help but remark on such a beautiful new face when I've been sur-rounded by the same hundred people since I was born."

I ducked my chin to hide the stain heating my cheeks. I assumed it was courtly flattery, but after yesterday's dubious welcome, it was more kindness than I'd been taught to expect.

"May I ask what you're doing out here alone?" He graciously ignored my blush. "And why you feel the need to go chasing after strangers along the Esplanade?"

"I'm lost," I explained. "I was trying to find the way to Dowser's chambers, but this palais is a maze. I hoped you might be able to point the way."

"Indeed," he murmured. He bowed absurdly low, sending his gaudy feathers flying. "Perhaps the lady will allow me to do even better, and lead her to her destination?"

I stared at the handsome lord, and swallowed hard. Already, Lullaby's lessons on comportment and decorum had flown from my head, leaving me with the awkward knowledge that I was almost certainly missing important social cues.

"You were on your way somewhere," I hedged.

"Nonsense." A broad smile creased his face, displaying a row of white teeth. "Allow me."

He proffered an arm clad in richest velvet and ringed with jewels. I hesitated the briefest second before reaching out and grabbing his arm with my hand.

"Easy!" he said, grin widening. "I'm not a crutch. Here: lightly, and from the inside."

Deftly, he showed me how to tuck my hand into the crook of his elbow, drawing me closer against him in the process. A rich, spicy perfume filled my nostrils, along with a subtler scent, like burnt grass. He led me firmly in the opposite direction, away from the open arcade and the sweeping jardins.

"I'm sorry," I blurted after a few minutes of walking in silence. "I apologize if I've offended you in any way. I barely know anything about courtly protocol."

"I noticed," he chuckled. "But I find it endearing. It serves to make the rest of us look rather foolish, prancing and bowing and preening like so many perfumed *paons*."

"*Paons?*"

"Ornamental birds we keep in menageries," he explained. "Slender and serene, with great sweeping tail feathers in kembric and blue. Ridiculous, as they cannot fly."

"Ridiculous?" I eyed the drooping feathers on his hat, and decided to lie. "Impossible. And I've seen the court. I can't imagine ever being so graceful and elegant."

"You're making a lively start, my lady," he said, with an incline of his plumed head.

A curving staircase choked in wisteria stole my breath for a few moments, and I took the time to mull over my new acquaintance's words. While his fashion and demeanor marked him as a courtier, he didn't seem overly concerned with my poor manners or rustic bearing. My behavior in the past few minutes would have sent poor Lullaby into a fit.

"I hate to pry, but you didn't recognize me when we met back in the hall," I said. "Weren't you in the Atrium yesterday? When I asked the empress for a place at court?"

"Ask?" he echoed. "From what I heard, your *request* took the form of an unmitigated demand, my lady Mirage. But no—I wasn't in the Atrium yesterday."

"Why not?"

"We take it in shifts."

"Why?"

"To better fulfill our great ruler's demands on us, of course." The smile on his face remained even despite a sudden tightness around his eyes. "And so she doesn't grow weary of our tiresome faces."

"Is that likely to happen?"

"It's happened before." He dropped me a sideways wink. "Although with such a face as yours the empress will surely be clamoring to see you more often than the rest of us."

I frowned, trying to see past the flattery.

"It's happened before?"

His laugh was a few seconds too late.

"Of course not. Merely a figure of speech, my lady." He released my elbow and bowed toward a passage glowing with quartz, where milky statues cupped blazing torches. "I'm afraid I must leave you for other, far less enjoyable pursuits. But Dowser's chambers are just down this hall."

"Oh!" A glimmer of recognition sparked in my mind. "Thanks for your guidance. I don't know how to repay you."

"No need. Your company is payment enough."

He dipped into another ludicrous bow, the feathers on his hat dancing. I tried to smile at the handsome man, but the expression felt forced. Beneath his courtly demeanor, I sensed he was avoiding some truth with his careful words.

"Then I am in your debt."

"And I yours."

He turned to go. And as his velvet-clad back disappeared between the crystalline chancels edging the luminous hallway, I remembered my vow to do whatever necessary to earn my place in this court of wagers and intrigue. As Lullaby had pointed out countless times, I was an unsophisticated gamine with no skill for secrets. I could use a friend like him. Someone shrewd, and glib, with a skill for flattery and a notion for guile.

It also didn't hurt that he hadn't been expressly ordered by an empress to treat me with civility.

"Wait!" I called. "One more thing!"

He spun, hazel eyes ripe with cautious curiosity.

"Your name," I said. "You never told me your name. I ought to know who to ask for when it comes time to repay my favor."

"Ah." The perfect smile faltered once more. "Of course. The empress and her court see fit to call me Reaper."

"Reaper?" I frowned. The name seemed uncharacteristic of the smiling, flattering young man standing before me. What could such a name represent? I imagined shining scythes cutting through fields of golden wheat, stealing plenty from the earth. My palms itched, scored by invisible blades.

"But since we're friends," he continued, reading the uncertainty on my face, "I hope you'll call me by my given name—Thibo." He brushed my chin with soft-gloved fingers. "Our little secret."

I meandered toward Dowser's rooms, lost in thought. I'd only spoken to a few courtiers at the Amber Court, but both Lullaby and Reaper seemed consumed with an inner turmoil I found puzzling. In the bloom-beribboned Atrium, everyone had seemed content in the luxury of the palais. And why wouldn't they be! Coeur d'Or was like paradise, glittering with wealth and magic and the promise of a thousand sun-smeared spectacles.

I was overlooking some intrigue or scandal. But did I risk my future at court by prying into business not my own?

Dowser's door of darkened wood snapped open of its own accord. The heavy scent of tabak underlaid with the tang of kachua assaulted my nostrils. I sneezed, wincing when the stays of my corset dug furrows between my ribs.

"Come in." His voice was as inscrutable as the layers of shadow swathing the study. I squinted, and stepped into the dimness.

SIXTEEN

"You're late," Dowser said. He leaned on a desk laden with dusty scrolls.

"I was busy," I said, cautious.

"Nothing you could have been doing is more important than learning to master your legacy," Dowser said. His voice was free of intonation. "Isn't that why you came? Or did you just want a new gown and a few spans of good feeding before crawling back to the Dusklands?"

"No!" My hands twisted into hard pebbles. "I want nothing more than to master my birthright."

"Birthright," he repeated, stepping closer. The light at the edge of the shrouded windows striped my gaze and hid Dowser's expression in silhouette. "Do you truly believe you deserve a place at court, by blood alone?"

"You tell me." The old familiar cinder of resentment flared to life, heating my blood. "You're the one who signed that writ, transferring my guardianship to the Sisters. You clearly know more about my past than I do."

"So you want to uncover your parentage," he said, shrewd. "You came here to find out if you're highborn, if you belong to a noble family. To claim a dowry? To marry a lord?"

"Frankly, I don't care about my parents." The ember burst into a bonfire, crackling through my veins and spinning runnels of smoke through my thoughts. "They abandoned me, discarded me at the edge of the daylight world like so much refuse. Even if they were still alive, even if they wanted me back, I wouldn't care. They don't deserve me."

"*Deserve.*" Dowser tasted the word, rolling it on his tongue. "And what, lady, do you believe *you* deserve?"

My breath caught. Staring around Dowser's closed-off chambers, I felt suddenly imprisoned within my own anger, a being of smoke and shadow trapped behind heavy curtains of resentment and humiliation. I scrubbed my aching palms down the front of my dress, fighting the sudden press of unpleasant memories: stinging slaps from children who could have been my friends, detached stares from women who should have been my mothers. I reached for the certainty I had riveted to my bones with each toiling step away from the Dusklands.

"I am a legacy of the Amber Empire." I forced my voice to stay calm. "You said so yourself—my bloodline is true. I may not have been born in a palais, but my bones were forged in the dusk and my veins are alight with dreams. Do not ask whether I deserve a place at court. Ask whether this court deserves me."

Dowser was silent, nothing more than a flash of spectacles in the smoke-dimmed chamber.

"You said the Sisters who raised you burned that Writ of Guardianship, to keep you from leaving," he murmured at last. "And yet here you are. Why didn't you obey them?"

"Obey the distant and sanctimonious Sisters who hid the secret of my heritage, denied my legacy, and locked me away when I dared ask questions?" I swallowed bile. "I'd had enough. I conjured shards of piercing sunlight and billows of glittering clouds. I blinded them with colors they'd never dared imagine, and escaped while they prayed for mercy from their Scion. I never looked back."

A frisson tripped brokenly down my spine: satisfaction prickled with guilt. I lifted my chin, and didn't tell Dowser about the waves of bone-deep exhaustion that had slowed my fleeing heels, or the jagged screams and curses that haunted my dreams for weeks after.

"You're ambitious," Dowser remarked. "You're arrogant. Perhaps even a little cruel. Whatever gave you the idea that you were owed so much, when you offer so little?"

My nostrils flared, and a low ringing teased at my ears.

"Poor abandoned highborn lady," Dowser said. "If only anyone wanted her around, she might be able to do great things."

I choked on my fury. "Why are you saying these things?"

"You have no discipline, barely any control over your thoughts or emotions. I want to see what happens when you lose what little control you have."

My breath hissed in my throat. Thorns needled my palms, and a familiar numbness coursed from my wrists toward my elbows.

"I'm not losing control!"

"Aren't you?" Dowser's hand lashed out. The flat of his palm struck my cheek. Pain exploded behind my eyes.

Shock twisted into rage in one dizzying instant. The sting at my cheek blended with the buzzing numbness coursing up my arms until I was roaring. Images and colors flickered and flooded and pulsed out of me in a perilous cascade.

Flaming sunlight. Cursed wasteland. The translucent whisper of jeweled fingers, pale as opals and sharp as glass. Flashing eyes. Runnels of shadow, unspooling like threads of smoke.

Darkness, hot and pulsing behind my eyes.

I must have fallen, because my knees were hard against the tile and my palms were slick with sweat. I shuddered, my head bursting with spikes of color and shadow.

"What were you saying about control?"

Dowser's voice was inches from my ear, composed as ever. My hands twitched with the urge to reach out and pitch him to the ground like the savage Dusker kids used to do to me. But I fought the urge, clamming my fingers and setting my jaw.

"You made me do that," I whimpered. "I was fine before you goaded me."

"I didn't make you do anything," Dowser replied. "No one can make you do anything, Mirage. Everything is a choice."

"That's not true." I pulled my feet underneath my shaking body and dragged myself upright. "I didn't choose to be abandoned at the edge of the world. I didn't choose to be raised by unloving zealots, praying to Meridian like he's about to swoop out of Dominion and save us all. I didn't choose this legacy coursing through my veins."

"Perhaps not. But you chose to abandon everything you'd ever known to travel halfway across the daylight world. You chose to reveal your legacy in a bid for recognition. And when I hit you barely hard enough to smart, you chose to lash out at me with the one thing that makes you powerful."

"I didn't *lash out*—"

"Which is it, Mirage?" Dowser's voice sliced my argument to shreds. "Did you lose control, or did you want to hurt and disorient me?"

Silence mingled with the rich scent of leather and tabak. The tremors wracking my chest subsided, and I forced my breathing to slow.

"I was angry," I finally admitted. "But I can't always choose when I use my gift. I don't know how to control it."

"And that is the most frightening thing of all." Dowser shifted in the shadows, a wraith in his black robes. "You let your legacy control you, instead of the other way around. That makes you powerless. And without power you have no control, no choice."

"I know." I shuddered in the dim. "That's why I need your help."

Dowser contemplated me. "Are you willing to work?"

"Yes."

A smile ghosted across his face. "Then let us begin."

SEVENTEEN

Dowser's lesson consisted of sitting, blindfolded, in the dark.

"Be still!" he snapped, again. From the ever-changing direction of his lashing tongue, I assumed he was stalking around his study like a cat.

I tried to obey, but I'd been sitting like this for what felt like an eternity. My neck ached with the effort of holding up my elaborate hairstyle, and I was reasonably certain the corset was cutting off blood flow to my legs.

"How much longer?" I whispered. "I thought we were working on my legacy."

"I am teaching you discipline," Dowser repeated. "Discipline comes before control. And control comes before capability. You have none of any of these things. So we begin with discipline."

"Is everything a moral lesson with you?"

"Must you insist on approaching every lesson with petulance and insubordination?"

"I'm trying—!"

"Find the stillness inside, Mirage. Still your mind, and the body will follow."

I lapsed into frustrated silence. Dowser's unceasing footsteps circled me. I chewed on my lips, and forced myself to think of nothing. But the instant I tried to think of nothing, every doubt and worry squawked and clamored for attention. Lullaby's lessons on etiquette, eddying into one giant pool of curtsies and addresses. The forced smile on Reaper's—*Thibo's*—handsome face when I asked for his court name. The sting of Dowser's palm on my cheek.

Sunder.

The bell for fourth Prime shattered the stillness, dispelling the images swirling between my ears.

"Enough. Get up."

I stumbled to my feet, dragging the blindfold off my face and swinging my arms to get my blood flowing. Dowser had lit long tapers in a burnished candelabra, and the guttering flames fractured his face into a patchwork of red and black.

"That was terrible, Mirage. You'll have to show more initiative if you ever hope to prove yourself for Dexter and win a permanent place at court."

Disappointment soured my stomach. "Tell me how."

"That's exactly what I'm talking about." He pursed his lips. "Come back tomorrow before Prime. We have a great deal of ground to cover."

I swallowed against the bitter tang of failure and reached for the clear-glass certainty that had carried me all the way from the Dusklands. *I belong here.* But the sensation was fractured and distant, like looking into a broken mirror and seeing someone else's face.

A flick of Dowser's fingers dismissed me. I plodded toward the door, confusion and dismay eating holes in the dristic cage I'd built around that ancient, desiccated heartache.

Discipline. Choices. *Control.*

"Dowser?" My voice sounded hoarse. I cleared my throat. "I know I said I didn't care about my parents, and I don't. But your signature was on that writ. Do you know why they left me? Why I was abandoned in the Dusklands?"

His obsidian eyes stared at me over spectacles flaring with reflected candlelight. Silence stretched chilly fingers to push at my chest.

"I'll say this, Mirage," Dowser said, at last. "It wasn't because your parents didn't want you. The rest of it, I would advise you to forget."

"I can't forget what I don't know."

"And what you do not know is less likely to hurt you."

"Hurt me?" A spark of curiosity burst to life inside me. "How—?"

"Merely a figure of speech," Dowser interrupted. "There is nothing in your past but forgotten ghosts and bad memories."

I shivered. He had no idea.

"If you truly wish to earn a place at court, you must focus. Learn the rules of your legacy. The rules of your station. Everything else is a distraction. Do you understand?"

"Yes," I said. I nodded my head, as much for myself as for Dowser. "I do."

Stepping out into the scarlet-striped passageway of Coeur d'Or was like being reborn. I leaned against the smooth alabaster wall and lifted my face to the shafts of coral light glimmering through a row of carved spandrels. Dowser was right. I had made myself a promise, in the shimmering waters of the baths, to do whatever it took to earn my place here. Too-tight corsets and mean little games and unspoken secrets—these were small prices to pay for the endless exhilarating exuberance of belonging. I was willing to work, I was willing to cooperate, I was willing to—

I jammed my hand into the pocket of my gown, where a small, smudged note had been burning a hole in the fabric since I shoved it there hours ago. The writing on the creamy envelope was nearly illegible at this point, crumpled and smeared. But I could still make out my name—my *new* name—spilling across the paper.

Mirage.

I gusted a breath and slid my fingernail under the edge of the envelope. The note inside was written on the same rich parchment, and when I lifted it to my nose I caught a whiff of something sharp and clean, like genévrier needles.

"Money," I muttered, to distract myself from the skein of trepidation unspooling in my belly. I wasn't sure I wanted to know what terrible price Sunder had decided to ask for his dubious sponsorship.

And wasn't sure I wanted to find out whether I was willing to pay it.

I sounded out the elegant words sauntering across the page. There were only a few.

Come to my residence. Belsyre Wing. Now.
Signed,
Sunder

I sucked in another gulp of that searing perfume, but this time, it tasted of bitterness and pain. My stomach soured. The vermilion light pouring in through the glass stained the fingers on my right hand, triggering a memory of Luca, and a guttering cook fire, and iron clouds scudding across a dim sun.

What had Luca said, when he'd told me the tale of the dust devil, with its terrible eternal thirst?

Maybe by paying a demon what he needs, you keep him from stealing what he desires.

I crushed the terse note into a crumpled ball of paper, and shoved thoughts of Luca from my mind. From what I'd heard and seen, this Sunder was little better than a devil himself. But what did he desire?

To inflict pain? To see me suffer? To watch me fail?

I tossed the hateful note behind a gilded statuette and stomped through an archway draped in velvet and strung with diamonds.

I wouldn't give him what he desired, and I might not be able to give him what he needed. But maybe I could give him a little something of what he deserved.

EIGHTEEN

Sunder's chambers were a wing unto themselves, a sprawling residence I only found after an hour of wandering in circles and cursing whatever vindictive architect had designed Coeur d'Or's curving hallways.

A blank-faced servant in black-and-white livery bowed me into a verdant foyer. Hanging terrariums spilled tendrils of green from a vaulted ceiling. Invisible fountains filled the air with the drowsy splash of water. A songbird trilled a soprano glissando that lingered sylphlike among the drooping heads of lush flowers.

"This way," prompted the servant.

We threaded down a hallway lined with polished silverwood and studded with carved ambric, and I couldn't help but wonder how rich my suspicious benefactor was. Just one of these exquisite finials or precious ornamentations was worth more than my life. And all of this together? A treasure trove unlike anything I'd ever imagined.

The servant led me out beneath a pergola draped in foliage. A crystalline chandelier dashed prisms against a pillar slim as a cygni's white throat. Gauzy veils tangled with rubies splashed blood across a glossy floor.

And at the center of it all was Sunder.

He was sleeping, draped along the curving tongue of a white chaise. His head was thrown back, and strands of pale kembric hair caressed the collar of a charcoal surcoat. Tall black boots left stark smudges on the couch. His lips, curled into a sneer the last time I'd seen them, were parted ever so slightly. Black lashes stained his high cheekbones with ink.

He was beautiful.

"I employ a portraitist, if you care to use his services."

He was also apparently not sleeping.

Sunder swung into a seated position, brushing hair out of his eyes. His gaze slashed up to meet mine. I glimpsed a vivid burst of pale green ringed in dristic before agony shuddered down my spine and clawed at my mind.

I gasped, clapping a hand to my forehead. But like before, the pain was gone in an instant, no more than a memory of suffering foaming on an ocean of unease.

"I apologize for the tickle," he drawled, rising to his feet and crossing to a low table tucked between two vine-wrapped pillars. "Some legacies are more volatile than others. And try as I might, I can't seem to look at you without wanting to hurt you."

A thrill of outrage heated my blood. Sunder sloshed liquid into a goblet before draining the glass in one long gulp. He refilled the cup, then turned to face me. I braced myself for the flare of pain, but it never came. He inspected me, cool eyes raking me from head to toe.

"A miracle indeed," he murmured. "You really are a talented fantast. An illusion to hide all that dirt—I'm amazed you didn't think to use it before."

A searing heat crept up the column of my throat. Sunder smiled at me over the rim of his goblet.

"Or did someone finally tell you about bathing?"

My newly buffed fingernails cut semicircles into the palm of my hand. The cursed corset tightened around my lungs. I couldn't drag enough air into my chest.

"You summoned me here, Lord Sunder," I managed between clenched teeth, dipping into what I hoped was the appropriate curtsy befitting his rank. I wouldn't respond to his insults. I knew he was trying to make me lose my temper, but I refused to let him know it was working. "And, as your note requested, I came."

"Forgive me, but did I neglect to specify a time?" His voice feigned innocence. He stalked closer. "When did I say you should come?"

He paused close enough for me to smell that sharp, clean scent wafting off him. I could see the dark embroidery etched along the ridges of his sleeve, and count the rings on his fingers.

"Well?" he prompted.

"*Now*," I admitted, reluctant. "The note said I should come *now*."

"Yes. And when was that?" His voice was an unstrung bow.

"Yesterday."

"Ah!" He snapped his fingers. His voice grew taut. "How strange, *now* being *yesterday*. Are Dusklanders unfamiliar with the concept of time? Or are you just as stupid as you look?"

Flames zinged out toward my fingertips, raising the hairs along my arms. My eyes cut up to his. "Sinking to my level, Lord Sunder? You insult my looks and intelligence so bluntly that no one would claim you are adept in the art of dealing pain." I dragged an insolent gaze around the lavish chambers. "Although subtlety hardly seems to be your forte."

His hand snapped out to wrap around my chin. His skin was cold. A low thrum of discomfort vibrated along my jaw, burrowing into flesh and bone. I met his gaze with as much malice as I could muster, and he smiled sharp as a knife's edge.

"It's alive," he whispered, leaning closer. "And it bites."

I held my breath against a choking flood of fury. Too late, Lullaby's warning about comportment echoed in my head. *Whatever you do, don't insult anyone.*

Too late.

"Tell me, my most clever lady Mirage." Sunder's hand trailed a cool, aching line along the column of my throat. "Do you understand the concept of reciprocity?"

I swallowed, hard, fighting the urge to shove his creeping, stinging hands away. Dread cooled the anger heating my blood. I'd promised myself I would do whatever it took to earn my place here. Corsets, cruel games, cold secrets—these were things I could endure. But this—this was asking too much.

"Let me remind you." He leaned closer. I felt the whisper of his breath in the shell of my ear, the brush of his hair against my cheek. "I offered you money. Power. Position. Now you offer me something in return."

I sucked air into my captured lungs, but still I couldn't seem to breathe. A shudder climbed my spine, vibrating against Sunder's fingers. His hand tightened, sending an icy twinge lashing along the plane of my collarbone.

"No," I choked out, taking one huge step backward. My skirts gasped along the slick floor as I wrenched my throbbing shoulder out of Sunder's grasp. "I owe you nothing."

"Nothing?" Sunder's hand drifted to his side. His smile was little more than a ghost. "You owe me everything."

"Your wager was with the empress, and so my debt lies with her."

"You will not repay me, then?"

"Only in vindication, lord."

He stared at me for a long moment, his gaze calculating. And then he swept me a deep bow I distantly recognized as being reserved for the most illustrious of nobility. But what must surely be mockery barely stung through the haze of surprise and confusion.

What just happened?

"Bane!" he shouted over one shoulder. "I win!"

I took another involuntary step backward as a willowy girl appeared from behind a curtain of blushing eglantine. She was the same lady I'd seen with Sunder in the Atrium, a chilling beauty with blond hair coiled high above her head and eyes like cut emeralds. The midnight damask of her gown made her skin look like marble. She wore satin gloves stretching to the elbow.

Sunder bowed over her elegantly proffered hand, then straightened with a half smile.

"You owe me." He gestured to the clock, which chimed as if on cue.

"I do not," she said. Her lovely red mouth twisted into a moue of derision. "You said it would take half an hour. Not that she wouldn't give in at all."

"But *you* wagered it would take only ten minutes. I think I win by default."

"If you insist." She reached into a delicate little purse to hand her companion something that glinted in the light. "But I'll have it back before the last hour of Nocturne."

"Care to wager on it?" Sunder shot back.

"Pardon me!" My voice was loud and raw. The two courtiers turned to me with looks that implied they'd forgotten I was even there. I twisted my fingers in my skirts so they wouldn't see me shake. "What just happened? Did you wager on how long it would take—how long—"

I choked, fury burning the words to ash even as I tried to force them from my throat.

"How long it would take me to seduce you?" Sunder cocked his head to one side and smiled like a serpent. "Why, does that bother you?"

Rage paralyzed every muscle in my body.

"Well, you did better than anyone dreamed." He lifted a sun-gilded eyebrow as he reached into a pocket and drew out a slim sheaf of parchment. He didn't even glance at the papers, just tossed them to the ground at my feet. "Apparently the Dusklands aren't populated solely by whores and thieves."

He turned on his heel and offered his elbow to the lady.

Every inch of my body trembled. I stared down at the sheaf of paper, catching a glimpse of sums inked on parchment. Carelessly scrawled signatures.

Promissory notes. Money. The sponsorship I was promised.

Tossed at my feet like so many scraps.

A sudden vivid memory seared my mind's eye—Sister Cathe's drawn white face, her trembling fingers as she'd unlocked the door to my room. She, of all of them, had been most frightened of me, of what I could do. Maybe she'd meant to set my dinner on the ground, but instead she'd flung the plate into the room, scattering morsels of food before slamming the door behind her.

I could still feel the dirt clinging to my scrabbling fingers, taste the dust coating my tongue. My vision flashed white.

Lullaby's warning sprinted like a mantra through my head. *Don't insult anyone. Don't insult anyone.*

Don't.

"Sunder," I called out, my traitor voice funneling all my furious thoughts into calmly uttered words. I couldn't think of anything beyond the blood pounding in my head, beyond the enormous sum of money thrown to me like leftovers to a begging dog. I couldn't remember why I wasn't supposed to insult anyone.

I just wanted to hurt him. Like he'd tried to hurt me.

Sunder paused, glancing over his brocaded shoulder. His lady followed suit, and I found myself admiring her smooth skin, her frosty hair, the jewel-bedizened choker collaring her white throat. She was perfect, and so different from me, with my faded dark hair, my travel-rough skin, my ungraceful manners.

"Are your lady's tastes so singular, then?" I asked, sweetly—and even as the words formed, I knew it was weak, I knew it was dull, I knew it wouldn't sting. "Or did you have to wager on her virtue too?"

His eyes widened, and I glimpsed a sudden, searing bleakness: a futile gasp of poisoned air, the cold moment before a last hope is dashed. For an aching moment, it was like staring into the violet-dark clouds above Dominion, dangerous and breathtaking and wild with impossible things.

I braced myself for pain.

But in another instant they were just eyes, and Sunder was just himself, arrogant and aloof and cold. He stared at me for one last moment, then stalked from the pergola with his lady, his boots loud as thunderclaps on the glassy floor.

I stood immobilized for what felt like an eternity before I found the will to crouch and retrieve the promissory notes. I felt particles of dirt stick to my numb fingers even though the marble floor was pristine. I thumbed through the sheaf, and even with my poor knowledge of numbers and finance, I knew the sum was enormous.

More money than an ambric mine could expect to earn in ten tides. More money than a Dusklander family would see in twenty lifetimes.

I took two shuddering breaths, then fled. I ran back through the porticos and vaulted halls, fighting the icicles stabbing at my eyes. No one stopped me, and the only sound to splinter the chirping of distant birds was the faint tap of my slippers on the pristine floors.

I made it nearly all the way back to Lys Wing before I collapsed between two carven pillars, shivering and shaking. Tears streamed down my cheeks, my eyes stinging as carefully applied kohl dissolved into salty mud.

I cried so hard I thought either the stays of my corsets must break, or my chest would explode. And when at last the tears subsided, the realization dawned.

I was rich. For the next three spans, at least, I was fabulously, ridiculously, unimaginably wealthy.

NINETEEN

When I finally made it back to my rooms in Lys Wing, Lullaby was waiting for me.

She wore a silver-blue gown, and matching metallic fingernails drummed a staccato on the arm of one of the many blossom-encrusted chairs thronging my chambers. An elaborate meal was laid out on the low table in my parlor; I smelled fresh bread, and dumplings, and more spices than my nostrils were used to.

Even caged in its prison of boning and silk, my stomach gave a yearning moan.

"You're an hour late," Lullaby snapped, water-blue eyes swirling. "Didn't you hear the bells for Compline? Or did you simply not care if I was kept waiting?"

"To set the record straight," I mumbled, folding onto a divan and giving my tearstained cheeks one last swipe, "I do know how to tell time. Despite what anyone says to the contrary."

"Pardon?" She leaned forward, her delicate brows coming together. "Who have you been speaking with? I thought I told you to keep a low profile."

"I tried," I said. "But Dowser thinks I'm a disappointment and a failure, and Sunder thinks I'm a mewling lowlife fit only to be tormented."

"Sunder?" Lullaby jerked out of her chair, and the delicate color of her skin drained to ash. "You saw Sunder? When? *Why?*"

"He summoned me," I reminded her. "He wanted to see me before he released the funds he promised me."

Lullaby relaxed a hair. "And?"

I jerked the cursed sheaf of parchment out of my pocket and flung it onto the table, where the pages lay wilting between charred greens and saffron rice. Lullaby hesitated for barely a second before grabbing them up, eagerly rifling through the pages. Her skin regained its color, then brightened with tinges of sapphire on her high cheekbones.

"Scion help us," she murmured. "I never dreamed it would be so much."

"Worth the price, I hope," I grumbled.

Lullaby's head snapped up.

"What did you say?"

"Nothing."

"Mirage." Her lovely eyes narrowed. "What did you do? Is there something I ought to know about?"

"More like what did *he* do," I said. Lullaby's gaze drilled holes in my forehead, and finally I sighed, fighting the urge to rip the pins out of my hair and tear the stays from my corset. "He slandered my birth, my intelligence, and my looks, then made a poor attempt at seducing me."

Lullaby's lips tightened.

"But that turned out to be nothing more than a sick wager between him and that icy witch he hangs around with, so he gave me the money and I left."

"And that was all that happened?" My mentor's dristic-flaked fingernails crushed the parchment. "You didn't say or do anything to punish him? For insulting you? For scheming to get you into his bed?"

I snorted. "I doubt there would have been any beds involved."

"*Mirage.*"

I blew out the air from my nostrils and jutted my chin forward, feeling like Luca's favorite brindled mule.

"I barely said anything at all. I only insinuated that his lover might not warm his bed by choice."

"Lover? What lover?"

"The girl. The frosty one. They're always together—I assumed—"

Lullaby jolted, then went still. "Mirage, no."

"What?" I rolled my eyes. "It's hardly even an insult, they're actually—"

"She's his *sister.*"

Shock sent a bolt of lightning up my spine, and I sat up so straight my corset ground against my ribs.

"His sister?"

"Worse." Lullaby's face was so pale I thought she might faint. "His twin. And they are most certainly not lovers."

"Oh." I cast my mind back over the events of the past two days, every second shifting in hue and shade until everything was awfully, blindingly clear. "Oh, no."

"Scion help us both." The multicolored light from the flower-stained windows turned the walls an ugly shade of mauve. "Oh, they will have their revenge for that slight."

"Who *are* they?" I had to ask. "You called him the empress's dog. He deals pain with a glance. He wagers on seduction with his *twin sister.* They're unimaginably rich. What am I missing here?"

"Who are they?" Lullaby's harsh laugh sent chills skittering down the back of my arms. "Only you would dare to ask that. Only you would dare not *know.*"

I waited.

"Most of Dexter refers to them as the Suicide Twins," she said, finally, a suggestion of fear in her lovely voice.

"Why?"

"Because you'd need a death wish to be on intimate terms with them." She took a breath. "Sunder and Bane. Pain and poison. They were born Aubrey and Oleander de Vere, and they're the last living heirs to the estate and great fortune of the Marquisate of Belsyre."

She looked at me, as if these names meant something significant. I had to shake my head. She sighed, deeply.

"Belsyre is the largest producer of dristic and kembric ore in the empire. Vast mines in the Meteor Mountains pump out nearly half the imperial supply of precious minerals. It's the wealthiest region in the land, and before the Conquest, the de Veres were dauphins in their own right."

I frowned, thinking of the gorgeous blond twins, tossing away fortunes to foundlings and wagering on intrigue. "If they have all that wealth and power, why are they here?"

"Is that a joke?" Lullaby stared at me like I'd sprouted extra eyes. "Their personal wealth rivals that of Severine herself. Their private militia is legendary in size and prowess. They control hugely valuable resources. Why would the empress want them anywhere *but* here?"

"Where she can keep an eye on them?"

"Where—" Lullaby's mouth twisted, and she dropped her voice, as though worried someone might be listening. "Where she can control them. Where she can use their power. Like she uses all of us."

"Uses you?" A memory nudged its way to the front of my mind—a handsome young man in a ridiculous hat, his smile fading when I asked why he and the other courtiers took it in shifts to dance attendance on the empress. *To better fulfill our great ruler's demands on us.* "What does she use you for?"

Lullaby's face shuttered like one of Dowser's darkened windows, and then she was prattling about place settings and cutlery and types of crystal and table manners, and I didn't have time to think about anything but keeping my back straight and my elbows in and my mouth shut.

But later, when the bells struck for second Nocturne and I was finally released from my aching tower of hair and my mask of cosmetics and my cage of a corset, I couldn't think of anything but the chilly slash of a gaze hard with dristic and infinite with green. And the sharp, clean scent of genévrier and pain.

TWENTY

The next week acquired something of a routine, and I was grateful for it.

I spent Matins with a grumpy Lullaby, rehearsing curtsies and niceties and flicks of the wrist, which seemed to be a language unto themselves. Comportment and address and carriage and diction. I tried on new clothing—Matin gowns and leisure gowns and Compline gowns and ball gowns. Underclothes and outerwear and shoes and accessories. Sunder's money had paid for a luxurious wardrobe that I—insulted but slightly relieved—was forbidden from having anything to do with selecting.

And there were my sessions with Dowser. Hours spent in that darkened study, breathing in the heavy scents of tabak smoke and kachua while he made me sit and focus, silent and unmoving, until I felt like one of the corridor statues forced to hold guttering torches from now until eternity. Hours dragging illusions from my uncooperative hands: a potted plant dissolved into flickers of ropy greenery; a glass paperweight snatched at the light before fading into shadow; a horn comb was a wisp of fog evanescing like a ghost at dusk.

I wasn't getting better.

Only once, after I managed to conjure the suggestion of an imaginary flutterwing, body like a diamond and wings like lace, did Dowser deem my work halfway satisfactory.

"Where do your illusions come from?" he demanded, frustrated. "What binds them to your mind, your body? Magic requires control, Mirage. Magic requires rules."

Rules. There had only ever been one rule with the Sisters—hide my legacy at all costs. Don't imagine, don't hope, never dream. And I'd tried. For so long, I'd tried to bind my power with the sinew of my will and suppress it beneath the weight of my fear. But control had always meant oppression. I didn't want rules; I wanted *freedom.*

I clenched my buzzing hands. Dowser was trying to help me hone my gift, and I'd sworn to do whatever he said. If he required control, then I'd learn control. I didn't know what the rules of my legacy were, but I'd find a way to learn them.

After my lessons I returned to my chambers in Lys for more hours with an increasingly nettled Lullaby, learning the differences between suppers, dinners, teas, and banquets. Socials, fêtes, soirées, and galas. The steps to dances long forgotten and yet to become popular. Card games. Gambling. Polite banter. Singing.

And although Lullaby swore the Suicide Twins would have their revenge for the slight I unwittingly—but not involuntarily—delivered, I saw nothing more of either Sunder or his icy sister.

But sometimes, when I woke at third Nocturne in a sweat and the edges of my shutters bled crimson, I knew all my nightmares were about pain and poison.

***

I burst into Lullaby's rooms without knocking, eagerness winning out over manners. After a whole week of practice, I'd finally mastered a complicated dance step, and I couldn't wait to show Lullaby. I hoped the progress would soothe her frazzled nerves—she'd developed purple bags beneath her eyes, and her once-manicured nails were bitten nearly to the quick.

I skidded to a halt in the foyer. Lullaby's sleek dark head was bent close to a cap of bronze curls under a rakish hat.

She was with someone.

Embarrassment heated my face, and I lifted my skirts to back out of the door. It was too late. Two faces stared up at me with matching expressions of guilty astonishment. And I recognized the second face—it was Reaper. *Thibo*. The gorgeous gallant who showed me the way to Dowser's. I glimpsed a flicker of parchment disappearing into his velveteen pocket, but I glanced away before they could catch me staring.

Even with my inferior manners and inelegant graces, I knew I'd interrupted something I shouldn't have.

"Oh, Lullaby," I mumbled. "I'm so sorry to barge in. I didn't know you had company, and—"

"Mirage?" Thibo's beautiful smile showed off every one of his perfectly white teeth. "Is that really you? I'd begun to think I dreamed you up in a fever, so deeply did you dazzle me with your beauty."

I knew it was worthless flattery, but his sugary words heated my cheeks. I ducked my head, embarrassed, but Thibo had already crossed the room on lavender-clad legs to bow over my hand. The feathers on his hat—silver today, edged in tiny black pearls—nearly brushed the ground.

"Thibo, stop," snapped Lullaby, from across the room. Annoyance darkened her turquoise eyes. "The last thing I need is for all that fawning to go to her head."

"Oh?" Thibo straightened with a flourish and a wink. "And what could possibly be the problem with her head?"

"The problem," sighed Lullaby, "is that no one else at court is going to treat her like that. I don't want her getting the wrong impression."

"Lullaby, it's fine," I cut in. "I'm not an idiot. I know it's just flattery—I know it's not true."

Thibo slapped a jeweled hand to his heart. "You wound me, fair lady! I would never say anything that wasn't true."

Both Lullaby and I fixed him with pointed glances.

"Fine," he pouted. "Perhaps I will leave the business of illusions to our famous fantast. Since mine seem so transparent as to be thought lies."

He sketched a bow before heading for the door.

"Thibo, wait!" In spite of the contrived compliments, I enjoyed his company, and after a week of no one but Lullaby and Dowser, I was antsy for fresh companionship. I wanted to hear about Coeur d'Or, about the parties and balls and courtiers. I was also desperately curious. Their whispered voices. The shred of paper shoved hastily into a pocket. "Won't you stay?"

He cocked his head, bronze curls swaying.

"Lullaby says your politesse is unparalleled," I lied. "We're practicing tea service and polite inquiry. Perhaps you'll lend some insight?"

He raised skeptical eyebrows at Lullaby, who stuck out a tiny pink tongue.

"Such beauty can brook no argument," Thibo said. "And by beauty, I mean you, not that fish-colored water sprite who delights in my pain and drinks all my wine."

"Fish-colored?" Lullaby's eyes narrowed into slits. "I'll have you know, songs have been written about the rare color of my exquisite skin."

"Now she's writing songs about the color of her own skin?" Thibo's wide eyes feigned shock. "The vanity!"

"I did *not* say—"

The pair devolved into comfortable squabbling, sniping at each other's insecurities with a skill that spoke of long familiarity. I rose and crossed to the bar, pretending not to listen as I poured a few generous glasses of ice wine. I might have invited Thibo to stay on a whim, but now that he was here I realized I was desperate for friends. Lullaby had been more than patient with me, but we hadn't exactly crossed the boundary into friendship. I didn't blame her. I was more an assignment than a companion, and my progress—or lack thereof—fell on her shoulders as well as mine. And she had more to lose.

But Thibo—Thibo brought forth an ease in Lullaby that I'd barely even glimpsed. Watching them bicker made me think suddenly of Luca and Vesh, separated by tides in age but so close in spirit. Melancholy clambered up my chest and tightened my throat. I could still only imagine what it must feel like to be so close to another person, to be understood so completely and loved so indescribably. To *belong*.

"Did you pour all three glasses for yourself?" Thibo quipped from the chaise. "Or is one of those for me?"

I snapped out of my reverie to see Lullaby and Thibo staring at me from across the room.

"She's a lightweight," Lullaby said, hiding a smile. "If she passes out drunk you have to carry her home."

"I won't," sniffed Thibo, indignant. "Besides, if anyone's passing out drunk, I can assure you it will be me."

I laughed, handing out the glasses before sinking onto the couch.

"You two seem close," I ventured, eyeing their arms, inter-locked at the elbow. "How long have you known each other?"

"Too long!" Lullaby rolled her eyes. "Thibo is here when I need him the most, and want him the least. He's a terrible friend and an outrageous nuisance. I've listened to his extravagant tales and outlandish compliments more times than I care to count."

"I would pretend to be offended by that." Thibo sipped from his glass. "But I really am an outrageous nuisance."

"Are you two—?" I cleared my throat, belatedly realizing it was probably impolite to ask such things.

Thibo frowned. Lullaby stared blankly at me for a moment before her face fractured into amusement. Her laugh was the sound of clear water rushing on stones, lovely and merry.

I couldn't help but laugh too.

"Oh, Mirage," she giggled, "that's not it at all."

Thibo choked on his wine. "Scion, you thought we were lovers? Lullaby, where did you find this simple-minded rustic? Does she also think babies are delivered by Dominion star maidens in the night?"

I flushed to my hairline.

"Don't be cruel," scolded Lullaby. Her soothing tones cooled the heat climbing my face. "Thibo prefers his, ah, *intimate companions* to be—hmm. Similarly male to himself?"

"Oh!" Another wave of embarrassment flared in my veins. "Why in the daylight world didn't you just say so?"

"I'm not sure Thibo's ever had to explain before," shrugged Lullaby, her tone wry.

"Speaking of which, I'm in love!" Thibo flung a mournful

hand over his heart, then sat up with an eager light in his eyes. "Lullaby, do you remember Mender?"

"How could I forget?" Lullaby shot me a spiky glance. "Mender is heir to the de Médeux estates."

"Compte de Médeux?" I wracked my brain. Just because we had company didn't mean Lullaby was going to stop being my mentor. "Cousins to the Isamberts? They export beech lumber from the Arduinne Forests."

"I'm impressed!" Lullaby turned back to Thibo. "What about him?"

"He's returned to court, and he's more beautiful than when he left!" Thibo sighed. "I want to steal the Moon herself from Dominion so I might hang her above his heart."

"I doubt the Sun would appreciate that," said Lullaby.

"Nor Meridian!" I added.

"Nor the Moon," we both said at the same time, before dissolving into giggles.

"This is why I don't fall in love with women," snapped Thibo. "You're so practical. No sense of the romantic."

"At least I know the difference between love and infatuation!" Lullaby scoffed.

"Did Blossom know that?"

Lullaby stiffened. Thibo froze.

Blossom. I sat up straighter. The girl who painted my rooms. The girl who was—*gone.*

"How *dare* you," Lullaby hissed. "If you had only done what I'd asked—"

"Now it's my fault?" Thibo's shoulders bunched. "You were the one who couldn't control her outbursts, it's no wonder—"

Thibo's white teeth snapped, slicing the words to ribbons. He cut his eyes to me, and Lullaby followed his gaze. I watched as courtly façades of feigned nonchalance descended over both their faces.

"It's well past Nocturne," murmured Thibo, rising to his feet. He bowed over my hand. "Mirage, let it be known your company was as exquisite as your visage. I hope to impose upon your pleasure time and again."

"The pleasure was mine!" I demurred, barely hearing my own words over the thunder of questions boiling inside me.

Lullaby didn't move as Thibo slipped out of the room. Her slender fingers were clenched in her lap, and her eyes shone like sapphires.

"Lullaby—" I began.

"Don't ask," she whispered, her voice cold as a frozen lake. "Please, Mirage, don't ask me to explain."

So I didn't. I eased out into Lys Wing's sun-bleached jardins, skimming my fingers over the heads of orange-painted callas and flushed asters. *Blossom.* The girl whose flowers crowded my walls might be gone, but she wasn't *gone.* Her presence rippled through my days, intangible but undeniable. Who had she been? And where was she now? What had happened to her, that she should be so discussed with so few actual words?

It's none of your business. I tamped down the curiosity spiraling through me. My place at court was still unsure. My progress with Dowser was almost pathetic, and I'd only recently made any headway with Lullaby. Whoever Blossom had been, she wasn't here now. And I couldn't let myself get distracted. Not now, not when I was so close to earning my place here, in the world where I belonged.

TWENTY-ONE

"What do you know about—?" I was already talking as I pushed my way into Dowser's study, waving my hand to clear the smoky haze souring the air.

Another week of twice-daily sessions with Dowser had cured my habit of knocking. But my voice shriveled in my throat when I saw who was already in my teacher's rooms.

Sunder stood across from Dowser, his arms braced on the broad desk. His suit was a crisp, stark blue: the color at the edge of the eastern sky. In the oppressive gloom of the study, he seemed uncanny—a creature blown from clear glass, or an icy breath on a cold morning.

They both looked up. Sunder's green eyes locked on mine, and I braced myself for pain. But there was none—just his cool, sheer regard and the throb of my own pulse in my ears.

"You're early," said Dowser.

"I'm sorry, I didn't—" I choked on my own words, suddenly flustered. "What is he doing here?"

"He," said Sunder, "happens to be your sponsor."

"Yes, but—" I struggled to maintain my composure, which felt suddenly frayed. "Why are you here?"

"To check on your progress."

"But you wagered against me. You're betting that I'll lose."

"That's a very simple way to think of a very complex investment." Sunder's voice was like polished marble, elegant and lavish and too slick to get a grip on. "And win or lose, the whole thing is bound to be entertaining."

The ember of resentment flared to life inside me, releasing a billow of rancorous smoke.

"Calm yourself, Mirage." Dowser stood smoothly, reading the mutinous fury that must have warped my features. "As your sponsor, Sunder does have the right to check on your progress. I would have updated him privately, but I'm afraid you interrupted us."

"And what were you going to tell him?"

"There's no need to tell me anything," said Sunder. "Why not just show me?"

Panic shivered hot through my veins, surely painting my skin in fevered shades. Since coming to Coeur d'Or, I had barely been able to conjure more than pathetic suggestions of illusions. Scraps of color, pulses of light. I would rather die than display my abundant failure in front of the lord who'd gambled on my virtue and wagered on my defeat.

"No."

"What are you afraid of?" Sunder bared his teeth in what might have been a smile. "Surely not me."

"Lord Sunder," Dowser interrupted, stern. "She is under no obligation to perform for you before Carrousel."

"I'm under no obligation to perform for you *ever*," I snarled, suddenly livid. "I don't care how much you paid—"

"Mirage."

"—if you think I'm some kind of dancing—"

"*Mirage.*"

The unexpected edge in Dowser's voice made me swallow my fury. My teacher was right. I shouldn't be wasting my time or my energy on this spoiled, sadistic man who called himself my sponsor. He was just a distraction, a stumbling block on the way to earning my place at court.

"No need to mince words on my account." Sunder cocked his head, amused, and the light from a guttering candle turned his hair to kembric. "I'm inclined to let the lady speak her mind."

"That's enough, from both of you," growled Dowser. "If you'll give us the room, my lord?"

Sunder tensed, and for the space of a breath I thought he might lash out. But then he bent into a practiced bow, inclining his bright head with such a degree of respect that even I recognized it as a taunt.

"I'd hate to be an impediment to genius," he murmured, brushing past me toward the door. I strained to keep my eyes unfocused, but the refined grace of his movements caught my gaze with jagged precision. He paused in the foyer.

"Lady Mirage?"

I gritted my teeth. "Yes, Lord Sunder?"

"Why are *you* here?"

The raw curiosity in his voice shredded my predictions. I dared to meet his eyes, and once again glimpsed the churning border of a bare kind of desperation I didn't have a name for. My heart lurched strange in the cramped cavern of my ribs.

"There's no need to tell you anything." I flung his words back at him. "In three spans' time, at Carrousel, I'll just show you."

Sunder's smile was a sharp blade in the dim. And then he was gone.

I exhaled.

"Have you heard nothing I've told you?" Dowser's voice was hard. "We've spoken of little else besides discipline. Restraint. And yet you lost every ounce of composure the moment you saw Sunder, and made no effort to regain that control."

"Did you hear what he was saying?" Pride quickened the coals of my resentment. "How could I allow him to treat me so disrespectfully?"

"You are so naïve." Dowser's words stung, more now than when he'd slapped me. "You understand nothing of this place, this world you are now a part of. You came here with your heart held in your palm, never realizing that this court was full of carnivores who would devour it in an instant. The things that mean nothing whip you into a frenzy, yet the important moments slip through your fingers like desert sand. You are weak, and simple."

"That's a lie!" Horror gripped me, and I fought for the words to explain how wrong Dowser was. "I am strong enough. I was raised in the grasping dusk. I discovered my legacy when a pack of feral village children beat me bloody into the dust. I survived a lifetime of being locked away and ignored by superstitious Sisters who treated me like I was cursed. I traveled a thousand miles with no money and little food to come to this place. I proved myself. Why isn't that enough for you?"

"Proved yourself?" Dowser chuckled grimly. The sound curdled my stomach. "If you've proved anything, it's that you still have everything to prove."

I tried to douse the dueling flames of humiliation and resentment.

"I don't know what else I'm supposed to do." I turned my head so he wouldn't see the gleam of tears in my eyes. "I came here because I thought this was where I belonged. Where I would be accepted. Where I would find the family I never had. But you're telling me that none of that means anything, and I'm just some weak child too stupid to understand the intricacies of a world she wasn't born into."

Dowser's expression softened, and his black eyes touched my face with something not too different from sympathy.

"You are weak," he said. "And you are a child. But none of that matters if only you could admit to yourself that you're both those things. Then try to be better. And try again, until you are wiser, and stronger. No one is born belonging anywhere. Nothing valuable is ever given. You deserve nothing that you haven't first earned."

"I am trying!" My gut ached. *No one is born belonging anywhere.* What if that was my fate—to belong nowhere, forever? Not at the frigid edge of daylight, not with the rumbling convoy of ore transports, not here in the palais surrounded by the legacies of an empire.

"Stop that." Dowser stepped closer. "Feeling sorry for yourself won't help."

"Why shouldn't I feel sorry for myself?" A hot hand clenched my throat. "I've been working as hard as I know how. But my illusions are just as weak as they were when I first arrived. *Weaker.* I'm supposed to be transforming into the Amber Court's prize fantast, not languishing in this study waiting for the empress or Sunder or whoever to toss me out on the street!"

Dowser sighed. He pulled his narrow spectacles off his face and polished them slowly on the hem of his robe.

"Your illusions," he said, after a long silence. "Where do they come from?"

"My bloodline." He'd asked me this question before—I didn't have a new answer. "Isn't that how legacies work?"

"That's not what I mean." His snapping eyes were a nighthawk's, keen as knives. "Where do the illusions originate? How do you conjure them?"

"I'm not exactly sure." I hesitated. "I pull them from inside me. There's a buzzing in my hands, and I push the illusions through my palms. Once I made a mask of a face—"

"How do you control it? What are its rules?"

I hesitated, struggling to find the words to explain. Every illusion I'd ever conjured was wrought in the dream-bright pulse of my quickening heart. A dream made real: ethereal symmetry unbound by earthly anatomy. Something of my very soul bursting out on the world. How did that have rules?

"I don't know," I whispered.

"How can you expect to master something you do not control?" Dowser shoved his spectacles back onto his face. "Perhaps if you assigned steps to the process, it might give your illusions structure."

"Steps?"

"You begin by imagining the object in your mind, yes?" That sounded right, so I nodded. "*Envision.* Then you must somehow use the energy of your body and mind to give the image shape."

I shrugged. "Maybe?"

"*Empower.*" Dowser looked pleased with himself. "And then you project the illusion outward. *Express.* Perhaps if you run through each step of the process with each new illusion, your legacy will adhere to the structure it so clearly needs."

Envision, empower, express. I rolled the words around my head. Dowser's new steps made logical sense, I knew that. Rules I hadn't intuited myself were probably better than no rules at all. But something rebellious and implacable railed against the rigidity of those three words. Three steps—three *rules*—for each new illusion, every vision I ever created.

"I'll try," I whispered.

Dowser studied me. "Perhaps that's enough for today. We'll give it a go tomorrow."

I bowed my head, gathering my skirts to leave. Surprise jolted my gaze back up when a heavy hand fell on my shoulder.

"Mirage." Something softened the spare, stern lines of Dowser's face. "I'm not unaware of what this means to you. You may think me harsh, but I only ask of you what I believe you can achieve. I have high hopes for what you might accomplish."

I scanned his face, but his eyes were unreadable behind his spectacles. "Why?"

"These Nocturnes, I dream too often of cold, pale faces and fractured heartbeats and invisible thieves," he mused. "But sometimes, come Matin, the sun breathes an ambric smile and I remember what it was like to dream in color."

Surprise pressed a shivering smile against my skin. I waited for Dowser to continue, but the only sound was the hiss of guttering candles and my hitching breath.

"That's not an answer," I said, at last.

"I suppose it isn't," Dowser agreed, before turning away to his desk. "Come back tomorrow, and be prepared to work."

TWENTY-TWO

"You're still mistaking the address for a duc with that of a compte, Mirage," complained Lullaby. "It's not complicated."

"Easy for you to say!" I groused. "I still don't even know what the difference is between the two."

"A compte—" Lullaby flattened her slender hands. "On second thought, I give up. Let's move on to wines, because frankly, I think I need a good, strong drink. You're hopeless."

But she was hiding a smile, and we both knew it. I had spent so many Matins ensconced with Lullaby that I was finally—if too slowly for my mentor's taste—acquiring something resembling good manners. My curtsies were no longer the wobbling stumble of a half-drunk goat, and I could pour a cup of tea without dumping hot water all over the table. Although I was still frankly incapable of telling a Belsyre ice wine from a coastal Cartoinne red, or a Devangelis ruby from a Sousine garnet.

"Goddesses!" Thibo swept into Lullaby's chambers with insouciant grace, clad in an outrageous suit the color of daffodils. "I come bearing gifts."

He tossed a few boxes of bonbons on the low table and flung himself dramatically on the chaise. Lullaby cooed over the patisseries, popping a handful of confections into her mouth. I'd asked her once how she ate such a staggering amount of sugar and maintained her slim figure, but she just patted her blue-tinged skin in obscure explanation.

I almost didn't notice the slender young man lurking in the foyer. I rose, curtsying in the manner appropriate for new acquaintances, and shot Thibo a questioning glance.

"Scion, I forgot you two hadn't met!" He popped back up, curling a proprietary hand around his friend's elbow. "Mirage, meet Mender. Mender, Mirage."

The name caught my attention, and I took the opportunity to study Thibo's new infatuation. He was indeed beautiful, all cool-dark skin with jeweled undertones, and firebrand eyes. He leaned forward and brushed a fleeting kiss on the back of my hand.

"Mirage enjoys being flattered," Thibo said to Mender in a theatrical whisper. "Here, I'll show you. Mademoiselle, today your beauty is as green and pliant as a newly grown leaf."

I snorted. Mender's eyes gleamed with humor as he leaned forward.

"Don't worry," he murmured in my ear. "Even I think he talks too much."

"I heard that!" Thibo griped, but the lithe young man was already slinging his arms around Thibo's lace-frothed neck and pulling him in for a kiss.

"Yeauch," Lullaby muttered, around a mouthful of chocolate. "Not in front of the children, please."

But I didn't mind. I liked Thibo, and I liked Mender, and I liked seeing them happy with each other. I tried to ignore the cold, dusky taste of loneliness coating my throat with dust. Once I earned my place here at court, then surely I'd find someone of my own. Someone who wanted to breathe my secrets and taste my hopes. Someone to share my world with, every soft-edged kiss and bittersweet sigh and pulsing promise.

"Let's play cards," said Lullaby. "Or something else. Anything, really, to force you two to keep your hands to yourselves."

"How about a game of peine?" Thibo extricated himself from Mender's embrace. "I only play cards if there's gambling involved."

Mender groaned. "But you always win."

"Do I?" Thibo favored me with a salacious wink. "That couldn't possibly be the case."

"I'm afraid I don't know the game," I admitted.

"Penance?" Thibo looked shocked. "Well, it's not difficult to learn."

"Not difficult to learn," said Mender, voice smooth as velvet. "Only difficult to avoid losing the entirety of your fortune to this thief."

Both were difficult for me, as it turned out. I had no head for cards nor for gambling, but I sipped my wine and obediently tossed Sunder's bronze écu on the pile of coins. Thibo won hand after hand of the viciously complicated game, bluffing and lying and cheating as the game actually required.

"Scholars at Unitas are predicting a Blood Rain," Mender said, eerily calm after losing yet another stack of coins. "Later this span."

"What's a Blood Rain?" I asked.

"Once per tide, a storm blows in from the Meridian Desert," Mender explained. "The deep red droplets deposit valuable minerals and nutrients across the land. Without it, crops wouldn't be able to grow beneath our dim sun. So it's usually a time of celebration and plenty."

"I think it's vulgar," said Thibo, nose wrinkling.

"That's just because you hate when your clothes get stained," Lullaby pointed out.

"I do at that." Thibo perked up, a wicked grin sliding across his face. "But a Blood Rain usually means a ball."

Lullaby jerked, nearly knocking over her wineglass.

"What's wrong?" I asked.

"Nothing," she lied. But sudden fear wreathed her gaze and sent a chill skipping down my arms.

"It's a good thing, Lullaby," insisted Thibo. I frowned—as usual, Thibo had leapt to some realization while I was still learning to walk. "Better a ball than the Gauntlet! Even if she makes a mistake—"

"How can you say that?" Lullaby looked stricken. "You heard what the empress said in the Atrium—"

The bell rang for Prime. I jumped to my feet before Lullaby and Thibo's bickering deteriorated into a brawl.

"I'm late for my lesson with Dowser. Anyone care to walk me across the palais?"

Lullaby shot Thibo a glance heavy with meaning, but Thibo returned the look with a peevish stare, throwing his cards onto the table and rising to his feet.

"I should be pleased to escort the fairest lady at court. Mender?"

"I'll stay for a bit." Mender gave Lullaby a smile like cool water touched with sunlight, and curled her hands in his. She instantly relaxed, her face smoothing like stretched silk. "We two should get reacquainted."

Thibo shrugged, and led me from the room.

"What was that about?" I asked as we strolled through a hallway streaked with malachite.

"It was nothing," said Thibo, but a muscle feathered in his jaw.

"You can tell me," I insisted, peering into his face. A frown marred his symmetrical features. "I know how to keep a secret."

"It's not a secret." Thibo shook his head, and his disgruntled expression slid away. "That's just Lullaby and me. We've fought like brother and sister since the day we first met. We disagree on practically everything. But we understand each other. And I would never trade that relationship with her, even if it is turning me grey before my time."

"Do you have blood siblings?" I asked. Thibo never spoke about his family.

"Yes," he said, with a queer finality in his tone. He glanced at me, and something softened in his eyes. "As I'm sure Lullaby told you, my father is Gilbert Montrachet, Duc de Beltoire. We are a notoriously fecund family, and my siblings and cousins are legion."

"And where is your estate?" I wanted to keep him talking— there was something strange behind his eyes, some apprehension or fear, faint as a whisper but dark as a Dominion shadow.

"South," he said, and brightened. "Come, I'll show you."

"Show me? But I'm late for my lesson with Dowser!"

But Thibo was already dragging me toward an unfamiliar annex of the palais. A narrow parlor opened into a sweeping hall, lined with high glass windows along both sides. A massive fresco soared in a grand arch high above—a stylized retelling of the Meridian myth. The Sun in his pale blue palais, the Moon surrounded by her starry-eyed handmaidens. And soaring between them, the Scion on his chariot of flames, flanked by his hounds and luminous with his Relics and his righteous fire.

"Not that." Thibo, impatient, tapped on the floor with the toe of his shoe. "*This.*"

I stared at the collection of tiny colorful tiles beneath my slippers for a long moment before I realized they were tesserae in a grand mosaic. I squinted at the vivid shards—emerald, turquoise, ambric, and pale glass—but I couldn't make out the picture. I didn't think it was a reflection of the Meridian myth above.

"What is it?"

"A map of the daylight world, of course!" Thibo stared at me. "You're telling me—"

"Don't," I snapped, holding up the flat of my palm. "I was raised by superstitious Sisters in the middle of nowhere."

"So I've heard," said Thibo, unsympathetic. "Here, I'll show you."

He dragged me toward the far wall, then spun me to face across the mosaic.

"This line of black tiles demarcates the edge of Dominion," he explained, pointing to our feet before nudging me forward. "This is you crossing the Dusklands." I nearly tripped over a hunk of ambric set into the tile. Thibo smiled. "The Amber City, of course. To your right—northward—are the Meteor Mountains. And to your left—southward—is Beltoire, the Montrachet lands." He pointed to a few sapphire-blue tiles scattered like jewels among the green. "*Terre du Lacs*. The lake country. Pretty women, *beautiful* men, and the most delicious delicacies you've ever tasted."

But I'd almost forgotten the original question. I stood transfixed by the daylight world, glittering with a million tiny colors. I could see it now, the sweep and flow of grasslands into forest, rivers trailing slow fingers toward the vast dazzle of infinite ocean. In the ruddy sunlight the mosaic glowed, chatoyant with light and depthless with shadow.

"Tell me more," I whispered.

"As you wish." Thibo led me around the room in a slow pavane, our slippers dancing between land and sea, desert and mountain. "Here—just off the southern coast, the Sousine Isles, where Lullaby's father lives. The water is blue as sapphires, and the worms who spin our silk are protected by powerful colonial warlords." We stepped into a vast golden stretch of mica-dusted tiles. "The desert ports across the Dura'a Valley, where the sand barges of Aifir and Lirias stop for supplies on their way to the Amber City."

"If you're planning on running away from Coeur d'Or," drawled a low voice from across the hall, "you're going to need a smaller map."

Thibo froze, his palm tensing against mine. We turned around at the same time, but I already knew who that refined tenor belonged to.

Sunder, flanked by his twin sister, Bane, and followed by a bouquet of finely scented lords and ladies. I faintly recognized a few from that day in the Atrium, but besides Lullaby, Thibo, Mender, and the oh-so-charming twins, my acquaintances at court numbered zero. The Suicide Twins were dressed to match—the rich verdure of Sunder's waistcoat made his eyes dark as genévrier needles, and Bane's pale green and silver gown looked sewn from frosted new leaves.

"Sunder." Thibo bowed with barely the appropriate level of respect due to the blond lord's rank. "Off to rip the tails from newborn kittens, I assume?"

"Reaper," replied Sunder, his tone acid. "Have you run out of lords to seduce, and so moved on to ladies? Narrow hips do not a boy make, despite what you may have heard."

Someone among the Sinister entourage giggled. I heard

Thibo's rough intake of breath, but couldn't look away from Sunder as his green gaze inevitably cut to me. I fought the urge to flinch as his eyes raked me up and down, lingering on my chevron-patterned gown of cobalt and rose.

"I see my money bought you clothing, but no taste." He quirked a disdainful eyebrow. "What are you doing roaming about the palais? I thought you were confined to your rooms until you learned to spell your name."

I did flinch then, and anger flared white-hot inside me.

"Wagered on any more seductions recently, my lord Sunder?" I made my voice as sweet as possible, ignoring the rage sending flames to burn my fingertips. "Or did they finally ban you from the stables?"

A courtier behind Sunder guffawed, elbowing his neighbor and sending a gratifying rush to cool my fury. But I was surprised to see most of the courtiers glance at each other with confusion. I was even more surprised to see Sunder flush nearly to his hairline before dipping into a low bow, his wrist quirked in an attitude I recognized as *points awarded*. When he rose back to his full height, he'd schooled his expression to its usual haughty scorn.

"As subtle and charming as always, demoiselle," he said, before turning on his heel and crossing the room, his cohort trailing him in a colorful convoy of satin and organza.

And as I watched his velvet back recede beneath the mural of Meridian, I wondered—why hadn't he told anyone about his sadistic plot to humiliate me in exchange for his sponsorship? I'd expected that to be the talk of court by now. But instead, my allusion to the wager had embarrassed him.

Who was Sunder? And what did he hope to gain by insulting and toying with me at every turn?

TWENTY-THREE

I arrived at Dowser's chambers late, flustered, and distracted. The room reeked of coquelicot resin, thin purple smoke lingering hazy in the air. The stench tickled my throat and burned my nostrils. I coughed.

Dowser jerked up from his chair, but when his eyes found mine across the room, they were dull and unfocused. He tried to rise to his feet, but his movements were jerky and uncoordinated.

"You're early," he groaned. His head lolled on the back of his chair.

"I'm not," I said. Surprise made my words slow. "You're just high."

I frowned, stepping farther into the chamber and waving the smoke away from my face. I'd met men and women like Dowser before, folk in the dusty villages along the Dominion border who sought refuge from the dusk in this insidious smoke poisoning them from the inside. Folk who called the stuff joie, or rêve, or lotus. Folk who thought they touched magic or foresaw tantalizing futures, but only found death.

"This place stinks." I flung the heavy curtains open. Ruddy light poured into the murky room. Another push sent the smooth panes of glass swinging outward. Cool air swirled the smoke into drifting specters, then banished them. Inexplicable disappointment shuddered through me. I had no right to scold my teacher, and yet—"How can you expect to serve your empress when you're floating in shadows like a nighthawk?"

"It helps . . ." Dowser's words were as sluggish as his movements. ". . . with the dreams."

Dreams. What had he said, the last time I was in his study? *These Nocturnes, I dream too often of cold, pale faces and fractured heartbeats and invisible thieves.*

Sympathy pierced my heart, reluctant but sharp. I'd never bothered to wonder what kind of life my teacher led. I'd been too busy disliking him. I'd hated the way he'd rifled through my memories, sifting shrewd fingers through shrouded secrets and drab dreams. But he couldn't have enjoyed it any more than I did. Was that how he spent his days? Diving deep in the resistant minds of spies and thieves and subversives, plowing their thoughts and harvesting their secrets?

He turned his head toward me, and beneath the blur of drug-induced stupor, there was pain in his eyes. Nausea soured my stomach. Perhaps if I dreamed in the splintered fragments of other people's stolen memories, I too would seek solace in a pipe of joie.

"Come on," I said, wedging one organdy-clad arm under his shoulder. He groaned again, but allowed me to haul him to his feet. His black ascetic's robes were long, and threatened to trip us both. "Let's go for a walk. This place needs to air out."

"Where?" he protested when I shoved him through the door and out into the gleaming corridor. It was still early in the day— hopefully we wouldn't run into anyone. I didn't want anyone to see him like this.

Unless . . . A thought sent outrage prickling in my belly.

Unless everyone already knew, and didn't care.

A broad hall narrowed into a corridor lined with agate and striated with amethyst. Beyond lay my favorite discovery since I'd arrived in Coeur d'Or—a sheltered grotto crafted from crystal. Mirrored trunks sent shards of burnished light to flicker between delicate leaves blown from clear glass. Prisms danced along lacy fronds. Water slithered down the walls like the phantom tears of invisible sylphs.

I eased Dowser onto one of the benches, then perched beside him. He stared around at the translucent jardin for a long, long moment. Finally, he smiled.

It was the first time I'd ever seen Dowser smile—really smile—and it was like a sunbeam slicing between thunderclouds, radiant and bright. It didn't matter that his teeth were stained with tabak and kachua, or that his lips were dull and cracked. He was happy, if just for an instant.

The smile disappeared, replaced by a more familiar frown. Though his eyes were still distant and a little cloudy, Dowser's gaze had regained some of its usual clarity.

"Why here, Mirage?" he asked.

I answered his question with one of my own.

"How often do you get out of your chambers?" I asked. "Be honest."

"Does escaping into hallucinations count?" His voice cracked, and he sighed, removing his spectacles to polish them on the front of his dark robes. "I'm sorry you had to see me like that. I never intended—"

"Don't apologize," I snapped, interrupting my teacher. "I've seen what that rubbish can do to a person, you know. If you truly felt sorry, you'd stop."

"It's not that simple," he growled. "It's never that simple, and if you've truly seen the effects of coquelicot, you'd know that as well."

We sat in silence, the only sound the chiming whisper of crystal petals.

"Who else knows?" I finally asked.

"How should I know?"

"Severine?" I pressed. "Does she know her closest advisor is an addict?"

Dowser was silent, but the corner of his mouth twitched. Horror prickled through me.

"She gives you the stuff?"

"That's enough!" Dowser surged to his feet, and in an instant I was reminded of his size and breadth, usually hidden behind a desk and a dark robe. His eyes were clear once more, as though he had willed away any lingering effects of the drug. "There are limits to the things you may discuss with me, and you would do well to remember that."

I took a deep breath, gazing around. The sky, a bruised mauve. The dazzle of a thousand crystal leaves. Glass flowers, beveled and faceted like diamonds. Water, streaming down gleaming walls.

"I know why I am kept at arm's length," I murmured, fighting against the drowning sensation of being always *outside*. "I know I haven't yet earned my place. But how can I play a game if I haven't been taught the rules? How can I navigate a web of intrigue if no one shares their secrets? Belonging is more than just existing somewhere."

"How can you be so sure this is where you belong?"

"How can you be so sure it isn't?" I spread my arms. "You spoke of sunlight and ambric smiles, of dreaming vast, colorful dreams. That's why I came here: to be part of that world. They named me Mirage, and that is what I am. Not a faint illusion that will quickly disappear, but a desire, and a promise, and a dream of something impossible. But only if I'm given the chance."

Dowser stilled. Beneath the ethereal shimmering branches, he was stark as a nightmare. Expectation glossed his gaze.

Control. I hissed Dowser's favorite word at myself. The dristic prison around my heart clenched. *Rules.* I bit my lip and tried to remember Dowser's steps. *Envision. Empower. Express.*

I squeezed my eyes shut and conjured up an image. *Envision.* I held it in my mind's eye as I tried to suffuse it with power from—where? I gritted my teeth as I imagined my blood pulsing with life, with *animation.* A tatter of energy was torn from my center, rent from my being. *Empower.*

And then I lifted my arms, and tried to create something that wasn't there. *Express.*

A cascade of crystal in a velveteen sky. Diamonds and dusk, ice wine and ambric. A dream of sharp edges, of hopes flown too high.

The illusion dribbled between my fingers like water down a drain.

Dismay hollowed out the space between my ribs even as vertigo blurred my vision and weakened my muscles. I dragged my heavy gaze to Dowser, but he wasn't looking at me, or even at my hands, where the illusion was barely a memory. He stared at the trees, at the smooth, polished trunks, mirroring our movements in distorted swoops and curves.

"Mirage," he murmured. "Where do your illusions come from?"

"I don't know," I said, choking on the hot tears smearing my rouge and clogging my throat. "I don't know."

"Go home," he said gently. "We'll try again tomorrow."

TWENTY-FOUR

S leep was like the Midnight Dominion, near enough to see but impossible to reach.

I drifted toward the window in a nightgown pale as the mythical Moon and soft as a lover's touch. The sunlight creeping beneath the curtains was red as the cinnamon Lullaby sprinkled on her kachua, and its touch on my skin made me feel feverish, as though I was burning up from within.

I didn't know how much longer I could do this. I'd come here believing so fully in the promise of a new life that I hadn't made space for the horrible possibility that none of this would work out. I might never step in time to the intricate choreography of courtly life. I might envision a thousand reveries—midnight and cold fire, bright sand and cobalt, amber and dusk—only to have them drift like wisps of fog from my fingertips. I might have dreamed of a perfect world that simply didn't exist.

A soft scuff at the door to my chambers jerked my attention toward the foyer. It was past second Nocturne. My staff never came to my rooms this late, and I thought I'd heard rumors of a big soirée tonight.

"Who is it?" I called softly.

There was no response, only another tap at the door. I gathered my dressing gown closer and ignored a warning throbbing in time with my heart.

Surely it's only Lullaby or Thibo, I assured myself. *Who else could it be?*

I opened the door, letting in a sliver of crimson light. I glimpsed a streak of white gold. A glitter of green.

Sunder.

Shock strung my bones at hard angles. My heart shuddered against my ribs.

"You." The word escaped me in a narrow hiss. The specter of remembered pain spangled white-hot against the back of my eyes, and I clenched my fists.

"Calm down," Sunder said, words clipped. And then, as though reading my mind: "If I wanted to murder you in your bed I probably wouldn't have knocked."

I gaped.

He glanced over his shoulder into the red velvet light, furtive, then brushed past me into my chambers. The scrape of his brocade jacket against my bare arm reminded me in an excruciating flash that I was dressed only in my flimsy nightgown.

"How dare you!" I snapped, crossing my arms over my chest and trying for haughty.

"Dare what?" Sunder turned on his heel, taking in my blooming chambers with slow disinterest.

"Dare—invade my privacy!" I spluttered. "What are you even doing here?"

"Offering you an opportunity." He gave an indolent shrug, and tossed a bundle of cloth at me. "Now get dressed."

I unfurled the cloak in a heavy exhale of green damask and black velvet. Curiosity and fear mingled with the sharp glossy tang of genévrier and frost, making me light-headed. I curled my fingers deeper into the cloth, remembering Dowser's admonishments. *Discipline. Control. Composure.*

"And why," I forced out, "would I want to wear this anywhere?"

"It doesn't much matter what you want. You're not supposed to be going where we're going. So you'll have to go disguised."

"Oh?" A flutter of intrigue tickled the nape of my neck, and I suppressed a shudder. I was suddenly desperate to leave my chambers—to go somewhere, do *something*. I'd been nearly a span at the Amber Court and had barely ventured out of Lys Wing. I didn't particularly fancy Sunder as a chaperone, but . . . he was the only one offering. "And where, pray tell, are we going?"

"I'm disinclined to ruin the surprise."

"And I don't like surprises." My voice was flat. "Tell me now, or I'm not going."

He hesitated, his eyes bright and rigid as polished dristic.

"The Gauntlet," he said at last. The word was a knife honed too sharp; brittle at the edges and so thin it might have been translucent. "Now hurry, or we'll miss the start."

※

It was after third Nocturne as we passed through eerily deserted palais halls. The constant glow of the sun steeped through glazed windows and stained panes, but torches and ambric lamps were extinguished, and gloom lurked in the silhouettes of things.

I hurried after Sunder, nearly trotting to keep up with his long, spare strides. The borrowed cloak was too long, flapping around my ankles and threatening to heave me onto the floor. It smelled like its owner too—a disconcerting bite of ice and greenery that crept up my nostrils and conjured vague visions of shadowed forests and frozen lakes. I shook my head, fighting the urge to hurl off the cloak and run in the opposite direction.

Sunder stopped suddenly in the shadow of a marble pillar along the Esplanade, flinging out an arm to halt my progress. I stumbled, knocking into his outstretched palm with my shoulder. I jerked away, but not before a coil of pain rippled down the length of my arm.

"Don't do that!" I yelped. I curled my hand around my wrist, but my fingers were cold and trembling and offered no comfort for a chilly ache that had already disappeared. "Don't you ever touch me like that again."

Savage shock pulsed raw across Sunder's face before he looked away. When he glanced at me again, his mask of practiced indifference was intact.

"You ran into me, demoiselle." His words were piercingly polite. "Perhaps you ought to ask Lullaby to school you in the sophisticated art of walking in a straight line."

"Perhaps *you* ought to—" I began, but Sunder's attention jerked away from me, and my hot words died in my throat.

Beyond the colonnaded arcade of the Esplanade, the terraced jardins of Coeur d'Or had been transformed into an arena. A broad oval court had been flattened and sanded, ringed by tiers of delicate benches draped in flaming pennants. Braziers of fire roared at both ends of the arena, melting the armor of stiff Skyclad Gardes into shades of amber and blood. I watched open-mouthed as courtiers paraded past in wild, revealing costumes and extravagant headdresses. I glimpsed a bare, muscular stomach painted like the gaping maw of a vicious beast; necklaces of thorns and bracelets of coals; tiaras of sharp glass and slippers of obsidian.

"What is this?" I whispered, but Sunder had already told me.

The Gauntlet.

The court began to file into the tiers of benches and seats. Their taut whispers filled the air with uncanny music, and their crystal goblets chimed like a hundred tiny bells. I reluctantly scanned the crowd, and recognized Thibo with a dreadful jolt. He stood with his arm slung around Mender, who was practically carrying his beau as Thibo sagged at the knees. I squinted: Thibo's eyes looked glazed and unfocused. I frowned. Even from here I could tell he was blind drunk.

I took one step forward.

"Don't." The quiet word was a dristic-tipped lash; when I turned my head Sunder's gaze was unforgiving. "Stay."

A manic energy throbbed through the crowd, and my own heartbeat quickened as my gaze fell upon the last courtier to join the gathering.

Severine. The Amber Empress.

She rode slowly out of the jardins on a massive chestnut destrier, wearing a dress of purest white and flanked by six feather-plumed chevaliers. The blazing braziers gilded the horse's coat with molten kembric and dazzled across the diamond-bright gown until Severine was a celestial vision astride a tongue of flame, outshining the dim sun. I could hardly breathe for the beauty of it.

She dismounted in a swirl of amber and took her place in a draped chair at the head of the arena. The crowd quieted.

"Tonight," Severine said, her voice ringing like the Compline bell, "we welcome the delegation from the Sousine Isles to our humble court. With vast bolts of rich silk and coffers full of jewels they thank me for my patronage—I intend to repay that thanks with hospitality! Let no request go undenied, no whim go unindulged, no fantasy go unrealized."

Sousine Isles. I scanned the faces of the group Severine indicated, looking for a hint of pelagic skin or aqua eyes, but besides the heavy medallions hanging around their richly clothed chests, the party looked no different from the courtiers. I frowned again. Why wouldn't the Sousine delegation include any native Gorma?

"So with no further ado," Severine was saying, "from Sinister, I choose . . . Bramble!"

A tall girl extricated herself from the crowd and prowled to the center of the sand court. She had sable hair coiled in a towering chignon and brown eyes ringed in kohl. Living vines entwined her torso, the creeping tendrils of green stark against her fair skin. She lifted her arms, and Sinister cheered and stomped. Her answering smile was cool with confidence and ripe with ruin.

"And from Dexter," purred Severine, "I choose . . . *Rill.*"

A cascade of some unspoken sentiment surged through my dynasty. Thibo lunged forward, only to be dragged gently back as Mender whispered hurriedly in his ear. I craned my neck to spot whoever the empress had selected. My stomach curdled when I saw him.

Rill couldn't have been more than fourteen. He had a man's height but a boy's body, all gangly limbs and skinny shoulders without an ounce of muscle. His eyes were huge in his face as he slowly descended to the arena. Bramble hissed at him, and he jerked away, trembling hard enough that a brisk wind could have blown him over.

"But, Sunder," I heard myself say, "he's just a child."

"Yes." Sunder's eyes went glassy with the reflection of some ancient torment. "Once upon a time, we were all just children."

"Let the pas de deux begin!"

The empress's cool clarion jolted my attention back to the ring. Bile climbed my throat in an acrid stream as I watched the duel progress, and end mere moments after it began.

Bramble dived at Rill like a desert cat pouncing on prey, shrieking with glad fury. Ropes of black-thorned vines sprouted from her fingertips, whipping through the air at the boy. They wrapped around his wrists and climbed his arms. Where they traveled, they raised painful welts that dribbled blood onto the sandy arena. Rill screamed, jerking his arms ineffectually against the tangle of barbed tendrils. A burble of clear water squirted from his palms in a pathetic attempt at defense, but that only seemed to egg Bramble on.

"Come on!" she screeched. "Is that the best you can do?"

Rill was crying now, leaking water from his face and skin as he fell to his knees in the sand. The thorns had climbed over his shoulders and snaked around his chest, pinning one of his arms to his side. He jerked, managed to free a hand, and with a sobbing gasp, pointed it directly at Bramble. A surge of water, stained pink with Rill's blood, punched the girl in the face. Her kohl smeared, and her tower of hair collapsed in a soggy mess. Fury contorted her face into harsh lines. She sneered, and stalked closer, whipping more green-black vines at Rill.

They slapped around his shoulders. Coiled around his neck. Climbed the sides of his face, punching ragged holes in his cheeks. He screamed with agony as the brambles invaded his mouth. He gagged as he wept for mercy. Still Bramble pushed forward, curling vines toward his nose, his ears, his *eyes*—

"Enough!" The empress's voice pushed through the choking silence. "Victory to Sinister!"

The vines retreated with Bramble, leaving Rill sobbing and broken and bleeding on the sand. A girl with Mender's cool-dark skin and lustrous eyes pushed out onto the court, dropping to her knees beside the boy and smoothing her hands over his lacerations.

With a sudden burst of vile heat I realized I was livid. My fingernails sliced into palms burning with fire, and when I glanced down I saw a jardin of creeping vines skulking at my feet. Their spiny leaves had long thorns that sprang sharp as needles from fat trailers. Drooping flowers hung tattered like Dominion shadows. Ichor dripped black as venom onto the marble.

Control. I bit down on the wash of hues. My chest contracted. The illusion disappeared. I looked up to find Sunder staring at me with brittle incredulity.

"Time to go," he said.

TWENTY-FIVE

I dashed after Sunder, hiking the borrowed cloak around my knees. Confused emotions roiled thick and sour through my head, slowing my thoughts to sludge.

"Wait!" I hissed as I struggled to catch up with his receding back. "Stop!"

He paused beneath an archway carved with crystal arabesques. I skidded to a halt beside him.

"Why did you show me that?" I demanded. "Why did you bring me to the Gauntlet tonight?"

Sunder opened his mouth to say something, but the raucous sounds of celebration ricocheted down the passageway. The shouting and laughter was gaudy in the muted Nocturne hush. My jaw hardened when I glanced over my shoulder and glimpsed smeared eye makeup, damp black hair, and a tight, gloating smile.

"Not here," said Sunder, and grasped my wrist.

I steeled myself for the jolt of pain. It never came. There was just the bracing frisson of his cool fingers against my hot pulse. My outrage at his touch bled away as my curiosity took over, and I let him lead me through a tangle of hallways. Finally, he pulled me into a shaded alcove dripping with breezy silks. They breathed and bloomed around us like captured clouds, caressing our skin with sleek, soft fingers and hiding us from view.

"Why didn't that hurt?" I blurted out.

A muscle in his cheek leapt as he clenched his jaw.

"Politic as ever, demoiselle," he said. "That's the question you want to ask me?"

"Now I do." A mulish stubbornness gripped me. "Can't you control your legacy?"

His eyes were metal. "Can't you?"

A blush painted my face with restless heat. "I'm an untrained fantast from the edge of the world. You've lived in the palais your whole life."

"You know nothing about me."

"I know they call you Severine's dog."

His head jerked back, sifting his pale hair between the drapes. His nostrils flared. He wordlessly turned to leave. I reached out, suddenly repentant, and snatched his wrist. This time, a sting zipped up my arm to my elbow. I dropped his hand like it was on fire.

"Your feelings," I guessed. I thought of how my own legacy ebbed and flowed with the tides of my emotional states—bursting out of me unbidden when I was frightened, or angry, or awestruck. I swallowed the uncomfortable sensation of having anything in common with the arrogant blond lord. "You can't control your legacy when your emotions are heightened."

"Our *gifts*"—he spat the word like it was poison—"are a reflection of our inner selves. Our inclinations, our experiences, our emotions. None of us are ever fully in control of our legacies. Some of us never are."

"But—"

"Enough." He forced a listless smirk. "Don't you have packing to do?"

"What?" Confusion rocked me off-balance.

"Packing," he repeated, enunciating the word until it was sharp and bright. "The process by which one readies one's belongings for departure."

"Departure?" My face twisted into a knot. "Who's leaving?"

"I assumed you would be." One burnished eyebrow lifted. "After everything you just saw—?"

"So *that's* why." Realization swelled, hued in faint shades of humiliation. "That's why you took me to the Gauntlet. To intimidate me. To frighten me away from the palais. To manipulate me."

"To give you an opportunity." Sunder stepped closer in the sighing silk sanctuary until we stood toe-to-toe. "The Gauntlet is more than just a political maneuver disguised as entertainment. It is a show of power. To the Sousine delegates, to the world, but most importantly, to *us*. At any moment, for any reason, any one of us could be called to the Gauntlet. Dexter versus Sinister. And the Gauntlet always has a winner. And a loser."

I shivered.

"I don't know why you came here, *Mirage*." His voice was barely audible. "Whether you want fortune or fame or you just have some dusk-addled fantasy about what it means to be aristocracy, I don't know. I don't care. But I don't want you here. And you shouldn't want to be here."

"I chose—"

"Make a different choice," he interrupted. "Leave the palais. Unless you're eager to find yourself lying in the sand of the Gauntlet in a pool of your own blood."

"Is that a threat?"

"No." I could taste his cool breath on my cheek. "But it might be a promise."

We faced off, as stiff as the breathless silks were pliant. I tried to banish the image Sunder's words had conjured back up—poor skinny Rill, covered in vicious vines as tears and blood and the water from his useless legacy pooled around him. Was that my fate? To be trussed up for slaughter and fed to another legacy, all for someone's twisted idea of entertainment? That wasn't the world I'd promised myself.

But no. Lullaby, Thibo, Mender—they were nothing like that. And I'd barely been at court a span—taking a single event like the Gauntlet out of context was jumping to conclusions at best, and social suicide at worst. I still had time to hone my legacy, to find my strength. Rill was young, nervous, weak. I'd gotten worse treatment from the mean brats in the Dusklands—I wouldn't let myself surrender to that fate.

What good are illusions against an army of thorny vines? whispered a traitorous voice in the shadows of my mind.

"I'm staying," I breathed. "This is where I belong."

Sunder loosed his breath and pushed his hair back from his forehead. His eyes blistered my skin where they touched my face.

"Who cares where you belong," he said, "if you're dead?"

And then he was gone, disappearing like a phantom in a shifting forest of silken trees. I almost pursued him, but a sudden fierce intuition rooted my feet to the ground, and I knew that if I followed him I would fall. Fall through a brittle glass floor onto bright, mirrored spikes, fall from a fragile dream into a waking nightmare, fall like an incandescent Meridian through the sheer blue riot of lingering dusk.

He isn't your friend, I reminded myself. *And he would see you ruined.*

I was nearly back to Lys Wing before I realized I still wore Sunder's borrowed cloak of midnight and pine. And even when I shucked it off and kicked it into a corner, I knew that I must now smell like cold fire and dristic and the sharp blade of anguish at the edge of cruelty.

I entered my chambers to find Lullaby perched on a cushion beneath the window. The colored glass cast such lovely shapes and contours on her face that for a long moment I didn't see how pale she was. Or notice her expression.

Dread was a living thing inside my breast.

"Where have you been?" Lullaby stood, and shoved something at my chest. It was a crimson envelope stamped in gilt and smothered in looping calligraphy. I couldn't have read it if I'd tried.

"What is it?" I asked, although some cowardly part of me didn't want to know, especially if Lullaby was so terrified.

"It's an invitation." Lullaby crossed behind me and glanced over my shoulder at the thick paper. "A grand ball, a week hence. Astrologists are predicting a Blood Rain. Everyone is to wear red, in honor of the occasion."

I frowned. "So?"

"So." Her lower lip trembled. "So, the invitation is for you, Mirage. The empress wants to see you. She wants to see your legacy."

"But—" Fear gripped me as my skin flashed hot, then bitter cold. "But what about Carrousel? I thought I had more time."

"Time is as fickle as a courtly game, Mirage." Worry made Lullaby's eyes stormy. "And the empress never plays by anyone's rules but her own. You'll have to be ready by the Blood Rain Ball. If not, we'll all pay the price."

And as she turned to leave, I heard the echo of her unspoken words: *I'll pay the price.*

TWENTY-SIX

Anxiety stole my sleep, and trepidation followed me on silent footsteps.

The following days were a flurry of activity. Fittings for an ornate gown in a fabric as scarlet as temptation. Instruction in the latest dances: tempête, jaconde, angoisse. Lullaby's eyes brimming with panic as I practiced the tiny twists of the wrist that meant much, much more than I would ever truly understand. Dowser, haunting the corners of his rooms like a ghost, insisting I *envision, empower, express.* Hours sitting on the floor of Dowser's study and attempting to conjure each of the objects he set before me: a small horn comb, delicate and fragile; a tabak pipe, smoothed with age; an old book, its spine broken and shredded by overuse.

I barely managed snippets of shapes and dribbles of color.

I couldn't bring myself to tell Lullaby that she'd have to be responsible for my failure.

Thibo sensed our collective unease, and attempted to distract me and Lullaby with various picnics and outings and adventures around the palais.

"I thought I wasn't supposed to roam Coeur d'Or yet," I hedged. Normally I would have jumped at the chance to escape my rooms, but I was sullen with dread.

"You received an invitation to the Blood Rain Ball from the Amber Empress herself," Thibo said, making his eyes comically round. "No one is going to bat their eyes at afternoon tea."

I glanced at Lullaby, who managed a brooding shrug.

"Come *on*," insisted Thibo. "We're going to the Solarium. If there's one thing that will cheer you two preening lumps, it's some sunshine and the mirrored images of your own vain faces."

Set in a little wilderness beyond the Weeping Pools, the Solarium was a tall, circular pavilion with a curving dome filigreed in bronze and kembric. We stepped through huge, swinging doors into a space thunderous with light. I gasped, throwing one arm up to shield my eyes from the brightness. The interior of the pavilion was edged and winged with mirrors—a hundred, a *thousand* mirrors, angled and curved and flared. Sultry sunlight poured in through an oculus above the door, striking one mirror, then reflecting again and again until finally it seemed to hang in a spectacular orb of kembric at the center of the dome.

I was so transfixed by the light that I almost didn't see Sunder. With one leg propped on a low bench against the wall, he leaned down to flirt with a lovely maiden in a cerulean gown. The hair pushed back from his brow glowed molten in the spectacular rays.

"It's Sunder," I said, grabbing Lullaby by the elbow. Wrath and embarrassment beat twin pulses in my heart when I remembered the last time we'd met. His cool fingers on my hot wrist, the taste of his derision in the back of my throat. *Who cares where you belong if you're dead?* "Let's go."

But it was too late. The blue-gowned lady's eyes had flickered to us across the room, and Sunder straightened to follow her gaze. His smile froze on his face.

"The most fearsome trio at court," he drawled. His low voice echoed around the dome, seeming to originate from everywhere and nowhere at once. "The Blue Man's daughter, the caterwauling Casanova, and our own filthy-faced Dusklander."

The familiar ember of rage scorched my blood. I stepped forward, quelling a brief flash of rational panic.

"Lord Sunder." I dropped into the curtsy reserved for royalty and hoped it looked sardonic. "I confess I'm not surprised to find you here, the one place in the palais where you can view your own reflection so many times. You must be in raptures."

Sunder prowled closer, until he stood with me beneath the false sun bathing us in brilliance. Behind him, his flirt edged closer, unease and curiosity warring on her face.

"So you admit," he purred, "that I am beautiful to look at."

"He who admires himself so confidently," I demurred, ignoring the hot throb at my temples, "must surely know more about beauty than one such as me."

Behind Sunder, the girl's mouth popped into a little O. Lullaby inhaled.

"You accuse me of vanity and poor taste in one breath." Sunder's droll tone hid an edge. "Perhaps, then, you might begrudge me your own explanation of beauty?"

I sucked in a breath of cool sunlight. Sunder's smirk oozed condescension, but there was something in the straightforward weight of his eyes that made me think he might actually care what I was about to say. But this line of bantering had grown far too philosophical for my tastes. Were we talking about vanity, or taste, or beauty? I didn't think so.

I only wished I knew what we *were* talking about.

"Beauty," I began, before abruptly deciding to be honest. "Beauty is all the things we can see, but cannot touch. Beauty is a way of seeing the world, unsullied by convention and free from coveting. Beauty is a stripe of amber light on a shoulder dusted with kembric. A breeze chiming through petals of glass. A distorted sun in a mirrored room."

"Beauty, by that definition," murmured Sunder, with a searing flare of his unfathomable eyes, "is your legacy manifest, is it not? What we can see, but cannot touch?"

I swallowed, and frost feathered the length of my spine.

"Perhaps you will favor us with a sample of beauty, then, my most talented lady Mirage?"

The ice turning my blood to sludge told me I'd made a mistake. I'd backed myself into a corner. I was trapped. There was no way to say no.

Control. I reached through the haze of panic for an image. Any image. *Envision.* A horned comb, or a jardin full of glass flowers, or an amber throne, or—

I dared a desperate glance at Sunder, expecting a sneer of scorn. But he just watched me with cool regard. Waiting.

I took a sunlit breath and let myself drift toward the well of impossible colors latched away in the dusky prison around my heart. They pulsed, hazy as amber and lazy as a heartbeat. These were the dreams that had carried me from the edge of the daylight world, but they were scorched with humiliation, shackled with thorny vines, stained with the gratuitous blood of gangling youths. I'd beaten them down so many times, throttling them and denying them, smothering them with rules even as I begged them to obey me.

Why couldn't I control them? It wasn't that the power wasn't there. I remembered a dim dusk edged in shadows, and then colors bursting blithe and brazen through the gloaming. I remembered the reverent cadences of an ancient myth, and then a lush blackness opulent with argent light. I remembered a vile burst of fury, and then an impossible wilderness of spiked vines and grasping tendrils.

The empress's voice echoed in my mind: *Let the pas de deux begin!*

A cruel joke; a beautiful veil for a hideous reality. Wrath burst to life within me, but so too did a bright, cold hope, clean-edged and gleaming like a silver thread in the dim. Another world, laid like a veil above our own: a scintillant hush of peace and harmony and calm.

A world where grace reigned. Where compassion dwelled. Where children weren't forced to fight to the blood.

I can do better than she can.

"Mirage?" Lullaby's voice, uncertain, pierced my reverie.

Envision. Empower. Express.

And I suddenly knew—I didn't want to mirror this world. I didn't want to conjure horn combs or paperweights or even glass jardins. I wanted to create my own worlds. Impossible, ephemeral, elusive worlds at the edge of imagining. Dreams, reborn and rebranded, set free from reality.

Something like that didn't have rules. And it certainly couldn't be controlled.

I opened my eyes and let instinct take over. A pair of dancers appeared with a gasp of light. I shaped them from breaths of rose-colored air and the contours of featherdown. I left them translucent, and the gilded edges of the false sun's rays cut them to ribbons before stitching them back together again. They glided, pellucid and lambent, through a breathless duet. Their feet never touched the ground. The mirrors caught their reflections and echoed them across the edges of other mirrors, until a hundred dancers whirled whisper-quiet through a world beyond touch.

Finally, the dancers drifted into oblivion. When I dared look at Sunder, I caught a glimpse of dazzled bemusement before his face smoothed into its cool mask once more. His eyes etched lines of fire on my face as he bent over my hand. The brush of his lips was the graze of a razor.

He returned his attention to the other lady, a gracious hand at her elbow. A second later Lullaby dragged me backward, away from the brilliance of the Solarium and out into the scorched dimness of our real sun.

"Scion, Mirage!" Lullaby burst out the moment the doors were closed behind us. "That was—why didn't you tell us you'd come so far? That was exquisite."

A whisper of pleasure heated my chest.

"But what in Dominion's name were you thinking, challenging him like that?" Practicality crept back into Lullaby's voice. "A philosophical discussion on the ideals of beauty with *Sunder*? That's like standing on the edge of a cliff and asking Meridian himself to push you over!"

"I think," said Thibo, smothering a gust of laughter and looping his arm through mine, "that you have proven yourself socially invincible in the most spectacular fashion on your first outing at court. I'm taking you everywhere from now on."

But as we trekked back to the palais, my friends bickering and laughing over my head, I couldn't think of anything but the chilly weight of Sunder's astonished gaze, and the perilous, tremulous sensation of working with my legacy instead of trying to control it. Look what I'd done: A new world had spilled jewel-bright from my fingertips. An impossible world, woven from patterns of dappled sunlight and the threads of old dreams.

A world that belonged to me, instead of the other way around.

TWENTY-SEVEN

I found Dowser almost by accident, after spending nearly all of Compline searching for my teacher to tell him the good news.

He stood in a broad hall with his arms loosely clasped behind his back. I'd never been to this wing before, and I couldn't help but catch my breath. Huge arching windows splashed rivers of amber light across a parquet floor. Lithe gilded statues twined themselves between jasper-limned pillars. Magnificent crystal chandeliers hung from a frescoed ceiling. And everywhere were portraits.

A hundred unfamiliar faces stared down at me. Smiling faces, severe faces. Laughing children with flower garlands and stern generals with medals spangling their jacket breasts and cool-eyed dames who'd seen the world. Dauphines astride destriers. Emperors dressed all in kembric. For a moment it seemed as though the weight of all that history and heritage would crush me to the earth and grind me into dust. But then I squared my shoulders, and strode toward my teacher.

"I heard about what happened in the Solarium." Dowser glanced away from the portrait of a man with laughing eyes and a peppery beard. A smile lingered around Dowser's mouth, a small ghost of the grin he'd given me that day in the glass jardin. "Congratulations."

I gaped at him.

His smile cracked wider. "News travels fast at court, Mirage. And I have eyes everywhere."

I turned toward the wall of portraits to hide a sudden awkward dazzle of mortification mixed with pride. *News travels fast at court.* Was everyone talking about me?

"I confess myself curious," Dowser continued. "What was it, in the end, that set your illusions free? Incandescent sunlight? The mirrors? Lord Sunder's unique attention?"

I barely registered the light teasing. Dowser's question had struck to the heart of my own seething conflict: What exactly had I done, and would I be able to do it again? All I knew was that I had relinquished the control I'd fought so hard for, and magic had happened. I chewed on my lip for a long moment. Finally, I flicked my wrist at a diamond-bright mirror wedged between two hulking portraits and dug deep for the words to explain.

"When I was a child, I kept a scratched and tarnished mirror under my pillow." I leaned forward until my own features loomed close. It was still a shock to see myself gowned and gilded, my hair an elaborate coiffure and my lips rouged. "I'd nicked it from a village kid and used to take it out when the Sisters thought I was asleep. I would trace the lines of my nose, the edges of my eyes, fascinated by the sensation of being in my own body, and no one else's."

Dowser gave a slow nod.

"But though my reflection may *look* identical to me, it is not me. She has no flesh, no blood. No thoughts, no opinions. No substance. She's not alive. She's merely a reflection of something that is alive." I sucked in a breath, focusing on the brilliant certainty that had soared through me at the Solarium. "Back in the Dusklands, the Sisters taught me that to control my legacy was to deny it. And when I came here you taught me that to control my legacy I had to give it rules. So I tried to bind it to reality—chain it up in the blood-hot space between sinew and bone. Make it *real*. But I am not a mirror, nor am I a god. I can neither reflect life, nor create it."

Dowser turned his head to regard me with quiet absorption.

"I am a fantast. My legacy is illusion—a blaze of strange colors born to rail against the pallid dusk. I *burn*, Dowser—with marvel and magic and a yearning I can't name. I finally stopped fighting for control. I surrendered to the impossible. I stopped trying to create the world I saw, and chose to create a world I wanted to see."

"And in that surrender, you have triumphed." Dowser's eyes glittered behind his spectacles, and I suddenly felt as though I was plummeting through a fathomless twilight: the boundless space between bright mirrors, lit by stars and hope and distant laughter. But then his eyes went flat and colorless once more, and he looked around the hall as though remembering where he was. Who he was. "Your success is my success, although I seem to have led you more wrong than right. I suppose you will no longer be needing my guidance now that you've found your own guiding light."

Disappointment plundered my heart. I looked up to stem a sudden well of tears, and caught a glimpse of the arching fresco adorning the ceiling. Another Meridian story—a fallen star and black mountains, the Blasting of the Wastes. I remembered another Scion fresco, and beneath it the spread of colorful tesserae in a mosaic of the daylight world. Thibo's easy explanation of lands I'd never heard of, never dreamed of. Lullaby's cool tones, picking out the weft and weave of the empire's political tapestry. The scrawled ink of Sunder's haughty hand.

I'd only just learned that the key to wielding my legacy was not control but surrender. Still, I allowed myself to hope. If I could finally prove I belonged here . . . I wanted all that—art, artifice, knowledge—for myself.

"Quite the opposite," I murmured. "I've unlocked my legacy, but I'm far from mastering it. I think I will need your guidance more now than ever. Also . . . it will come as no surprise to you that the Sisters were remiss in my education. The basic scholarship highborn sons and daughters attain—geography, politics, art—was denied me. If you wouldn't be opposed, I wonder if you'd be willing to spend some time . . . catching me up."

"I'd be more than willing." Dowser smiled again, but the expression looked suddenly strained. A tremor shook his fingers as he adjusted his spectacles. "But perhaps we can begin another day."

I frowned, glancing more closely at my tutor. Although it was hard to tell in the harsh blanch of amber sun, his eyes looked shadowed, and grey stubble flecked his jaw.

"Are you sick?"

Dowser splayed his hands, then clenched them tight. Another spasm feathered the muscles along his jaw.

"Only of you," he said, but the comment carried neither malice nor humor.

And then I remembered Mamie, the woman who used to sweep for the Sisters. When the peddlers were late or weather delayed the convoys, she would turn grey and quivery, her teeth chattering even in the warmth. *The ague*, she used to insist, *it's just the ague.* But when the peddler jangled through the village and replenished her secret stash of coquelicot—rêve, joie, lotus, whatever you wanted to call it—her face warmed and her muscles strengthened.

"Thank you," I whispered into the sun-washed crush of strange faces and untold stories. "Thank you for trying."

Dowser didn't say anything, just lit his tabak pipe with trembling fingers. The ember flared as he turned to leave, releasing a billow of sour smoke that followed him out of the portrait gallery.

I took the winding, less-populated route back through Coeur d'Or to Lys Wing, caught in the colorless wasteland between pity and compassion. An imprecise sensation nettled me, like being given a gift I hadn't known I'd wanted. For I had never known anyone quite like Dowser: the man who cloaked himself in black robes and resided in the shadows, searching for magic in everyone but himself.

TWENTY-EIGHT

From my perch on the roof of Coeur d'Or I could see to the red river where it burned between the foothills. Bloated clouds rolled in overhead, snarling like shadow wolves. The wind whistled, tasting of moisture and foreign lands and the distant brush of midnight.

For three Nocturnes I'd practiced my illusions here, amid the gleaming spires of cool crystal and brushed bronze. Bribing the Gardes had cost me more of Sunder's kembric livres than I cared to admit, but it was worth it. Up here, I could almost imagine I was an empress of bright dreams and brittle hopes, awash in the clamoring perfume of a million soul-safe secrets drifting upward from the city below.

I had practiced surrendering to my legacy, slowly unraveling tides' worth of restraints upon the power belling inside me. I shattered fetters forged from fear and unlocked shackles chained with humiliation and inhibition. It was thrilling, to feel the unencumbered swell of strange pictures and dreamworlds, bigger and more fantastical than ever before. But it was unnerving too, to release the control that for tides had been a safeguard against punishment and a weapon for survival. The sensation was almost like falling: I felt as though I flung myself from the lip of the roof, again and again, with nothing but the pliant promise of ephemeral hope to catch me.

But it was working. Illusions of cities: glass spires and jeweled staircases, faceted with crisp clarity and translucent in the fantastical haze of an inky night. Great birds with feathers of onyx and wings of cold fire, sheared sharp as flaming swords. Liquid landscapes, rippling like pale honey below azure skies. Milk-white plains beneath cobalt mountains. Thrones of amber, drenched in blood.

I blinked, and scrubbed my palms against the slick brocade of my gown. High above, the wine-dark clouds grumbled, promising a deluge. And soon.

I'd nearly reached the edge of the palais roof when the thunderheads burst and showered me in blood.

Fat droplets splatted down, liquid roses blooming on the slanting tile. They struck my face and my arms, staining my bodice and skirt. The liquid dripped along my spine and between my breasts until I was red, as if my skin had been flayed from my body and I was nothing but glistening muscle. I imagined that soon even the muscle would disappear, and I would be nothing but bone, gleaming pale and white.

And when I looked down to see Coeur d'Or drenched in blood, I felt remade, as though I was forged of illusion, and always had been. An illusion of muscle draped over bone, covered in an illusion of flesh and hair and clothing. And at the heart of it all, an illusion of a soul, of a being, of a person.

I was nothing but what I had made myself.

The chime for sixth Nocturne hung in the air like a warning.

I hesitated near the top of the staircase leading from the roof to Lys Wing and glanced over my shoulder. The storm cast a pall of purple shadow over the unlit stairwell, and my scarlet footprints glittered dull like a trail of real blood.

Scion, but it looked like someone had been murdered. I muttered a curse. The Gardes would never let me up on the roof again if I trailed a broad river of red from their abandoned post straight to my rooms. Or worse—they'd be punished on my behalf, flogged for indulging the well-paying whims of flighty aristos.

I sent a prayer toward the Scion, and stripped. My ruined dress slapped to the ground, and I kicked the gown and my slippers behind the archway leading to the roof. Even if the Gardes discovered the garments, I'd paid for silence as well as discretion. I shivered for a long minute in nothing but my underthings, my bare feet cold against the floor. Then I made a dash for it, sprinting through the echoing halls of the deserted palais with my heart clogging my throat.

I shoved into my chambers. The panic clutching at my chest loosened, and my limbs turned liquid with relief.

"The Dusklander has wheedled her way into someone's bed," drawled a voice from the depths of my shuttered room. "Will wonders never cease?"

I started, violently, banging my shoulder against the corner of the foyer. My eyes dredged at the gloom. A streak of white gold. A glitter of green.

Sunder.

Fury turned my blood molten. I sucked in a breath of twilight-tinted air, remembering at the last second that I was essentially naked. I wrapped my arms around my torso, ignoring the shudder wracking my spine.

"Lurking in dark corners?" I hissed. "Appropriate behavior for a spider like you."

Sunder's splash of pale hair loomed closer. I glimpsed a midnight-blue waistcoat, a glint of amber, and those fierce, fathomless eyes.

"I came to surprise you." He lifted a languorous hand toward my shoulder and trailed a gloved finger along my collarbone. The tip of his finger came away scarlet, as if he'd dipped it in blood. His voice twisted in a taut spring—if he had been anyone else in the world, I would have named the intonation jealousy. "I confess, demoiselle, that you have surprised me instead."

I took a purposeful step backward. My skin buzzed as though he was still touching me.

"Surprise me?" I made my voice chilly. "And what, pray tell, have I done to deserve such an honor? Insulted a beggar? Kicked a small animal?"

"Do I seem like a man who needs a reason to do anything?" A smile stretched his voice but stopped short of his eyes. He pivoted on his heel and stalked behind me. I followed him with my eyes, insolent. "I'm your sponsor. I wanted to give you something for the upcoming ball."

"I don't want anything from you." I shoved the words between clenched teeth.

"And here I thought women enjoyed being showered in gifts." He stepped close, pushing the sopping mass of my hair over my shoulder. His splinter of a laugh raised the hair on the nape of my neck. "Drenched, even."

A snake of chilly metal slithered around my throat. My breath hissed between my teeth, and every muscle in my body tensed. Sunder's cool hands coiled the chain, clasping the necklace at my nape. I glanced down. A waterfall of kembric and rubies nestled between my ichor-striped breasts, topped by an ambric jewel the

TWENTY-NINE

The Blood Rain bewitched Coeur d'Or with a dark, sweet languor.

I barely recognized the palais as I trailed Lullaby to the ball. The ink-stained clouds had darkened steadily all day, thrumming thunder through the halls and birthing secrets in the shadows. Ambric lamps pulsed a sullen red, and my heart quickened to match the throb of the light. We passed beneath two heavy doors into the transformed Atrium.

It was like standing inside a Devangelis ruby. The glass ceiling arched high above, stained crimson by the bloody rain falling from the wounded sky. The air tasted thick as nectar and sweet as wine. A curved and coiling chandelier hung from the apex of the ceiling, glass tendrils in black and scarlet grasping toward the floor. Silhouetted against a churning sky of violet and tangerine, Severine sat atop her ambric throne.

I glanced around the Atrium, fighting a nebulous sensation of exposure and shame. I tugged at the bodice of my gown, cut viciously low. I'd wanted a higher neckline, but the moment Lullaby set eyes on Sunder's dubious gift she summoned my seamstress and demanded she slit the bodice nearly to my navel. Satin skirts billowed around my legs, the color smoothing from black at the hem to a lustrous maroon near the hips. A grindingly narrow waist. That obscene plunge of a neckline. Bare shoulders. Sunder's jewels, heavy as iron manacles around my neck.

I suppressed a shiver. Courtiers pressed close, bedecked in the same brazen finery as me. Gowns in ebony and violet and scarlet. Wine-red lips and lusty eyes. Some danced slow, purposeful steps to the sultry strains of unseen musicians. Others lounged on cushions strewn in purposefully dim corners. Still more whispered behind their fans, watching me with brutal deliberation.

Lullaby shoved a wineglass into my hand. The liquid was sweet, and cool, and I drank gratefully. My throat was parched, and the air in the room seemed too thick—too solid—to drag into my lungs.

We edged around the room. Lullaby introduced me to friends and acquaintances, and I curtsied and nodded as politely as possible, striving to obey the modes of decorum demanded by the politesse of the court. No one mentioned my infamous introduction that day in the Atrium, and I was glad. But curious glances followed me around the room, and I heard my name murmured behind my back more than once.

Finally, Lullaby pulled me behind a gilt-limned pillar.

"Stay," she ordered. "Don't talk to anyone if you can help it. I'm going to get us both something to eat."

Her words roused an answering grumble of hunger from my cinched stomach.

I waited, taking everything in. Nearby, a pale statue of a half-naked man acted as a strange candelabra; lit tapers of red and black dribbled waxy trails down his shoulder and around his uplifted wrist. I drifted closer, admiring the sculpted contours of his marble torso. His eyes cut to mine. He shifted his weight.

I jumped backward, shocked and embarrassed. It wasn't a statue—it was a person, wearing real candles pouring hot wax onto skin painted to look like marble. I forced my gaze away, but when I gazed around I saw other men and women posed as living candelabras, tapers clinging to their skin.

Disgust battled with curiosity. How dare the empress order

these servants—these *people*—to stand for hours as melting wax stained the planes of their well-formed bodies? Didn't it hurt? I imagined the sensation, a hot drizzle prickling across my skin before cooling and solidifying. The thought sent a burst of warmth through my belly, and my eyes skittered across the room. I realized who I was looking for a moment too late.

Sunder, standing elegant and unsmiling beside his sister. Their pale hair gleamed diamond-bright amid the churning sea of red and black.

I shuddered. It was impossible not to admire the Suicide Twins, so alike in appearance and demeanor. But I couldn't help but curse my traitor gaze, seeking my sadistic sponsor out across a room full of people just as handsome and rich.

I rubbed an absent thumb against the faceted cabochon of ambric resting over my heart.

Almost as handsome and rich.

✦

The lazy hours of Nocturne crept by. I ate, and drank more wine. I met more courtiers—Vida, Mender's curvaceous sister; a glowering Sinister lord named Haze; River, a young man with a laugh like sunlight on water. I drank a little more wine. I danced, my too-high slippers an easy excuse when I fumbled a step. I flicked my wrist and simpered; my dance partner laughed and handed me another glass of wine. Finally, I stumbled upon Thibo, tucked beneath a rose-draped alcove with a deck of cards and a coterie of rakishly handsome young men.

"Mirage!" he cried. In his poppy-colored suit studded with rubies, Thibo looked every inch the libertine. His ringed hand rested on Mender's slender thigh. "Tonight you are exquisite in the way of new flowers and old money."

I curtsied. "And your compliments are as fleeting as wind in the desert or a roué's kiss."

The gentlemen all laughed.

"We're playing peine, Mirage," said Thibo. "Would you care to join us?"

"I have no head for gambling, nor a face for bluffing," I mused. "But I am of a mind to waste some Belsyre coin."

"A noble ambition," Mender said, nodding gravely.

"Indeed!" A wicked gleam brightened Thibo's eye. "Altruism at its finest."

I'd just been cleaned out when the empress rose from her throne of luminous amber and waved to the musicians, who ceased their slow sarabande. I raised my sluggish head from where I'd propped it on my hand to watch Thibo bluff his way into another stack of livres.

"A bountiful Blood Rain to you all!" the empress called, her voice as fluted as I remembered. She was resplendent in a gown glowing like molten kembric. "May it bring you luck in love and audacity in ardor!"

The courtiers all clapped, and turned to plant light kisses on their neighbors' cheeks. One of Thibo's foppish friends leaned in, but I pushed him away, wrinkling my nose. Not a tradition I cared to ascribe to.

"The Blood Rain comes but once a tide, carrying with it important nutrients and minerals from the Meridian Desert. Without this rain, our crops could not flourish. So it is a time to celebrate fertility and fortune." Severine paused, and cast her eye over the crowd. "It so happens that my greatest fortune is you! My prized court, full of beauty and wit and talent. But we should also remind ourselves that sometimes fortune comes from afar, and we don't know we have it until it knocks on our door." She smiled. "Sometimes literally. Mirage, where are you?"

I was pleasantly drunk, warm and buoyant with wine. The sound of my name ringing like a bell across the silent Atrium sobered me in an instant. Thibo and his friends stared nervously at me over their cards. I stood up automatically, a marionette with strings attached to my arms and legs. The courtiers in front of me moved away, clearing a path to the raised dais where the empress waited.

My unsteady steps in my precarious shoes rang loud on the marble floor. I swallowed against a throat that felt suddenly dusty, and I cursed the amount of wine I'd drunk. What I wouldn't give for a cool glass of water. I clenched my trembling hands in the skirts of my revealing gown, wishing I had fought harder to keep the design modest. I felt excruciatingly exposed, as though the assembled courtiers could see through all the satin and boning into the kaleidoscope cavern of my soul.

I reached the bottom of the dais. I slid into my best curtsy, lowering my coiffed head in the posture of utmost deference. I waited there, spine screaming and waist aching, for a long, miserable moment.

The empress's chiming laugh rang in my ears like a seductive curse.

"How our fantast has changed!" she exclaimed. "What a difference a span makes! Those eyes! This dress! That necklace!"

I fought the scarlet flush climbing my exposed décolletage. I didn't know whether to be flattered or offended.

"Rise, child."

I obeyed, forcing my tottering knees to behave as I pasted a smile on my face.

"You are much changed in appearance, Mirage," remarked the empress. "But tell us, are you so changed in ability as well? The last time you appeared before us, your abilities seemed to render you . . . rather faint."

Yes, if you called collapsing on the Atrium floor *rather faint*.

"I beg Your Highness not to torment me so," I simpered. "Surely my teacher keeps you apprised of my efforts."

"But you're wrong," said Severine, a bite to her tone. She tapped her closed fan against the side of her thigh. "My Dowser has maintained an irritating silence on the matter. Perhaps he hopes to shield me from disappointment."

"Or perhaps he hopes merely to raise your anticipation."

The court sucked in a shocked breath. Someone laughed. It rang in my ears, sounding appreciative, but I knew it must be mocking. I dropped my gaze and silently ran through every curse word I knew.

Why are you bragging? I snarled at myself. *This is your opportunity to prove you've earned a place here, not act the arrogant upstart with absurd ambitions.*

"Perhaps," agreed Severine, but her voice was too smooth, a desert pard closing in on its long-awaited prey. "Either way, we're all dying to know. Won't you favor us with a little sample of your talent?"

"I'm at your command, Majesty," I murmured around a mouthful of ashes. *You knew this was coming.* "But perhaps another evening? I wouldn't want to diminish the glory of this exquisite ball."

Again that braying laugh, loud and earnest. And with a sinking feeling, I realized I'd done it again—I was *bragging*. I insinuated that my legacy was so astounding that the ball would pale in comparison. My pride conspired with my mouth and left my brain out of the decision.

"Impossible," purred the empress. "Really, Mirage. I must insist."

No escaping that.

I sucked in a deep breath of crimson air. Around me, courtiers retreated, leaving a wide berth. I trawled my gaze around the room one last time, looking for a familiar black robe and smooth pate.

Dowser wasn't here.

I didn't expect him to be. Ever since he learned I would be presented at the Blood Rain Ball, Dowser warned me he might not be there. He insisted I practice my chosen illusion over and over, until it was perfect. Perfect from every angle, in every light, under the tightest scrutiny, since I wouldn't be able to rely on his presence to calm and strengthen me.

No one wants me there, he said. *And I don't want to be there.*

I closed my eyes. I didn't expect it, but part of me had hoped he would show up anyway. For my sake.

I slowed my breathing, focusing on the cool cluster of icy whites and blue golds swirling in the space beneath my heart. In honor of the Blood Rain, I had decided to show the court a vision of a world bursting with vast, wild oceans and cold cascades. It began simply enough: a pool of clear spring water bubbling up from the floor. I closed my eyes and focused on the glass-bright water, the murmuring plash, the blush of sullen light on a ruffled surface. I tasted the fresh, cool kiss of water against my lips.

I surrendered to the sensation, falling into the illusion as I waited for the glister and gleam to spill forth.

Nothing happened.

THIRTY

A snake of dread coiled around my spine.

I tried again, dredging the coruscant reservoir of light and color.

Nothing happened.

Panic shoved my composure to the side and dug pointed fingers between my ribs.

I pushed away the carefully choreographed illusion and reached for any of a dozen half-dreamed reveries. *Control.* The treacherous thought slithered into my mind, and I obeyed it without thinking, tethering the images to the sinew of my will. I throttled my legacy, forcing grand, impossible visions into its silent depths. A flying ship with bones of glass and wings of steel. Kembric cliffs slicked with lakes of obsidian. Alabaster skin and crinoline eyes, hewn from pale rock and towering like a mountain.

Nothing.

My hands, cold as ice, dropped to my side. A bare few seconds had passed, but already the court was beginning to rustle and whisper, curious and contemptuous. I dared not raise my gaze, but I could feel the empress's keen eyes on me.

Reality, heavy as a slab of iron, compressed my lungs. It was no use. Despite the intoxicating thrill of finally unlocking my impossible dreams, my legacy had refused to perform when I needed it most. Anything would have been better than this. A small, simple illusion. A pathetic half illusion followed by unconsciousness—even *that* would have been better than this. This . . . nothing.

I had failed.

"Mirage?" Severine's voice forced my gaze up to hers. Her smile was luminous. "Is something the matter? Did you misunderstand my directive?"

I shook my head, slowly, putting off the terrible moment of admitting my failure. *Failure.* Oh, Scion. *Lullaby.*

She stood to the side of a grinning Sinister lord. Even from here I could see she was crying—her lovely face wet with tears and her mouth twisted in a grimace of disappointment. I hadn't just failed myself—I'd failed my mentor. *Keep close to her,* the empress had said that day in the Atrium. *I blame you for her mistakes.*

I took a deep breath and shoved my pride beneath the sickly blossom of failure and dread blooming in my chest. I dipped into a deep, fawning curtsy.

"Majesty, I apologize," I murmured. "I seem to have forgotten how to conjure the smallest illusion. I can only account for it by saying that I have drunk far too much wine."

"Too much wine?" The empress raised a delicate hand to cover her smile. "Indeed. I can safely say there are many here this Nocturne who understand the feeling. Drinking too much wine can often lead one to, ah, *underperform.*"

The assembled courtiers roared with sudden laughter, and all the tension drained from the room. The empress gestured, and a sprightly minuet cascaded from the corner, sending men and women lining up across the Atrium. A young lord shoved me out of his way, not unkindly, but without a second thought. I turned a shocked stare to the empress, but she wasn't even looking at me as she returned to her throne, gilded skirts gathered in jeweled hands.

I was the entertainment of a moment ago. A disappointing one, at that. Time to move on to the next momentary pleasure.

Disappointment and shame and relief and irritation boiled up inside me in a great, heaving stew. I turned on my heel, scanning the crowd for Lullaby. After everything she'd done for me—all the work she had put into my appearance and my comportment—I had to apologize for my pitiful performance.

But my eyes didn't find Lullaby.

They found Sunder.

He stood by the heavy Atrium doors, a sullen ambric globe brightening his hair to a halo. He was staring right at me, his dristic-ringed gaze a sharp lash in the dim.

My hand flew to my throat. My fingers closed around an expensive jewel, set in kembric and edged with rubies. Sunder smiled like he'd break the world, if only he could grasp its bones.

My heart faltered, then jolted forward in double time. Sunder's words echoed in the rough-hewn valley between my sense and my sentiment.

You'll wear it to the Blood Rain Ball.

A command. He ordered me to wear his gift to the ball, and like a rustic half-wit, I obeyed. For a span, Lullaby had warned me the Suicide Twins would exact their revenge for my insults. Yet I had blindly agreed to wear his talisman in front of the entire court. I had even thought well of him for it.

But now—now it seemed so painfully obvious. I didn't know how it worked—or even what it *was*—but this waterfall of gems and precious metals around my neck was no mere ornament. I closed my fist around the necklace, the crisp facets of the jewels biting into my palm. I'd pull it off, I'd march back over to the empress, I'd insist I was enchanted, I'd demand another try, I'd—

Sunder was gone.

A raging beast frothed in my chest. I shoved through the crowd, pushing dancers and servants out of my way as I marched toward the end of the Atrium. Sunder's sword-sharp smile carved a bleeding gash in my composure, and I couldn't banish the sound of his voice convincing me to accept his gift. What had possessed me to trust him?

Part of me already knew. I had dreamed him up. Not the hard line of his jaw, or the chilly slash of his evergreen gaze, or the elegant sweep of his broad shoulders. But I must have imagined the uncertain pulse of bleak remembrances behind his eyes, the jealous tone that cracked his voice like agate, the blur of hesitation whenever he touched me.

That Sunder had to be an illusion. Because I couldn't fathom a world in which both of these men existed.

❧

I stalked Sunder through the palais.

Outside the Atrium, it wasn't hard to spot his bright head bobbing between the sultry red lamps lining the dusky halls. He didn't glance over his shoulder as he strolled through bands of gloom and glow, although my heels clicked loud on the marble behind him. He knew I was following him, and his indifference stoked the flames of my fury like a bellows. By the time we reached the collection of suites I'd come to know as Belsyre Wing, I burned with a rage that blistered my skin and hollowed my bones.

Sunder pushed through a gate that appeared to be fashioned from long runnels of ice. I followed, curiosity drawing my gaze and pouring cold water over the embers of my anger. It wasn't ice at all; the gate was cunningly crafted from glass and jewels and suffused with moisture to make it gleam. My fingers, when I dragged them along the pointed spines, came away wet.

Sudden doubt raised the hairs along my arms. I ignored it, shoving through the flimsy gate into a jardin made from winter.

We had winter in the Dusklands, where the earth froze hard as forged metal and the rugged vegetation bloomed with flowers of frost. But I'd heard stories of other kinds of winter, in the Meteor Mountains—where blankets of white fell heavy on broad-limbed trees, where waterfalls froze into châteaux of ice, where the cold was a living thing. I'd dreamed of that winter world.

Sunder's jardin was like waking up in that dream.

Pillows of purest white piled high on the glazed trunks of black trees. Shimmering blossoms of bright ice dangled like secrets between the stark boughs. My breath clouded the air before me. Silence hung thick enough to taste, a hush as tangible as a name or a wish.

"What is this place?" I breathed, and Sunder turned to face me.

In this white womb of ice and solitude, Sunder finally seemed fathomable. His black waistcoat was the same stark ebony as the trees reaching bare, mournful arms, the silver tooling like frost trellising bark. His defined cheekbones were carved of ice, his skin like snow. And his eyes—his eyes were winter. Cold metal and harsh memories, frozen behind frosted glass.

Abruptly, I remembered I was supposed to be livid with anger. I grimaced, wrapped my hand around the hateful necklace hanging from my neck, and pulled. The clasp snapped with an audible pop. Jewels cascaded into my palm. I raised the necklace to catch the flat white winter light, then flung it at Sunder. It struck the ice-glazed floor and slid with a whisper to knock against his boots.

Sunder glanced at the jewelry, then returned his unreadable gaze to my face.

"Well?" I snapped, frustration making me impatient. "What are you waiting for? What do you have to say for yourself?"

"I beg your pardon," he said. "I was waiting to see if you were going to take off the rest of your clothes and fling them at my feet."

The gibe was rude, and consummately Sunder, but fell flat, as though his heart wasn't in it. A smirk died in the corner of his mouth. He turned on his heel and stalked farther between the snow-draped trees. I opened my mouth, then stormed after him. I would not be denied an explanation.

"You tricked me!" I snarled. "You gave me that enchanted necklace to stop me from performing illusions. You wanted me humiliated in front of the empress and the court. See?"

I held out my hand and conjured the illusion I'd practiced with Dowser. The clear, bright water poured from my finger-tips, easy as breathing. I closed my fist, and the illusion trickled away. Sunder watched, unimpressed. His shoulders curled into a shrug.

"So?"

"So?!" I spluttered. I took another step, but I felt off-balance, as though every time I found myself on sure footing the path veered in another direction. "So why did you do it? Was it revenge, for what I said about you and Bane? Were you trying to punish me? Are you still trying to manipulate me into running away from the palais, like that Nocturne at the Gauntlet?" Another thought sidled into my mind, a thought that dragged my mouth open in horror. "Or did the empress *command* you to do it? Were you under orders to shame and humiliate me in front of the entire court?"

Sunder sighed, and lifted his gaze to the black trees. Wind whispered, and a shower of snow flurried between the branches. The flakes danced before my face, and when I looked close I could see the individual crystals, meticulous and fine. I reached out my palm, but the snow disappeared before it alit, insubstantial as one of my illusions.

"I had this place enchanted," Sunder murmured, and I wasn't sure whether he was talking to me or to the trees. "There was a girl—a Dexter girl—named Shiver. All she ever wanted to do was create places like this. Beautiful, cold, intricate sculptures. She loved the touch of ice, the brush of snow, the way winter never promises anything it doesn't intend to give. So I had her build this jardin for me."

"Why?" I asked, to fill the drowning silence.

"It reminds me of home." His eyes cut to mine. "Belsyre. It's not a forgiving place. Icy winds scream between valleys scooped from black rock. We tear out the bones of the earth and forge them into wealth. It's always cold. Death is a constant companion. But the pines are old and sturdy. The tigers are white as snow, and clever as men. There is something clean, and precise, and fair about winter. It has no patience for wealth, or power; it only values vigilance."

I listened, astonished. I'd never heard Sunder put so many sentences together in one breath, and there was none of the sneering lord in his tone. For the first time since our regrettable meeting, I believed the words falling from his mouth.

"And the girl?" I said, at last. "What happened to her?"

"She needed help." His fingers twitched tersely toward the edge of the trees. "So I helped her."

My eyes followed his indication. A white statuette of a slender girl leaned between the trunks. Her head was bowed, and icicles fell from her eyes and down her nose, making her look as though she was crying.

A corresponding trickle of ice trailed down my spine. Curiosity and horror battled for dominance within me. Horror won. I yanked my gaze away from what I thought was marble, but could just as easily be flesh and ice and impossible magic.

"No," I whispered. "You wouldn't. You couldn't."

"I helped her," Sunder repeated, and his gaze on my face was flat and unpitying. "Has the thought ever occurred to you that I might be trying to help you too?"

"Help me?" Disgust twisted my face. I fought for control over my expression. "If that's your idea of help, I don't want anything to do with it!"

"No, I suppose you wouldn't." Sunder's face hardened into its usual mask of disdain and cruel amusement. "You can leave now. You're bleeding on my snow."

Shock forced my gaze to the ground, and I saw he was right, in a way; the wine-dark hem of my gown, drenched in melting snow, had left great lacerations of dye across the bone-white floor of Sunder's winter jardin. I gathered the sodden hem in my hands, but that only served to smear the bloody gashes further. I bit my lip and did as I was told, retreating to the gate. Sunder paced a step behind me.

I paused outside the gate, emotions whirling within me. I only distantly remembered why I'd come in the first place, and the interaction had left me feeling cold and disappointed, as though I expected something different from what I was given. I whirled on my heel to once more meet Sunder's dispassionate gaze.

"Why—?"

"Do you know what my sister does, on evenings like these?" Sunder asked, his voice the unexpected slice of a sharpened blade.

My head jerked back. Again, I felt as though the path I took here had veered suddenly in a different direction, leaving me stranded in an unfamiliar wilderness. I shook my bewildered head.

"On evenings like these," Sunder murmured, "other courtiers, drunk on wine and lust, seek pleasure in each other's company. They flit behind pillars and steal sweet kisses. They use touch like a weapon, their hands on each other's bodies, stroking and exploring. Their breath mingles, warmed by shared desire."

His words ignited a thrill of heat in my veins.

"My sister, on evenings like these," Sunder continued, "retreats to her chambers. She tears pins from her hair and scrubs rouge from her lips. She hides in her bed, and she weeps. She weeps because her breath is venom, and to taste it would mean sickness and pain. She weeps because a single touch from her finger would drive a person mad. She weeps because her lips are poison, and a kiss from her turns a man or woman into a pile of rotted, putrid flesh."

"And you?" His words scored my heart with lines of ice, but I couldn't ignore one obvious fact: He was trying to manipulate me. As usual. "What do you do, on *evenings like these*? Play vicious pranks on unwitting Dusklanders? Deal pain with a touch? Make a game of seduction? Yes, my lord, you have my deepest sympathies for your sad plight."

"Do not mock what you don't understand." His eyes were a glacier, cold and unyielding. "We are bound to our power, just as it is to us. And every legacy has its consequences."

"Prestige, fortune, and admiration," I hissed. "Consequences indeed."

"You think you understand this world, demoiselle," he whispered, leaning closer. That sharp tang of genévrier needles slapped me in the face. "You think you hear Dexter, or Sinister, and you know what that means. Good, evil, *legacy*. Pain, poison, *power*. You imagine these words bound up and trussed away, with clear outlines and hard borders. But they are alive, seething with a complexity you refuse to acknowledge."

I opened my mouth to keep arguing, but Sunder reached a finger toward my lips. He hesitated at the last second, curling his hand back to his side. An involuntary gasp tore at my throat.

"There are worlds of understanding you have failed to envision," he said. "We are only as blind as the things we refuse to see."

The ice gate swung shut in my face, leaving me dripping scarlet dye in an empty hallway and wishing I'd never, ever come.

THIRTY-ONE

I tottered back along the Esplanade toward Lys, my thoughts choked with poison and ice.

I didn't want to believe one insidious word out of Sunder's twisted mouth. But I didn't think he was lying—not about Bane, at least, and the consequences of her legacy. I couldn't exorcise the image of her scraping cosmetics from her perfect face and weeping because she could never be touched, never be held, never be kissed.

What had he said, the Nocturne of the Gauntlet? *None of us are ever fully in control of our legacies. Some of us never are.*

Surely the touch of Sunder's hand was not inevitably laced with pain. I'd heard rumors of his conquests, his seeming parade of paramours. I doubted many maidens enjoyed a lover's gaze that seared with actual fire. I suddenly wondered what it would be like to kiss him, whether—

I tripped, the spiked heel of my shoe catching the soggy hem of my gown. I cursed, throwing out a hand to steady myself against a fluted column. I bent at the waist, reaching for my slipper.

A low moan snagged on the edge of my hearing. I froze.

Again—a throaty sigh, followed by a soothing murmur.

Blood rushed to my face, and Sunder's words rang in my ears. *Courtiers, drunk on wine and lust . . .* I had almost stumbled upon an assignation. I ducked deeper into the shadow of the pillar, gathering my skirts and preparing to make a stealthy exit.

One of the trysting lovers laughed, a melodious, bell-like

sound that struck a chord of familiarity even as it raised the hair on my arms.

Curiosity overcame discretion, and I dared to peer out from behind the column.

Caught in a wine-stained swathe of stormy light, the empress's golden gown looked mottled with blood. A luminous smile lit her face from the inside, and her violet gaze was fixed on the man in her embrace. He had his head thrown back with pleasure, and he was moaning, breathy and indistinct.

Fear prickled white-hot at my temples and pulped my muscles. If the empress caught me spying on her rendezvous, it wouldn't matter that I had stumbled here by accident. I couldn't afford her wrath, not after what had happened at the ball.

I tiptoed away, tensing at every rustle and sweep of my traitorous gown. Finally, I reached the edge of the Esplanade.

But as I turned to flee, I caught a glimpse of the empress's hands, her long, elegant fingers tipped in blood-red nails. And I realized she wasn't embracing her beau after all: She had her hands coiled tight around his neck, and his muffled moans weren't from pleasure.

They were sounds of pain.

<hr />

I waited for Lullaby in her silent, empty chambers as the bells chimed for fifth Nocturne, then sixth, then Matin. I waited for the chitter of footsteps on cobbles, the brush of satin in the marble foyer, the sweep of midnight hair. I waited for my friend to collapse beside me on the divan and stuff her face with chocolate while complaining about Thibo.

I waited until I was sick with guilt and unease.

I needed to apologize for my abysmal performance at the ball and explain why my legacy had failed me. Failed *us*. I needed to tell her about Sunder's ice jardin, about the strange things he'd said. About Bane's tortured ill fortune. To ask her about the consequences of legacies, the penalties for power.

But most of all I was desperate to tell her what I should never have seen in that darkened hallway. I couldn't banish the image of Severine's slim fingers wrapped around the exposed throat of a faceless man. Her blood-red nails. His moans. Lullaby must know *why*—why the empress skulked in shadows without a retinue. Why the sting of Sunder's touch made me shiver with a thrill I couldn't name. Why a legacy was sometimes a curse.

I must have fallen asleep.

The door slammed, jolting me awake. Soft, burnished light crept beneath the curtains. Lullaby limped into the room, leaning on Thibo's scarlet shoulder. I surged to my feet, and they both stopped. In the window's rosy flush I could see my friend was crying; tears cut channels through her makeup, and swollen pillows nearly hid her eyes.

"What are you doing here?" Thibo asked, not unkindly.

"I—" The apologies and explanations and questions choked me. "I waited for hours."

"Lullaby's not well." Neither his gaze nor his voice was as heavy as my heart. "She doesn't feel like talking. You should go."

I nodded, mute. My eyelids stung as I watched Thibo half carry Lullaby to her bed. I scoured her body for any sign of injury, a cut or scrape or brindled bruise that could make her whimper like that. I saw nothing. I dug my teeth into my lip and fled outside.

The storm had passed. Gauzy clouds draped a veil across a new-forged sun. Lys Wing rang with quiet birdsong and the patter of lingering red moisture. Sudden disgust soured my stomach as I hunched by Lullaby's door. How could a place so beautiful, so serene, be filled with so much pain and sorrow? I closed my eyes against the rush of images. A sandy arena stained with a child's blood. Bane scraping cosmetics from her face. Lullaby's cheeks striped with tears. Blood-tipped nails digging—

A hand brushed my shoulder. In the ruddy light, Thibo's face was drawn and exhausted.

"Go home, Mirage," Thibo said. "It's been a long Nocturne for everyone."

"What happened to her?" My voice sounded ugly in my own ears. "It's my fault, isn't it?"

"You couldn't have prevented this."

"That's not what I asked."

Thibo hesitated as he squinted into the light, hazel eyes distant.

"I won't be here much longer," he finally said. I frowned, not understanding. He unslung a locket from beneath his cravat and opened it to reveal the miniature portrait of a girl with his same deep complexion and bronze hair. "My youngest sister has come of age. She's talented, and ambitious. She wants to take my place here, to represent Beltoire at the Amber Court."

"But—" Shock slowed my words. "But there are other siblings at the palais. Sunder and Bane. Mender's sister Vida—"

"Mender's coming with me," he interrupted. He jerked his gaze to mine, his gorgeous features a discordant clash with the caustic anguish swelling in his eyes. "Scion, Mirage, can't you see? I *want* to go. This is my chance to have something for myself, for once in my miserable life. I haven't been back to my father's estate since I was a child, but I know there's an old farm south of the lake where the vines are unkempt and the fields lie fallow. And Mender—" Emotion choked him. "I would marry him, if he'll have me. We could look after my nieces and nephews, and maybe someday have children of our own. We could grow grapes, build barns, dance at country festivals. I want all those stupid, mundane, ordinary moments, Mirage—I want them so much it hurts."

I was quiet, but I was beginning to understand.

"And yet," he whispered. "And yet when I think about leaving I can't help but feel as though I am stealing something that doesn't belong to me, something I don't deserve, something I can never truly have."

"You're not a thief, Thibo," I interrupted, fierce. "Not for reaching for a world where you know you belong."

"We are all thieves here, Mirage," Thibo breathed. "We steal a thousand scintillating moments of drinking and dancing and laughter and pretend that there will never be any cost for the choices we make. But the price of love is heartbreak. The price of pleasure is pain. And the price of power is always corruption."

I shuddered. Thibo cupped my face in his hands, his touch tender. His fingers tightened against my cheekbones, and for a moment I imagined that sharp blades traced the edges of my memories, shining scythes slicing sheaves of golden wheat. But then Thibo dropped his hands to his sides and turned away.

"Sometimes—sometimes we all must pay the cost for what others have stolen," he murmured. "And the empress always collects when a debt is owed."

THIRTY-TWO

A breeze sifted motes of ruddy sunlight through a vivid curtain of bougainvillea. I leaned back on my elbows, letting fingers of light and shadow stroke my face. The air was redolent with hot honeysuckle and freshly mown grass. A fat bee hummed around my head, mistaking the silk flowers on my hat for real blossoms. I blinked drowsy eyes.

The day was hot, the sky clear save for a few salmon clouds bellying toward the horizon. Most of Dexter sprawled across the manicured lawn edging the Weeping Pools, sipping lemonade and munching on dainty cakes. The picnic was River's idea; I could see him floating great, undulating spheres of clear water across the grassy sward. A few courtiers, clad in gossamer skirts and light linen waistcoats, danced and darted after the liquid globes. They tried to pierce the limpid surfaces with the tips of their fans, shrieking with glee when the spheres exploded, scattering droplets across the lawn. Puppies borrowed from the palais kennels wobbled and flopped in their wake, bounding and nipping at skirts and heels.

The last fortnight had been *pleasant*. After the disconcerting events of the Blood Rain Ball, I'd expected a cascade of unpleasant consequences. But when I'd approached Thibo to ask how best to make amends to Lullaby for my failure, Thibo had cut me short.

"She doesn't remember." He'd drained the contents of his wineglass in one long slug, sending the feathers on his velvet hat sweeping. "So leave it alone, Mirage."

He'd been right. Lullaby was her usual self—if slightly glazed—and had no recollection of the night. And I didn't have time to ponder her lacquered smile, because my social calendar was suddenly and astonishingly full.

Events filled my days from Prime to the latest hours of Nocturne. Feasts with mountains of delicious foods: fragrant salmon with thyme and lemon crème fraîche; delicate tomato bisques; sweet, rich mousse. Salons where giant tabak pipes with sinuous necks smoldered, and guests drifted sylphlike between curtains of fragrant smoke. Soirées with literal fountains of spiced wine, which I learned the hard way made my head feel like it had been kicked in by one of Madame Rina's mules.

And if I sometimes glimpsed Sunder standing in the shadow of an opalescent pillar, sipping from a goblet and watching me, I bit my lip and lowered my eyes. Because when my eyes snagged on his, I saw they were full of a jagged expectation that made the tips of my fingers and the depths of my heart cold with ice.

I didn't owe him anything. I'd fought for my place in this world, and earned it. I deserved this serenity, this opulent luxury. Amid the flurry of graceful nobles and redolent perfume and gossamer fancies, I could almost forget the splatter of ruby blood on sand, crimson-tipped fingernails clutching bare throats, icy maidens weeping frozen tears. I could almost forget the chill of dread tripping brokenly down my spine when I counted the days until the Fête du Carrousel, where I would either prove I'd earned my place here, or shame my mentor and my dynasty before losing everything.

I could almost forget the word that lingered in my mind and stained the edges of my dreams: *gone*.

I shook my head to clear the miasma of worry, and looked for my friends. I spotted Thibo with his gaggle of preening pop-injays, regaling them with one of his favorite yarns—an embellished lark involving seven chickens, a prince in disguise, and one very long sword.

I saw the messenger before anyone else did—a palais courier, long-legged and tan. She crossed the lawn at a lope, cutting between the sphere chasers, who paused in their revels to watch her pass. The conversation and laughter died to a murmur as Dexter waited to see who the urgent message was meant for.

It was for Vida. I didn't know Mender's healer sister well, but she seemed kind, with her gleaming eyes and slow smile. That smile faltered now, as she reluctantly accepted the slim envelope from the courier. A bated hush descended over the courtiers. Her fingernail popped the seal on the envelope, and she raised the paper to her face.

The wail that ripped from Vida's throat was the sound of someone's world tearing apart. She collapsed to the grass like a marionette with its strings cut. The picnic shattered into chaos, courtiers rushing toward and away from Vida. A fight broke out between several young men; one of them yelled at the top of his lungs, while three others tried to catch his flailing arms and hold him down. Glass shattered, and the sound of weeping sucked all the light from the jardin, leaving it pale and colorless.

The hair rose along my arms, and I was suddenly cold. I hesitated for a moment, biting my lip between my teeth, before dashing out from beneath the fall of foliage toward the wrecked picnic.

No one paid me any attention. I cast about for Lullaby or Thibo, but in the mayhem it was difficult to tell one silk-clad figure from the next. Finally, I caught sight of Thibo, whose extravagant hat broadcasted his location. He was crouched in the group beside Vida.

"He's gone!" She screamed the words over and over, a terrible mantra that sent horror to claw deep fissures in my heart. "Mender's gone!"

Thibo stroked a hand over her bright head and whispered too low for me to hear.

"Did something happen to Mender?" I asked, my voice breathless. "What can I do?"

His eyes twisted to mine, but they were unfocused and sad. It took him a moment to recognize me.

"Go away," he murmured, without malice. "You don't belong here."

Hurt splintered through me like shards of broken mirror glass, leaving me empty and breathless and wretched. I careened up the grassy rise toward the palais, where lawn gave way to exquisite topiaries twisting against the rouged sky. The strange, leafy animals stared down at me and seemed to echo Thibo's words: *You don't belong here.*

I smeared an uncharitable tear from my cheek. Why was I crying? Thibo and Vida had just experienced a tragedy of unimaginable significance. I should be filled with compassion for their troubles, not consumed with self-pity and embarrassment for my own idiocy. Nothing that happened to me was anything but my own fault. I came here. I threw myself at the mercy of the empress. I begged to be a part of her court.

I should have known this world would always be out of my grasp.

I marched along the Esplanade, gripping my voluminous skirts. Dowser—Dowser would know what was happening at the Amber Court. Why my footsteps interrupted sibilant whispers and hurried conversations. Why Lullaby couldn't—or wouldn't—remember the empress punishing her for my failure at the ball. Why a place that had once seemed like a haven for magic and wonder had transformed into a nightmare of pain and lies and disappearances.

I rounded the corner. I recognized every crook and twist of the pallid arms clutching their fitful torches. I lifted my hand to rap on Dowser's door. My fist froze in the air when I heard voices floating from behind the door.

Voices raised in argument. One was Dowser's. The other was female, rich and cultured and authoritative.

The Amber Empress. And she was shouting at my teacher.

I knew I should back away—*I absolutely must not eavesdrop on the empress*—but my amber heels were glued to the floor. The image of slender, red-tipped fingers wrapped around a male throat haunted my mind's eye.

"I will not be put off any longer, Dowser!" Severine paced in front of the door, her voice growing louder and softer. "I want what you promised me, and I want it now!"

A low murmur indicated that Dowser had replied to his liege, but I couldn't make out the words.

"Time?" Dristic sharpened her voice. "I don't think you realize the urgency of this. We have only the briefest of windows, and the weapon *must* be ready in time."

Weapon? I leaned closer, struggling to make out Dowser's low voice, but it wasn't any use.

"No," snapped Severine. "There is no one else, and you know that as well as I. The Zvar corsairs are devouring my operatives nearly as quickly as I can conscript them, and that decision has not been without retaliation and reprisals from my nobles. Word has gotten around, and we've seen no new volunteers—"

Dowser's soft murmur interrupted her.

"Scion, who cares?" she snarled. "If I had to guess, it would be Reaper, but—"

A sudden ringing in my ears drowned out the empress's muffled words. *Reaper.* But that was Thibo's court name.

Panic jolted me away from Dowser's door. A shudder quaked through me, sending Severine's disjointed words skittering around my skull, teasing me with half-understood meanings.

I shouldn't be here. I couldn't be here.

I turned and fled.

My skirts whispered against the walls, and my heels tapped louder even than my panicked heart, flinging itself against my ribs. The outstretched sconces seemed to twist and reach in the dimness of the hallway, as real as the human candelabras at the Blood Rain Ball, ready to catch and hold me until the empress could punish me.

"You're imagining things," I whispered to myself. And I had to laugh, as I gazed around the halls of Coeur d'Or—at the marble veined with the blood of an empire, the murals depicting brutal battles and savage conquests. This whole world was an illusion, and I, the fantast, had been the only fool to believe it for so long. Lullaby, Thibo—all their actions and comments had hinted that everything was not as it seemed. But I'd been seduced by the glamour and the games and the heady, tremulous feeling of finally belonging to the world I'd always longed for.

Even Sunder had tried to warn me, that Nocturne in his ice jardin. *Has the thought ever occurred to you—*

The necklace. I thought he was trying to sabotage me, by dampening my legacy, but what if—like he said—he was trying to *help* me? To protect me?

But from what?

Or who?

I closed my eyes against the whirlwind of uneasy realizations and vague guesses. The only thing I knew . . . was that I knew nothing. And if I wanted answers, I was going to have to go right to the source.

THIRTY-THREE

By the time I arrived at Belsyre Wing my fancies had expanded into paranoias. Everywhere I looked, I saw curious eyes: the lowered gazes of servants flickering as I passed, the studiously blank eyes of the Garde suddenly keener. Even laughing courtiers seemed to mark my passage, their manners suddenly false and pretentious.

I fought to control my breathing as I was bowed into Sunder's residence, but my corset strangled my chest and my palms buzzed with Duskland shadows. I clenched my hands and calmed my expression.

"My lady?" asked the demure servant garbed in the black-and-white argyle of Belsyre.

"I will see Lord Sunder at once," I said, arching my eyebrow in the imperious manner I'd seen the court ladies use with the servants.

"I'm afraid he's—"

"I'll find him myself," I snapped, brushing past the girl. Her protestations fell on deaf ears as I marched through Belsyre Wing. I didn't know if I'd be able to find Sunder in this disorienting sprawl of opulence and splendor, but I was tired of only ever meeting him on his terms. This time, he'd be the one off guard and off-balance. I'd have the upper hand.

The idea sent nerves stitching up and down my arms. I shivered, and smiled.

I found him in the covered pergola where he had wagered upon my virtue. I thought he was actually sleeping, this time;

his lean frame was once again draped along the curve of the couch, but his hair was mussed, his fine features slack. His gleaming boots were kicked off, and his shirt was open, baring the pulse leaping in the hollow of his throat.

The servant made a nervous sound behind me, so I turned to her with a seductive smile and laid my finger gently across my own lips, hoping she'd assume this was a tryst. She hesitated for a moment, then curtsied and left the arbor.

I stepped closer to Sunder. In sleep, without his courtly mask of hauteur and sneering politesse, I could almost picture what he must have looked like as a boy. His lips were slightly parted, and his burnished brows slashed together in an expression both anxious and vulnerable. His pale hair drifted in the genévrier-scented breeze, and I imagined what it would be like to run my fingers through it, to smooth it away from his forehead and smooth away that frown with it.

Stop. I clenched my hand until my nails bit into my soft palm. The burst of pain cut through the absurd fantasy. *He's* Sunder. *Even if he actually is trying to help you, he'd just as soon hurt you.*

I uncurled my fist, reached for the half-empty goblet at his elbow, and dashed it to the ground in a shower of brazen prisms.

Sunder's eyes flew open. He jerked back against the chaise. For a long moment there was nothing but shock and fierce confusion in those sharp eyes. Then they narrowed, shuttering against emotion, and he was the Sunder I knew, cold and haughty. A smirk tugged at the corners of his mouth.

"Hasn't anyone ever warned you?" Sleep made his voice dark and husky. Cool fingers latched around my wrist, sending a whisper singing toward my elbow. "Never wake a sleeping tiger, unless you want to be bitten."

"Oh, I don't know." I made my expression scornful, and raked my eyes up and down his lithe body, lingering at his pale hair. "I've heard the white snow tigers of your precious Meteor Mountains are all born without teeth. I'm not particularly worried."

"I don't need teeth," he said, his smile sharpening into a knife, "to make you scream."

I snatched my hand from his grip and stepped away, willing my pulse to slow.

So much for the upper hand.

"I need to talk to you," I muttered, rubbing at my wrist.

"No," Sunder said. He dragged a hand through his sleep-mussed hair. "I don't *talk*."

"I'm serious," I hissed. "Something's going on in this damned palais. Everyone knows about it but me, but they refuse to tell me about it."

"That's because you don't belong here," said Sunder, without expression. The words were Thibo's, and they sent a streak of pain to bleach the colors swirling around my heart.

"But I am here."

"Unfortunately."

"Stop!" I clenched my jaw, battling against the ember of fury Sunder's needling words invariably kindled within me. "I know what you're trying to do, and I know why you're trying to do it."

"Oh?" Sunder leaned down to retrieve his boots, and his shirt fell open around his torso. I caught a glimpse of a lean, muscled chest and a hard stomach before I jerked my eyes to the floor, fighting the surge of heat climbing my cheeks. When I finally dared look up, he was watching me. Amusement glinted deep in his shrewd eyes. "A glass of wine."

"*What?*"

"Fetch me a glass of wine," he ordered, gesturing toward the shards of broken crystal glittering on the tile. I opened my mouth to retort in anger, but he added, "And get yourself one too, if you must," before leaning back on the couch and examining his fingernails.

I did as he asked, fighting to extinguish the slow burn spewing flames in my belly. If acting like his servant bought me some answers, I was willing to pay that price.

I sloshed what I now recognized as Belsyre ice wine into two glasses, then marched them across to Sunder. He accepted his glass without thanking me. I sat across the room with a huff of annoyance, and sipped gingerly at the crisp liqueur.

"Do you know what Severine's legacy is?" he asked.

The sudden change in subject paired with the casual and familiar use of the empress's first name rocked me off-balance.

"No," I said, remembering Lullaby's bright flare of panic when I alluded to it that first day in the Atrium. "No one does."

"Exactly," said Sunder. His eyes flicked left, right, and up. He gave a tiny shrug, as if to say, *You never know who might be listening.*

I narrowed my eyes on his face. Was he trying to tell me something about Severine? Or was he trying to tell me that he thought he—or I—was being spied on? I couldn't see past the courtly mask.

An idea occurred to me. I shut my eyes, and dreamed up a thunderstorm: the drowning thrum of ponderous rainfall, the hissing splash of a million raindrops striking parched earth.

A phantom tempest roared down, drowning out the whisper of leafy branches and the twitter of unseen songbirds. Surprise flickered across Sunder's face. He held a hand out between the dashing droplets, but the rain passed through his flesh, ghostly and insubstantial.

"Indiscreet, demoiselle," he shouted over the grumble of the storm. "Unspeakably so."

I huffed, and dissolved the illusion. I chewed my lip, dredging the lucid swirl of fantastical visions for something more appropriate.

"Go on," said Sunder, with half a smile. He ran one long finger around the rim of his goblet. "Impress me."

I imagined the sound of a soirée: voices raised in merriment, a trickle of laughter, the clinking of glasses, a strain of distant music. The pergola sang with it.

"You may be irritatingly loudmouthed," Sunder laughed, "but even you don't produce this much noise."

"Fine," I snapped. The ghostly party disappeared. I wasn't fond of these straightforward fancies, these fleshless daydreams. They reminded me of my early lessons with Dowser: pale copies of paperweights and leather-bound books drifting like ghosts in flat vermilion light. Worlds bound by terrestrial rules, the rules of reality. *Control.* I longed for oceans blazing with fire, armies wrought of diamonds and dust, clouded worlds cracking open like eggs.

I sighed, and surrendered to a world identical to our own in all but a few ways. The chirrup and warble of birdsong amplified. Sunder frowned upward at the arbor, searching for birds that weren't there. The slow trickle of the fountain splashed louder, almost distractingly so. A brisk breeze disturbed the lush foliage surrounding the veranda, and the leaves' whispered gossip grew louder. I imagined thick cotton blanketing the space between Sunder and me—a density of space where sound didn't carry.

Sunder blinked. I saw his mouth move, but the words were too muffled to hear. He rocked back in his seat, smirking as he beckoned me closer. I approached, dropping gingerly onto the edge of the chaise. The curve of the seat deposited me nearly in Sunder's lap. He didn't seem to mind, leaning closer so his mouth was at my ear.

"Better," he said. Even this close, his voice was distorted, as though we were speaking underwater. "Now, to sell the illusion. May I?"

I found myself nodding. Sunder reached up and yanked a few pins out of my coiffure, tumbling my hair around my shoulders. His fingers threaded through the locks, spreading them to drape around our faces.

"There." His cheek brushed mine, and he glided his hand around the base of my wrist. A frisson of energy raised the hairs along my arm, and I suppressed a shiver. "You wanted to talk. So talk."

I tried to focus on the reason I'd come in the first place, but it was hard to think with Sunder's cool fingers drawing zinging circles against my pulse. I swallowed, focusing on the edges of the illusion and ignoring his hands on my skin.

"What's happening?" I thought of Lullaby's friend, whose room I now lived in, and Vida's tears. *Gone.* I thought of Thibo's dour expression when he thought no one was looking. "People are frightened. Why?"

"Don't you remember the Gauntlet, Mirage?" Sunder's sardonic laugh was chilly on my cheek. "We are more than just legacies. We are weapons, wielded by our empress."

"Weapons?" I jerked with surprise. His arm tightened around my waist.

"Don't," he whispered. "Where do you think my sister is right now?"

I tensed. "How should I know?"

"She is with the diplomatic delegation from the Sousine, in the arms of the Compte du Verre."

"But—"

"Yes. He'll be dead by Matin. No one will dare question why. But without his vocal opposition, the Aifiri embargo will be signed by the remaining Senat, and Severine will have her alliance. Do you see?"

"Not really." I closed my eyes, trying to shut out Sunder's intoxicating closeness. I focused on the words he was saying, willing them to make sense. *Sousine. Senat. Alliance.* "The empress sent Bane to assassinate a political opponent?"

"Eloquent as ever, demoiselle," purred Sunder. "Now think of how many *political opponents* the empress of the most powerful empire in the daylight world has. Rulers of distant lands. Desert corsairs. Peasant dissidents. Her own unruly nobles."

"You're saying—" Sunder's words bloomed into realization. "We're an army."

"A silent, *secret* army," corrected Sunder, "beholden only to Severine herself. And not just the courtiers in Coeur d'Or. Most of the time, we are merely her insurance."

His words summoned up a conversation I'd had nearly two spans ago with Lullaby: *We are her insurance*, Lullaby had said. *Our presence guarantees that our noble parents and families behave according to her wishes. Do you understand?*

I hadn't then. But I thought I was beginning to. I shifted on the chaise to relieve a cramp above my knee. Sunder took the movement as an invitation, his hands smooth as quicksilver as he circled my waist and lifted me onto his lap. I yelped a protest, but it was too late; I was straddling him, my gown bunched around my thighs in a billow of floral chiffon. I glared down, my dark hair a curtain separating us from the world. His steel-edged eyes flashed with savage mirth.

He's just trifling with you, I snapped at myself. *It's all a game. Get your answers and get out.*

"Why now, then?" I hissed down at him. "If she's been leveraging her court of favorite sons and daughters all this time, why are courtiers suddenly disappearing? Why is she taking legacies from Coeur d'Or?"

"Skirmishes in the Dusklands: the shadows of Dominion, testing the strength of our borders. Zvar corsairs uniting under a single banner, threatening Lirian trade barges crossing the desert. Barges that are more valuable than ever before, because of the civil war in Aifir. Tensions rising between colonial government and natives in the Sousine." Sunder's face hardened, and the touch of his skin to mine vibrated with a stinging thrum. "We are on the brink, Mirage. The threat of war strains the empire's bones and hums in its veins. Severine is clutching at weapons she dared not use before."

"But—" A grim thought chased my words away. *Insurance.* The word had been burrowing deep within me, and suddenly I realized why—

I had no connections. No family, no relatives to keep in line or leverage as a weapon. I was just a penniless fantast who turned up out of the dusk.

"Me," I said, out loud, and the word resonated in my chest like a death knell. "She wants me. No one will care if I disappear. No one will weep when I'm gone. No one will threaten revolution if I die in the dusk or the desert."

Sunder's eyes on my face were empty of menace, only calm pity.

And that's when I remembered the necklace—a fat amber gem nestled at my throat, a waterfall of kembric and rubies swinging between my breasts. *Has the thought ever occurred to you . . .*

"You did help me," I said, forgetting the bracelet of his cool, nettling palms. "You weren't lying. You gave me that necklace to dull my legacy. To hide my abilities from the empress. So she wouldn't steal me away to fight her battles. Yet."

Sunder's eyes sharpened on mine.

"Carrousel is a span away," I whispered, and panic opened its eyes, a frightened beast awakening inside me. I clenched my hands into fists. "Like it or not, I'm going to have to perform for the empress. She'll know how far I've come. What should I do?"

"Do?" Sunder's expression didn't change. "I've been telling you since the Nocturne of the Gauntlet—*leave.*"

"Leave?"

"Yes, you stubborn half-wit," he snarled. "Get out of this labyrinth of lies while you still can."

He shoved me out of his lap without ceremony. I stumbled backward, half falling before catching myself on the slick floor. Humiliation stirred my blood to a boil and sent flames to lick at my cheeks. The illusion shattered around us, birdsong and trickling fountain and stirring trees calming as the bubble of silence evaporated. I glared as Sunder crossed to his sidebar and sloshed out another glass of ice wine.

"How dare you—" I breathed, but Sunder turned a gaze so cool and disinterested on me that I jerked back in shock.

"Enough," he said. "You may go."

I rocked back on my heels, searching for something appropriately scathing to say. But my chest and throat were empty of anything but a sinking bewilderment. I smoothed my rumpled skirt with shaking hands and turned away without a word.

I was nearly to the edge of the veranda when Sunder's crisp voice halted me in my steps.

"Demoiselle?"

I turned, suspicion battling with a strange, sour hope. Sunder lifted his glittering goblet toward the elaborate chandelier turning lazy circles above his chaise. The low red light dappled one quivering teardrop of true ambric dangling from its base.

"Shield enchanted that pendant," said Sunder, naming a Sinister lady I'd never met, only seen from afar. "Its magic shields this room from prying eyes and ears. Anything said—or done—beneath its protection cannot be heard or seen by those without. But never let it be said I didn't enjoy your company."

He drained his glass and turned on his heel, disappearing between the blooming lianas.

My embarrassment was swallowed whole by fury. Images came thundering at me like a terrible tide. My lackluster joke of an illusion. Sunder's guile in convincing me his fingers in my hair were *necessary*. His lips brushing my ear. His hands gripping my waist, sending lines of fire racing toward my heart.

A game. A vicious game to take my trust and transfigure it into something else. Something that now nestled chilly against my heart, beckoning me even as I fought to shove it away. Something bleak and delicious and horribly, wonderfully tempting.

I never should have trusted him.

I stalked out of Belsyre Wing with desire seething in my blood and hate searing my heart. Nothing Sunder did or said was trustworthy. Even his words about the empress and her legacies could be nothing more than an elaborate ruse to drive me out of the palais. To win whatever sadistic bet he'd wagered on my failure.

And whether I left or stayed, I knew I'd been outplayed. I thought suddenly of peine, the complicated card game Thibo had taught me. No matter how good my cards were, or how sure I thought my win was, Thibo always found a way to beat me. And sometimes, the only way to keep a bluffer from cleaning you out . . . was to fold.

Scion damn him.

Has the thought ever occurred to you . . .

Something stopped me in my tracks. I stared up at an archway swathed in cold, undying flames, and reached for the notion teasing at the back of my skull.

Dark trees tracing calligraphy against a backdrop of white. Frost. An ambric necklace skittering across a floor of ice.

And I realized: I asked Sunder whether he gave me the necklace to protect me from Severine.

I never thought to ask him *why he cared.*

THIRTY-FOUR

The bell for third Nocturne was nothing more than a memory, and still I worried.

Light burned through Blossom's painted glass window, casting orange shadows on my face. I fingered the planes of my ambric amulet, throbbing in time to my hurried pulse. Its weight against my chest was unfamiliar, like a memory I thought I'd forgotten, only to recall when I least expected it. It was so different from the gaudy spill of Sunder's Blood Rain gift, and yet I preferred its ancient contours, worn smooth by unremembered lives and time's steady strum.

The scratch at my door was so soft I almost thought I imagined it. I jumped to my feet. Reluctant hope untangled the knots in my chest.

The door whispered open at my touch. A broad-shouldered man stood in the shadow of the doorframe, nothing but darkness edged in blood. He stepped closer. My lungs gasped for air.

I saw a palais servant's pewter livery. A mop of curling, dark hair. Brown skin kissed by the sun. And burnished eyes gleaming like kembric in the shadows.

He wasn't who I thought he'd be.

"Luca?!" The name ripped out of me.

He kicked the door shut and crushed me against his chest. I gasped, and curled my arms around his neck. The kiss he planted on my cheek was rough with stubble. He smelled of musk and incense and the city, a scent so different from the fine perfumes of the palais that I nearly wept.

"Luca!" I repeated. I could hardly think of any other words. He set me to my feet, although he seemed reluctant to release me completely—his hands lingered at my waist. Heat climbed my cheeks when I remembered I was wearing nothing but my filmy nightgown. "Do you *work* here now?"

"Of course not." His smile was a flash of white, startlingly bright and achingly familiar. "I came to see you."

"But—" I paused. I hardly knew what to say. I never expected— "But I thought you were leaving the city with the convoy over a span ago! And how did you get into the palais? What if—?"

"I get caught?" His smile, if possible, grew brighter. "I hoped you—the famous fantast the city can't stop talking about— might be able to help with that."

"Famous—?" I barely got the word out before shock bubbled up into laughter. I clapped a hand over my mouth. "You're joking."

"Care to find out?" Luca stepped closer, holding out a mass of fabric—the same color and weave as the outfit he wore. Servants' livery.

"How—?"

"My friend Garan. The servant. He snuck me in and lent me these." Mischief brightened his eyes. "Come on. The palais may be asleep, but the Amber City is still awake. The city is *always* awake. What do you say—a reprieve from this prison of silk and secrets?"

Reality sent a sharp knife slicing through my fizzing exhilaration. Luca shouldn't be here. Luca *couldn't* be here. Not in the palais, and certainly not in Lys Wing. And I couldn't leave, not mere weeks before Carrousel.

Couldn't I? Sunder's cool voice echoed in my mind. *Get out of this labyrinth of lies while you still can.*

"Sylvie. Don't you trust me?" Luca whispered, and the name froze me. *Sylvie*. Again, I caught that scent of him, like burnt wood and sun-kissed skin and infinite skies. The scent of outside.

My teeth worked at my lip, and I remembered the day we arrived at the Amber City. The convoy transports, rattling along broad boulevards and narrow alleyways. The rush of unfamiliar sights and sounds. A thousand colors glittering like jewels in the ruddy light of a dim sun. A million people, with joys and pains and secret dreams.

I never got to see any of it.

"Just an hour." I grabbed the servants' livery from his hands, fixing him with my sternest glare. "If I'm not back before Matin I will personally have you executed by the Skyclad Garde."

His muffled laugh sent a flare of pleasure blazing up my spine. I ducked into my room and dressed quickly, shucking off the gossamer nightgown to step into the linen livery. After spans of dressing in only silks and lace, the fabric was rough on my skin. I repressed a shudder of doubt, and shoved my carefully curled hair beneath a nondescript cap.

"Ready," I whispered, ducking out. But Luca had moved toward my sitting room. His long, dark fingers splayed against the jardin of painted flowers draped about my chambers.

"Did you do these?" In the dimness of my shuttered room, his eyes gleamed like the bronze écu in my chamois purse. "I didn't know you could paint."

"The girl who lived here before me painted them."

"Where's she now?" He caressed a splash of white lilies.

"I don't know." *Gone.* I swallowed a bright burst of grief. *Mender.* I still hadn't been able to bring myself to approach Thibo after the picnic, but I wanted— No. I shoved the moil of emotions beneath the unexpected thrill of seeing Luca. "She . . . left before I arrived at the palais."

"Ah." Luca nodded, as though he understood something I didn't. He crossed to my side, twisting his arm through mine. "Let's go."

"Luca—" I hesitated one last time, but Luca spun to face me. He pressed one warm finger to my lips, his calluses brushing the tender skin. I swallowed, hard.

"Hush," he laughed. "No more excuses."

❧

We drifted like shadows through the halls of Coeur d'Or, keeping to the inner passages and secret doors the servants used to get quickly from one wing to the next. I jumped at every footstep, but Luca's hand was firm on the small of my back, pushing me forward.

A flight of hidden steps; the quiet whisper of a wooden door; the dank press of an ill-lit tunnel. And finally, a splash of burnished light on pitted cobblestones. The distant murmur and chatter of a city that never slept. A breeze laden with the complicated smells of a million citizens and their daily lives.

Outside.

Luca didn't let me catch my breath. We raced down streets where close-set houses frowned like distant Sisters. We squeezed along alleyways slick with moisture, where unseen creatures scuttled in the shadows. The air screamed in my lungs, and I was utterly lost.

"Where are we going?" I hissed at Luca's pewter-clad back,

barely visible in the shadow of a warehouse with busted windows like a gapped smile. "We shouldn't go too far!"

"Don't worry." Luca tossed the words over his shoulder. "I want to show you something."

I swallowed my uncertainty and followed my friend, avoiding the refuse beginning to slop at my boots. I breathed through my mouth to avoid the insidious whiff of waste teasing at my nostrils.

Finally, we wedged between two twisting heaps of scrap metal, and then all of my senses were simultaneously assaulted by noise and light and smells and the crush of thousands of people. Hundreds of booths and tables and blankets crowded together. Smoked meats and candies and breads piled between glorious bursts of exotic fruits and spices and wines. Cloth and jewels and food and trinkets and junk. People of every race and age and height and breadth moved between them, shouting and laughing and chatting.

So many people.

And behind the vast market, humped like the massive head and shoulder of a sleeping giant, was another city. Buildings and houses and streets and ladders, stacked and heaped and towering like the violet mountains at the city's back. My palms itched with a sudden tremor of delight.

"What is this place?" I heard myself shout. The crowd picked us up in its current and yanked us into the throng.

"This is the Thieves' Emporium," Luca shouted back at me, "and *that* is the Paper City."

THIRTY-FIVE

I stuck close by Luca. After I was nearly carried away by the shove of the crowd, he laced his callused fingers in mine and tucked me against his side. I could hardly believe it was third Nocturne—the Emporium was as lively and crowded as if it was Prime.

"You should see it at Prime," he shouted when I said as much. "It's deserted!"

Luca paused at this stall and that stand bartering and negotiating in garbled dialects I didn't understand. Coins flashed between fingers, and keen eyes flashed toward my face, my clothes. I yanked the cap farther over my hair, panic stitching hot threads down my arms.

Finally, when I couldn't bear the crowd any longer, Luca ducked between two booths, down an alleyway, and up a flight of rickety stairs. An alcove in the shadow of a dead vine brushed cool air across my face. I could still hear the shouting of a thousand voices, and smell the crush of unwashed bodies and perfumed hair, but people no longer pressed against my shoulders and stepped on my feet.

Luca's face swam into view. Worry dragged his brows together. "All right?"

"Fine," I whispered, sucking in another lungful of humid air. After two spans in the palais, I wasn't used to the sounds and stenches pouring over me like a waterfall. "Now can we go back?"

"Back? No." Luca's mouth lifted in a crooked grin. "Now, we go up."

The Paper City was a mountain made of the debris and detritus of an entire civilization. Tiny cottages of wood and stone were crushed beneath towering suites built from corrugated metal. Dristic and steel were neighbors to slipshod masonry daubed between vast tracts of cobbles. The city was alive beneath my feet, breathing like a slumbering beast of legend.

Luca took a circuitous route of ladders and ledges toward the roof of the city. We were never alone—faces peered from behind tattered curtains, and untethered voices drifted like phantoms. A flock of startled birds flew at our faces, and we had to beat away the barrage of feathers and beaks. The creak of improvised levers and pulleys warned us to whizzing buckets full of refuse and dirty water. Dampness slapped cold, clammy hands on the back of my neck. A child wailed, and somewhere I heard the frenzied barking of a trapped hound.

And finally, when the muscles in my legs burned and the dank air seared my lungs, we reached the top. Luca clasped his hand around my forearm and hauled me up onto the final rooftop. A sudden wind yanked the cap from my head and flung it away. I turned to reach for it, and froze.

An ocean of rooftops fell away from my feet, heaving up toward the foothills and churning down to the city gates. An entire city laid out before me like a tapestry, many-hued and knotted with the threads of a million human lives.

It was awful, and beautiful. I'd never seen anything like it.

Luca's muscled arm curled around my waist as the wind whipped his dark curls against my cheek. The press of his chest against my back was warm, but a shiver wrenched at my spine. I trained my eyes on the horizon, where a line of wine-stained clouds billowed in a honeyed sky.

"Careful," Luca whispered, his breath hot in the shell of my ear. "We should sit. The Amber Empress would never forgive me if I pushed her prized fantast off a roof."

❧

We sat on top of the city, our legs pressed against each other and our hands entwined.

Luca spread his trove of purchases around us. A small jug of tize, enough for two. Tiny fireworks that shrieked and spun circles before sputtering into nothing. Sweet buns bursting with fruit and honey and tasting nothing like the rich, fine foods of the palais.

"Do you like it?" Luca's eyes flitted, grazing the dirty bricks and the flushed horizon and the glowering clouds. "Living in Coeur d'Or, I mean."

The question caught me off-balance, and I swigged tize to delay answering. The tangy fermented liquid heated my blood and loosened my words.

"It's not what I expected," I admitted. I reached for my throat, where my old amulet hung for the first time in spans. I felt suddenly split in two—the innocent Dusklander with towering dreams and a hundred incandescent worlds living inside her, and the pampered courtier with muddled doubts and mounting secrets. How could I be both girls, and yet neither? "Everything is so beautiful—a paradise. I can still hardly believe I live there."

Luca's eyes glittered. "And the Amber Court? Have you found your place bowing and scraping at the empress's feet?"

"That's not—" Air hissed between my teeth. "It's complicated. I'm still navigating the intricacies of court life."

I thought Luca would say something—something like *I told you so*, or *What did you expect?*—but he just bared his teeth at the city ebbing away from our feet.

"And you?" I asked. "That day in the Mews, you told me your mother's convoy was leaving in two weeks. You were meant to go with it. Why are you still in the Amber City? What about Madame Rina? Vesh?"

Luca surged to his feet, stalking to the edge of the rooftop, where the wind snatched his hair from his face.

"Maman and Vesh are safe in the Mews," he said, "until the whispers of violence are silenced."

"Violence?"

Luca's eyes on my face were filled with curiosity, disappointment, and something else—something like pity. Even when I was poor as the dust rolling beneath the wheels of his mother's ore transport, I never saw that look in Luca's eyes. It sent the scant sips of tize roiling in my belly. Bitterness coated my throat.

"They sure keep you sheltered, up there in the Heart of Gold," he said. "How can you not hear the murmurs? Civil conflict in Aifir restricts shipments of the valuable weapons and machinery the empire trades for its natural resources. Famine and plague ravage colonies in the Sousine Isles, forcing up the price of luxury commodities like silk and kachua. More Zvar corsairs in the Meridian Desert, scuppering imperial sand skiffs and threatening trade along the Amber Road. Moneylenders are struggling to raise enough capital to fund the pursuits of honest merchants and traders like Maman. The empire is hemorrhaging capital even as the empress raises taxes and encourages her nobles to bury themselves in debt to finance continuously lavish lifestyles."

I leaned back. Sunder's words echoed through me. *We are on the brink, Mirage.*

He'd told me of the troubles in Aifir, and the threat posed to trade across the Meridian Desert. But Luca made it sound so much worse. I gnawed on my lower lip, thinking of the sheaf of promissory notes Sunder had tossed at my feet when he sponsored me. It was hard to imagine anyone in the palais being in debt to the empire, but now that I knew how Severine treated her legacies, I wasn't too surprised to hear she encouraged her nobles to rely on her financially as well as politically.

"You and those—those *courtiers*, and the empress—none of you bother to see how your actions affect the people," Luca spat. "The people like me, and my family, who eke out a living from the meager castoffs of the rich and never ask for more than we deserve. When contagion blackens trade ships, we are the sailors who sicken. When corsairs launch fire globes at sand skiffs with only a few weak legacies for protection, we are the men who must fight with swords against magic. When soldats require free mounts, we are the horse breeders who die."

"Legacies?" My heart gave a bewildered leap toward the word. "What legacies?"

"Of course you would only care about the legacies." Luca's harsh laugh scraped inside my chest. "I shouldn't have expected you to stay the same. How could you? You have everything, when you used to have nothing."

"I *was* nothing." I found my voice. "Penniless and indigent, with nothing to my name but bad memories. Now I have a place where I belong. Would you really begrudge me that?"

We stared at each other. My pulse throbbed with the rumble of thunder, and I imagined my heart as dark and purple as the horizon. I clenched my fists against a sudden buzzing thrum.

"There's more." Luca dragged a hand through his mop of curls. "Maman postponed our departure date indefinitely, saying it would give us time to gather supplies and contracts for a more prosperous trip. But I was restless. I wandered the city from Matin to Nocturne, from Unitas to the Concordat, Jardinier to the Paper City. I visited teahouses and wine bars and lotus dens. And in the shadows—wherever the light of the palais doesn't reach—there are whispers."

"Whispers?" My throat rasped dry. "Of what?"

"Of revolution."

"*Revolution?*" The incredulous word slipped out louder than I intended.

Luca's expression flamed. "For tides the Amber Empire has flourished enough that even the poorest of her citizens didn't want for much. When your children are fed and your house is warm you may gripe about the excesses of the aristocracy, but taking up arms to overthrow an imperial family with a vast and powerful army is nothing short of madness."

"It *is* madness. The Skyclad Garde is highly trained and armored. Any attack on the palais would fail. A war would never—"

"Not a war. *Assassination.*" The word had been forged by unrest and cooled with patience.

"Assassination?" I repeated. The word tasted like poison on my tongue. "The empress?"

"Who else?"

"But what will that do?" I was on my feet, my voice a fierce hiss. "She isn't even the reason most of these things are happening. Like you said—it's civil war in the Aifiri Archipelago, plague in the Sousine Isles."

"Why are you defending her?" Luca was on his feet too, a bonfire in his eyes. "In the seventeen tides since she came to power she has run the empire halfway to the ground. She dissolved her Council ages ago. Any nobles who defied her promptly disappeared or met with accidents, only to be replaced by a farce of a Senat filled with the nouveau riche. She personally instituted the harshest immigration and refugee laws in history. Taxes on ores have soared, while technological innovation has plummeted. She's a tyrant, Sylvie. She needs to be stopped."

"I'm not defending her," I protested, swallowing down the taste of bile. I closed my eyes against the sick rush of images Luca's words conjured. I hadn't had the most pleasant experiences with Severine, but these revelations brought her into clearer focus. But even if she was a despot, did she deserve to die? Did anyone deserve to die without a proper trial, without justice? "Assassination just seems—*extreme*. And like you said, there's no Council. She has no heir or consort. Murdering her will leave a hole at the heart of the empire. Who will fill it?"

"Not another power-hungry aristo, that's for damned sure," Luca snarled. "Maybe we can finally throw off the yoke of imperial rule and build a government ruled by the people, for the people."

Realization finally hit.

"We," I repeated, rolling the word over my tongue and tasting everything it implied. "This isn't theoretical. You're not just telling me what people in the city are saying. You're a part of this. You want to assassinate the empress."

I couldn't ignore the froth of eagerness in Luca's eyes.

"You're not a revolutionary, Luca!" My voice came out shrill and desperate. Every muscle in my body trembled. "I remember the day you told me that your father chose you to be a Tavendel Guardian. You were handpicked to honor the ways of your land. To remember the songs of your people. To honor your family by defending them. Where is the honor in assassination? In revolution?"

A shadow darkened Luca's face. "There is honor in standing up for a cause. In protecting people who cannot protect themselves. There is honor in making the world a better place."

"There is also little to no chance you will ever succeed," I hissed. "If you fail—if you're captured—you will be tried and sentenced as a traitor, Luca. You will be publicly executed."

"I'm not afraid to die."

"What about Vesh?" I whispered. I felt a shred of jagged satisfaction when Luca flinched. "Your brother is barely seven tides old. You may not be afraid to die, but how will your family survive seeing your head mounted on a spike by the city gates? Who will teach your little brother how to be a man after you throw your life away on a futile cause?"

"Stop," growled Luca. His hot hands cuffed my wrists, his pulse thrumming in counterpoint to mine. "You're making this about something it isn't. Revolution is a distant possibility. War could not be further from my mind."

"Then what is this?"

"Do you agree the Amber Empress needs to be stopped? She's tearing her empire apart from the inside out."

Luca's words opened a yawning chasm between my ribs. I closed my eyes, and sifted through the bloodstained images painting themselves against the back of my eyelids. Sand and flaming torches, black vines and torment. Wine-scorched clouds and sharp red nails gouging a bare throat. Lullaby's swollen eyes and stolen pain, a scar of oblivion on the landscape of her mind.

The empress always collects when a debt is owed.

"You want something from me." I didn't pretend it was a question.

"I snuck into your wing by disguising myself as a servant," Luca said. "But that won't work with a bigger group. And Garan said the empress is heavily guarded from Matin to Nocturne. We won't get halfway to her chambers before being slaughtered by Skyclad."

"Bigger group?" Horror strained my voice. "How many of you are there?"

"Enough to make sure the job gets done, and well." Luca's voice was grim. "But we can't do it without you."

"Me?" Surprise rocked me backward. "What can I possibly do?"

"You're a fantast—an illusionist. You could shield us. Make us invisible. Lead us there and back without anyone seeing us."

"So you can kill the most powerful woman in the daylight world?"

"And possibly save that world in the doing."

"Luca—" I snatched my hands out of his grasp, choking on a hundred objections. "Even if I wanted to help you, this plan is insane. My legacy creates worlds from dreams—I'm not sure I'm capable of cloaking one person, let alone a group. And even if I could, I'm far from Severine's inner circle. I can't go waltzing into her private chambers unguarded."

"Planning can overcome all sorts of limitations. Just say you'll do it."

"I won't." I plucked at my collar, sudden heat burning me up from the inside. "I can't."

"If you won't do it for me, Sylvie," said Luca, and his face was suddenly hard, "and you won't do it for the citizens of the empire, poor and starving and diseased as they are, then do it for yourself. I've heard about your precious legacies disappearing in the night, whisked away to fight *her* battles. Those who have the most to lose are always the most selfish."

"And manipulating a friend to do your dirty work?" I stared at him. Dread cast a shadow over my heart. "That's not selfish at all."

Luca's eyes dropped. I clenched a hand to a belly suddenly roiling with nausea.

"I want to go home," I whispered. "You promised to have me back before first Matin."

Luca gathered up the last of our scanty picnic without meeting my eyes. When he helped me from the rooftop his hand was chilly against my palm. I imagined ice creeping upward from my fingernails all the way to my heart, and when frosted lace crackled like cobwebs around my wrist, I hid my hand behind my back.

We descended through the Paper City. We slipped down on loose shingles, and caught ourselves on rusted railings torn from listing balconies. Ladders fashioned from creeping lianas. Mortared shells curled tight like ears full of secrets. It grew warmer, the miasma of the city settling around us like a humid, stinky cloak.

I stopped Luca at the pitted wooden door leading to the servants' wing.

"I wish you hadn't come," I whispered. "Our friendship was made for guttering campfires and dusty songs and half-remembered legends, not assassination and intrigue and manipulation. I wish you would have let me remember you the way you were."

"Sylvie—" Luca sucked in a deep breath. "You must know I didn't want it to be this way. I wanted—"

"Go back to Madame Rina and Vesh," I pleaded, daring to press my hand against his chest. I couldn't feel his heartbeat beneath the layers of cloth. "The convoy. Go back to the girl at the depot—what was her name? Anaïs? Let this talk of revolution and assassination die before it destroys you."

"I would, Sylvie." He inhaled. "If you came with me."

"What?"

"My offer still stands. Same as it was in the Mews. Run away with us. With *me*. I would be willing to forget all this—radical discourse, revolution, assassination—if I knew it meant having a chance to be happy with you."

I forced my gaze to meet his. And when the sun-bleached kembric of his eyes dulled with sudden uncertainty, I knew he was lying. He realized it the same instant I did. Panicked denial jarred his expression. His fingers found my wrist. His arm curled around my waist. My heart lurched. His fingers cupped the side of my face, and his lips pressed against mine.

A taste of salt, and grit, and bitter discontent. A clash of tongue and teeth and lips. The tang of desire, soured by the promise of violence.

He jerked away first. I stumbled back, and pressed an involuntary hand to my mouth. My gaze cut up to his, and when our eyes met something stretched and snapped in the air between us. Something delicate, and barely formed, like hope or a dream of distant stars.

"Garan says the court ladies hang handkerchiefs in their windows to signal their lovers," Luca said. "If you change your mind, hang a red one. I'll know what it means."

Tears prickled the back of my eyelids. We both looked away at the same time. Luca nodded once, then disappeared around the corner.

We both knew that was hardly a kiss.

That was goodbye.

THIRTY-SIX

I didn't sleep that Nocturne, nor the next.

My conversation with Luca raged like a storm within me, thundering through my bones and striking lightning in my veins. The need to do something—*anything*—was a pulse within me, but with every thrum of that pulse I was thrown in another direction. Side with Luca. *No.* Betray my erstwhile friend to Severine. *No.* Confide in Dowser. *No.* Run, run, run away and never look back.

And so I did nothing. I let my servants coil black Sousine pearls in my lacquered hair and varnish my lips until they gleamed like Devangelis rubies. I trod on polished marble shipped from quarries in the foothills of the Meteor Mountains. I perched on divans and drank Belsyre ice wine from crystal goblets crafted by artisans in Lirias. And every gesture—every glint of polished ambric or brush of fine silk—reminded me that just by being here, I was complicit in all the evils my empress committed.

Every miner dead in a mine blast—*my fault.*

Every sand skiff scuppered by Zvar militants—*my fault.*

Every child starving in the stinking shanties of the Paper City—*my fault.*

But when I passed through the gilded halls and peered from beneath my darkened lashes at the woman who ruled over us all, laughing behind her fan and tossing her auburn head, I didn't think I could do it. Did she deserve to be overthrown? Possibly. Did she deserve to die? Maybe. But could I be the one to do it?

Could I forge the sword that spelled her destruction, and hold it to her throat?

I came to this place because I believed in a towering, tremulous, intoxicating world of beauty and grace. The world where I knew I belonged. Much as I'd fought for it, I hadn't found that world here, where shadows spawned secrets and justice was a kind of farce. Hope smeared sunlit colors against my heart when I thought that maybe it wasn't the world at fault, but *her*. If I destroyed the empress, cut out the cancer at the heart of the empire, maybe this world could fulfill its uncertain promise.

But even contemplating the assassination of an empress meant that the world I'd sought from the start might simply not exist.

And I wasn't sure I was willing to admit that to myself.

❦

"Scion's breath, Mirage!" snapped Dowser, yanking his spectacles from his face and fixing me with his sternest glare. "I said show me a tree bending in a breeze, not shred a forest with a hurricane!"

I dragged my attention away from the illusory tempest spinning cyclones of black mist through copper-boughed trees. I imagined the tangled branches lashing at my arms and face, raising painful welts on the delicate skin.

"What did you say?" I shouted over the sound of the wind.

"I said, *stop!*" roared Dowser.

I released the illusion. Pennants of fog drifted away into the shadows. I rubbed my hands together to dispel the faint sensation of nerves buzzing along my palms.

"What's wrong with you today?" Dowser's eyes flickered with annoyance. "Your worlds are all spinning out of control. It's less than a span until Carrousel."

"I haven't been sleeping well," I said, which was miles away from admitting the truth. I shuddered to think what my teacher would say if he knew I had spent the past few Nocturnes staring at the ceiling and contemplating treason. "Bad dreams."

Dowser's expression softened. "I don't blame you for being nervous, after what happened at the Blood Rain Ball."

That wasn't my fault, I wanted to scream. But how could I explain that to my teacher?

"You must focus on the illusion you intend to perform at the fête," he continued. "Your empress, not to mention your dynasty, is counting on you to be your best. As am I."

One of Luca's accusations against the empress surfaced in the muddied ocean of my irresolute thoughts. *She dissolved her Council ages ago . . . any nobles who defied her promptly disappeared.* But Dowser had been a chevalier to the imperial family since before Severine's coronation. His signature on that Writ of Guardianship proved as much. Surely he would know the truth about such an accusation.

I couldn't forget that Dowser was the empress's creature. What would he do if he suspected I plotted against his mistress?

"Everyone speaks of Severine with such admiration and pride," I mused, making my way to the wall, where maps new and old clustered thick as wallpaper. I examined the crisp edges of continents dark against pale oceans. I traced my fingers along charter lines vivisecting the land. Names swam into view, names of cities and oceans and mountains.

"But what of the old emperor?" I continued, casually. "What was his name?"

I dared a glance at Dowser, and saw his eyes flatten with something like surprise. He hesitated, then sank into his worn leather chair. He polished his spotless glasses on the front of his black robe.

"Sylvain Sabourin was a decent man, and a good emperor. He died too young, and with many things left undone."

"Too young?" I frowned. "How old was he?"

"Barely forty tides," Dowser murmured, "and until his heart gave out on him we thought he'd live to see eighty. A stronger, healthier man you never would have thought to meet."

"How did the empress take it?" I asked. "She couldn't have been older than . . . ?"

"Severine was seventeen," Dowser replied. His eyes sharpened on my face. "She was your age. And she was as distraught as any young dauphine losing her father ought to be. What have you been hearing?"

"I haven't heard anything." My pulse quickened, and I cursed my lack of tact. "I just wondered—"

"You shouldn't listen to rumors, Mirage," Dowser interrupted, fixing me with a severe stare. "Every palais physician ruled Sylvain's death as nothing more than a weak heart and bad luck."

I tried to hide my surprise. "I didn't—"

"And before you even ask, the dauphin was always a sickly child. He never would have been considered an appropriate heir to the throne even if he had lived to see his majority. And even had any *natural* children existed, they never would have been deemed suitable to succeed Sylvain."

What dauphin? What natural children?

I turned back to the wall of atlases to hide the twin serpents of curiosity and dread coiling around my heart. My fingers trailed toward the north of the empire, to the range of hard-edged peaks jutting from the earth like giants' teeth. The Meteor Mountains. I traced the tips of those snowcapped mountains, sounding out their strange names. *Dom. Le Brigand. La Belladonne.* And there, nestled in the cupped valley between two massifs: *Belsyre.*

I snatched my hand away as if I'd been stung.

"You're right," I said to Dowser. "I shouldn't have listened to the rumors. It's none of my business."

Dowser's gaze searched my face. "If you must know, you're better off asking someone who knows what really happened."

My head snapped up, and I stared at my mentor. Was he trying to tell me something? Was he giving me an opening to ask whatever I wanted? I opened my mouth to ask the question I was dying to ask—*Did Severine disband her Council and murder her dissenting nobles?*—but the bell chimed for Compline and Dowser looked away.

The moment was over.

"Get some sleep," Dowser commanded. "And come back tomorrow with your head full of illusions and empty of rumors. We're running short on time."

Dowser's bald pate gleamed in the dimness, and I couldn't help but wonder how many secrets were stored in that head, stacked like books and dusty with disuse.

"Your tremors," I remarked, tentative. "They've stopped. Should I be pleased, or worried?"

"Inquisitive *and* intrusive today." He rubbed an ink-stained thumb over his brow. "I still wonder why you feel obliged to care."

I thought of my teacher, sitting day after day—tide after tide—in this dim, musty study, tattered books and bad dreams his only company. A colorless life punctuated by demands on his legacy and his loyalty.

"Do you have a wife or husband? Children?" My words conjured something doleful in his gaze. "Well, then. Everyone ought to have someone who feels obliged to care. I guess you're stuck with me."

Dowser's eyes glittered behind his spectacles, and a tenuous understanding seemed to bridge the space between us.

"I'm trying," he finally muttered. "If you must know, I'm still trying."

<hr />

I paced back toward Lys, curiosity and frustration tangling within. Dowser hadn't answered any of the questions I'd intended to ask; he'd only raised more questions. How had I never heard the rumors about Severine? A father, dead much too young. A sickly brother, dead before his majority. Illegitimate half siblings. A Council, dissolved. Nobles, disappearing.

Maybe Dowser was right. Maybe it was cruel speculation and idle gossip.

Or maybe it was something more.

I thought of Luca's face, resolute in the light of our weary sun. His eyes bright with the promise of violence. His tongue heavy with conviction and death.

And for the first time, I stopped to consider if he might be right. Maybe violence did demand violence. Maybe death begat death. If the empress truly murdered and connived her way onto the throne of an empire, then what kind of world would I be condoning by letting her get away with it?

I gnawed on a lip already raw with my uncertainty. After everything he'd said to me, I wasn't sure I trusted Luca's judgment. I had to know the truth before I condemned anyone—empress or pauper, noble or thief—to the Scion's mercy.

Much as I hated to admit it, there was only one person I could ask. I didn't trust Sunder. But something about the unflinching way he looked at me made me think that maybe—if I could just ask the right questions—he might tell me the truth.

THIRTY-SEVEN

I stood in the shadow of a clematis-draped arch and watched Sunder fight.

I'd only recently discovered that many courtiers made a game of dueling with their legacies as a precaution against being called to the Gauntlet. Angled sunbeams sliced the sandy arena into wedges. It was hot, and most of the men had thrown off their overcoats and vests in a pile of brocade. They loitered in the long green shadows of boxy hedges, sipping from flagons of ale and exchanging bets as they watched their friends spar. A coterie of ladies lingered nearby, clad in pale linen and hiding their gossip behind colorful fans.

Sunder stood in the center of the arena, hair blazing gold in a bar of ruddy sunlight. His white undershirt was rolled to the elbow. Muscle corded along his forearm when he lifted his hand. He saluted his opponent—a glowering Sinister lord named Haze—then bowed. Anticipation hummed in the air as they slid into crouches. The game turned dangerous.

Sunder lunged, his long fingers snaking toward his opponent's heart. Haze blocked the blow with his elbow and aimed a pennant of dense fog at Sunder's face. He danced away, his steps quick and sure in the sand. He circled Haze, wary, then lashed back in. His fingers found his opponent's wrist. Haze roared with sudden agony and kicked Sunder in the stomach. Opaque smog rolled outward, disorienting Sunder as he searched for his foe.

It was a dance of death, meticulous and savage and ancient as the sun. Each step was choreographed, each maneuver deliberate. Point, counterpoint. Attack, parry, riposte. I was transfixed, hypnotized by the measured sway and dart, leap and flicker. They orbited each other in elegant circles, flashing in and out of bars of light and shadow. There was no sound, only their silent legacies singing promises of blood to the thirsty earth.

A misstep; an ankle rolling. My heart beat a fervent pulse as Haze stumbled. Sunder was a viper, striking fast and sure. He tackled Haze to the ground, who hissed with pain. Scarlet bloomed like a flower on a white shirtsleeve.

Sunder won first blood.

The pair separated, breathing hard. Polite applause scattered across the arena; coins exchanged hands. Sunder saluted. Haze did the same, although the look on his face verged on murderous. Sunder sneered and turned away, flagging an attendant as he dragged a hand through hair dark with sweat.

I swallowed hard, and stepped from the shadow of the archway.

I saw Sunder's face in the split second before the rest of the courtiers spotted me. And it occurred to me that if I had wanted to keep this meeting private I should have waited deeper among the hedgerows.

Sunder stalked toward me with a vicious smile. Behind him, I saw the courtiers turn to each other with raised eyebrows. One girl flicked her wrist at her friend in a gesture I recognized as *true love*. A sarcastic smile coiled in the corner of her mouth.

Sunder cut me an ironic bow, then pushed me back against the curve of the archway in full view of the courtiers. My breath caught as he captured my wrist with a hand and pinned it against the bricks. He covered my body with his own, sliding his knee between my legs and bunching my skirts against the backs of my thighs.

"What are you doing?" I gasped out. Every inch of me was molded to him. I could smell the hot musk of sweat and sand clinging to his skin, see the moisture beading the fine hairs at the base of his neck. I could barely think.

"Assuaging the rumors while saving both of our reputations," he breathed against my throat. I shuddered; I couldn't help it. "How dare you approach me here, in front of everyone? I'm not your friend, my most graceless demoiselle."

"I need to talk to you," I snapped. His insult cleared my head, and I shoved at his chest. He drew back, slowly, trailing his fingers along my wrist and his eyes over the curves of my body. He gave me a leisurely smile, but it didn't reach his eyes, and I knew it wasn't aimed at me.

"And I told you I don't talk," he replied, too soft for his friends to hear. "Did you come here to spite me? I can assure you—only your own position at court will suffer."

"This isn't about revenge." Spite was just an added bonus. "And I'm not concerned with either of our reputations. So if you don't answer my questions *now* I'll do something that will actually give you something to be embarrassed about."

Sunder's eyes blazed. Pain needled up my spine.

"Don't you dare," I commanded.

He clenched his fists, and the sensation was gone, nothing more than a memory.

"My apologies," said Sunder. "You make a compelling argument. But I'm going to need you to simper."

"What?"

"Do it."

I hesitated, then did as he said, dropping into a curtsy and tilting my head in a gesture of deference. I forced my wrist to swirl in the attitude for *quiet admiration*. I gritted my teeth at the sound of muffled tittering from the watching courtiers.

"That will do." He offered a hand to guide me toward the path. Out of the corner of my eye, I saw him turn on his heel and cut an extravagant bow to his friends. They all burst out in laughter. I fought a hot flush threatening to climb my cheeks.

"What was that?" I snarled as soon as we were out of sight.

"Window dressing," he snapped. "You may be content with the dubious state of your own reputation, but mine has been eighteen tides in the crafting. I will not allow an unrefined provincial upstart to ruin it with her meddling."

"I assume that's supposed to describe me?"

Sunder said nothing, just led me between the high walls of a hedged labyrinth. My captured pulse sang against his cool fingers. Finally, he dragged me up a shallow flight of stairs and through a set of glass doors, flinging me away from him and slamming the metal frame shut behind us.

I stared around, rubbing my wrist. Potted trees marched in regimented rows, globes of orange and yellow and green peeking between neatly trimmed branches. The air was cooler than outside, but humid; the strands of hair loose around my face were already starting to curl. Low honeyed light slanted in from the curved glass ceiling, casting dappled patterns across the tile. A marble fountain plashed pleasantly at the center of it all, echoing off the paned walls.

"What is this place?" I murmured, half to myself.

"The Orangerie," replied Sunder, before dunking his whole head into the basin of the fountain. He flicked his head back, and water cascaded down his neck and shoulders, soaking his white shirt and gluing it to the planes of his chest. I coughed and turned away, staring into the quiet army of citrus trees to avoid looking at the only thing I wanted to look at.

"Why did you bring me here?"

"There's no dress code," he drawled, raising an eloquent eyebrow at my blue gown, "and I can keep an eye on the door."

"What's wrong with my dress?" I snapped, indignant, before throwing my hands up and shaking my head. "Never mind. I won't let you bait me. That's not why I'm here."

"No?" He leaned against the fountain, propping one leg against its curving basin. "I'm dying to hear why you thought it appropriate to accost me publicly, in front of my friends, in the middle of my leisure."

"Fine friends," I muttered, before dropping my voice to a whisper. "It's about the empress. I heard something, and it's important to me that I find out whether it's true or not."

"Ask someone else."

"I did. I asked Dowser, but I couldn't tell whether he was trying to hide something from me, or tell me something else entirely."

"Clearly you didn't ask the right questions," said Sunder, looking bored. "Why in the Scion's name do you think I'll be any different?"

"Because—" I hesitated, suddenly uncertain. When I'd decided to ask Sunder—before I scoured half the palais looking for him—I'd thought my reasoning was sound. But now, standing in front of him, I wasn't sure I dared voice it. "Listen, I don't know exactly who or what you are. Some people say you're the empress's dog, and you bark or bite at her command. Some people say you're a dissolute libertine with decadent and depraved tastes."

The barest hint of a smile coiled in the corner of his mouth.

"And I know you don't care about me," I plunged on. "I could fall down a flight of stairs to my death and you'd call for another glass of wine. But I know what you do care about. Maybe the only thing you care about: Bane."

Sunder looked away, the smile dropping from his lips. With his wet hair slicked away from his face, he was a collection of hard lines and harder angles. He looked like someone who rarely slept, and never deeply.

"You're not the only one who understands pain, Sunder," I whispered, and ventured a step closer. "Bane's pain is your pain. And who makes Bane hurt? The empress. Severine takes the thing your sister loathes most about herself and uses it as a weapon. And Bane isn't like you, is she? She isn't as strong as you."

"Enough." Sunder's voice was rough, and when he lifted his eyes to mine they were empty of that familiar sardonic spite. They were empty of anything—an abyss I didn't dare stare into. "What do you want to know?"

"Severine's rise to power," I said quickly. I wasn't going to question my luck, or Sunder's cooperation. "I need to know what she did, and how it all happened."

"Sedition, seduction, and slaughter." Sunder's eyes flickered left and right, but there was no one here but us—nothing but a vast circle of orderly trees and a glass dome to eavesdrop. "But how else do you think the rulers of the daylight world get their power? They steal it."

"Did she—?"

"Murder the old emperor?" Sunder pressed his thumb and forefinger into the corners of his eyes. "By all accounts the young dauphine was whip-smart, persuasive, and ravenous for power. Sylvain was wise, merciful, and moderate in his government. Sacrifices had to be made. As a matter of fact, rumor has it my own father, Guislain de Vere, possessed a legacy strikingly similar to my own. I'd ask him if the empress ordered him to assassinate Sylvain, but of course, he's dead."

"She didn't—?"

"She did." Sunder's smile was a rictus of death. "Nearly half of her court—and most of her Council—suspected what she had done. There were . . . alternate opinions regarding succession, and plans in motion with those ideas in mind. But mere weeks before her coronation all of her dissident nobles dropped dead or disappeared in the dead of Nocturne."

"Your parents." Sunder's gaze flickered, a chink opening into the bleak expanse lurking behind his eyes. A dristic fist clenched my heart. "Sunder, I'm so sorry. I didn't know."

"I was barely old enough to remember them. It doesn't really matter."

The sudden silence was broken only by the plink of water in the fountain.

"What about—" I paused, fighting the sudden lump in my throat that threatened to crack my voice. "What about her sibling? Did she murder him too?"

"*Sibling?*" Sunder's laugh was a serrated knife. "Try siblings."

"There was more than one dauphin?"

"The dauphin was sick and weak, and if she hadn't killed him someone else would have," Sunder said without passion. "There were more pressing concerns. Sylvain had appetites. He married, once, but Seneca and Severine's mother died in childbirth, and let's say the emperor liked to keep his options open. Very, very open. By the time Severine came to power, there were seventeen tides' worth of options to worry about."

"Illegitimate children?" I gasped. Dowser's words trickled through my memory: *Even had any natural children existed . . .* "But if they were illegitimate—"

"In the Sousine Isles," interrupted Sunder, "the Gorma tell tales of a fearsome creature in the depths of the ocean. With its sharp teeth and cold eyes, it devours anything it comes across. But after it mates, a chilling ritual begins. A dozen littermates fight for space, and even in the womb, the unborn monsters have teeth. The biggest and strongest gobble up their brethren, growing larger and larger until finally, there is only one left to be birthed. Only the strongest, and the cruelest, and the hungriest offspring survives the womb."

A shudder wracked my spine. "How many?"

"No one knows," Sunder said with a shrug. "But rumors suggest that Severine makes that cannibal shark look like a magnanimous vegetarian."

A numb wave sent needles to prickle at my arms and legs. A low hum teased at my ears, and my palms tingled. I rubbed my hands together, shaking my head to dispel the buzz.

Luca was right. Worse—Luca's accusations were too kind. Severine wasn't just a tyrant, she was a butcher. Not only did she murder her father, her brother, and countless nobles, but she hunted down scads of children whose only crime was being sired by a lusty emperor.

I was beginning to think assassination was too kind.

"And you're sure about this?"

"Nothing is ever sure, especially not in Coeur d'Or," said Sunder. "But dig deep enough, demoiselle, and even beneath marble you are certain to find dirt."

I lifted my eyes to the glass ceiling. Spears of light lanced between the staid rows, and I felt suddenly as though I was one of these captive citrus trees, cultivated and pruned, my world reduced to the space between four glass walls and one arched ceiling. Luca was right to scoff at this place and everything it stood for. But revolution? Assassination? Could death and destruction ever lead to peace? To a world where dreams had wisdom and hopes had depth?

"Thank you." My words sounded distant and feeble to my own ears. "And for what it's worth, I'm sorry about your parents. I'm—I'm just sorry."

My footsteps were soft on the tiles as I turned toward the door.

"Mirage," said Sunder, and it was the first time he used the word as my name and not as a weapon. Surprise spun me toward the sound of his voice.

He closed the distance between us in a few spare strides. He looked down at me, and the press of his canny eyes on my face sent a thread of heat unspooling through my veins.

"I confess that I find you nearly as surprising as I find you annoying," he murmured. "But not all surprises are good, my most unexpected lady. So whatever decision I just saw cross your face, I suggest you reconsider."

"Decision . . . ?"

"On one so unerringly brash as yourself, coyness is an unflattering mask." He stepped closer, and a bar of low sunlight bleached his skin to marble and brightened his eyes to turquoise.

"However highly you may consider yourself, I can assure you: Whatever you're planning, you are outnumbered, outpaced, and outwitted. You are neither as brave nor as clever as you imagine yourself to be."

I couldn't stop the breath of air that hissed between my teeth. Was I so obvious? Or was Sunder bluffing?

"I'm not afraid," I whispered. "Not of the empress, and certainly not of you."

He bared his teeth in a laugh. "You should be."

"Isn't fear what allows people like her to seize power?"

"Fear is what keeps people like me alive," Sunder said, "when all around the world is dying."

"You're a coward," I hissed.

Sunder's hand jerked toward my face, and I flinched away from the anticipated jolt of pain. But he just brushed a strand of hair off my cheek. His cool fingers skimmed the curve of my ear.

"And you're a fool," he whispered. "And there's nothing I fear so much as a fool."

He brushed past me, tossing his brocade jacket over one shoulder and striding between the glass doors.

Thirty-Eight

I stood for a few long moments, inhaling the sultry scents of mulch and bright citrus and sorting through the coil of emotions looping inside me. Maybe Sunder was right—maybe I should be afraid. But when I closed my eyes all I could see were the snapping jaws of an underwater monster, hungry for flesh and hungrier for power.

I pushed out into the jardins. A line of heavy clouds had rolled in over the palais, casting dull shadows over the crisp lines of rosebush and hedge. I didn't know exactly where I was—between the Gauntlet arena and the Orangerie, I'd gotten lost in Coeur d'Or for the first time in spans. Crystalline spires and ambric domes glinted over my left shoulder, so I headed that way, cutting through a wild copse edged in lavender and sedge. My broad skirts were loud in the underbrush, and I almost didn't hear the staccato rustle of someone else's footsteps retreating through the scrub.

I jerked my gaze toward the sound.

A maze of slender trees sliced my vision into shreds of brown and white and grey. I squinted. I glimpsed limp feathers clinging desperately to sharp twigs. I didn't understand what I was seeing. A bird, caught in a trap? Pity clogged my throat, and I lifted my skirts to move closer, scattering dried leaves and moss behind me. But no—beneath the silvery brush of pale feathers I saw dove-grey velvet and fawn-colored chamois. My bemused gaze lingered on a glister of jeweled rings before drifting to the curled sweep of bronze hair beneath a rakish hat. Hair I recognized. A hat I recognized.

The cold anticipation of trauma gripped my spine with barbed fingers and turned me on my heel. I took two shaking steps, as though I might undo a thing before it happened, just by walking away. But the thing was already done. I felt it in the drumming pulse at my temple, the sick roil of acid in my stomach, the keening horror unfurling thunderous wings inside me. I turned slowly back.

It was Thibo, beautiful and lavishly dressed and *empty*. He lay askew in the shadow between two trees. His hazel eyes stared toward the sky. I dropped to my knees beside him with a crunch of dead leaves. Terror bubbled hot below a slick sheen of denial.

"Thibo." I curled my hand around his shoulder. "Thibo, what are you doing out here?"

His only reply was silence.

"Is this supposed to be a joke?" I shook him, hard. His head lolled.

"Thibo, stop it." Panic made my voice shrill. I shook him again, my fingernails breaking as they crushed the rich nap of his waistcoat. "Thibo, this isn't funny!"

He blinked, slowly. Too slowly. My hands crept to his neck. His pulse—fast but even—throbbed in time to the desperate litany clogging my mind.

No, no no. No, no no.

But I couldn't wish this away. This—in the churning confusion of disbelief and nausea I could hardly fathom what *this* was. Thibo injured? Thibo dying? My hands fluttered uselessly, and I shook him once more, just to give them purpose. A burnished circle on a kembric chain slipped from beneath his cravat.

Thibo's locket.

I snatched at it with more force than I meant to, and the locket came away in my hand, the delicate chain slithering around my fingers. Disjointed words bubbled upward. *My youngest sister.* Mender. *I would marry him, if he'll have me.* Reaper.

And finally, like a boot to the gut: *gone.*

I jolted to my feet and took off at a run. I hiked my skirts around my knees and sprinted, faster than I'd ever run in my life. Branches slapped at my shoulders and raised welts on my face, but I didn't care. A strange, serene world of smooth velvet and chilled wine threatened to drown me in the dead, muffled silence of despair. I pushed the glassy calm away, forcing my leaden legs faster. The wilderness gave way to a sward of smooth green, and I glimpsed sky-bright chips of armor pacing calm along the palais wall.

"Help!" The word was jagged in my throat, a strip of raw metal tearing me from within. "Help!"

The Skyclad Gardes spared barely a glance at my rich jacquard gown and coiffed hair before jumping to my aid. They asked brief, pointed questions. I answered as best I could through the bewildering fog of grief and shock as I backtracked toward the copse, retracing steps that felt painfully slow. My thighs burned as my corset dug pitiless fingers into my waist. I fell to my knees in the grass, tearing with my fingernails at the prison of satin capturing my ribs, the rigid stays stealing away my breath.

The pair of Skyclad Gardes paused, confusion marring their trained impassivity as I shredded the bodice of my gown.

"Go!" I screamed at them. I realized I was weeping; hot tears left scalding tracks against my cheeks. I pointed a trembling finger at the pale trees rimming the copse. "Save him!"

They sprinted away. Others had heard the commotion and came running—servants in palais livery and courtiers in organdy and moiré. More Skyclad Gardes. They flickered through the trees like fireflies in the dusk, their calling voices a quivering lament.

Reaper! Reaper! Reaper!

And I—I churned with sorrow in the blanched glare of the staring sun. This was my fault. Instead of comforting my friend in the wake of his lover's disappearance, I had cavorted through the Paper City with a rebel. I had wrenched sick secrets from a lord who only spoke in riddles. I had thought only of my own desperate longing for an impossible world, dreaming of belonging when the people who mattered to me were scraping and scrambling to simply stay alive.

I should have kept him close. I should have watched his back. I should have protected him.

I wasn't sure whether it was minutes or hours before the Skyclad Gardes returned to me. Their eyes were full of pity and disbelief and a distant kind of scorn. I knew what they would say before they had a chance to say it.

They weren't able to find the body I'd *supposedly* stumbled upon. There was no one in the copse, or the jardins beyond. Their final verdict splintered my bones.

Thibo was *gone*.

I trudged to Lys Wing, where Lullaby greeted me with mussed hair and tearstained cheeks. And even before she flung her arms around my neck, my heart was shattered into pieces of broken mirror glass.

"He's gone," she wailed, her words garbled and hoarse. "She finally took him. Thibo's gone."

We held each other as we wept, but the tears streaming down my own cheeks seemed cheap in comparison to the grief of my friend. And when we finally broke apart, exhausted by grief, I could barely look her in the eye.

"I don't—" I choked on a fresh flood of tears. "I don't understand what *gone* means. Is this what happened to Blossom? Mender?"

"More or less. No one ever saw them . . . before. Or after. They just disappeared."

"Are they dead?"

"Dead? Probably," agreed Lullaby, and the set of her mouth was grim. "Or worse."

The skin on my face felt too tight. "What's worse than dead?"

"You're the fantast. Use your imagination."

We lapsed into silence.

"I think *she* takes them," Lullaby finally whispered. "Do you know what Thibo's legacy was?"

"I only knew his court name, and how much he hated it. I never wanted to ask."

"He stole memories." Her voice was terrible. "He could reach in and pluck them away. Gone. He loathed it. He used to say he was worse than a thief because no one even knew what he had stolen. But he was one of Severine's most useful tools. She'd been using him more and more, as a spy, as an assassin, for whatever she wanted. And he kept trying to refuse, but she knew how to get to him. She sent two of his sisters to the Dominion border, never to be heard of again. When Mender . . ." Lullaby paused, shaking her head. "Thibo was done, you know? Tired of fighting, tired of losing. Part of me wonders if he was ready to go. Ready for her to take him for good."

I shuddered with anguish, rolling my thumb over the dented surface of Thibo's locket. *I would marry him, if he'll have me.* He'd been so close to his perfect life, only to have that precious, mundane, ordinary world stolen from him.

It was almost too much to bear.

"I'm never going to see it again, am I?" Lullaby suddenly said. I jerked my eyes to her, and realized that she was staring at the curling drapes kissing the deep blue walls of her painted room. "The ocean. I dream of it every Nocturne, you know. The crash of the tide kissing the beach. The red sunlight piercing the waves. My father's voice, like coils of seaweed and echoing caverns and the infinite line of the horizon. But I'm never going to hear it again, Mirage."

"You'll see the ocean again," I said. The promise etched itself onto my ribs with pulses of light. "You'll hear your father's voice. I swear it."

And so too did I silently swear that this time, Severine had stolen too much. And if there was no one else, then I would be the one to collect the debt.

Oh, I would collect.

And when I finally returned to my chambers, my hands barely shook as I knotted a red silk handkerchief to flutter between my curtains.

I'll do it.

THIRTY-NINE

The next few days passed in a haze.

I didn't write to Luca for fear of my correspondence being opened or intercepted—I had no idea whether Severine was spying on me, but it would be stupid to assume she wasn't. But I took to wandering along the Esplanade in the last hours of Nocturne, and if more than one shadow lurked between the towering pillars there was no one nearby to notice.

We conspired in hurried whispers, sketching a plan that between the two of us might actually work. Luca crushed my hands in his and smiled like I'd been sent by the Scion himself. And with his lilting voice and eager eyes, words like *infiltrate* and *assassination* sounded less like sedition and more like a promise of change.

"And no one else will die?" An image of Lullaby's lovely face stained with blood instead of tears brushed the edge of my mind. "Promise me the courtiers will be safe."

"Only the empress," Luca swore. "There will just be a few of us. We'll be like ghosts."

But once he slipped back through the darkened halls in his stolen livery, doubt crept close. Regardless of the right or wrong of it, we were plotting treason. And if either of us was caught, we would both die.

I distracted myself by practicing my legacy with Dowser. It wasn't difficult to convince my mentor to help me learn camouflage instead of projection; when I suggested the idea of invisibility and cloaking, he stared at me in surprise.

"I don't know why I didn't think of it first," he muttered, polishing his spectacles.

Neither of us mentioned my questions from the day before, or the threads of obscure understanding stitching us closer together.

But mastering another aspect of my gift was more challenging than I expected. It was like learning to write with the wrong hand, or speaking an unfamiliar language.

I practiced long into the Nocturne hours, begging off parties and concerts in favor of standing in front of my mirror and trying to turn myself invisible. I surrendered to a world where I was made of glass, only to have my skin sparkle like crystal. I fell into an illusion where I was formed from breaths of air, only to have my skin smear on the breeze like pink paint in water.

I gritted my teeth and tried again. And again.

I awoke in the dead of Nocturne from a dream of rippling birdsong and ice wine and cool hands encircling my waist. Belsyre Wing. Epiphany slunk around the borders of my consciousness. I'd hated the literal practicality of that illusion, the passionless labor of reflecting a world that already existed. It was everything I'd loathed about Dowser's methods: reflecting the world I lived in, instead of creating my own. But I'd done it, and well.

I jumped out of bed and stood in front of the mirror. I closed my eyes, and imagined a bedroom identical to my bedroom, but without me in it. The gloom behind my shuttered curtains. The rumpled sheets. The constant press of hand-painted flowers. I surrendered to my absence, shearing away from the cavernous grasp of existential dread.

I opened my eyes. I wasn't there.

A cool smile of relief pressed against my skin. I squinted, and thought I glimpsed the outline of an arm, the impression of a grin. But it was faint, like a scrap of parchment scraped clean, only to be written on once again.

I released the illusion.

It wasn't perfect.

But maybe with a little practice, it would be good enough.

❧

I spent every moment of the scant few days before Luca's plan was to go into effect practicing my illusion of invisibility.

I practiced in my room until the bells for Matin chimed, then kept on practicing until I was famished and my eyes swam with half-imagined illusions. I practiced in the halls of Coeur d'Or, standing stock-still and imagining another identical world over-laid on my own—a world that simply didn't show me. I practiced until my face didn't swim distorted in polished crystal vases and gilded statues.

Once, a Dexter maiden brushed too close, inside the bounds of the illusion. Her eyes flew open so wide I thought they'd pop out of her skull. I dropped the illusion at once, but she stared at me like I was an apparition of Meridian himself.

"Mirage!" she shrieked. "You came out of nowhere! I could have sworn—"

But I simpered, and made up a lie, and she laughed at herself, her unease turning into embarrassment. It was almost too easy.

Moving was the hardest part. Once I'd mastered making myself invisible at a standstill, I tried moving. Tiny steps, in one direction at first, slitting my eyes and imagining the illusion moving with me. Then faster, walking from one end of my room to the other, the world sliding around me as if I wasn't there.

So gradually that I hardly noticed it happening, the process of being unseen became like second nature. And when I realized that I'd intentionally rendered myself nearly as *gone* as Thibo, I had to laugh. Laughter that quickly turned to tears that turned to resolve when I remembered how ruthlessly my friend had been stolen from me.

The Matin before I was meant to let Luca into the palais with his cadre of assassins, I set myself one final test. Elodie and Matilde dressed and primped me, but the moment they left my room I undressed to my shift and corset. I shoved the gown in a wardrobe where no one would find it, then opened the door out into Lys Wing.

The sun burned a harsh red, unmarred by clouds. Razored shadows lined the passageways, untouched by the dull glow of ambric lamps. I breathed deep, and let the veil of my second world fall around me. I cleared my mind, ignoring the froth of my nerves, and stepped out into Coeur d'Or.

I drifted like a phantom through the halls. No one turned their heads or wondered why the newest courtier was prancing through the palais in her undergarments. And slowly, as instinct replaced control, I began to enjoy myself.

I eavesdropped on a group of servants gossiping about their vexatious mistress. I paused in the shadows and saw pretty Vida steal a kiss from Wing, who blushed to the tips of her bejeweled ears before returning the embrace with gusto. All around me, life in the palais kept marching forward. I was nothing more than a fleeting fancy, an unexpected breeze raising the hairs along napes. A whispered footfall and a distant laugh, a flash at the corner of an eye.

And even though I knew it was petty, I couldn't help but exact one small revenge.

I found Sunder leaving the Gauntlet, flushed and sweaty, a silver-embossed jacket slung across his shoulders. He seemed pensive, his brows slashed together over eyes focused on some distant thing. His stride was rapid, but I jogged up behind him, hugged my illusion tight around me, and jerked the jacket from his shoulders.

The expensive brocade fell to the packed dirt of the jardin with an audible thump, raising a cloud of dust.

Sunder turned on his heel, frowning at the limp pile of fabric. He bent, reaching for the collar.

I twitched the hem, and the jacket pulled away from his fingers.

Sunder's hand closed into a fist, and he raised himself to his full height. His nostrils flared, as though he were scenting the air, and he tilted his head. His glittering eyes narrowed to slits as he stared right at me. I stood perfectly still, every muscle tensed as I focused on making the illusion perfect—my very existence a hallucination.

Gravel crunched as he stalked from the jardin, leaving me standing trembling beside an abandoned pile of expensive embroidered jacquard.

Later, after I dashed back to my room and laced my gown with fumbling fingers, a churn of laughter bubbled up and spilled from my lips. I laughed until tears prickled at my eyes and my corset dug a painful groove into my waist. And when I stepped back out in the palais, fully clothed and entirely visible, I could almost convince myself that seeking out Sunder was a stupid prank, a childish bit of revenge.

Because when he turned on his heel and stared straight into my eyes, I almost felt like I was trying to say goodbye.

FORTY

The hours before first Compline passed so slowly I wondered if time was working against me.

Luca and I had agreed in one of our secret conferences that the only thing stranger than me marching up to Severine's personal quarters and requesting a private audience was me doing it in the dead of Nocturne. So I inquired, idly and discreetly, about the empress's daily rituals, and a courtier was more than happy to gossip about Severine's schedule.

She spent the hours of Matin ensconced with the cabal of cronies she called advisors. Prime, she whiled away in the Atrium with favored courtiers dancing attendance on her every whim. Most of Nocturne she spent sampling the pleasures of whichever salons, dinners, and concerts piqued her capricious interest. But first and second Compline she usually spent alone in her private chambers.

I scouted the Imperial Wing once I'd mastered my trick of passing unseen and unnoticed through the real world. Severine kept her chambers at the very center of the labyrinth of Coeur d'Or, past Belsyre Wing. The entrance was marked by a huge door, emblazoned with the Imperial Insignia: a massive sunburst gilded with kembric. Two Skyclad Gardes flanked the door, armed and alert. I waited until Severine exited her chambers for the delights of Nocturne, and caught a glimpse of a long passageway, curved like the inside of a shell and lit by ambric torches. Four more Gardes, two on each side of the hall. And one final door, slender and filigreed, edged in hard dristic.

Six Gardes, two armored doors. Getting in might not be difficult, not with my new ruse. But getting out was going to be a challenge.

Finally, sixth Prime tolled, and anticipation frothed within me, fueling the flames of my anticipation. I grabbed a cape with a deep hood and slung it over my shoulders, then turned to cast my eyes around my borrowed room. If everything went according to plan, I'd never return to this place. I lingered on the painted flowers slowly fading around the windowsills, and I couldn't help but think of poor Blossom's memory fading away with them. Bile burned in my throat when I thought of Thibo, passing in the same direction.

Would Lullaby miss me, when I was gone? Did I deserve to be missed?

I ran my fingers slowly over the surface of my vanity, touching the pots of cosmetics and jars of perfumes as if they were talismans. My collection of jewelry winked up at me, diamonds and rubies and amber purchased with Sunder's spare change. I considered shoving a few of the expensive necklaces in my pocket as insurance, but I clenched my hand into a fist instead. The less of this place I brought with me, the better.

I did one last sweep, then fished my amulet from its place beneath my mattress. The worn amber winked up at me, and I clasped the cool chain around my throat, tucking the pendant into the bodice of my dress. Then I stepped out into the last day I'd ever spend in the palais.

My steps carried me through Coeur d'Or, quiet in the lull before Compline. I paused at the Esplanade, gazing across the manicured jardins and vaulting topiaries. *Thibo.* Sudden sorrow knocked the breath from between my ribs. I'd met him here, that first day in the palais. He'd smiled at my mistakes and made me feel at ease in an unfamiliar place. He'd been *kind* to me, kinder than I probably deserved.

Coeur d'Or's insistent beauty crushed down on me, suddenly oppressive. I'd wanted so badly to belong here, for the promise of this place to be more than a wish or a dream. But I could no longer ignore the taint of death and violence lurking in this glittering heart. Wanting something badly enough doesn't make it real. And it certainly doesn't make it right.

I turned myself invisible as bitterness coated the back of my throat. Maybe it was easier to pretend I was already gone than spend another moment pretending I belonged.

I wound slowly toward one of the small gates set into the high wall surrounding the palais compound. It was rarely used, but I'd seen a few couriers ducking through it into the wealthy neighborhood just outside, and the palais side was wooded and shadowed. Unless Luca's group of revolutionaries were spectacularly imprudent, no one should notice anything amiss between when they arrived and when I made them disappear.

I crouched in the shadow of a crooked laurel to wait. The heat of the past few days had ebbed, and a bank of thick grey clouds shrouded the Amber City, turning the light of the sun eerie. A cool breeze kicked at my loose curls, and I dragged my cloak tighter.

Finally, I heard it: what sounded like a strange birdcall followed by a series of taps on the gate. I unlocked it quickly, using the code I'd memorized while surveilling an oblivious courier. I grasped a bare impression of height and breadth before a figure shoved by me, and then another, and another. Dread curled icy fingers around my heart as more and more hooded figures tromped through the gate. Finally, I spied a familiar crop of curling black hair over golden eyes, and I reached forward to grab Luca's hand.

"What's going on?" I hissed. I stared over my shoulder at the militia forming in the shadow of the palais walls: nearly twenty men and women, muscled and grim. Weapons glinted from belts and shoulders. Inked tattoos crept above collars and along corded forearms. "Who are all these people?"

"We call ourselves La Discorde," replied Luca. His fingers crushed my hand. "And we're going to change the face of the Amber Empire."

"I don't care what you call yourselves, there are too many of you. I can make you and one other person invisible. *Maybe* two." Panic threaded my voice as disquiet chilled my blood. "The rest of them can't come. What are they even doing here?"

"They have another mission," said Luca, his tone unforgiving. He motioned to two figures, a stocky man and a copper-haired woman. "Denis and Petra are coming with us."

"This is not what we discussed," I snapped, trying to infuse my voice with authority. "We planned a bare-bones mission. In and out. Simple, quick."

"Plans change, Sylvie." Luca's eyes shone with fever.

"But—"

"Stop whining," Luca snarled. "They're striking at the armory. None of your precious aristos are going to die. Not if they don't get in our way."

"The armory?" My knees were unsteady, as if the earth was crumbling beneath my feet. "I just told you, I can't turn them invisible. If anyone sees them, our plan falls to pieces!"

"If anything, it will be a diversion." Luca's voice was

impatient. "We're losing time. Our plan stays the same. Don't back out now, *Mirage*."

I stared at the dark-haired boy—*man*—and regret made my limbs heavy and weak. Regret for what I'd done. Regret for what I was about to do. I opened my mouth to say I wouldn't do it, I couldn't do it, but the words were distant and impossible. Something in my face must have given me away, because Luca nodded sharply to a muscular, bearded man.

The fighters disappeared into the hedgerows surrounding the outer jardins. I watched, mutinous, as the shadows swallowed them whole.

"Sylvie, come on." Luca gestured to Denis and Petra, standing silent and still as statues. "We don't have a lot of time."

I swallowed against the rock of dismay clogging my throat. *Our plan stays the same.* But I couldn't banish the image of twenty renegades cutting a swathe through the palais. I remembered the glint of weapons, the harsh tang of hatred souring the air.

I shook my head. It was too late to change that now. I had to trust that Luca wouldn't be a part of wholesale slaughter. They were here for weapons. They had their own mission.

Our plan stays the same.

"Fine." My voice was dry as a bone. "We'll take the quickest route to the center of the palais, to Severine's chambers. I'll be visible, but for you to remain unseen you'll have to cluster close together and move as one. You'll also need to walk in front of me."

"Why?" interrupted Petra.

"Because I don't have eyes in the back of my head," I growled.

"I thought you rich snobs had everything," the girl sneered.

"I'm not—"

"Petra, shut up," said Luca, a warning in his voice. "Sylvie, continue. We're listening."

"Luca, stay in front of the other two," I forced between my teeth. "If we reach a turn in the hall, I'll snap once for left and twice for right. If we meet anyone coming in the other direction you'll need to stop, and stay dead still. I'll take care of the rest."

"And once we get to the Imperial Wing?" asked Luca.

"Follow my lead, don't say a word, and wait until we're inside before you do *anything*." I fixed Luca and each of his comrades with a stare. "Do you understand?"

They each nodded. I sucked in a breath that didn't begin to fill the hollow growing shadowy as the Midnight Dominion between my ribs.

The bell for Compline rang.

It was time.

Sharp black clouds scudded across the curtained sun, throwing strange shadows as we darted across the lawn. The second we were beneath the pillars of the Esplanade, I cleared my throat, and the trio tightened formation, Luca standing in front with Denis and Petra flanking him. I conjured the illusion. The revolutionaries blurred against the background, then disappeared.

The palais was calm in the lull before Nocturne, and we kept to quieter passageways. I had to focus nearly all my attention on maintaining the illusion—it was far more complicated hiding three strangers than keeping myself out of sight. I concentrated on the gleam of the floors, the glow of ambric lamps, the flicker of torchlight on gilt. I couldn't afford to make a mistake. A mistake would mean death not just for Luca and his friends, but for me.

We were lucky. We only passed one servant, and he stepped

aside and bowed his head as I passed. I was so nervous I almost greeted the boy.

Stay calm, I whispered to myself, like a mantra. *You're in control.*

Finally, we were in spitting distance of the Imperial Wing. This deep into Coeur d'Or, the passageways curved inward, leading toward the most secure part of the compound. I couldn't see the sunburst door yet, but I recognized the color of the torches, shifting from pale gold near Belsyre Wing to the deep red favored by the empress.

I was so focused on what was around the bend that I didn't notice a pennant of shadow detach itself from an archway and step into the hall.

"Fairest Compline, demoiselle," said Sunder, and the smile on his face was as poisonous as his sister's touch. "What brings you to this side of the palais? At this hour? Pleasure, I hope."

Luca and his fellows stopped dead. I froze a bare second later. The illusion stuttered, but I clenched a panicked fist and the hall-way was empty once more. Fury and fear beat twin fists against my heart. A trickle of sweat trailed cold from my temple down the line of my jaw.

"Sunder," I choked out. "What are you doing here?"

"How could you forget?" He quirked an eyebrow and stalked closer. So close his sleeve nearly brushed Petra's hidden shoulder. "I live here."

My voice was a caged moth in my chest, and I could only stare in mute horror at the catastrophe unfolding in front of me. Tension was a living thing, a grotesque specter hovering in the air between us.

"Not *here* here, of course," he amended, clicking his teeth. "Obviously I don't live in the hallway."

Sunder lashed out, one hand disappearing as he thrust it into my illusion. A horrible sound like grinding bones split the air. Someone screamed. The sound sheared off abruptly. Petra fell to the floor in a heap, the entire left side of her body bent at an unnatural angle.

Chaos splintered the hallway into fragments of shape and movement. Figures darted in and out of the illusion. I gasped, raising arms that felt heavy as bricks. The emptiness dissolved.

Denis punched at Sunder, and Sunder wrapped one long-fingered hand around his fist. I heard the sound of all of Denis's fingers breaking at once. Horror surged in Denis's eyes in the split second before Sunder's hand coiled around his throat and turned his head backward.

Luca leapt onto Sunder's back. A blade flashed like kembric in the torchlight. I opened my mouth and flung out a hand, but it was already too late. Sunder disarmed Luca in a flurry of expertly placed blows, and the dark-haired boy's knees hit the marble floor with a crack. Sunder twisted his arm behind his back, bones grinding in protest.

"So this is your Tavendel lover?" Sunder wasn't even winded. A flower of hostility blossomed in my chest. "I expected him to be taller."

"Please," I heard myself whisper. Water dragged cold trails down my frozen cheeks. "Don't hurt him."

Sunder sighed, and rolled his eyes. "An empire's trash is a revolution's treasure, I suppose."

His fingers dug into the space between Luca's jaw and

skull. Sudden agony flashed across Luca's face, then his eyes lost focus and his head rolled forward. Sunder dumped him in a heap on the tile.

"What did you do to him?" A sob escaped my chest, rising into a wail. "Is he dead?"

"Bane!" called Sunder. "Do you mind?"

Bane emerged from the opposite side of the archway where Sunder ambushed us. For once, the pale girl wasn't wearing gloves. Her bare fingers were long and white as albino spiders.

Bane gave her brother a questioning look. His shrug was fluid with apathy.

Fear poured adrenaline into my veins. I took a shaky step away, and prepared to flee.

Bane raised one liquid wrist to her mouth, and blew me a kiss. Her breath gusted across her fingers, black as dusk. I whirled as the inky particles glided toward me. My shoes slipped as I scrabbled for purchase on the slick floor.

It was like a bad dream. The cloud of poison surrounded me, and I was too slow. My steps clomped ponderous and strange, as though I was slogging through mud. My heart beat dull and sluggish, and I couldn't seem to draw enough breath. The vapor hemmed me in, clinging to my nose and prying at my mouth.

I collapsed to my hands and knees on the floor, coughing as Bane's venom invaded my system. My vision blurred.

Conviction crowded out any lingering uncertainty: This was the end.

I fumbled for my ambric necklace with numb fingers, and clutched its familiar, worn planes as darkness settled in.

FORTY-ONE

Consciousness dug sharp fingernails into the edges of my mind, and *pulled.*

My sense of hearing returned first, sending a constant clatter thundering into my brain. The sound was scraped raw of context or meaning, jarring me to my bones. I stirred. My muscles wailed in silent agony. I shifted my jaw and tried to open my eyes. Light screamed in like shards of glass. It prickled raw along my tender skin. I moaned, and curled away from the onslaught of sensation.

Slowly, the world settled around me. My head ached like I'd been drinking wine for three days straight, and I couldn't open my eyes more than a slit. I peered around, trying to make sense of the clatter and sway jolting me side to side. A carriage? I pressed my palms to the plush cushion beneath me.

"You're alive," remarked a cool female voice.

I forced my eyes to focus. A blurry face sharpened. Red lips. Ice-white hair coiled in complicated spirals.

Bane.

"What—?" I croaked out, but my throat was so dry I couldn't manage another word. I swallowed. It was like gulping razors.

"Pithy," said Bane. Her tone was cruel, with none of Sunder's bite of humor to warm it. "Sunder never said you were a philosopher."

"Water?" I managed. Pitiful.

Bane sighed, and tossed me a heavy skin sloshing with liquid. I raised it to my lips, sucking at the water like a greedy child. It was cold—so cold my teeth ached—but it was clean and pure and tasted like paradise. Finally, I capped the bottle and wiped a hand across my mouth to clear the droplets from my lips. My palm came away black.

Memory came flooding back. The Imperial Wing. Sunder. Violence and death. Luca. Bane, breathing poison, chasing me down the hall.

"What did you do to me?" I spat. The fingers I brushed across my eyes and nose came away filmy with fine black soot.

"Scion, you're a mess," she sneered. She looked away and curled a voluminous fur ruff closer to her face. She was clothed all in furs, pale grey and white framing her face and draping her slender figure. "Sunder's taste in women really has taken an unfortunate turn."

"Bane!" I snapped. She cut frigid emerald eyes to me, and her mouth formed a moue of scorn. "Feel free to insult me at your leisure, but would you mind telling me what happened? What did you do to me? Where's Sunder? What happened to Luca? Where are we, and where are we going?"

"Who are you? What time is it? What's a bath?" she mocked.

"You only *tried* to kill me," I hissed. Fury sent lines of fire to kindle my chest, and I felt suddenly myself again. "I can make you wish you'd succeeded."

"Ooohhh," said Bane, rolling her perfectly lined eyes. She lifted a velvet-gloved hand to tap idly at the white lace of frost spreading across the carriage window. "I didn't try to kill you. Sunder asked me to incapacitate you."

"But—you're—"

"Poisonous? Yes, I poisoned you. Don't worry, the effects

aren't permanent. You'll feel mildly ill for another day or two before you return to your natural state of loathsome vulgarity."

"And Luca?" I swallowed the wave of nausea rising in my stomach. "Did Sunder kill him, like he did the others?"

"The Tavendel ore trader?" Bane curled her lip into its accustomed sneer. "Sadly, no. My brother seemed concerned about how you might take that news."

I leaned forward, sudden hope fizzing in my chest. "Where is he? Luca?"

"In a great deal of pain, if I know Sunder." She smirked at my stricken look. "Oh, calm down. I haven't the faintest idea."

"And the empress?" The words were blades in my throat, and I dreaded the answer. "Did she learn of our attack?"

"I'm sure she'd be *soooo* surprised to discover the Dusklander trash she let into the palais turned out to be a traitor."

"Is that why I'm here? Are you taking me somewhere to torture me, or to—"

"Kill you?" Bane's eyes glittered. "Scion, I wish. But I'm afraid that's Sunder's decision."

I bit back the vicious words rising in my throat. She was baiting me—her eyes had the same savage glint as her twin brother's. I suddenly remembered what Lullaby called them when I first arrived at Coeur d'Or: *the Suicide Twins*.

I smothered a desperate, humorless laugh.

"Something funny?" Bane snapped.

"You are," I spat back, and was rewarded with a barely masked flash of curiosity. "If you're not going to kill me, then where are you taking me?"

"We're a day's ride from Belsyre," she said, returning her wintry gaze to the frost stitching a cold tapestry on the glass window. "I hope you like the cold."

❧

We spent most of the journey in uneasy silence, Bane and I.

Soon after our delightful conversation, I suffered a bout of nausea so intense I could do nothing but curl against the seat and close my eyes. The constant rocking and swaying of the carriage soured the empty cavern of my stomach, and for the first time in my life, I was glad I hadn't eaten anything.

When the nausea finally ebbed, the chills set in.

I shuddered in the corner with my teeth chattering before Bane finally took pity on me and tossed me a length of pale fur so soft and luxurious I could barely believe it wasn't an illusion. The moment I wrapped it around my shoulders my shivers faded away and delicious warmth folded me in its arms. I spared a thought for whatever fluffy winter animal gave its life for my comfort, and snuggled deeper into the fur.

The travel became almost hypnotic. I couldn't see anything out the frost-glazed windows, so I could only guess where we were. Sometimes I felt the pull of gravity as we crested a rise or turned a corner, but for all I knew we were driving around in circles a mile outside the palais. I settled into an uneasy stupor as my body slowly detoxified from the poison scouring my insides. I only moved when a leg went numb or the edge of the carriage jarred my shoulder. Bane seemed lost in her own thoughts, and neither of us was eager to engage the other in conversation.

We stopped only once, when—much to Bane's disdain—I had to relieve myself.

She rapped on the ceiling of the carriage, and the equipage slowed to a halt. A footman handed me down. Ice bloomed on the dark fur of his hood and rimed the tips of his mustache.

My palais slippers crunched through a thick layer of frigid snow as I trudged toward a copse of trees. But I barely noticed my cold toes or the chill air sucking the warmth from my cheeks. Hulking mountains rose up like giants, jagged heads and shoulders disappearing into clouds stained bloody by a hidden sun. Snow lined the branches of black trees. Everything was bright, and sharp, and crisp beneath the muted light. I stared around in awe even as the cold robbed the breath from my lungs.

"Hurry up!" shouted Bane.

But nothing could take away the mute wonder settling in my breast as we left civilization behind and climbed into a strange world of winter. And when I finally fell into a restless, broken sleep, I dreamed of red blood spilled across milky snow. Stone black as hate. Cold so fierce it snapped your bones.

And Sunder, with my name on his lips.

FORTY-TWO

I jolted awake to the sound of shod hooves striking cobblestone and the vague certainty that someone was trying to talk to me.

"Huh?" I grunted, shoving myself into a sitting position and closing my gaping mouth.

"Ever the poet," said Bane, but for once the jibe wasn't laced with poison. She rubbed the sleeve of her coat across the window and stared outside, joy polishing her face to a jewel and lighting her up from the inside. "I said, *We're here.*"

I reached for the handle of the carriage door. Bane slashed a hand toward me and frowned.

"Careful," she snapped. "Unless you want to lose a finger to wolfbite."

I snatched my hand away. "What?"

"It's colder here," warned Bane. "You're not used to it, and you're not dressed warmly. The cold steals from those who don't respect it." She tossed me fur-lined gloves and a pair of woolen socks. "Stuff those in your shoes. They're ruined anyway. We'll find you better clothes once we're inside."

I did as she said, swathing myself in layers of warmth. When I was cocooned to Bane's satisfaction, we stepped from the carriage.

Belsyre flung ice and light into my eyes, shattering my sight into razored shards of broken mirror.

Perched on a craggy rise nestled between two black ridges, Belsyre jutted strange and pale, slicing through a veil of icy fog like the teeth of some forgotten monster. The château seemed to grow up from the stone, rugged outcroppings smoothing upward into sharp towers and looming walls. Slender bridges arched across steep ravines, the crash of fast water thundering through a shroud of grey. Black trees drew lines of ink across a bone-white canvas of drifted snow.

And between the shadows of these looming mountains, I could almost imagine the sun had set forever.

"Isn't it beautiful?" whispered Bane at my shoulder.

And when I turned to look at her I realized she wasn't speaking to me at all. Her face was turned up in rapture to gaze at her home. The tears at the corners of her eyes were already frozen. They glittered like perfect diamonds.

I shivered deep in my borrowed fur, and watched as servants clad in the stark argyle of Belsyre unloaded the carriage. A team of ink-black horses, their forelegs and hooves flocked in white, stamped impatiently. Their breath sent clouds of steam to mingle with the fog.

"My lady." An older servant bowed low over Bane's gloved hand. "Welcome home at last."

"Thank you, Bertan," she replied. "How are your girls? Did Mireille ever coax that oleander plant to bloom?"

"She did, lady," said Bertan, "and its loveliness reminds us of you every day."

If I didn't know any better, I'd think the smile that ghosted across Bane's face was kind.

And as I trailed Oleander de Vere through the austere gates of her childhood home, I found myself wondering that I ever thought the Suicide Twins cold or cruel.

A wolf wasn't cruel when she killed for her meal. A

nighthawk wasn't cruel when he ripped his talons through the still-warm body of a mouse. Winter wasn't cruel when it blanketed the land in snow and stole the warmth from your bones.

Sunder and Bane might be cold, but they weren't cruel.

They were merely as nature made them.

❄

The inside of Belsyre was as forbidding as its outside.

Our footsteps reverberated strangely across the vaulted foyer. High above, white stone twisted in shadow-wreathed archways. Slender ambric lamps pierced down like blood-dipped icicles, throwing garnet jewels across the bare, smooth walls. I shivered.

Bane marched across the gleaming tile to a spun-sugar staircase coiling up toward a gleaming balcony. She didn't say anything as she took the steps at a trot, her gloved fingers skimming the balustrade.

"Wait!" My voice chimed like a bell in the echoing space. "What am I supposed to do now?"

"Do?" Bane paused, her face a blurry circle of white in the muted glow. "Why should I care?"

"Because—"

"You're not a prisoner." A huff of impatience. "Leave, for all I care. The wolves are always hungry."

"But—"

"Sunder should be here in a few days. He'll deal with you then."

She was nothing more than a flurry of velvet and fur

disappearing into the labyrinth of her frosty home. I considered following her, but she clearly wanted privacy. To ice her heart or bathe in milk, or whatever girls like her did to look like that.

So I wandered the empty halls of Belsyre like an unseen ghost. Many rooms were closed off—tables and chairs draped in thick white cloth. Still more stood empty of anything, except perhaps ghosts. I passed through a great audience chamber, where two ironwood thrones stood proud, limned in dristic and polished to a sheen, as though their occupants had only just left and might return at any moment. Banners chased with the stark emblem of the marquisate hung silent on the walls, untouched by wind or time.

In another wing of the château, a vast banquet hall played host to nothing but shadows. Unlit lamps glittered like unshed tears between the frosted boughs of captive genévrier. Grand empty dining tables were lined with perfectly maintained crystal and silver. Not even dust dared sit where royalty once feasted.

Belsyre was like an enchanted palais from legend, stark and elegant and eerie. I half expected to find a beautiful dauphine sleeping upon a bed of thorns, or a penitent king disguised as a monster. But beneath the crisp austerity lurked something desolate, and the bare walls seemed to pulse with the remembrance of lost things. And with every step I felt as though I was forgetting something important.

Or perhaps it was just the feeling of being forgotten.

Finally, a blank-faced equerry cleared her throat and led me up a twisting spiderweb of staircases to a fine bedroom with a bed piled in furs and a curving window looking out over the shrouded valley. A great fire roared with heat, and a plush carpet warmed my frigid toes. Toasted black bread lay beside a steaming pot of stew. The scent of mulling spices reached my nose, and I was suddenly starving.

Only later, when I was stuffed and clean and warm and tucked into a lush bed, did I let myself fall prey to the gnarled knot of worry and fear and sorrow pushing crooked roots into my heart. And when I swiped at my wet eyes with trembling fingers, I couldn't help but imagine my hands coming away red with the blood of lost lives.

❧

I spent the next three days pacing the halls of Belsyre in a haze of anxiety. I didn't catch a glimpse of my merciless hostess again, but Bane's words echoed in my mind.

Sunder should be here in a few days. He'll deal with you then.

Images of the fight in the hallway raged through my mind no matter how I tried to quell them. The scream of bones snapping. Petra and Denis dispatched with the ease of an assassin. Pain curdling Luca's gaze as his head fell forward and he slumped to the ground. Sunder, eyes unforgiving as he sent his sister to incapacitate me.

You're not a prisoner, Bane had promised. But then, what was I? Why was I here? The luxurious suite of rooms at my disposal was unlike any prison I'd heard of. I had food, and warmth, and a wardrobe full of gowns hastily altered from Bane's castoffs. But the natural environment of Belsyre was its own ruthless fortress. I shivered just looking at the austere banks of bone-white snow, the cold, leaden mountains, the hungry trees. I was as much a captive here as if actual bars of steel hemmed me in.

I considered finding Bane and demanding answers, but every time I approached her wing of the château, a gracious servant intercepted my progress and led me away.

So I was left alone to obsess about what Sunder did, and why he did it.

And most importantly, what he was going to do to me.

FORTY-THREE

The sound of footsteps jerked me from a nightmare of snapping jaws and breaking bones.

Furs fell away from my shoulders, and a chill kissed my collarbone. My eyes flew to the front of my room. A black silhouette skulked in the open doorway. Cold fingers ran the length of my spine.

Sunder stepped into the dim red light pouring through the window. He wore black furs and carried the scent of outside with him: ice and iron and pine. Melting snow puddled on the fine nap of the carpet, leaving dark stains beneath his boots. The flickering glow of the banked fire painted the angles of his face in shades of blood, and his eyes were forged dristic.

"Where have you been?" I asked, and immediately cursed my stupid traitor voice.

"Cleaning up your mess," he growled, voice hoarse. "Explaining to the empress how a score of rebel thieves managed to break into the palais compound without a single Skyclad Garde noticing. There's talk of canceling Carrousel."

"What about—?"

"Your foolish assassination attempt? You'd better hope she never finds out, or your lovely head will find its way onto a very sharp pike."

We stared at each other across the darkened room. Fear spackled my thoughts with mud and slowed the churn of questions within me.

"What are you going to do to me?" I asked finally. I'd thought of little else besides crunching bone and bursting blood since that awful fight in the hall outside the Imperial Wing.

"*Do* to you?" His startled brows clenched. "What in the Scion's name has Oleander been telling you?"

"Nothing," I whispered. "I haven't seen her since we arrived."

Sunder muttered a curse, then tossed off his coat and slumped into the fat-armed chair beside the fire. He lowered his head into his palms. His lips moved, but I couldn't hear what he mumbled under his breath.

Hesitantly, I swung my legs from under the crush of blankets and stood up, wrapping a length of snowy fur around my bare shoulders. I moved on quiet steps to the fireside, hovering an arm's length away from Sunder.

"How did you catch us? How did you know they were there, without seeing them?"

"My legacy. I can hear the throb of hearts, feel the rush of blood, smell the stink of fear."

I smothered a flash of revulsion.

"Where's Luca? Did you hurt him?"

"Your Tavendel beau is fine," muttered Sunder, without lifting his head from his hands. "Better than fine. He's back in the Paper City, probably planning the next ill-fated revolution."

"He's not my beau." My hands trembled with relief. "What happened to the other rebels?"

"The ones who weren't slaughtered by the Garde will be tried and executed as traitors."

"What if—"

"They divulge your involvement?" He sighed. "One of Bane's poisons blots out memories. It's not as elegant as—as some legacies, since it blots out most other cognitive functions too, but it gets the job done. By the way, the court thinks you were grievously injured during the attack and had to repair to Belsyre for recovery. When we return, everyone will assume we're lovers."

Silence clogged the space between us. I attempted to sort through the roil of opposing thoughts and feelings. Sunder had protected the empress from our assassination attempt, but hadn't told her of the danger to her life or the part I played. And if he was loyal to her, then why was I here, and not in some drafty dungeon awaiting my execution? Why was Luca alive?

"I don't understand anything," I said out loud.

"Never were truer words spoken!" He jerked his head up, fixed me with his sharp eyes, and barked a desperate laugh. "You inconceivable fool. You have no idea the trouble you've caused me these past spans. You have single-handedly and unwittingly dismantled tides' worth of planning, just by being you. You've nearly ruined everything."

"I don't know what you mean." Annoyance chased away my fear. "And if you were planning something so important, then you should have told me instead of letting me *ruin* it so efficiently."

"Tell you?" Sunder's eyebrows winged up toward his hairline. "Tell *you*, an ignorant, unreliable, loudmouthed provincial with delusions of grandeur and an entitlement complex as big as this château? Your grasp of the intricacies of intrigue boggles the mind."

"If you're just going to insult me, you can leave," I snapped, wrapping my fur tighter around me to keep from throttling him. "I'm sorry if my ignorance offends you."

"Everything about you offends me," Sunder said, and though his words rang harsh the look in his eyes was unguarded, ragged with expectation. "I don't understand how you can be the way that you are. You are brash, and thoughtlessly brave. You do exactly the thing that is the least expected and the most destructive. You are a puzzle and a curse."

"If I didn't know any better, I might think you were complimenting me," I snapped, lacing my tone with poison as I turned toward the door. "I'd rather sleep with the wolves than spend another moment being verbally abused by a haughty lord with knives in his fingertips and deceit in his soul."

"Stop." Sunder was on his feet in an instant. His fingers whispered around my wrist, holding me back from the door. I spun to face him. In the shadowed archway, his eyes glinted like silvery coins. "I—I'm sorry."

"Say it like you mean it," I hissed through my teeth.

"I do," he whispered, and the strain in his voice made me want to believe him. "I shouldn't have said those things. But you must understand the chaos you have wrought in my life since the moment you marched into that cursed Atrium."

"I don't understand," I said again. The familiar coil of ignorance and frustration soured my stomach. "You're going to have to explain it to me."

"I will." He suddenly looked unspeakably tired, as if the weight of the daylight world rested on his shoulders. "But you're going to have to sit."

Reluctant, I did as he said sinking into an armchair and tucking my legs beneath me. Sunder tossed a log on the banked fire, which spat yellow sparks before flaring. He poured himself a tall glass of wine from a decanter, raising a questioning eyebrow at me. I gave my head a hard shake. He shrugged, and paced to stand across from me.

"I'm astonished you haven't figured it out yet," he mused.

"Assume I'm as stupid as you imagine me to be," I managed around the resentment gluing my teeth together. "Start from the beginning. Don't leave anything out."

"If you're certain." Sunder cast pensive eyes to the crackling fire. "Dowser and a secret group of like-minded nobles have been plotting a coup against Severine almost since the moment she seized power. Recently, those plans have acquired a clearer sense of urgency and agency. Wheels are turning. Assets are in play. Everything is in motion to remove her from power. Or was, until you waltzed up the steps of the palais and announced yourself as a legacy in front of the court."

"Me?" I asked, incredulous. I felt suddenly dizzy as my world shifted beneath me. Dowser, plotting against the empress. *Sunder*, on the same side as me? I clenched my teeth and tried to focus. "What do I have to do with your plans?"

"You mean *besides* leading a score of frenzied revolutionaries in a rash and ill-planned assassination attempt at the heart of the palais?"

I gritted my teeth so hard I thought my jaw might crack.

"You were never supposed to leave the Dusklands. Did it never occur to you that whoever hid you away at the edge of the world had a good reason for doing so? Did you never read the Writ of Guardianship Dowser left with the Sisters?"

"They burned it," I whispered. Curiosity poured water over the embers of my rage, and brought with it a strange, dazed sense of inevitability. I knew there was *something*. I knew—

"Who am I?" I asked, a numb certainty breathing rainbows against my heart.

"You were *supposed* to be our secret weapon," said Sunder, his voice bitter. "You, and that hunk of rock hanging around your neck."

My hand flew to the familiar planes of the skin-warmed necklace. The bubble of anticipation exploded into a firework of nerves. "Why?"

"You're the last surviving child of the dead emperor, and besides the empress, you're the only living—if currently illegitimate—heir to the Sabourin dynasty." Sunder's voice was a kembric bell tolling in the dusk. "And that ambric necklace is a Relic of the Scion. Mirage, you alone have the power to change the face of the Amber Empire."

FORTY-FOUR

Shock turned my insides liquid with heat.

"What?" I spluttered. "But I've had this since I was a child! It's the only thing my—"

Sunders eyes sparked on mine, and things began to make sense.

"Oh." My heart stuttered in my chest like some invisible force had a fist wrapped around it.

"Dowser was a junior advisor in the emperor's cabinet when Severine reached her majority," said Sunder, his voice pitched low. "Barely out of Unitas. He saw the warning signs of her rabid ambition before anyone else did, not least because he briefly shared the then-dauphine's bed."

"What?" My head jerked up. "Dowser was Severine's lover?"

"He isn't a monk, you know," said Sunder, wry. "He grew even more worried in the spans following Seneca's death."

"Who?"

"The dauphin, the frail but well-liked heir to the Amber Empire. He was poorly throughout his childhood, but the fatal illness that struck him weeks before his twentieth birthday seemed suspicious to Dowser. He expressed his concerns, but the emperor was healthy and his Council busy administrating a vast empire Sylvain had largely left in their able hands in order to pursue . . . other interests."

"His mistress," I guessed.

"*Mistresses*," corrected Sunder. "A veritable harem of official and unofficial concubines, spread across the empire."

"My mother—?" The word was strange on my tongue, and I choked on the question before I could finish it.

"Is long dead." Sunder's eyes sliced back to the fire. "Madeleine Allard. A courtier. The Allards hailed from a charming estate in the Rose Valley. They're all dead now, purged in the same cull that severed the roots of my family tree."

Sudden regret for the family I never knew—and would never know—washed over me.

"I'm sorry," I whispered.

"There's no point in being sorry," muttered Sunder. "Regret changes nothing. Only action can undo the ravages of the past."

The fire spat sparks into the silence.

"Emperor Sylvain never legitimized any of his natural children," he continued, "but he made his affection for a great many of them obvious to the world. And to an ambitious heir, such blood ties can be unpredictable and dangerous. Severine didn't directly target her half siblings until after she dealt with her father, but she prepared for the moment in advance—making lists, identifying threats, keeping tabs on potential problems. Dowser tried to head her off. He counseled many of the emperor's mistresses to flee, to protect themselves. But few listened, and the few who did were slow to run and ill-equipped to remain in hiding for long.

"Madeleine was barely pregnant when Severine seized the throne. Dowser smuggled her away to the edge of the world, hoping she would escape Severine's notice. Madeleine arrived on the doorstep of the Sisters of the Scion in a dusty hamlet outside Piana with a squalling infant, a Writ of Guardianship carrying the Imperial Insignia, and a Relic of the Scion."

"What is it?" I leaned forward, the ambric pendant thumping against my ribs. "And why is it important?"

"I hardly know," said Sunder, scrubbing a hand across his tired eyes. "Dowser is the Scion scholar. But it's been in possession of the imperial line for tides. When wielded by the right legacy, it supposedly confers untold power, especially when paired with other Relics."

"Other Relics?" I frowned. "How many are there?"

"I don't know. Some say as many as ten. Others put the number at three or four. Some don't believe they exist at all. The Sabourins claim to possess at least one other."

"Fine," I said, trying to place all this information in order. "But if they're so all-powerful, why didn't the old emperor ever use them?"

"Maybe he did." Sunder shrugged. "Or maybe he didn't need to. Regardless, Severine was cut from different cloth. Dowser didn't want any more power falling into her greedy hands, so he sent the Relic with you. If nothing else, he hoped the symbol would inspire the Sisters to guard you with every superstitious bone in their bodies."

"A true believer yourself, I assume?"

"Some call it faith. I call it credulity," Sunder snarled. "When Meridian descends from the sky in a chariot of fire with the armies of Dominion at his back, I'll believe in the Scion."

I bit back a laugh. For once, I had to agree with him.

"So what happened?" I pressed. "Did Dowser's plan work?"

"Madeleine is long dead, and you're at Coeur d'Or instead of waiting patiently to be fetched when the time is right," snarled Sunder. "So, no. Severine's spies followed Madeleine to the Dusklands and slaughtered her on the steps of the cloister. They demanded the Sisters give you up, under threat of death. The Sisters obeyed."

Confusion muddled through the churn of horror and regret.

"They did? Then I'm not—"

"Disciples of the Scion may be pious zealots, but they are willing to risk almost anything in the service of their idol. Sabourin blood flowed through your veins, direct from Meridian's mythic line. You wore the Scion's mark around your neck. In their eyes, the choice was clear." Sunder swallowed, and looked away. "A child was handed over. A child was murdered. That child was not you."

Disgust and outrage washed over me, tinged with creeping sympathy for the hard, distant Sisters who raised me without kindness or warmth. I remembered the desperate looks on their faces when I declared my intention to leave for the Amber City, the way they burned the writ and tried to lock me in my room. In their eyes, protecting me was their sacred duty, the thing that brought them closest to the man or god they'd devoted their life to worshipping. Nothing had been too great a sacrifice to keep me safe. And even if I didn't believe in it, I could see how in their eyes, I had betrayed that faith.

"And Severine assumed she'd rid herself of the last of her blood," I supplied. It wasn't hard to guess what happened next—I lived it. "And I grew up on the edge of the darkness, never knowing who I was. Safe. Sort of. But what did Dowser intend for me? Was he ever going to rescue me from the dusk?"

"Eventually, yes," Sunder said, with frustration. "We needed the promise of another Sabourin heir to motivate reluctant dissidents. Few are willing to overthrow a tyrant without the promise of a better ruler. But we also needed to keep you hidden, and keep you safe until Severine could be deposed."

A better ruler. The full gravity of the situation hammered down on me. I wasn't merely a legacy of the empire. I was *royalty*. Except for Severine, I was the last living descendant of the Sabourin line. Even illegitimate, I was the daughter of an emperor. And that came with responsibilities. Responsibilities I could hardly comprehend. A world of hard lines and vast promise bloomed at the edge of my imagination. I shook my head, tucking away the thoughts to revisit later.

"If you've been planning this coup for tides, why haven't you let the sword drop? Why is Severine still sitting on that throne, bleeding her empire dry and culling her legacies one by one?"

Sunder's eyes grated on mine. "Do not underestimate the difficulties of launching a secret coup on a ruler with a tyrannical death grip on her security, her advisors, and her nobility. You may think felling a regime is as easy as smuggling three illiterate rebels into the empress's inner sanctum. It's not."

"We were almost there!" I bristled. "We could have succeeded."

"You think you're the first person to attempt an assassination on Severine?" Sunder's laugh was a fingernail on slate. "Not by a long shot. The empress is wily, and she has secret weapons."

"What weapons?"

"They wouldn't be much of a secret if everyone knew," Sunder said. "First: Dowser feels certain she has another Relic in her possession. She always plays her hand close to her chest, even with her closest advisors, so he isn't sure what it is or what it does. Regardless, if it makes her more powerful, then it makes her a greater and more unpredictable foe."

"Powerful at what?" I asked, thinking of Lullaby's horrified look when I asked the empress about her legacy.

"That's the second weapon," Sunder said, and there was something like disgust muddying his gaze. "Her legacy—no one knows how it manifests. No one has ever seen her use it. Not her childhood playmates, not Dowser, none of her courtiers or advisors. But she has walked away unscathed from every attempt on her life. Poison. Dristic. Magic. No one has ever managed to harm a single hair on her head."

"What about you?"

Something brittle splintered in Sunder's eyes. "I prefer to keep my *gift* as a last resort."

"You seemed more than willing to snap the necks of those rebels."

"Yes." Sunder surged to his feet. "Because you were about to march straight up to Severine and, once the assassination was inevitably foiled, announce yourself as a threat. Severine would have tracked your origins to the Temple and realized who you were. What you were wearing around your neck. Then everything Dowser and I had fought for would be ashes and dust. I consider that the definition of a *last resort*."

I jutted my chin out.

"She's already trying to trace you," muttered Sunder. "She isn't stupid. The second you walked into the Atrium she knew there was something about you. We all did. Even covered in dust, you were too powerful and beautiful and proud to be a fluke."

Heat washed over me, and it wasn't from the fire. I remembered that day in the Atrium, everyone laughing behind their fans at my common manners and dirty hair. Sunder stepping forward to sponsor me . . . for the opposing dynasty. I pushed down the old shame, trying to see the situation in a new light.

"You knew who I was," I said slowly. "When you sponsored me. How?"

"Dowser's legacy allows him to speak mind to mind," said Sunder, as if it was common knowledge. Surprise jolted me back against the seat. "He saw your unexpected arrival as a miracle and a promise. I saw it as a curse. I tried to drive you away. I tried to make the palais miserable for you. I thought if you left we could still keep you hidden, safe until we needed you. But you were too determined, too sure of yourself. And by the time I started trying to help you, it was too late. You had your own plans."

"Do the others know?" I asked. "Lullaby and the rest? Are they in on the plot? Was Thibo?"

"A few are," said Sunder carefully. "It's dangerous. Some in Dexter are sympathetic to the cause. Reaper was a great asset, especially considering his family connections. Some in Sinister too. But it's easier to deal with nobles who don't have an active presence at court. Most people are not adept at secrecy and espionage."

"So what's next?" I leaned forward. Now that I knew everything Severine had done, to me, to my friends, the family I never knew, *Sunder's* family . . . I wanted to see her ruined, her power shattered, her sick grasp on her nobility dissolved. "What can I do to help?"

Sunder drained the last of his wine and ran a harried hand through his perfect hair, leaving jagged golden strands sticking in every direction. He looked suddenly too young, too overwhelmed, and much too tired to be carrying so much weight on his shoulders. A burst of pity cooled the eagerness climbing my ribs and knocking at my heart.

"I don't know," he said. He stood abruptly. The dull glow from the window turned his hair the color of rust. "I need to think. And you need to rest. We'll all need our strength, whatever happens."

I opened my mouth to protest, but the door whispered shut and his footsteps echoed away down the hall.

I turned back toward my bed, but my eye snagged on the heavy fur Sunder had tossed over an empty chair and forgotten. I stepped closer, hating the sudden impulse to touch it, to wear it. I ran my hand over the thick ruff, sinking my fingers into the coarse black fur. I raised it to my face and breathed in the scent of Sunder, faint but unmistakable. Crisp. Sharp. Genévrier and ice. A spark of desire ignited in my belly.

I dropped the fur to the floor and dived back into the pile of blankets on my plush bed. I buried my head deep between the feather pillows and willed myself to sleep.

But much as I wished I could drift away, thoughts of treason and assassination and legacy and dynasty whirled like snowflakes caught in a stiff wind, and it was many, many long hours before I found rest.

FORTY-FIVE

I spent most of the next day pacing in my chambers and avoiding both of the de Veres.

I replayed Sunder's revelations from the previous Nocturne over and over again. Not only was I a legacy, and highborn—which I had always guessed—but I was the emperor's sole surviving natural daughter. I kept having to sit down and force myself to breathe. Sunder hadn't told me the entirety of his and Dowser's plot to overthrow Severine, but if everything went according to plan my own future might look exceedingly different from what I originally had in mind.

Empress. Amber Empire. *Empress*. Sabourin.

The words were a litany in my head. I never wanted that kind of power. All I ever wanted was a world where I belonged. A world forged in reveries and quickened with wonder, as sublime as the kaleidoscope glow bathing my soul in light. I'd fought to be part of that world, and once I'd realized it was an illusion of someone else's making, I'd fought to create my own worlds. And wasn't that what royalty—what *power*—was? Building something—creating something—from nothing more than clear-glass conviction and ephemeral power?

But what did I know about ruling?

I felt suddenly, righteously furious at Dowser. Part of me understood that he had sent me to the Dusklands as the best chance of escaping my half sister's campaign of fratricide. But couldn't he have done more to ensure I wouldn't grow up a half-literate rube from the edges of the world? Couldn't he have given me some small hint that someday, someone would come for me? That I wasn't a forgotten orphan destined for nothing but what I seized for myself?

I was staring at the spume of water feathering upward from the river gorge and feeling deeply sorry for myself when a tentative knock came at the door.

"My lady?" A servant poked her silvery head through my door. Everyone in Belsyre was pale and blond—as though the white landscape leached the color from all it touched, including its children.

"You don't have to call me that," I said, a touch unkindly. Uncertainty and anxiety had frayed my nerves to the point of snapping. "What is it?"

"His Lordship and Her Ladyship request your presence at supper, my lady," she said. "I'm to help you dress and prepare, if you please."

My mood grew forbidding as the black mountains crouching silent on the horizon. The last thing I wanted was to participate in some charade of politesse while the fate of an empire hung in the balance. But my only other option was to sit up here like a prisoner and sulk.

I honestly didn't know which was worse.

I struggled to choose a gown from the haphazard selection of dresses the staff of Belsyre had culled from Bane's wardrobe. They were all exquisite, but they were tailored for Bane's willowy frame and designed to suit her icy complexion. Jewel-bright velvets; metallic satins. None of the light, soft Dexter styles that flattered my sable hair and warm complexion.

Finally, I selected an elegant, if slightly eerie gown. A pale skirt drifted like snow, etched in lines of pewter like the bare, spreading branches of a winter forest. Leafless twigs in dristic and charcoal crept up from the wrists and the narrow waist, branching across the bodice and twining around the arms.

The girl coiled my dark hair into a twisting braid and planted tiny, glinting jewels among the tresses. She glazed my lips and smeared kohl along the curve of my lashes. Diamonds like chips of ice winked from my ears. And when I stared at myself in the burnished mirror, I felt suddenly as though I'd become a part of this cold, lonely place. I imagined walking out those lofty doors and being swallowed up by the hungry forest, a pale dauphine made of nothing more than ice and brittle wood, blood and snow, frozen water and strange desires.

I descended the looping staircase with nerves tangling in my belly.

The Suicide Twins waited at the bottom, sipping ice wine and talking. They glanced up at the sound of my footsteps, Bane very pale against the deep violet of her low-cut gown, Sunder angular and polished in black and green. He cut a small bow and offered his free arm. I took it, laying light fingers against the cool brocade. I didn't look at him, staring straight ahead with my chin high, but I felt his eyes graze my face, my neck. I was suddenly and intensely conscious of the transparent branches twisting across my chest, barely hiding the breathless rise and fall of my rib cage. I fought the flush staining my cheeks.

Dinner was an uneasy affair. We three sat at one end of the vast dining table in that echoing feast hall, barely talking. Servants served mountain hare doused in a rich sauce spiced with genévrier and sour-sweet lingonberry. Savory squash and roast vegetables. Smoked salmon with cream and dill. Cloudberries with cream.

Sunder ate quickly, his manners elegant but cursory. Bane cut her food into smaller and smaller pieces, then nibbled daintily. I was starving, but the second I piled my plate high, bile climbed my throat and I could barely eat a thing.

Finally, Bane pushed her chair away from the table.

"I'm going to bed," she announced, turning on her heel.

"Oleander—" Sunder began, but his sister was already gone. His eyes cut to mine, and for a moment I thought he was going to say something to me. Then he too rose from the table and stalked away through Belsyre.

I sat mute and uncomfortable, suppressing another blush. Irritation and impatience sliced through my shame, and I shoved back from the table and stomped after Sunder.

He wasn't hard to follow—his boots sent crisp echoes ricocheting off the cold tiles. I had a sudden, sharp memory of following him down another hall in another palais; a crimson storm and a jardin made of ice. I quelled a burble of nervous laughter.

Sunder stepped through a pair of tall glass doors onto a secluded balcony. I followed, bracing myself for a frigid bite on my nearly bare arms, but the air was only pleasantly crisp, not freezing. I glanced around the terrace. Hot water cascaded down the walls in crystal sheets before gathering in broad shallow basins at the base of the walls. Plumes of steam billowed up from the pools, heating the air above. Tiny red blossoms twined along swan-slim pillars, droplets of blood against ice.

Sunder stood in the shadow of one marble pillar, staring out across his estate. Two black-and-white mountains dipped low to the churning froth of a coursing river. The low sun peered between the peaks, sending vermeil fingers to caress the snow-draped hills.

"You call her Oleander here," I remarked when the silence grew too heavy.

"It's her name, demoiselle."

"Should I call you Aubrey?" I asked. The name felt clumsy on my cold lips.

"No. That's not who I am anymore. Maybe it never was." His eyes rose suddenly to mine, and a tangle of indecision fractured his features. "I wanted—"

He hesitated. I waited.

"I wanted to apologize. For Lullaby." His voice rasped, rough as unpolished marble. "The Nocturne of the Blood Rain Ball, after you left my jardin—"

Horror and rage flashed white-hot. I remembered her eyes swollen with tears as she limped to bed. Thibo's haunted gaze: *We are all thieves here.*

"What did you do to her?"

"I broke every one of her fingers. Twice." A drowning abyss opened in his eyes. "Severine commanded it, as punishment for your failure. I tried to dissuade her, but she was rabid with fury. She smiled as I—" He choked on the words. "But Lullaby never once screamed. She just wept silent tears. For hours."

Wrath and outrage and misery pulped my heart. I wanted to blame Sunder, to scream and push and cry, but a cold, calculating corner of my mind tallied Lullaby's torture and Sunder's guilt and my own failure to protect my friend onto the empress's ever-growing list of sins. Her debt was growing.

"Lullaby doesn't remember," Sunder added. "Reaper took the memory away. After. All she knows is she was punished, not how. But I thought you ought to know that it was me. And that if I could—if I could somehow take that pain away, take it onto myself, I would."

Reaper took the memory away. I sucked in a deep breath of pine-scented steam, feeling as though it was I who took my friends' pain onto myself, not him. That old ember of fury blazed up, but this time it was new. Different. It was hard as diamond and sharp as dristic. Polished and faceted as a ruby, it burned with a smoldering, scorching intensity. It burned like a spark that wanted to set the world on fire.

When the time was right.

"I forgive you," I finally said. I didn't think I was lying.

"Why?" Sunder's shoulders curled, and he dragged his bleak gaze back to the expanse of snow. "How can I be redeemed for causing that kind of pain?"

"I didn't say you could be redeemed," I whispered. "I said that I forgave you. I'm sorry if that's not enough."

Hot water trickled. Red flowers shuddered in the breeze. I considered leaving.

"Have you decided?" I asked, instead. "What happens next?"

"Yes," he said. "I'm sending you away."

"Oh?" My hands curled into fists. "Where?"

"Somewhere you and the Relic will be safe until we find a way to deal with Severine."

"No," I said. The ember glowed red-hot. "I'm going back to the Amber City with you."

Sunder cut his eyes to me. The blackness of his pupils seemed to swallow all the green. "Why?"

Why. I fumbled for some way to explain that ember smoldering within me. The rage, and the dread, and the steady throb of inevitability I felt whenever I thought about where I belonged. The world I'd fought for, and now felt responsible for. I took a deep breath, and tried.

"Growing up in the Dusklands, all I knew was dust, and twilight, and the desolate edge of the known world. Out there, you can never trust your eyes. Distances are strange and difficult to measure. Shadows betray. Colors are dimmer, without light."

Sunder turned his head to look back over the crags of his domain, but I knew he was still listening; his head tilted to one side, and pale strands of hair drifted in the steam-warm air.

"There were children, from the village," I continued. "Grubby little things. Just like me, I guess. The Sisters let me play with them, sometimes. One boy bullied me: jabbed me with rocks, teased me, pulled my hair. Once, things went too far. He pushed me to the ground. Punched me, kicked hard at my ribs. I remember terror and anger and humiliation all curled up inside me, whimpering like an animal that's been beaten." I paused, letting the soul-etched horror of that moment wash over me and then drift away. "That animal snapped. Something let go inside me and there were colors all around. It wasn't a thing, or a shape. It was a dream, a muddled collection of sounds and feelings and colors crushing and shifting against each other. It was vibrant, intense. Beautiful."

I opened my palms, and that dream spilled out, as vivid now as it was then. A song in color, a gossamer impression of violet clouds and silver wind and the keening feeling of being alive. Sunder's eyes widened.

"The children ran, screaming like I was a monster. And in that moment, I knew I was different. Not in degree, but in *kind*. I dreamed of a world graced with light and redolent with color, and I yearned for it. To see those brazen shades again, experience that strange joy, wield that kind of power: That's what I wanted. That's what I *deserved*."

Sunder nodded, terse, as though he understood something he hadn't a moment ago.

"I will not sit idly by while the world changes around me," I murmured. "I don't know whether my blood is a gift or a curse. And I don't relish breaking the world in order to remake it the way I see it." I took a deep breath. "But I will if I have to. Does that make me a monster?"

Sunder turned away from the ledge and stepped toward me, until he was close enough that I could have reached out and touched him. In the cavern of his frost-limned eyes I saw some sheer part of myself reflected back.

"Do you know why our gifts manifest in such different ways?" he murmured. "Pain, poison; healing, song. Illusion."

I shook my head.

"No one does. Some think it's passed parent to child, shifting and warping as blood binds to blood. But no one is born wielding magic. Our legacies only manifest after we grow and mature, experience the diversity of joy and pain life invariably brings."

I frowned. "What do you mean?"

"Oleander and I were barely older than babes when our parents were killed." Remembered pain chiseled Sunder's features. "But we both understood too well what had happened. I remember she used to sit in the greenhouse beneath the flowering oleander, our mother's favorite flower and my sister's namesake.

The flower is lovely, but poisonous in all its parts. She would sit, and weep bitter tears, plucking the blooms from their stems and crushing the petals between her little hands. And I—I would wander the woods beyond the ravine, setting traps for rabbits and foxes because I wanted them as my pets. I wanted them as my *friends*. But I didn't know how to catch them without maiming them. And even the animals I eventually caught, and tamed, and kept, were afraid of me. Because I had broken their bones, spilled their blood across the snow."

An arrow of sympathy laced with shock sang toward my heart. Sunder leaned closer.

"I believe that, instead of arising from our blood, our legacies are shaped by who we are. Our abilities rise and shape to our own inclinations. For better or for worse, I *want* to cause pain, even to the things I love."

His hand drifted toward me, slow enough that I could slap it away if I wanted to. I didn't. His fingers hovered above my collarbone. A crackle of energy passed between us.

"And me?" My voice was breathless. "If that's true, what do my illusions mean?"

"Perhaps you have deceit in your soul," whispered Sunder. His hand floated higher, raising the hairs along my neck. "Or perhaps you want to show the world something only you can see. Something lovely, and strange, and just a little bit monstrous."

"So you don't mind," I managed, "if I'm a monster?"

"No." He rocked closer, and his closeness sent a thread of desire stitching up my spine. "Because I'm a monster too."

I kissed him. It was as simple as turning my head and pressing my lips against his. For a moment, time waited. My heart stopped. His hands stilled. His lips brushed against mine, cool and soft and light as a flake of falling snow.

Time stuttered. And started again.

He deepened the kiss, his lips a promise: a covenant of the sublime. His hand found my waist and crushed me against him. Our heartbeats thundered side by side. I slid my palms up the front of his coat, finding his collar. I tugged, pulling him closer. Strands of his hair whispered against my knuckles and sent my thoughts whirling away into the dusk. He nudged me backward. My shoulders hit the edge of the pillar. I gasped.

The clouds of our breath mingled as he drew away, eyes snagging on mine. And for the first time since I'd met him, I saw Sunder utterly unmasked and unguarded. I saw the deep well of torment pooling behind eyes dark with want. I saw desolation, and desire, and an icy, endless strength.

He captured my lips with his once more. But this kiss was laced with desperation, and something else: a zinging ache that jolted the skin across my face and tightened my muscles. His hands glided down the column of my neck and left scorching trails in their wake. A high ringing pierced my ears. My palms itched. I clenched my hands into fists and shoved him away.

"No," I breathed. "Not like that."

A cold breeze off the mountains gusted between us. Sunder stared at me. He was breathing hard, and spots of hectic red stood out high on his angular cheekbones. He shuddered, and pushed the spill of white-gold hair off his furrowed brow.

"I'm sorry," he said.

And I believed him. Because I was sorry too.

"You're cold," I whispered, because he was shivering in his fine brocade, shivering like he'd break apart, shivering like he'd never be warm again.

"I'm always cold," he replied.

"We should go inside." I laughed. The sound was as hollow as my heart. "Before you catch your death."

"Death," he repeated, and turned his face toward the mountains. The low sun drenched him in blood. "I've dreamed of dying so many times. Sometimes, I can't help but think that somehow, somewhere, it must have already happened."

He straightened, turned, and smiled like an ice wolf.

"Come on." He brushed past me and into the château. "We have much planning to do if we ever hope to outsmart that lying witch and steal the throne from under her nose."

I watched him disappear back into Belsyre. Another icy wind stole the breath from my lungs. I couldn't help but feel like something else had been stolen from me too.

FORTY-SIX

We planned until Compline turned to Nocturne and a sweep of freezing fog shrouded the valley.

"To mount a successful coup," Sunder said, "we're going to need the Amber Court on our side. We don't have time to requisition the noble families from their country estates, so we'll have to rely on our peers. Sinister is ruthless and fierce, but their loyalties can be unpredictable. There are a few courtiers I've been grooming to turn against the empress. I can try to motivate them with favors or fortune."

"Most of Dexter is furious and deeply resentful about all the legacies the empress has been seizing from their ranks," I added. "I might not be able to incite them myself, but now that Thibo—"

Sunder nodded. "The Montrachets have no great love for imperial rule—they were annexed during the Conquest, same as the de Veres. From what I hear, half his clan has already been drafted for the empress's petty battles. Use his disappearance if you can."

"And Luca—"

"We are not involving that feckless ore trader!" Sunder's eyes slashed up to meet mine. "He nearly ruined all our plans. Besides, we want to replace the empress with an heir *we* control—"

"Control?" My voice was icy.

"You know what I mean." Sunder sat back against his chair. "We don't know how many militants La Discorde has in its ranks, nor how much support they have among the commoners. If we cede any part of this overthrow to Luca and his friends, we could have a revolution on our hands, instead of a clean coup with relatively few casualties. Do you want to eviscerate the Amber Empire, or just remove its head?"

"Fine," I snapped. "Maybe you're right. But we could still use them without telling them what we're doing. They could create a diversion—draw away the Skyclad Gardes while we put the rest of our plan into motion."

Sunder opened his mouth, then closed it again. He grimaced, and put his head in his hands.

"That might actually be a good idea, demoiselle," he muttered. "Discuss it with Luca when we're back in the city. But no promises."

"Agreed." I glanced up to find his eyes lingering on my face. My mouth parted, and the silent press of heightened emotions threatened to collapse the frigid wall we'd built between us since that moment on the terrace. I looked away first. "Will you speak to Dowser, or should I?"

"I will," he said. "He's not going to like any of this. He's been trying to find out for tides what Severine's legacy is, and has spent almost as long trying to find out which of her treasures is the second Relic. He's going to counsel us to wait until you're stronger, until we have more information, until we know we can win."

"Do you think he's right?"

"That depends on you." Sunder splayed his hands across the table. "For this to work, you won't be able to lead the dissident courtiers against the Skyclad Gardes to secure the palais. The nobility know me; they fear me. They may or may not be willing to follow me, but they most certainly won't follow you. Furthermore, we're going to have to separate Severine from those among her court who remain loyal. She knows how to manipulate them, how to bend them to her will. No—you're going to have to be the one to vanquish Severine. Alone."

"I know," I said, and even as the words left my mouth I realized that ever since I had discovered who I was—who my father was, and what Severine had done to my mother, my innocent siblings—I had known that I was going to have to be the one to face the empress. The ember inside me spat sparks. "I need to remind everyone—commoner and noble alike—what she did to seize power, so I can discredit her. I need to find out what her legacy is, so she can't use it against me, or the rest of the court. And I need to defeat her, in whatever way I can."

Sunder's gaze flicked with jagged awe. "And how do you plan to do that?"

I smiled. "I have a few ideas."

We spent hours planning moves, and countermoves. Attack, parry, riposte. We mapped out every player at our disposal, and tried to predict where our enemies would be, and how they would act. We planned until my head swam with so many plots and gambits that I could barely remember my own name, much less who I could and couldn't trust, and under what circumstances.

When the bells for Nocturne turned to Matin, and the fog turned to feathered blasts of downy snow, our plans were finally complete. We rose from the table in the gloom, the silence between us fragile as glass.

"Have you thought at all—" Sunder began, tentative. He cleared his throat. "You said that you would break the world, if you had to; to remake it the way you see it. What will that world look like, when you sit upon the Amber Throne?"

I opened my mouth to say I hadn't thought about it. But when I met his eyes—taut with expectation and bright with brittle hope—I realized that wasn't true. In a strange way, it was all I'd ever thought about. From the moment I learned what I was, I'd dreamed of that world. I'd crossed an empire for that world, only to realize that if I truly wanted a place to belong, I'd have to create it.

I can do better than she can.

"I don't have easy answers," I whispered. "And I know next to nothing about ruling. But when I close my eyes I dream of a world where beauty is an intention, not a pretense. Where grace reigns. Where compassion dwells. I can't promise to make this empire great again, but I can promise—I can *try*—to make it *good* again. I have to believe I'm capable of that."

"Then I have to believe it too."

Sunder reached for me, one last time. His hand brushed against mine. I flinched. He had to look away to hide the pain twisting his face into something desolate, broken, and more than a little monstrous.

FORTY-SEVEN

C oeur d'Or was so busy and full of activity that our return a week later was barely remarked upon.

The remaining members of La Discorde had been publicly executed. The sight of their gore-striped heads adorning spikes on the city gates striated my bones with cold-hot blades of fear and fury. Nausea punched holes in my stomach and bile seared my throat, but I refused to look away, forcing myself to memorize their agonized, disfigured faces.

This, I whispered to myself, *this is the price of failure.*

And when at last I turned away, I thanked the Scion that Luca's dark-curled head did not hang among them.

Carrousel was going forward as planned, preparations turning the palais into a carnival. The jardins bustled with tradespeople and artisans and artificers building grand pavilions and gazebos and magical mechanisms to transform the landscape. Trees and shrubbery swarmed with decorations: bright lanterns flapping like strange colored birds, streamers gossamer as captured cobwebs, white lights glittering like the stars of legend.

I went directly to my seamstress. I didn't have time to waste if I wanted the gown for my performance to be perfect. I tipped her handsomely to have the gown ready by the end of the week, and tipped her even better for her discretion.

Lullaby greeted me with narrowed eyes.

"Where have you been?" she demanded, and I fought the

urge to cry. I'd left her without a word, abandoning her like I'd abandoned *Thibo*—

No. Nothing I could have done would have saved Thibo. I gathered my memories of my friend into a precious bundle and stored them in the quietest corner of my mind. I'd grieved and would continue to grieve him. But the best thing I could do now was stick to the plan and make sure that murderous witch didn't steal any more of my friends.

I told Lullaby, as concisely as possible, about my time at Belsyre. About Sunder, and Bane, and Severine. Everything I knew. Everything we planned. How I hoped she'd fit into that plan.

When I was finished, Lullaby sat back against the divan. She barely looked surprised.

"I'm glad." Her mouth hardened. "I'm only sad Thibo isn't here to be a part of it. He's been talking about this for spans, he—" She broke off, and that determined mouth quivered. "He said he was in contact with a spy in Sinister, someone planning something big. He guessed it was Sunder. I always said he was insane. Shows you what I know about intrigue."

"I'm sorry. I'm sorry I was too late."

"Don't." Lullaby turned to look out the window, her gaze distant. "He used to say: *I reap what others have sown; I am the scythe they least expect.* I suppose now you—*we*—have to be that scythe."

I tamped down the flames of anger and pain and futility, glazing them along the facets of that ember smoldering beside my heart. A cinder that a single spark would reignite into an inferno of sunlight and perilous dreams, jewel-bright visions and monstrous hopes.

And when I left Lullaby with a strong embrace and a handful of instructions, I saw that fire reflected in her own water-blue eyes.

"Mirage?" she said as I turned away.

"Yes?"

"Make her pay for what she did to Thibo."

❋

A letter. A handful of écu here, and a few kembric livres there. Whispered conversations.

I signaled Luca with our old method of red handkerchiefs in the window, and when he stalked out to meet me along the Esplanade I told him about the plan. Just enough about the plan, just enough to get him excited, like I knew it would. His smile flashed sharp as a dagger forged in the red light of our sun. His eyes didn't flicker as he agreed to involve La Discorde, whose recent loss had only strengthened their resolve. He didn't even flinch when I told him he'd have to work with Sunder.

And that's when I knew my friend—the boy with the wild curls who somersaulted from Madame Rina's convoy and snuck me crusts of bread because he knew how hungry I was—was gone forever. He'd transformed into a man I'd once glimpsed long ago by the uneven light of a guttering cook fire. A man scarred by tragedy and transformed by rage, with death in his eyes and revolution in his soul.

My disappearance with the Suicide Twins was talked about, but not in the way I would have expected. As Sunder predicted, everyone at court assumed he and I were lovers. I tried not to dwell on the various twisted and unspeakable speculations regarding the nature of our relationship. Eyes raked my back when I passed through the corridors of Coeur d'Or, but I straightened my shoulders and lengthened my stride.

Sunder was—*Sunder*. He inhaled wine and exhaled insults. We saw each other at parties and salons and concerts, and if he leaned too close to whisper something in my ear, or curled a proprietorial hand around my waist, I only smiled, and simpered, and hid the bleak, delicious flare of heat burning through my veins.

What was it he said, that day beneath the pergola? *To sell the illusion.*

Because that's all it was. Yet another illusion in my growing repertoire of fancies and delusions. A cheap facsimile of something that, for a moment, felt real. *Was* real. Wasn't it? But even now, mere days after my time at Belsyre, those moments seemed to be slipping away, like a half-remembered dream. I closed my eyes, and tried to remember, but it was like reaching for someone else's memory. A broken promise, a good dream turned bad; blood on the snow where before there were red flowers.

So I focused on the plan. I ran through it again and again, every step, every illusion, over and over. I practiced it until I dreamed it. And then I practiced again.

FORTY-EIGHT

I paced the annex with the mosaic floor, my eyes trained on the frescoed ceiling. I tried to concentrate on the Sun in his sapphire throne, the Moon flanked by her star-eyed maidens. The Scion on his chariot of flames. But the images blurred behind the film of tears prickling hot at my eyes, and all I could think of was the first time I came to this room. Thibo, laughing at my ignorance. Thibo, dancing me across a map sparkling with gems and mica. I rubbed a thumb over the locket I'd started carrying in my pocket. Thibo—

"Don't cry on my account, demoiselle." A cool voice cut through my misery.

I whirled. Sunder stood across the mosaic of the daylight world, clad in a kembric-gilded waistcoat so bright he could have been the Scion himself. For the first time in days, his entourage of Sinister lords and ladies was nowhere to be seen.

"We met here, once," Sunder mused, his tone bittersweet. His polished boots carried him across the Dusklands toward the Meteor Mountains, where my jeweled slippers nudged tiles of onyx and opal.

"I remember," I muttered. Uncertainty battled with a sour, brittle yearning. "Didn't you accuse me of pawning your money for tacky gowns?"

"Maybe." He smiled, whisper-thin. "But you accused me of defiling innocent horses."

I choked on a laugh. Mirth tinted with old embarrassment

chased away the last tatter of my sorrow. "More fool you for matching wits with me."

"A lesson I've learned time and again." His boots paused by my slippers. His dristic-edged eyes searched mine, but he didn't touch me. "And you were dancing that day, were you not? With your friend. With Thibo."

I opened my mouth to correct him, to explain that Thibo was only showing me the map. But Sunder suddenly bowed, hand out and palm up. I hesitated, staring at the long, elegant fingers, the ridge of callus where a sword hilt fit. His hand trembled in an unspoken question.

I bit my lip, and slid my hand into the curl of his palm.

A thrill sang up my arm. The world tilted on its axis as he dipped me, the brush of his hands at my waist featherlight. He swirled me across the mosaic, the tiles blurring in a circle of kembric and blue. He was deft, deliberate, stepping in time to the echoes of some forgotten music. I drifted, my feet barely touching the floor, hypnotized by the measured sway and dip of our first dance.

He eased me back into a niche between two pillars. I gasped in a breath of that sharp, clean scent of him. He closed the gap between us. I could hear the thud of his heart, too fast. His lips brushed my ear, sending a shiver dancing toward the base of my skull. My mind went smooth and hard with desire.

"Someone requires your presence," he murmured. The wall behind us clicked audibly, then swung open.

I stumbled and almost fell into the cramped, dingy room behind me. A single ambric lamp lent a fitful glow. A dark shadow loomed, light glinting off oval spectacles.

Dowser.

I set my jaw and glared at Sunder, who leaned against the wall and avoided my eyes. I'd evaded my teacher since I'd gotten back from Belsyre, because I knew what he'd say about all this. He'd tell me—

"You're not ready!" he roared, slamming his fist on the table. As my eyes adjusted to the dimness, I saw he was incandescent with rage. Angrier than I'd ever seen him. "The time isn't right!"

"What do you propose?" I snapped. Exhaustion and grief and duplicity cut my fuse short. "Wait another seventeen tides for you to leave that smoke-filled study and discover how to defeat your old lover?"

He stiffened. "You are an absolute fool if you think you can face the empress and survive."

"How would you know what I can survive?" The old resentment stirred, smooth and polished by tides of use. "You abandoned me at the edge of the world to wait patiently for a destiny that might never come. Out there they treated me like a monster, a freak. They reviled and abused me for the one thing that made me strong. But I survived. I traveled halfway across the world. I fought tooth and nail for everything I've been given. This is me fighting to create the world I want to live in. You have no right to tell me I'm not ready for that."

"*The world you want to live in?*" His voice was appalled. "By the Scion, you actually *want* this. Not just to oust the empress, but to take her place."

"I do." My skin flared hot and cold. "I will remake this world. It's my birthright."

"The birthright of the Sabourin dynasty is lust and blood and death. After everything I taught you, is that who you want to be?"

"Take me or leave me," I snarled. "I know you'll do your part regardless."

He rocked back on his heels, shocked into silence. I turned on my heel. I was tired of going around in circles. Everything had already been decided.

"When you first came," Dowser whispered. Something in his voice stopped me in my tracks. "When you first came, I thought you were like your father. Lavish, but generous. Unthinking, but brave. Selfish, but ultimately kind. But every day I see it more and more. The single-minded pursuit of a world only you desire. A world only you can see." He took a deep breath. "You're just like her."

Ice crackled the length of my spine when I realized who he meant. "You don't mean that."

"You're right: I will do my part." His voice trembled, then cracked. "But I hope you are very careful when you look your sister in the eye. You don't want to see yourself staring back."

Outrage and grief and a terrible sucking dread filled the cavern of my heart. I felt Sunder lift his eyes to my face.

"Dark seeks dark, Mirage," Dowser whispered, and his words were like a song of undoing, an elegy for a disappointed hope. "And pain seeks pain."

My gaze slashed up. Sunder's eyes crackled with ice, and again I glimpsed that unending expanse of desolation held back by pure, steely will. Cold fire and a monstrous longing crackled in the air between us.

I shoved out into the annex, gasping for breath like I'd been underwater. I stalked away without looking behind me, choking on bitterness and conviction and the glass-bright shards of soul-deep fear.

FORTY-NINE

arrousel arrived at last.

A Matin like any other, except for the buzz of anticipation buoying Coeur d'Or. The sky was clear, strung with distant clouds of lavender and mauve. Even the sun seemed to pulsate with slow excitement.

My handmaidens helped me prepare for the day. Sunder had bribed Severine's hairdresser with an astonishing amount of livres to divulge the style the empress requested for the day, and I asked Louise to imitate the same coiffure. It took shape slowly, a complicated tower of curls and braids, elegant and bold. I did my own cosmetics, lining my eyes in heavy kohl and glossing my lips until they were ripe and plump. I took kembric leaf I bought off an artificer and spread it along the contours of my face: the edge of my hairline, the tops of my cheekbones. I dusted crushed gold powder along my collarbones, the line of my nose, and my décolletage, until I glimmered like a gilt statue in the red light filtering through the window.

Elodie cinched my corset until I was gasping for breath, and helped me into the extravagant gown. The skirt was pure kembric, a cascade of liquid satin glowing molten in the lamplight. A bodice of thick black lace twisted up over a golden underlay, clinging tightly to the contours of my chest. A black capelet hung from my shoulders, with a deep hood. I didn't want to be recognized until my big reveal in front of the entire court.

The bells for Prime rang, and the gates to the palais thundered open. I couldn't hear it, but I could feel it in my bones—the juddering rush of hundreds of feet pouring across the pavement, up the stairs, into the palais. Boots tromping across the jardins, spectators crushing the shrubbery and peering into the ponds. Voices raised in eager chatter.

This was the custom: One day per tide, on Carrousel, the gates of Coeur d'Or swung open and anyone who could afford the entrance fee was allowed to come, and admire, and take part in the rollicking merriment organized by the Amber Empress and her court. Peasant, pauper, merchant, fool. All were welcome. Carrousel was a day when anyone could imagine they were anything. A housewife could imagine she was a beautiful courtesan, gowned in expensive silks and crowned in the jewels of her patrons. A lord could imagine he was a merchant stuffing his face with sausage and beer, with no lands or legacy to plague him. The secret child of a dead emperor could pretend she wasn't about to intentionally turn the world on its head. She could pretend she was the person she used to be: nobody.

I wandered through the festivities with my face hidden beneath my hood. It was strange to see the jardins and the Esplanade and the Hall of Portraits packed with strangers. Men and women jostled for space, clad in everything from plain cotton to velvet, linen to brocade. Strange, vain, elaborate costumes. Simple rags. Masks. Stilts. An air of merriment and revelry quickened my heartbeat and tightened my fists.

Pavilions erected on the lawn offered curiosities from distant lands: baubles, trinkets, ornaments, and oddities. A fortune-teller with eyes white as snow and hair forged from dristic promised true love for the low cost of one deadly secret. A troupe of tumbling children flipped and whirled, a motley, gymnastic rainbow. Hawkers peddled spices from across the sea: the powdered horn of an incubus, said to raise your mettle in the bedroom; the liquid tails of captured sea-stallions, guaranteed to speed any journey. Vials of flaming sand enchanted by a desert *d'haka*. Liquors to make you drunk; elixirs to turn you sober once more.

Near Compline, Skyclad chevaliers paraded along the Esplanade, their prancing destriers decked in armure chevaline, spiked armor forged from dristic and steel. The chevaliers' extravagant coats and polished armor sent spears of light to pierce at watching eyes, and the plumes dancing from their helms frothed like great clouds in hues of raspberry and tangerine.

Finally, the bells for second Compline rang, and the crowd hushed. Whispers sprinted around the edges of the courtyard as the merrymakers waited. Finally, someone pointed, and the crowd cheered, clapping and waving and howling at the palais.

From a balcony halfway up the tower Severine emerged, her gown glowing like its own sun in the brilliant light shining at her back. Her kembric crown was a stylized sunburst, alternating straight and curving rays to affect a gleaming corona around her head. She waved, and smiled, elegant and benevolent, then stepped off the edge of the balcony.

The crowd gasped. Someone shrieked.

Severine didn't fall. She floated gently down, her gown billowing and belling around her. She alit like a feather, her pointed slippers delicate on the manicured lawn.

The crowd roared its pleasure, and the empress curtsied deep, her violet eyes sparking. I peered at the balcony to see which legacies had been drafted to forge this illusion, but the courtiers lurked out of sight.

"Welcome!" she called. The onlookers quieted, craning and pushing. "The wonderful Fête du Carrousel returns once more.

Sample the delights we offer you, for nothing is too grand or too decadent on this festival day! And when you are sated, follow me to the Golden Grotto, where my most talented courtiers will entertain us all with the glory of their legacies!"

She curtsied once more, and again the crowd roared its approval. She danced across the lawn toward the little wilderness and the amphitheater beyond, where the evening's performances would be held. Ladies and gentlemen frolicked in her wake, but not too close—a platoon of Skyclad Gardes shadowed her every move, a grim reminder that even on this day of celebration, the empress didn't fully trust her own people.

I let the crowd part around me, and stared up at the balcony, letting my imagination soar. Severine's entrance was just a show. I knew it, and the crowd knew it. But everyone loved a show.

At least, that's what I was hoping.

❧

Past the Weeping Pools, the trees grew closer together, their untrimmed branches shadowing the sun. A narrow pathway coiled between the boughs, shimmering globes strung along the darkened trail. Veils of flowers festooned the trees, light and color swaying between the looming shadows of crooked branches. The scents of jasmin and lavender drifted thick in the languid air.

I trailed at the back of the crowd following Severine to the Grotto. Because of the famous wager and the buzz surrounding my performance, I'd been designated to appear last. I had an hour, if not two, before I had to prepare. I wanted to see a few of the other courtiers perform—Lullaby was singing, and I had missed her last concert—but part of me wanted to linger here, to savor my last moments of relative anonymity, before chaos descended and the world burst apart with noise and color.

I glanced quickly over my shoulder, then stepped off the pathway into the shadows. I lifted my skirts, moving quietly through the clinging underbrush, until I looked back and couldn't see the path anymore. I gazed upward through the reaching branches, glimpsing a sky stained with rust and wine. A sudden breeze sent leaves rustling on the trees, and I couldn't help but think of bare branches etched in pewter on a pale floating skirt, the nip of an icy wind, the steam of someone's breath mingling with my own.

A heavy hand fell on my shoulder.

I stifled a scream and spun on my heel. A dark hooded figure loomed between the trees. I swallowed my fear, steadying myself on the trunk of a tree. He wore all black. He knew what I was wearing. He was—

The figure held out a placatory hand and brushed the hood away from his face. Dark brown skin. A glimmer of spectacles.

A wave of residual anger crashed against sweeping disappointment. He wasn't who I hoped he would be.

"Dowser." The ragged edge of resentment made my throat hoarse. "What are you doing here? Come to scold me one last time?"

"Scion's breath, Mirage." He stepped closer, lowering the hood of my capelet with wary fingers. His eyes took in the kembric leaf slicked along my skin, the shimmer of golden dust along my neck, the elaborate coiffure. "You really do look like her."

"I have to get to the Grotto." Bitterness and misery made my voice foreign.

"I know," he murmured, and stepped away. His throat bobbed

as his hands folded into their black sleeves. "You must know I never meant to say those things. And I didn't mean a word."

Something collapsed inside me. "Yes, you did."

"Some of it," he amended. "But it's hard not to be frightened of how powerful you've become. This place has changed you. Not just your legacy, but your sense of self. You came here to fight for a place in this world where you thought you belonged. Now you fight for a new world—a world you think you can create. You are formidable in so many ways, Mirage. I only hope you can remember why you really want the things you strive for."

"I—" I choked on my words, casting my eyes to the jeweled hem of my dress and fighting for composure. "I understand what you're saying. But this place hasn't changed me. It's just given me the opportunity to show the world who I really am. And I won't apologize for being who I'm not. And never was."

"I remember I once said you were ambitious, arrogant, and even a little cruel." Dowser turned his eyes to the burnt sky high above. "I wasn't far off. But I hadn't realized yet how deeply the pains of this world reverberate inside you. How they are transformed, in you, into something sublime. Transcendent. That, Mirage, is your gift."

A fragile seed burst into tenuous bloom inside me. I tried hard not to think about another Nocturne. *Perhaps you want to show the world something only you can see. Something lovely, and strange, and just a little bit monstrous.*

"I just hope you remember how much good there is in this world, although too often it is obscured behind shadow and pain." His voice cracked with all the things he would never tell me. "I hope you remember how much good there is in *you*."

"I never wanted to be good," I muttered.

"That's what makes it so special." He smiled, a clear-glass swell of pure joy. "I want you to know how much it meant to me that you cared. About me. I never—" He cut off abruptly, staring at the ground and polishing his spectacles on his sleeve. His eyes gleamed with varnish. "I never had a child, Mirage. But—"

"I know," I whispered. The words were a strip of splintered wood tearing at my throat. "I know."

He leaned down, slowly, and brushed a breath of a kiss on my temple. Hot nettles prickled my eyes as I flung my arms around his neck. When he drew back, some of my makeup had smeared on his cheek, leaving a swathe of golden stars glittering against his night-dark skin.

"Here," I said. I couldn't help but laugh as I lifted a gloved thumb to swipe away the dust. "You'll give me away."

He chuckled, but we both knew it was for show.

Something made me reach into my pocket and draw out a small velvet pouch. I placed it in Dowser's palm, and before I could change my mind, I curled his fingers around it.

"Keep it for me," I whispered. "You'll know what to do with it, if anything—if anything happens."

He nodded, grave. "Please, Mirage. Be careful. If not for your sake, then for mine."

"I promise."

He disappeared between the trees, silent as a wraith. But as I turned and faced toward the Grotto, I felt like an iron band had been unfastened from my heart, and I smiled through the film of tears turning the world soft as watercolors.

FIFTY

The Golden Grotto was riotous with light. Built into the edge of an old quarry, the amphitheater rose in sloping tiers. Hidden fountains gurgled and plashed, releasing the scents of fresh mint and spring water. Hundreds of floating lanterns mixed a cool white glow with the red burn of the sun. The crowd was raucous and merry, half-drunk and well pleased by the performances of the empress's captive legacies: a festive aria sung by a radiant Lullaby, whose dulcet tones had most of them dancing like enchanted marionettes in the aisles; a watery display by River, who floated undulating globes and sent liquid javelins lancing in great arcs; Tangle, who grew an entire brambled jardin into a spiky château, then made giant blossoms float to the heavens like colorful balloons.

And finally, my turn came.

An uneasy silence fell as I stepped out onto the stage. I was still wearing my cloak and hood, but I heard a few murmurs about my dress, so similar to the empress's outfit. I cut my eyes to the great lady herself, careful to keep my face out of the light. She perched on the top tier of the theater, voluminous skirts arrayed and sunburst crown gleaming. Courtiers fawned over her.

The lacquered ruby sleeping by my heart spat a spark.

Strains of music rose from the edge of the stage: the Meridian Suite, by a composer well known in court. The piece began slowly as I lifted my arms and surrendered to my illusion.

Night. A swathe of purest black, impenetrable save for

distant stars prickling like chips of diamond. I made the night vast, stretching from one end of the amphitheater to the other, blocking out the sun. I imagined the Midnight Dominion, and it was so.

A soft moan of appreciation rose from the crowd.

I showed them the moon, drifting pale and cold and distant across the night. And then I shifted the night into day, black bleeding slowly into red, bleeding slowly into bright, eye-stinging blue at true Prime. I'd never seen such a sky, but then, I'd never seen true night either. And in that azure sweep I put the sun, a giant globe of pulsating orange.

The crowd gasped, and clapped.

I spun the illusion, slow then fast. Dawn, day, dusk, night. Day. Night. Sun. Moon. And as I spun I subtly transformed the sun and moon into figures—people, dressed in elaborate costumes. I finished the metamorphosis, placing the figures at opposite ends of the amphitheater, facing each other across the dusk.

The crowd murmured, a touch uneasily.

They finally understood what I was doing. It was a modified version of the Meridian story, the legend we'd all heard so many times from the cradle that most of us could recite it verbatim. But I'd altered it. Instead of making the Moon a lovely woman floating in a pearly palais, I'd made her a man, clad in a fine silvery coat. He wore an elaborate plumed hat, and a mask shaped like adjoining crescents covered his face. And instead of making the Sun a man—a king in a golden château—I'd made the Sun a woman. More specifically, I'd made the Sun Severine—the illusion wore her radiant gown and elaborate hairstyle, bedecked in a sunburst circlet. The only difference: The Sun wore a kembric mask around her sparking violet eyes.

I chanced a glance at the empress, but she just swept her fan in slow circles around her smiling face.

I reenacted the legend of Meridian. The Sun chased the foppish Moon, but he rebuffed her love. Now that the story was well under way, the crowd was enjoying itself again, laughing and clapping at the charade. Finally, the Sun grew angry and sour, heartbroken that the Moon would not be hers.

The crowd grew somber. Everyone knew this part.

I made Meridian a towering Skyclad Garde. There was the flaming chariot, the weapons forged to catch and destroy the Moon. I projected a glorious, heartrending chase across the sky: a flaming star inscribing an elegant arc in the night, a long tail of sparks streaming out behind it. The Moon fled, flickering between his phases, but the dristic-clad lord was too slow. At last, the chariot approached the Moon.

The crowd held a single breath.

But my Meridian didn't fall in love in a single glance. He didn't spare the Moon. He didn't fall to earth with his weapons of destruction. My Meridian caught the Moon. His net of glittering kembric snared the dancing lord, crushing his curling hat feather and bearing him to the ground. Meridian lashed the lord to his chariot and flew him back to the Sun.

Uncertainty pulsed through the watching revelers. This was an unfamiliar twist. I dared another glance at the empress. She was no longer smiling. Her fan flicked like the tail of an irritated house cat.

I took a deep breath, and focused all my energy on the next part of the illusion.

The Sun empress stepped from her shining throne to where the Moon lord knelt at her feet. She yanked the hat off his head, spinning him to face the audience and exposing his features for all the world to see. There was cropped red-brown hair. A trim beard on a handsome—if grizzled—face. And piercing, wise eyes a shade somewhere between grey and violet: a shade darker than my own blue-grey eyes, a shade paler than the empress's stunning gaze.

It was Sylvain, the old and very dead emperor. I'd studied his portrait for hours, searing the image of my murdered father into the flesh of my brain. I faced him toward the audience long enough for the crowd to react.

An anxious laugh. A shriek of surprise. Severine rose to her feet.

The empress's fantasy doppelgänger took a dagger from her waist and plunged the blade into her father's heart. A fountain of blood spurted out, drenching the onlookers seated in the first row with phantom gore. They scattered and jumped away, even though the scarlet droplets were nothing but illusion.

Chaos erupted. The crowd surged to its feet, shouting and screaming. I thought I heard clapping, and a possible roar of approval, and a grim smile crossed my face when I turned my gaze to the empress. She was livid with fury, snarling orders at her courtiers and her Skyclad bodyguards. Three of the silver-cloaked soldats detached from the phalanx and pushed through the crowd.

Time for the final act.

I dissolved the illusion, and the Sun and the Moon and Meridian all faded like a lover's promise. There was only me, standing cloaked and gowned at the center of the stage. The crowd quieted, waiting to see what I would do. Even the Skyclad Gardes slowed their booted steps. Would I plead for my life or shout murder at the empress? Would I weep, or laugh, or rant like a madwoman?

Would it all be a strange joke, a twisted prank among bored aristos?

Behind me, the music swelled. Slowly, theatrically, I drew back my hood and let the cape fall. The crowd leaned in, confused. My hair, though a few shades darker than Severine's, was coiled in the precise manner of their empress. A sunburst circlet sat on my head. A golden mask covered my features. With one smooth gesture, I tore away the black lace overlay of my gown. The cloth whispered to the ground, exposing a gown identical to Severine's.

Silence hung thick enough to choke.

I reached into the pocket I had specially commissioned on my counterfeit dress and drew out my ambric pendant, the Relic everyone seemed so eager to possess. It glinted dully in the light, rotating gently on the end of its golden chain.

At the top of the amphitheater, Severine's violet eyes went wide with rage and greed.

I pulled off the glittering mask obscuring my features and dropped it to the ground. There was no mistaking me now—without the mask I was most assuredly not the empress. My grey-blue eyes were closer set, my skin more tanned, my lips fuller. Anyone who lived in the Amber City—a city emblazoned with banners sporting their ruler's face—would know in an instant that I wasn't the empress.

I was just announcing to the world that I ought to be.

The Grotto exploded with noise. People rushed toward and away from the stage, shouting and roaring in a maelstrom of emotion. Severine was no longer content to let her lackeys do her bidding; she hiked her voluminous skirts to her knees and marched down the tiered theater, murder in her eyes and destruction in her soul.

I was so focused on the empress striding through the humanity churning at her feet that I nearly didn't see the Skyclad soldat remove a crossbow from his back and notch a bolt. The string drew back. The trigger pulled.

A straight, true shot. The arrow flew toward my pale breast, exposed above the plunging neckline of the replica gown. The bolt pierced skin, flesh, bone. I fell backward.

And dissolved into a cloud of fantasy and imagination.

The real me stepped out of the shadows at the edge of the stage, still clad in a cape and black lace. I held up the pendant and gave it a gentle swing. The empress screamed, her eyes venomous with spite. The Skyclad Gardes drew their weapons and loped toward me.

Now, I whispered in my head. I imagined the thought winging out across the palais jardins, piercing stone and marble and amber to hit its mark. *Now, Dowser.* NOW.

A half mile away, Coeur d'Or exploded with a rumbling thrum that shook the earth and sent a cloud of fire and ash climbing toward the sky.

FIFTY-ONE

M elee.

Shouting. Screaming. Wailing. Shoving.

The Skyclad twisted to stare at the plume of smoke disfiguring the red sky, their usually impassive faces distorted with confusion and fear. Only the empress stalked forward, her eyes fixed on me and the dull glow of the Relic around my neck.

I turned on my heel and left the Grotto, heading in the opposite direction of the explosion. I counted—*one, two, three*—then glanced over my shoulder. Severine followed, hunger in her eyes and only two Skyclad at her shoulder. She must have sent the rest to the palais.

I quickly turned myself invisible as I sent a copy of myself streaking across the lawn at an angle. She was fast, and the Skyclad Gardes didn't hesitate before giving chase, cocking their crossbows and moving with practiced ease. Only the empress paused, her eyes fixed to the spot where she'd seen me standing a moment ago. She'd noticed what the Skyclad Garde had not— my illusory double wasn't wearing the Relic.

Trust Severine to notice the difference.

I winked back into view. Severine frowned and whirled to call her guards, but they were already out of earshot, chasing their false prey. I kicked off my heels and took off at a trot, brutally aware that the real me was much less graceful than my imaginary twin. I had to trust that my actual half sister was seventeen tides older, hours drunker, and more burdened by her voluminous skirts than the dress I'd had specially made for tonight.

I led her across the lawn and through the trees, cursing my heavy legs and thumping heart. I shed first my hooded cape, then the swathe of black lace differentiating my gown from Severine's. How strange we must look, if anyone were to see us: two nearly identical women in identical outfits, sprinting across the palais jardins like the world depended on it.

I choked on a breathless, bitter laugh. Maybe the world did depend on it.

I reached the Solarium with strides to spare. The empress was flagging, her long train slowing her progress. I dashed into the pavilion, darting my gaze around the arched room. I'd had Sunder's men shift the high mirrors, angling and tilting them in a design of my own concoction. I just hoped my calculations were correct.

I spared an anxious moment to catch my breath and calm the reedy thrum of my heart. Then I darted to the back of the room, slid behind a mirror, and projected myself throughout the circular room. I made two of me, four of me, eight: the angled mirrors made me sixteen, twenty-eight, fifty.

I was legion.

I waited, trembling in the corner, for Severine to arrive. And in some twisted corner of my mind, I heard Sunder's voice, tight with irony and rich with humor.

Finally, not-Sunder drawled. *Mirage earns her name.*

And even though I knew it wasn't really Sunder, even though I knew it was some crazed corner of my fearful mind playing tricks on me, the words sent a veil of calm settling over my frayed nerves.

The empress burst into the Solarium, and stopped dead. I almost laughed at the look on her face, but the laugh died on my lips when I saw her eyes narrow and murder creep back into her gaze. She stalked toward the center of the room, examining each of my replicas in turn.

I didn't skimp. A copy of the Relic hung around each doppelgänger's neck. It took all of my concentration, but each time she approached one of the illusions, I had it back away. All the others twisted and shifted in different directions, their reflections spinning in a kaleidoscope of echoing reflection and deflection.

It worked. Irritation and confusion twisted the calm mask on my sister's face, transforming her into a vengeful demon.

"Come out, you coward!" she shouted, her fluted voice loud in the cavernous space. "Are you going to hide from me all Nocturne? Or are you too afraid to face a woman twice your age, unarmed and unguarded?"

I gritted my teeth and settled deeper into my crouch, fighting the flare of pride her words ignited. I knew she was trying to bait me into fighting her on equal footing, but that wasn't going to happen. I needed to buy Dowser, Sunder, and Luca more time. And I needed to find out how Severine's legacy manifested. If we couldn't find a way to defeat her power, then all of this would be for nothing.

I nudged one of my replicas forward to turn and frown at the empress. She lifted her gold-dusted arms in a placating gesture. I spoke, and in the echoing room, it was impossible to tell where my voice came from.

"I'm frightened," said the copy. "I didn't know it would go this far. If I surrender, will you grant me mercy?"

Light sparked in the empress's lucent eyes, and she crossed to the illusion in two fast strides. Her hands lashed up, so fast I barely saw them move. One grabbed for the Relic, and the other curled into a claw latching around the illusion's throat.

The other me dissolved into mist. The copies around her shifted and turned, their reflections rotating in a disorienting rush.

Severine screamed, the inhuman sound exploding from her mouth and reverberating around the room. I gasped, clapping my hands over my ears and fighting for control. I tried to sort through what I had just witnessed. When Severine thought she had me in her reach, she went straight for the Relic. But she also reached for my throat, like she wanted to choke me. Like the Nocturne of the Blood Rain Ball, when she'd wrapped blood-tipped nails around the throat of a man I'd thought was her lover.

I wasn't big, and I didn't know how to fight. But I was nearly the same height as my half sister, and with her slender frame and slim arms, I didn't doubt I could break her hold in an instant. So her legacy was either enhanced strength, or—

What? What else?

Think, Mirage, think, I whispered to myself. *Time is running out.*

"I know who you are!" called the livid empress. She stalked through the labyrinth of mirrors and illusion, her composure untangling as her patience faded. "You're one of his brats! One of the many litters whelped on his kennel full of bitches."

I caught my lower lip between my teeth, and tried to smother the kernel of fury spitting sparks. *Not yet.*

"I should have noticed," she continued. "You look like him. You even look a little like me, if I'm feeling especially generous. But mostly, you look like her. Madeleine Allard, wasn't it? The one who *almost* got away. I say almost because she didn't, of course. Do you know, she begged to trade her life for yours, in the end? Before she bled out slowly on the steps of a cloister." She chuckled. "Isn't that ironic? Maybe if she'd gone to the nunnery first she wouldn't have gotten herself knocked up with my father's indiscriminating seed."

Something tore inside me. Flames licked at my heart.

"Yes, you look like her. The same unfocused ignorance around your close-set little eyes. The same vulgar air of entitlement, like the world owes you something. She thought she deserved special treatment because she rutted with royalty. Well, she got what she deserved. It just wasn't what she expected."

A hot tear squeezed down the ridge of my nose.

"And you," she screamed. She punched one of my illusions, haphazardly, and missed. I wished I could make the replica punch her back on my behalf. "That's what all this is about, isn't it? You think you deserve *my* throne because you were born with *his* blood in your veins. Blood means *nothing*. He thought his blood kept him safe. He sat on his throne with his merciful laws and moderate policies, and delegated the empire away to his Council while he tried to bed every girl who'd have him. He thought he deserved what he was given just because he was born to it."

"And you weren't?" The cinder pulsed hotter. My voice echoed from every direction. "You were a dauphine. An heir to an empire. Isn't that the definition of bloodline? Of entitlement?"

"I would never have sat on that throne if I hadn't earned it," Severine snarled. "I never wanted what I was born to—*second in line*. No one deserves anything. The only things worth having are the things you take."

"Don't you mean steal?" I screamed. My voice rasped hoarse, and I knew I should be more careful, but the kernel of rage had splintered into chips of ruby, singeing my veins. "You stole your brother's life. You stole your father's life. You stole the lives of countless children for no other reason than your own self-loathing. You're nothing but a thief."

Her high-pitched cackle spangled through the room.

"I'd wager more thieves wish they could brag of the bounty of an empire."

"And I suppose you'd have to be a thief," I shouted. A voice inside me kept telling me *Stop, no, it's too soon*, but I was incandescent. Too hot, too bright. "Since you have no legacy. There's no use pretending you even know how to use this Relic." I forced myself to laugh, and it was a wretched, savage sound. "You may rule an empire, but you can never steal the one thing that even the lowliest of legacies possesses: *magic*."

"You have no idea what you're talking about!" Severine screamed at the ceiling.

"You're giftless!" I continued, savage. "Not one magical bone in your body. Or perhaps it's a pathetic legacy so useless you'd be derided until the day you died! Why else hide it, unless it's so weak you can't bear anyone to know what it is?"

Severine stood quiet for a bare second, surrounded on all sides by copies of me. Then she thrust her arms outward.

The room exploded.

A hundred angled mirrors burst instantly, sending needles of glass winging into every corner of the room. I threw my arms up in time to protect my eyes, but shards of pain erupted along my bare arms, in the small of my back, the base of my neck. I sucked a sharp breath of air into paralyzed lungs, and when I lowered my stinging arms Severine was standing right over me. A long shard of mirrored glass smiled silver against her palm.

"Say hello to our brothers and sisters for me," she snarled, and slashed her makeshift dagger toward my throat.

FIFTY-TWO

Instinct pushed me out of the way and rolled me along the floor.

I felt the wind as the dagger sliced by my ear. Lines of pain flared along my waist and shoulders as scattered mirror shards cut me. I was on my feet in a moment, crouched low in the tatters of my once beautiful gown.

"No legacy?" The empress smiled. "Wrong guess."

She lifted her arms, and the piles of broken glass trembled and lifted, hovering in the air like a frozen rain of tiny daggers. I conjured up four illusions of myself, and sent them running around the room as I dashed for the door.

But Severine was smart. She sent the shards flashing through the air toward the real me, the only one who fled straight for the door. I cursed my panicked idiocy, and flattened myself to the floor.

A thousand needles whistled inches above my head. Fear was a tremulous pulse forcing me up, pushing me up by my bleeding palms, revving my flailing muscles. *Run.* I took off for the door, but the heavy slab slammed shut in my face. I pounded my bloody hands against the door. It didn't budge. I whirled, planting my stinging back against the wood.

"You have something I want," purred the empress. She stalked closer. She didn't seem to mind that her hand was slick with blood where the mirrored shard dug into her palm. Her violet eyes glued to the cabochon of ambric bouncing above my breast. "Give it willingly and perhaps I'll be merciful, in the end."

"How stupid do you think I am?" I hissed through my teeth. Every breath stung—one of my ribs must have broken.

"Very, very stupid," she said as she took one final step and grabbed at the Relic.

Her blood-slicked fingers brushed through empty air, dissolving the illusion like mist and leaving smears of red across my chest.

"Not that stupid," I croaked. I launched myself at my half sister, barreling into her with all the force of the rage and fear and pain boiling up inside me. She screamed as she fell, and we tumbled across the floor, shredding our gowns and flaying our skin. She scrabbled at me with sharp fingernails, slashing across my face. My head snapped back. I fought for a grip around her wrists, but she was stronger than she looked. She slapped my fumbling hands away and jerked her clawed hands toward my neck.

"Nothing that is mine will ever be yours," she snarled. "But know that I will steal everything you ever loved."

Her fingers encircled my neck. Her nails dug sharp grooves in my skin, and she squeezed. She was strong, viciously so. The room blurred.

Nothing but a thief.

My hands flailed at my side, even as my vision darkened. Distantly, I felt the prickle of tiny shards against my fingertips. Prick. Snick. Slide.

In the weightless, vital space between breath and blood, I heard an echo of Thibo's voice: *We are all thieves here.*

A long laceration along my hand jolted me. I blinked at the ceiling. A chunk of the central mirror remained intact, and I saw a woman in a kembric dress throttling the life out of another woman in a kembric dress. Blood-tipped nails left welts against her bare throat.

Nothing but a thief.

I thought of disappearing courtiers, of sand and blood and bramble, of Thibo's empty, staring eyes. And then I felt as though I was being lifted out of myself, my colored heartbeats separating and floating apart. Weightless, as though something warmer than air and more vital than blood was being lifted from my chest.

I am the scythe they least expect.

Thibo had stolen memories. What if—

A firework epiphany exploded in my mind. Severine wasn't trying to murder me. She was trying to *steal my legacy.*

My hand closed around a shard of glass.

Somewhere, someone dreamed of dying.

That someone wasn't me.

We are all thieves here.

I tightened my hand. Pain carved through my bones, but I bit down on the final scrap of myself left and lifted the shard. It slipped against my bloody palm.

I shoved it home.

Severine grunted, and loosened her grip. Air rushed into my lungs. Warmth spilled down the front of my dress, but it wasn't my blood.

It wasn't my blood.

Consciousness returned in a spiral of pain so agonizing and brutal that for the sparest moment I wished I had died. I rolled my sister's jerking body off me. She flopped back onto the glass-littered floor, staring at the ceiling. A long needle of broken mirror winked at me from its home deep between her ribs. Her mouth worked. She coughed, wetly, and a bubble of blood splattered down her chin.

"Scion curse you," I spat at her. "I hope our siblings are happy to see you."

FIFTY-THREE

I limped to my feet. The door swung open at my touch. Outside, the world was red and smoke-tinged, stained with distant sounds of screaming. My head spun, but I sucked in deep breaths of air until my wooden limbs moved and I didn't think I was going to collapse.

The trek back to Coeur d'Or was torment. I could barely move; every inch of me hurt, and each step sent flares of pain smashing against the back of my skull. My slashed palms dripped steady rivulets of blood onto the grass. My dress was so shredded that it hardly counted as clothing, but I wouldn't have cared even if my body didn't feel like someone had flayed me, then boiled me.

Finally, the trees cleared and the Esplanade swam into view.

What was left of the Esplanade.

A whole wing of the palais was burned away to nearly nothing. Splashes of red marked where fire still burned amid the rubble. Thick black smoke climbed away from the charred hunk of what was once expensive marble and gilt.

Luca's diversion, timed precisely to coincide with the finale of my illusory drama, and set to blast its way into the vault buried at the heart of the palais. The vault where Dowser suspected the empress's other Relic was stashed. It was the other half of our careful plan, and the signal to Lullaby and all the other sympathetic legacies to drop what they were doing and keep the Skyclad Gardes from getting to Severine, Dowser, or Luca.

Sorrow and regret and a blistering disappointment stitched

cold threads down my spine. Was this what it took, to remake a world? Was this what change looked like, in a world forged of metal and stone instead of flimsy wishes? This wasn't what I'd dreamed.

I tried to hurry my hobbling pace. I skirted the worst of the damage, ducking into an unharmed hallway and coughing against the spume of black smoke clogging my lungs. The palais churned in disarray. I heard the sounds of distant shouting. Servants and Gardes sprinted by me in the opposite direction, but I couldn't tell what was going on. How long was I gone? My clash with Severine felt like an eternity, but it could have been mere moments, or an hour. I had no idea.

Anxiety pushed through the haze of pain clouding my thoughts. Sunder was supposed to come to the Solarium when he was done rallying Sinister to his cause. Luca too. Anyone who wasn't fighting was supposed to retreat to the Solarium, in case I needed help against the empress.

No one had come.

I quickened my steps, pushing through the agony tearing me from the inside out. Hallways flashed by, marred by grim scenes of destruction. Skyclad Gardes, facedown and bloodied. Courtiers, unrecognizable beneath the curling feathers on their fine velvet hats. Smoke. Ash. Blood.

Too much blood.

I recognized the golden torches grasped in motionless hands. Dowser's chambers. I limped faster, reaching for the dark wooden door that had become so familiar to me.

"Mirage!"

The voice was distraught, thick with tears. I spun. Lullaby nearly barreled into me, a flurry of black hair and blue skin and blood. Blood on her hands. Tears cutting long trails through the soot on her cheeks.

A slab of iron sank into my stomach. Bile surged toward a throat already tightening with fear.

"Everything went wrong," she wept. "Come quickly. Sunder's hurt."

I forgot my pain and flew on my friend's heels as she dashed through the palais. She hurried me through the vast doors of the Atrium. I heard the thunder of them being barred behind us.

Entering the Atrium was like plunging into a nightmare. The cavernous chamber was thick with smoke. Sooty sunlight crept in through shattered windows; colored glass lay smashed on the floor. The cinders of burnt flowers hung like shrouds from the walls, filling my nostrils with an acrid stench.

Sunder lay halfway up the dais, prone in Bane's lap. Her shaking hand held a bloodied bandage to his ribs. Red stained his lips, and his breath rattled.

"No," I whispered. I fell to my knees beside him. My hands fluttered, useless. I grabbed one of his limp hands in my own. "No!"

"He was badly hurt," murmured Dowser, and I jumped to find him looming behind me, grave and severe. "His injuries are beyond my medical abilities. We need to find a healer at once."

"How—?" I choked on a bitter mixture of tears and blood. "What happened?"

"The explosion collapsed one of the passageways," spat Luca. He paced along a shallow tier, hands shoved deep in his pockets. He looked unhurt, but bitterness twisted his features. "Sunder's legacies were cut off from La Discorde. It was a blood-bath. The Skyclad Gardes slaughtered my men out of hand."

"What about the dissident legacies?"

"The ones that weren't killed in the blast dispersed," said Lullaby. "It was the right thing to do—in all the chaos the Gardes won't know which courtiers aren't loyal to the empress."

"And you?" I glanced up at Dowser. Dismay slowed my blood to an anxious trickle. "Did you find the other Relic?"

The older man gave his head one hard shake. He lifted my ambric necklace out of his pocket, the velvet-wrapped Relic I'd left with him for safekeeping. "This is still the only one I know of."

"Then it was all for nothing?" My voice came out high and hysterical as I took the amulet from Dowser. I squeezed Sunder's hand, hard. "Nothing happened the way it was supposed to."

"You're alive," groaned Sunder. His eyes glinted between slitted lashes. "And strong enough to crush the bones in my hand to dust. So that's something."

My hand flew to my mouth. Tears burned the back of my throat.

"Lullaby!" I called. She was at my side in an instant. "Do you know if any of the legacies still alive are healers? Vida, maybe?"

"Maybe." Her mouth flattened into a line. "But they're scattered. I don't know where anyone is."

"Please," I whispered. A tear squeezed beneath my eyelids. "Please find someone to help him."

Her eyes flickered toward the blond lord, leaking blood on the marble. I could almost hear the mental tally of Sunder's past sins as Lullaby pondered my request. Finally, she nodded.

"For you, Mirage." And she disappeared into Coeur d'Or.

"What happened to you?" Bane snapped. "I hope Severine came out worse for wear. If that's possible."

"I killed her," I whispered. The dam broke, sending a waterfall of pain and misery and ashy disenchantment gushing down my cheeks. For a long while, all I could do was cry, replaying the moment like a bad dream. Her hands digging into my neck. The shard of mirror lacerating my palm. Stab. Gush.

Finally, I tuned back in. Thunder shook the Atrium doors: the stomp of boots and the shouts of Gardes.

"We'll stay with you." Bane wept over her twin brother. "Lullaby's finding you a healer."

"Dowser and I will be fine," croaked Sunder. "Go with Mirage. She needs your help more than I do."

"What?" I jerked my head up and dashed the tears from my cheeks. "No one's leaving. The empress is dead. I'm Sylvain's daughter. I have to declare my intention to ascend the throne immediately."

"That's too dangerous," said Dowser. "The Skyclad have taken the palais. If they see you, they will kill you."

"He's right," growled Luca, still pacing like a wild animal. "Even looking like you do, that dress is too recognizable. If the empress is truly dead, the best thing we can do is retreat and regroup."

"Astonishingly," managed Sunder, "I agree with him. You need to go. Belsyre. Our militia can protect you. Wait until I send word. You're our jewel in the crown, our one shot at doing this right. We need you to stay safe."

"And I need you to stay safe!"

"Dowser is above suspicion," Sunder croaked. "As for me, even if I was seen with the dissident legacies, we're all too valuable to be butchered out of hand. And I've never met a dungeon guard who couldn't be bought with the right amount of kembric."

"But—" I leaned closer, fighting another spill of tears. "I can't leave you. Not like this."

His free hand drifted up to hover over my cheekbone, where crinkled kembric foil peeled away like burnt skin. "I'll survive," he said, and smiled. Even though his teeth were bloody and his hair was black with soot, he was beautiful. "I always do."

"We need to go," urged Luca. "*Sylvie.*"

"*That's not my name,*" I cried, fighting back anguish. A cool touch brushed against my wrist, soothing.

"Come here, demoiselle," whispered Sunder. His eyes were distant, clouded with pain. I leaned in, and he wrapped shaking fingers around the sides of my face. An ache numbed my skin and clenched my teeth, but for once I didn't care. I was wracked with so much pain already that a little more wouldn't kill me.

"I'm here," I choked out, resting my forehead against his. His eyes fluttered shut.

"I know this isn't what you wanted," he rasped. "This isn't the world you dreamed of, long ago in that pallid dusk."

I choked on a soot-stained hallucination of a perfect city, a perfect life.

"But you deserve the chance to live in that world," he said. "You deserve a chance to create it. And even if I can't be redeemed, I *know* you can be."

He struggled to sit up, propping himself onto his elbows. He leaned forward, and brushed his lips against mine.

I plummeted into the kiss. I didn't care that we both tasted of blood and desperation, or that pain needled my skin from a hundred shallow wounds. I fell like I'd never dared to fall before—through a riot of bright, fragile hopes toward a cool promise of belonging.

"My monster," he whispered against my mouth. "Show me what you dream, when you dream of new worlds."

And he cut his gaze to the hulking ambric throne sitting empty at the top of the dais.

I climbed the shallow steps with shaking footsteps. I brushed my palm against the smooth beveled surface, polished smooth and glowing from within. It hummed against my hand. The amulet between my breasts throbbed. I turned, hesitant, and sank down onto the sleek, curving throne.

Radiance painted my bones in sunlight and drowned my eyes in dusk. I roared with the prismatic pulse, sending threads of light and shadow toward the corners of the room. A covenant of colors: Dominion's black heart, warming to violet; crimson glow against pale ambric; sanded kembric and sheer towering blue; dristic and genévrier and cold white. And at its center breathed a city. A city gilded with kembric and bathed in amber light. A city sharp as a wish and dazzling as a secret. A city where I dreamed of belonging, and where that dream came true.

I smiled into the blinding promise of what might never be. I smiled, and engraved an oath upon my heart with lines of amber fire.

It might not be today, or tomorrow. I would wait a thousand tides if I had to. But I would show this world my dream. My dream of a world that was lovely, and strange . . . and just a little bit monstrous.

ACKNOWLEDGMENTS

Publishing this book is a dream come true for me. But there were times I felt like I was sleepwalking more than anything else, and if it weren't for the incredible support of so many people, I would probably have fallen to the bottom of a (metaphorical) well.

To my amazing editor, Lisa Sandell, for seeing what this book could be, instead of what it was, and easing me through that transition so smoothly that it almost felt effortless. I cannot thank you enough for your enduring faith in Mirage's world, even when it felt like mine was flagging. To Olivia Valcarce, for always knowing what I was trying to say even when the words on the page weren't quite there yet—your intuition is invaluable. And to Scholastic, for taking a chance on me, and this book I love so much.

To the entire Curtis Brown family, but especially my agent, Ginger Clark: I am in awe of your humor, experience, wit, wisdom, and strength. Whether I need tough love or pep talks, you're always a speedy email away. There will never be enough wombat photos to thank you for your help in bringing this book into the world.

To my critique partner, Roshani Chokshi, for reading everything I write in record time and never failing to gently eviscerate my drafts with your genius. You are eternally gorgeous and flawlessly wise, and I would never have made it without your lengthy emails and perfect GIFs. To M. Evan Matyas, for being a roommate, friend, sounding board, commiserator in chief, and for holding my hand since the beginning—thank dog for Craigslist, amirite? To Spellbound Scribes past and future, but especially Shauna Granger, Nicole Evelina, and Liv Rancourt— your experience, humor, sophistication, and scholarship cannot be overstated, and I feel lucky to count myself among you. To the Table of Trust, otherwise known as PitchWars 2014, for being an unparalleled wealth of information and advice, as well as an excellent place to vent.

To Tammy Meyers, Ann Dunn, Dr. Ewert, Dr. Harpold, Kevin Hyde, Dragan Kujundzic, Professor O'Neill, and all the other educators who attempted to mentor me despite myself.

To Jess, for bone crushing, Darcy-ing, and infinite snuffa loving—arf arf arf! To the Marshall "frat," for mead halls, horsey dances, and late-night games of Fishbowl. To Michelle, for never reading all the words. And to Hannah, Lauren, and Sonia, my F4: for a decade and a half of weird fan fiction, inappropriate Dracos, dollar-store prank gifts, black licorice in my shoes, too much Frontera, *Bachelorette* fantasy leagues, and unconditional love.

To my parents, Monica and Michael, for teaching me the value of a library card from such a young age, always reading to me at bedtime, and listening to all my wacky dreams. To my siblings, Sarée, Erik, Siobhán, and Shane, for never not giving me a hard time. You keep me sane and grounded. Our expanding family makes me feel so wealthy in music, laughter, and limitless love.

And finally, to Steve: for castle Christmases and woodland wanderings, for black-and-white music and midnight musings, for anticipating plot twists and always sympathizing with my villains. I love you to Olympus Mons and back.

LYRA SELENE was born under a full moon and has never quite managed to wipe the moonlight out of her eyes. When she isn't dreaming up fantastical cities and brooding landscapes, Lyra enjoys hiking, rainstorms, autumn, and pretending she's any good at art.

She lives in New England with her husband, in an antique farmhouse that's probably not haunted. *Amber & Dusk* is her debut novel.